Short Stories
volume two

Born in 1903, in Cork, Frank O'Connor had no formal education and his only real ambition was to become a writer. Aged twelve, he began to prepare a collected edition of his own works and, having learnt to speak Gaelic while very young, he studied his native poetry, music and legends. His literary career began with the translation of one of Du Bellay's sonnets into Gaelic.

On release from imprisonment by the Free State Government for his part in the Civil War, O'Connor won a prize for his study of Turgenev and subsequently had poetry, stories and translations published in the *Irish Statesman*. He caused great consternation in his native city by producing plays by Ibsen and Chekhov: a local clergyman remarked that the producer 'would go down in posterity at the head of the pagan Dublin muses', and ladies in the local literary society threatened to resign when he mentioned the name of James Joyce. By profession O'Connor was a librarian and his other great interest was music, Mozart and the Irish composer Carolan being his favourites. He will long be remembered for his collections of short stories. Frank O'Connor died in March 1966.

Also by Frank O'Connor in Pan Books:

Short Stories volume one

An Only Child and My Father's Son
an autobiography

Frank O'Connor Short Stories

volume two

Pan Books
in association with Macmillan

Masculine Protest and other stories first published 1969 in *Collection Three* by
Macmillan and Company Ltd

The Mad Lomasneys and other stories first published 1964
in *Collection Two* by Macmillan and Company Ltd

This collection published 1990 by
Pan Books Ltd, Cavaye Place, London SW10 9PG
in association with Macmillan Ltd

9 8 7 6 5 4 3 2 1

Masculine Protest
Acknowledgements are due to the following publications in which these stories first appeared:
*Harper's Bazaar, John Bull, Mademoiselle, New Yorker, Penguin New Writing, Saturday Evening Post,
Woman's Day.*
The text of 'A Story by Maupassant', which first appeared in *Penguin New Writing* in
1945, is the completely revised version published in *Winter's Tales 14* in 1968.

ISBN 0 330 31517 X

Printed and bound in Great Britain by
Cox & Wyman Ltd, Reading

Contents

Foreword

For Frank O'Connor the most important single element in any
story was its design. It might be years between the moment of
recognizing a theme and finding the one right shape for it – this
was the hard, painful work – the writing he did in his head. But
once he had the essential bony structure firmly in place he could
begin to enjoy the story – to start 'tinkering' with it. It was this
'tinkering' which produced dozens of versions of the same story.
The basic design never changed, but in each new version light
would be thrown in a different way on a different place. Frank
O'Connor did this kind of rewriting endlessly – as he admits
in the Introduction to *Collection Two*, he frequently contined
it even after a story had been published. Though this confused
and sometimes annoyed editors, reviewers and bibliographers,
the multiplicity of versions was never a problem to him. When
there were enough stories to form a new collection he didn't start
trying to choose between the many extant versions of them – he
simply sat down and prepared to rewrite every story he wanted in
the book.

That particular rewriting was directed towards a definite aim –
which was to give a book of stories the feeling of being a unity
rather than a grab bag. He believed that stories – if arranged in
an 'ideal ambience' – could strengthen and illuminate each other.
This unity was only partly preconceived, he contined to create it
as he went along. He never wrote a story specifically to fit into
a gap in a book – nor did he change names or locations to give
superficial unity. Rather it was as though the stories were bits of
a mosaic which could be arranged harmoniously so that the pattern
they made together reflected the light which each cast separately.
Ultimately this unity probably sprang from his basic conviction
that the writer was not simply an observer: 'I can't write about
something I don't admire – it goes back to the old concept of the
celebration: you celebrate the hero, an idea.'

This means, of course, that Frank O'Connor had very definite ideas about the contents and arrangements of each new book of stories. If he had lived, this might have been a different book. As it is, I have had to choose, not only which and how many stories to include, but also which of the many versions of each story to print. There was also the problem of that 'ideal ambience' and the comfort of the knowledge that even his own 'ideal ambience would be shattered by the time the book appears'.

I do not doubt that I shall have to answer to the author for each of these decisions. But for the stories themselves no one need answer. They are pure Frank O'Connor.

Harriet O'Donovan (Mrs Frank O'Connor)

Masculine
Protest

Contents

Masculine Protest

For months things had been getting difficult between Mother and me. At the time we were living in Boharna, a small town twenty miles from the city – Father, Mother, Martha, and I. I had managed to put up with it by kidding myself that one day Mother would understand; one day she'd wake up and see that the affection of Dad and Martha was insincere, that the two had long ago ganged up against her, and that I, the black sheep, the clumsy, stupid Denis, was the only one who really loved her.

The revelation was due to take place in rather unusual circumstances. We were all to be stranded in some dangerous desert, and Mother, with her ankle broken, would tell us to leave her to her fate. Dad and Martha would, of course, leave her, with only a pretence of concern. I could even imagine how Dad would look back regretfully, with his eyebrows raised, and shrug his shoulders, as much as to say that there was nothing he could do. But I, in my casual way, would simply fold my hands about my knees and ask listlessly, 'What use is life to me without you? It's all very well for Dad and Martha; they have one another, but I have only you.' Not a word more! I was determined on not having any false drama, any raising of the voice. I was never one for high-flown expressions; the lift of the shoulder, the way I pulled a grass-blade to chew (it needn't be a desert), and Mother would realize that though I was not demonstrative – just a plain, rough, willing chap – I had a heart of gold.

But Mother had a genius for subjecting hearts of gold to intolerable strain. It was the same as with Flossie, our dog. We had been brought up with Flossie, but when Dad had to go on a long trip and Mother wanted to accompany him, Flossie got in the way. She was sent to the vet, and I wept for hours over her.

It wasn't that Mother was actively unkind, for she thought far too much of the impression she wanted to make to give one of unkindness. It was just that she didn't care; she was more and more away from home. She visited friends in Dublin and Galway, Birr and Athlone; I never met a woman with so many friends or one so fond of them. All we saw of her was the flurry between one foray and the next as she packed and unpacked. Dad was absorbed in his work, but that was different. He never gave you the same impression of invulnerability as Mother. He came in while she packed, looking like an overgrown schoolboy, in spite of his moustache, and stood with his hands in his trouser pockets and his long neck out, making jokes at her in a mock-vulgar accent. Then, when she grew serious, he put on a blank face and shrugged his shoulders while his thin voice grew squeaky with anxiety – a bit of a nonentity, really, as you could see from the way she took him.

But I who loved her realized that she expected me to be a nonentity, too. She thought Dad made too many demands on her, which you could understand, but she thought the same of me, and sometimes I thought this was also how she must have felt about poor old Flossie.

Things came to a head when she told me she couldn't be at home for my twelfth birthday. There was no particular reason why I should have gone off the handle about that more than about anything else, but I did. The trouble was that the moment I did so, I seemed to have no reasons on my side. I could only sob and stamp and say she hadn't done it to Martha. She looked at me coldly and said I was a pretty picture, that I had no manliness.

'And you did the same to Flossie!' I shouted, stung to madness by her taunt.

I thought she'd hit me, but she only drew herself up, looking twice as noble and beautiful, and her lip curled. 'That is a contemptible remark, Denis,' she said, 'and one I'd expect only from you.'

Then she went off for the evening with the Clarkes, leaving Martha and me alone. Father was still at the office. Martha looked at me half in pity, half in amusement. She was never really very disappointed in Mother, because she expected less of her.

'What did I tell you?' she said.

I went up to my room and cried like a kid. It was the taunt about my lack of manliness that stung me most. I simply felt I couldn't live in the same house any longer with a woman who had said such a thing. I took out my Post Office savings book. I had four pounds fifteen – enough to keep me for a month or more till I found some corner where people wanted me, a plain, rough-spoken chap who only needed a little affection. If the worst came to the worst I could always make for Dublin, where Auntie May and my father's father lived. I knew they'd be glad to help me, because they had never even pretended to like Mother, and though I had resented this in them, I now saw they might have been right. It would be something just to reach their door and say to Auntie May in my plain, straightforward way, 'I see now I was wrong.' Then I dried my eyes, went downstairs, and took out my bicycle. It was equipped with dynamo lamp and everything – a smasher!

'Where are you off to?' Martha asked.

'You'll soon see,' I said darkly, and cycled off.

Then I had my first shock, because as I cycled into Main Street I saw that all the shops were shuttered for the weekly half-day and knew that the post office, too, would be closed. Apart from what I had in the bank I had nothing, and I knew I couldn't get far without money – certainly not as far as I hoped to get, for I intended not to come back.

I stood for ten minutes outside the post office, wondering wildly if one of the clerks would turn up. I felt that I simply couldn't return home. And then the idea struck me that the city was only twenty miles away, and that the post office there was bound to be open. I had been to the city a couple of times with Mother, so there was nothing very unfamiliar or frightening in the idea of it. When I got my money I could either stay the night at a hotel or cycle on through the dark. I was attracted by the latter idea. It would be good fun to cycle through the sleeping villages and towns, and see the dawn break over Dublin, and arrive at Auntie May's door, in the Shelbourne Road, while she was lighting the fire. I could imagine how she would greet me – 'Child of Grace, where did you come from?' 'Ah, just cycled,' I would reply, without any fuss.

It was very pleasant, but it wasn't enough. I cycled slowly and undecidedly out the familiar main road where we walked on Sunday, past the seminary and the little suburban houses. I was still uncertain that I should go on. Then something happened. Suddenly the countryside struck me as strange. I got off my bicycle and looked round. The town had sunk back into its black, bushy hills, with little showing of it but the spire of the church and the ruined tower of the abbey. It was as though it had accompanied me so far and then silently left me and returned. I found myself in new country, with a little, painted town sprawled across a river and, beyond it, bigger, smoother, greener hills. It was a curious sensation, rather like the moment when you find yourself out of your depth and two inclinations struggle in you – one to turn back in panic to the shallows, the other to strike out boldly for the other side.

The mere analogy was enough for me. It was like a challenge, and that moment of panic gave new energy to my cycling. The little town, the big red-brick mansion at the end of a beech avenue, the hexagonal brown building on top of the smooth hill before me, and the glimpses I caught of the river were both fascinating and frightening. I was aware of great distances, of big cloud masses on the horizon, of the fragility of my tyres compared with the rough surface of the road, and everything disappeared in the urgent need to get to the city, to draw out my money, to find myself food and a bed for the night.

For the last ten miles I hadn't even the temptation to look at my surroundings. Things just happened to me: the road bent away under me; wide green rivers rose up and slipped away again under my tyres; castles soared from the roadside with great arches blocked out in masses of shadow. I was lightheaded with hunger. I had been cycling with such savagery that I had exhausted myself, and the spires of the city sticking up from the fields ahead merely presented a fresh problem – whether or not the post office would be open.

Though that is not altogether true. There was one blessed brief spell when the rocky fields closed behind me like a book, and the electric-light poles escorted me up the last hill and gently down between comfortable villas and long gardens to the bridge. The city was stretched out along the other side of the river – a castle by the bridge, a cathedral tower above it, a row of warehouses, a terrace of crumbling Georgian houses – and I felt my heart rise at the thought that whatever happened I had proved I was a man.

But now emerged the greater problem of remaining one. Beyond the bridge the road climbed to the main street, two long façades of red-brick houses broken by the limestone front of a church. As I passed, I promised God to come in and thank Him if the post office was open. But as I crossed its threshold I knew my luck was out. Only the stamp counter was open, everything else was shut. At the stamp counter they told me I must come back next morning. They might as well have told me to come back next year.

Stunned and miserable, I pushed my bike back up to the main street and looked up and down. It was long and wide and lonesome, and I didn't know a soul I could turn to. I knew that without a meal and a rest I couldn't set out for Dublin. I was whacked. I had proved to myself that I was manly, but what good was manliness when Irish post offices wouldn't remain open after five o'clock?

It was just because I was so tired that I went to sit in the church – not out of any confidence in God, who was very much in my black books. I sat in the last row, at the end of the church. It was quiet and dark, with a red light showing far away in the sanctuary. And it was then that the thought of Dad came to me. It was funny that I hadn't thought of him before, even when thinking of Grandfather and Auntie May. I had thought of them as allies in my campaign against Mother. Dad seemed so ineffectual that I hadn't thought of him at all. Now, as I began to imagine him, with his long neck and weak face, his bowler hat and his moustache, which made you think of a fellow dressed up in a school show, his puerile jokes in his vulgar accent, everything about him seemed attractive. And I swear it wasn't only the hunger and panic. It was something new for me; it was almost love. Full of new energy, I knelt and prayed, 'Almighty God, grant I can talk to Dad on the phone!' The sanctuary lamp twinkled conspiratorially, like a signal, and I felt encouraged.

It wasn't as easy as that, though. The first place I asked permission to telephone they just hooshed me out, and the feeling that I was obeying an injunction of Heaven gave place to indignation. The sanctuary lamp had no business making signals unless it could arrange things better. I dawdled hopelessly along the main street, leaving my bike by the kerb and gazing in shop windows. In one I found a mirror where I could see myself full-length. I looked old and heartbroken. It was like a picture. The title 'Homeless' suggested itself to me and I blinked away my tears. There were nice model trains in the window, though – electric ones.

Then, as I passed a public house, I saw a tall man in shirt-sleeves by the door. I had a feeling that he had been watching me for a good while. He winked, and I winked back.

'Is it a pint you're looking for?' he asked in a loud, jovial tone, and I was disappointed, because it struck me that he might be only looking for trade.

'No,' I said, though I shouldn't have said it if he had asked me whether I was looking for lemonade.

'I'm sorry,' he said. 'I thought you might be a customer. Are you from these parts?'

'No,' I said modestly, conscious that I had travelled a long distance, but not wishing to boast, 'I'm from Boharna.'

'Boharna, begod!' he exclaimed, with new interest. 'And what are you doing in town?'

'I ran away from home,' I said, feeling I might as well get that in, in case he could help me.

'You couldn't do better,' he said with enthusiasm. 'I did it myself.'

'Did you?' I asked eagerly. This seemed the very sort of man I wanted to meet. 'When was this?'

'When I was fourteen.'

'I'm only twelve,' I said.

'There's nothing like beginning young,' he said. 'I did it three times in all before I got away with it. They were fed up with me then. You have to keep plugging away at it. Is it your old fellow?'

'No,' I said, surrendering myself to his experience and even adopting his broad way of speech. 'My old one.'

'Ah, cripes, that's tough,' he said. ''Tis bad enough having the old man on your back, but 'tis the devil entirely when you haven't the old woman behind you. And where are you off to now?'

'I don't know,' I admitted. 'I wanted to go to Dublin, but I can't.'

'Why not?'

'All my money is in the savings bank and I can't get it till tomorrow.'

'That's bad management, you know,' he said, shaking his head. 'You should have it with you.'

'I know,' I said, 'but I only made up my mind today.'

'Ah, cripes,' he said, 'you should have a thing like that planned for months ahead. 'Tis easy seen you're not used to it. It looks as if you might have to go back.'

'I can't go back,' I said despondently. ''Tis twenty miles. If I could only talk to Dad on the phone, he'd tell me what to do.'

'Who is your dad?' he asked, and I told him. 'Ah, we might be able to manage that for you. Come in.'

There was a phone in the corner, and he beckoned me to fire ahead. After a few minutes I heard Dad's voice, faint and squeaky with surprise, and I almost wept with delight.

'Hullo, son,' he said. 'Where on earth are you?'

'In Asragh, Daddy,' I said lightly. Even then I couldn't make a lot of it, the way another fellow would.

'Asragh?' Dad said, and I could almost see how his eyebrows worked up his forehead. 'What took you there?'

'I just ran away from home, Dad,' I said, trying to make it sound casual.

'Oh!' he said, and he paused for a moment, but his voice didn't change either. 'How did you get there?'

'On the bike, Dad.'

'The whole way?'

'The whole way.'

'Are you dead?' he asked with a laugh.

'Ah, just a bit,' I said modestly.

'Have you had anything to eat?'

'No, Dad.'

'Why not? Didn't you bring any money with you?'

'Only my savings-bank book, but the post office is shut.'

'Oh, hard luck!' he said. 'And what are you going to do now?'

'I don't know, Dad. I thought you might tell me.'

'Well, what about coming home?'

'I don't mind, Dad. Whatever you say.'

'Hold on a minute now till I see when the next bus is . . . Oh, hullo! You can get one in forty minutes' time – seven-ten. Tell the conductor I'll meet you and pay your fare. Is that all right?'

'That's grand, Dad,' I said, feeling that the world had almost come right again.

'Good! I'll have some supper ready. Mind yourself now.'

When I finished, the barman was waiting for me with his coat on. He had a girl looking after the bar for him.

'Better come and have a cup of tea with me before the bus,' he said. 'We can leave the old bike here.'

The lights were just being switched on. We sat in a brilliantly lit café, and I ate cake after cake and drank hot tea while the barman told me how he had run away. You could see he was a real reckless sort. On the first two occasions he had been caught by the police. The first time he had pinched a bicycle and cycled all the way to Dublin, sleeping in barns and deserted cottages. The third time he had joined the Army and not come home for years. It seemed that running away was not so easy as I had thought. On the other hand, it was much more adventurous. I felt the least shade sorry that I hadn't planned more carefully, and resolved to have everything ready if I did it again.

He put me and my bicycle on the bus and insisted on paying my fare. He also made me promise to tell Dad that he had paid my fare and that Dad owed me the money. He said in this world you had to stick up for your rights. He was a rough chap, but you could see he had a heart of gold. It struck me that only rough chaps like us were really that way and I promised to send him a letter.

When the bus drew up before the hotel, Dad was there, with his bowler hat, and with his long neck anxiously craned to find me.

'Well, the gouger!' he chuckled in his commonest accent. 'Who'd think the son of a decent, good-living man like me would turn into a common pedestrian tramp? Did you get an old bone in the doss-house, mate?'

I felt it was only right to keep my promise to the barman, so I told him about the fare, and he laughed like a kid and gave me the money. Then, as he pushed my bike down the main street, I asked the question that had been on my mind since I had heard his voice on the phone. 'Mummy back yet, Dad?' What I really meant, of course, was, 'Does she know?' But I couldn't put it like that – not to him.

His face changed at once. It became strained and serious again. 'No, son, not yet,' he said. 'Probably won't be in before ten or eleven.'

I was torn with the desire to ask him not to mention it to her, but it choked me. It would have seemed too much like the very thing I had always blamed Martha for – ganging up against Mother. At the same time I thought that maybe he was thinking the same thing, because he mentioned with careful casualness that he had sent Martha to the pictures. We had supper when we got home, and when we washed up together afterwards, I knew I was right.

Mother came in, and he talked as though nothing had happened, questioned her about her day, shrugged his shoulders over his own, looked blank and nervous. He had never seemed more a nonentity than then, but for the first time I realized how superficial that impression was. It was curious, watching him create understanding between us, understanding in more ways than one, for I realized that, like myself and the barman, Dad, too, had run away from home at some time in the past, and for some reason – perhaps because the bank was shut or because he was hungry, tired, and lonely – he had come back. People mostly came back, but their protest remained to distinguish them from all the others who had never run away. It was the real sign of their manhood.

I never ran away again after that. There was no need for it, because the strands that had bound me so inescapably to my mother seemed to have parted.

A Minority

Denis Halligan noticed Willy Stein for the first time one Sunday when the other fellows were at Mass. As Denis was a Protestant, he didn't go to Mass. Instead, he sat on the steps outside the chapel with Willy. Willy was a thin, seedy little chap with long, wild hair. It was an autumn morning; there was mist on the trees, and you could scarcely see the great ring of mountains that cut them off there in the middle of Ireland, miles from anywhere.

'Why did they send you here if you're a Proddy?' asked Willy.

'I don't know,' said Denis, who felt his background was so queer that he didn't want to explain it to anybody. 'I suppose because it was cheap.'

'Is your old fellow a Catholic?' asked Willy.

'No,' replied Denis. 'Is yours?'

'No,' Willy said contemptuously. 'He was a Proddy. My old one was a Proddy, too.'

'Where do they live?' asked Denis.

'They're dead,' Willy said, making the motion of spitting. 'The bloody Germans killed them.'

'Oh, cripes!' Denis said regretfully. Denis had a great admiration for everything German, particularly tank generals, and when he grew up he wanted to be a tank general himself, but it seemed a pity that they had to kill Willy's father and mother. Bad as it was to have your parents separated, as his own were, it was worse having them dead. 'Was it a bomb?' he asked.

'No,' Willy replied without undue emotion. 'They were killed in a camp. They sent me over to the Cumminses in Dublin or I'd have been killed, too. The Cumminses are Catholics. That's why I was sent here.'

'Do you like it here?' asked Denis.

'I do not,' Willy said scornfully in his slummy Dublin accent, and then took out a slingshot and fitted a stone in it. 'I'd sooner

14

Vienna. Vienna was gas. When I grow up I'm going to get out of this blooming place.'

'But what will you do?'

'Aw, go to sea, or something. I don't care.'

Denis was interested in Willy. Apart from the fact that they were the only Proddies in the school, Willy struck him as being really tough, and Denis admired toughness. He was always trying to be tough himself, but there was a soft streak in him that kept breaking out. It was breaking out now, and he knew it. Though he saw that Willy didn't give a rap about his parents, Denis couldn't help being sorry for him, alone in the middle of Ireland with his father and mother dead half a world away. He said as much to his friend Nigel Healy, from Cork, that afternoon, but Nigel only gave a superior sniff.

'But that fellow is mad,' he said, in his reasonable way.

'How is he mad?' asked Denis.

'He's not even left go home on holidays,' explained Nigel. 'He has to stay here all during the summer. Those people were nice to him, and what does he do? Breaks every window in the place. They had the police to the house twice. He's mad on slingshots.'

'He had one this morning,' said Denis.

'Last time he was caught with one he got flogged,' said Nigel. 'You see, the fellow has no sense. I even saw him putting sugar on his meat.'

'But why did he do that?' asked Denis.

'Said he liked it,' replied Nigel with a smile and a shrug. 'He's bound to get expelled one of these days. You'd want to mind yourself with him.'

But for some reason that only made Denis more interested in Willy Stein, and he looked forward to meeting him again by himself the following Sunday. He was curious to know why the Germans would want to kill Stein's father and mother. That seemed to him a funny thing to do – unless, of course, they were spies for the English.

Again they sat on the steps, but this morning the sun was warm and bright, and the mountains all round them were a brilliant blue. If Stein's parents were really spies, the idea of it did not seem to have occurred to him. According to him, his father had been a lawyer and his mother something on a newspaper, and he didn't seem to remember much about them except that they were both 'gas'. Everything with Stein was 'gas'. His mother was gentle and timid, and let him have everything he wanted, so she was 'great gas'. His father was sure she was ruining him, and was always on to him to study and be better than other kids, and when his father got like that he used to weep and shout and wave his hands, but that was only now and then. He was gas, too, though not, Denis gathered, great gas. Willy suddenly waved his hands and shouted something in a foreign language.

'What's that?' asked Denis with the deepest admiration.

'German,' Stein replied, in his graceless way.

'What does it mean?' asked Denis.

'I dunno,' Stein said lightly.

Denis was disappointed. For a fellow like himself, who was interested in tanks, a spatter of German might one day be useful. He had the impression that Stein was only letting on to remember parents he had lost before he was really old enough to remember them.

Their talk was interrupted by Father Houlihan, a tall, morose-looking priest. He had a bad belly and a worse temper, but Denis knew Father Houlihan liked him, and he admired Father Houlihan. He was violent, but he wasn't a stinker.

'Hah!' he said, in his mocking way. 'And what do you two cock sparrows think you're doing out here?'

'We're excused, Father,' Denis said brightly, leaping to his feet.

'No one is excused anything in this place till I excuse him,' snarled Father Houlihan cheerfully, 'and I don't excuse much. Run into Mass now, ye pair of heathens!'

'But we're Protestants, Father!' Stein cried, and Denis was half afraid of seeing the red flush on Father Houlihan's forehead that showed he was out for blood.

'Aha, what fine Protestants we have in ye!' he snorted good-humouredly. 'I suppose you have a Protestant slingshot in your pocket at this very minute, you scoundrel, you!'

'I have not!' Stein shouted. 'You know Murphy took it off me.'

'Mr Murphy to you, Willy Stein,' said the priest, pinching his ear playfully and pushing him towards the chapel. 'And next time I catch you with a slingshot I'll give you a Catholic cane on your fat Protestant backside.'

The two boys went into chapel and sat together on a bench at the back. Willy was muttering indignantly to himself, but he waited until everyone was kneeling with bowed head. Then, to Denis's horror, he took out a slingshot and a bit of paper, which he chewed up into a wet ball. There was nothing hasty or spontaneous about this. Stein went about it with a concentration that was almost pious. As the bell rang for the Consecration, there was a *ping*, and a seminarist kneeling at the side of the chapel put his hand to his ear and looked angrily round. But by this time Stein had thrown himself on his knees, and his eyes were shut in a look of rapt devotion. It gave Denis quite a turn. Even if he wasn't a Catholic, he had been brought up to respect every form of religion.

The business of going to Mass and feeling out of it made Denis Halligan completely fed up with being a Proddy. He had never liked it anyway, even at home, as a kid. He was gregarious, and a born gang leader, a promoter of organization, and it cut him to the heart to feel that at any moment he might be deserted by his gang because, through no fault of his own, he was not a Catholic and might accidentally say or do the wrong thing. He even resented the quiet persuasion that the school authorities exercised on him. A senior called Hanley, whom Nigel described sarcastically as 'Halligan's angel', was attached to Denis – not to proselytize, but to give him an intelligent understanding of the religious life of the group. Hanley had previously been attached to Stein, but that had proved hopeless, because Stein seemed to take Hanley's company as a guarantee of immunity from punishment, so he merely involved Hanley in every form of forbidden activity, from smoking to stealing. One day when Stein stole a gold tie-pin from a master's room, Hanley had to report him. On Hanley's account, he was not flogged, but told to put the tie-pin back in the place from which he had taken it. Stein did so, and seized the opportunity to pinch five shillings instead, and this theft was discovered only when someone saw Stein fast asleep in bed with his mouth open and the two half-crowns in his jaw. As Hanley, a sweet and saintly boy, said to Denis, it wasn't Stein's fault. He was just unbalanced.

In any other circumstances Denis would have enjoyed Hanley's attention, but it made him mad to be singled out like this and looked after like some kid who couldn't undo his own buttons.

'Listen, Hanley,' he said angrily one day when he and Nigel were discussing football and Hanley had slipped a little homily into the conversation. 'It's no good preaching at me. It's not my fault that I'm a Proddy.'

'Well, you don't have to be a Proddy if you don't want to be,' Hanley said with a smile. 'Do you?'

'How can I help it?' asked Denis.

'Well, who'd stop you?'

'My mother would, for one.'

'Did you try?'

'What do you mean, Hanley?'

'I mean, why don't you ask her?' Hanley went on, in the same bland way. 'I wouldn't be too sure she wants you to be a Proddy.'

'How could I ask her?'

'You could write. Or phone,' Hanley added hastily, seeing the look on Denis's face at the notion of writing an extra letter. 'Father Houlihan would let you use the telephone, if you asked him. Or I'll ask him, if you like.'

'Do if you want to,' said Denis. 'I don't care.'

He didn't really believe his mother would agree to something he wanted, just like that, but he had no objection to a free telephone call that would enable him to hear her voice again. To his astonishment, she made no difficulty about it.

'Why, of course, darling,' she said sweetly. 'If that's how you feel and Father Houlihan has no objection, I don't mind. You know I only want you to be happy at school.'

It was a colossal relief. Overnight, his whole position in the school changed. He had ceased to be an outsider. He was one of the gang. He might even be Chief Gang Leader in the course of time. He was a warm-hearted boy and he had the feeling that by a simple gesture he had conferred an immense benefit on everybody. The only person who didn't seem too enthusiastic was Father Houlihan, but then he was not much of an enthusiast anyway. 'My bold young convert,' he said, pulling Denis's ear, 'I suppose any day now you'll start paying attention to your lessons.'

Yet the moment he had made his decision, he began to feel guilty about young Stein. As has been said, he was not only gregarious, but he was also a born gang leader, and had the feeling that someone might think he had deserted an ally to secure his own advantage. He was suddenly filled with a wild desire to convert Willy as well, so that the pair of them could be received as a group. He saw it as even more of a duty of Willy's than of his own. Willy had been saved from his parents' fate by a good kind Catholic family, and it was the least they could expect that Willy should show his gratitude to them, to the school, and to Ireland.

But Willy seemed to have a deplorable head for theology. All the time they talked Denis had the impression that Willy was only planning some fresh mischief.

'Ah, come on, Willy,' he said authoritatively, 'you don't want to be a blooming old Proddy.'

'I don't want to be a Cat either,' said Willy with a shrug.

'Don't you want to be like the other fellows in the school?'

'Why don't they want to be like me?' asked Stein.

'Because there's only two of us, and there's hundreds of them. And they're right.'

'And if there were hundreds of us and two of them, we'd be right, I suppose?' Stein said with a sneer. 'You want to be like the rest of them. All right, be like the rest of them, but let me alone.'

'I'm only speaking for your own good,' Denis said, getting mad. What really made him mad was the feeling that somehow Stein wasn't speaking to him at all; that inside, he was as lonely and lost as Denis would have been in similar circumstances, and he wouldn't admit to it, wouldn't break down as Denis would have done. What he really wanted to do was to give Stein a sock in the gob, but he knew that even this was no good. Stein was always being beaten, and he always yelled bloody murder, and next day he came back and did the same thing again. Everyone was thinking exclusively of Stein's good, and it always ended up by their beating him, and it never did him any good at all.

Denis confided his difficulties to Hanley, who was also full of concern for Stein's good, but Hanley only smiled sadly and shook his head.

'I know more about that than you do, Denis,' he said, in his fatherly way. 'I'll tell you if you promise not to repeat it to a living soul.'

'What is it?' asked Denis eagerly.

'Promise! Mind, this is serious!'

'Oh, I promise.'

'The fact is that Stein isn't a Proddy at all,' Hanley said sadly.

'But what is he?'

'Stein is a Jew,' Hanley said in a low voice. 'That's why his father and mother were killed. Nobody knows that, though.'

'But does Stein know he's a Jew?' Denis asked excitedly.

'No. And mind, we're not supposed to know it, either. Nobody knows it, except the priests and ourselves.'

'But why doesn't somebody tell him?'

'Because if they did, he might blab about it – you know, he's not very smart – and then all the fellows would be jeering at him. Remember, Denis, if you ever mentioned it, Father Houlihan would skin you alive. He says Stein is after suffering enough. He's sorry for Stein. Mind, I'm only warning you.'

'But won't it be awful for him when he finds out?'

'When he's older and has a job, he won't mind it so much,' said Hanley.

But Denis wasn't sure. Somehow, he had an idea that Stein wanted to stay a Proddy simply because that was what his father and mother had been and it was now the only link he had with them, and if someone would just tell him, he wouldn't care so much and would probably become a Catholic, like Denis. Afterwards, when he did find out that everything he had done was mistaken, it might be too late. And this – and the fact that Father Houlihan, whom Denis admired, was also sorry for Willy Stein – increased his feeling of guilt, and he almost wished he hadn't been in such a hurry himself about being converted. Denis wasn't a bright student, but he was a born officer and he would never have deserted his men.

The excitement of his own reception into the Church almost banished the thought of Stein from his mind. On the Sunday he was received he was allowed to sleep late, and Murphy, the seminarist, even brought him comics to read in bed. This was real style! Then he dressed in his best suit and went down to meet his mother, who arrived, with his sister, Martha, in a hired car. For once, Martha was deferential. She was impressed, and the sight of the chapel impressed her even more. In front of the High Altar there was an isolated prie-dieu for Denis himself, and behind him a special pew was reserved for her and his mother.

Denis knew afterwards that he hadn't made a single false move. Only once was his exaltation disturbed, and that was when he heard the *ping* of a slingshot and realized that Stein, sitting by himself in the back row, was whiling away the time by getting into fresh mischief. The rage rose up in Denis, in spite of all his holy thoughts, and for a moment he resolved that when it was all over he would find Willy Stein and beat him to a jelly.

Instead, when it was over he suddenly felt weary. Martha had ceased to be impressed by him. Now she was just a sister a bare year younger who was mad with him for having stolen the attention of everybody. She knew only too well what a figure she would have cut as a convert, and was crazy with jealousy.

'I won't stand it,' she said. 'I'm going to be a Catholic, too.'

'Well, who's stopping you?' Denis asked.

'Nobody's going to stop me,' said Martha. 'Just because Daddy is fond of you doesn't mean that I can't be a Catholic.'

'What has Daddy to do with it?' asked Denis with a feeling of alarm.

'Because now that you're a Catholic, the courts wouldn't let him have you,' Martha said excitedly. 'Because Daddy is an atheist, or something, and he wanted to get hold of you. He tried to get you away from Mummy. I don't care about Daddy. I'm going to be converted, too.'

'Go on!' growled Denis, feeling sadly how his mood of exaltation was fading. 'You're only an old copycat.'

'I am not a copycat, Denis Halligan,' she said bitterly. 'It's only that you always sucked up to Daddy and I didn't, and he doesn't care about me. I don't care about him, either, so there!'

Denis felt a sudden pang of terror at her words. In a dim sort of way he realized that what he had done might have consequences he had never contemplated. He had no wish to live with his father, but his father came to the school to see him sometimes, and he had always had the feeling that if he ever got fed up with living at home with his mother and Martha, his father would always have him. Nobody had told him that by becoming a Catholic he had made it impossible for his father to have him. He glanced round and saw Stein, thin and pale and furtive, slouching away from the chapel with his hand in his pocket clutching his slingshot. He gave Denis a grin in which there was no malice, but Denis scowled and looked away.

'Who's that?' asked Martha inquisitively.

'Oh, him!' Denis said contemptuously. 'That's only a dirty Jew-boy.'

Yet even as he spoke the words he knew they were false. What he really felt towards Willy Stein was an aching envy. Nobody had told him that by changing his faith he might be unfaithful to his father, but nobody had told Stein, either, and, alone and despairing, he still clung to a faith that was not his own for the sake of a father and mother he had already almost forgotten, who had been murdered half a world away and whom he would never see again. For a single moment Denis saw the dirty little delinquent whom everyone pitied and despised transfigured by a glory that he himself would never know.

(1957)

The Face of Evil

I could never understand all the old talk about how hard it is to be a saint. I was a saint for quite a bit of my life and I never saw anything hard in it. And when I stopped being a saint, it wasn't because the life was too hard.

I fancy it is the sissies who make it seem like that. We had quite a few of them in school, fellows whose mothers intended them to be saints, and who hadn't the nerve to be anything else. I never enjoyed the society of chaps who wouldn't commit sin for the same reason that they wouldn't dirty their new suits. That was never what sanctity meant to me, and I doubt if it is what it means to other saints. The companions I liked were the tough gang down the road, and I enjoyed going down of an evening and talking with them under the gas-lamp about football matches and school, even if they did sometimes say things I wouldn't say myself. I was never one for criticizing; I had enough to do criticizing myself, and I knew they were decent chaps and didn't really mean much harm by the things they said about girls.

No, for me the main attraction of being a saint was the way it always gave you something to do. You could never say you felt time hanging on your hands. It was like having a room of your own to keep tidy; you'd scour it, and put everything neatly back in its place, and within an hour or two it was beginning to look as untidy as ever. It was a full-time job that began when you woke and stopped only when you fell asleep.

I would wake in the morning, for instance, and think how nice it was to lie in bed, and congratulate myself on not having to get up for another half-hour. That was enough. Instantly a sort of alarm clock would go off in my mind; the mere thought that I could enjoy half an hour's comfort would make me aware of an alternative, and I'd begin an argument with myself. I had a voice in me that was almost the voice of a stranger, the way it nagged and jeered. Sometimes I could almost visualize it, and then it took on the appearance of a fat and sneering teacher I had some years before at school – a man I really hated. I hated that voice. It always began in the same way, smooth and calm and dangerous. I could see the teacher rubbing his fat hands and smirking.

'Don't get alarmed, boy. You're in no hurry. You have another half-hour.'

'I know well I have another half-hour,' I would reply, trying to keep my temper. 'What harm am I doing? I'm only imagining I'm down in a submarine. Is there anything wrong in that?'

'Oho, not the least in the world. I'd say there's been a heavy frost. Just the sort of morning when there's ice in the bucket.'

'And what has that to do with it?'

'Nothing, I tell you. Of course, for people like you it's easy enough in the summer months, but the least touch of frost in the air soon makes you feel different. I wouldn't worry trying to keep it up. You haven't the stuff for this sort of life at all.'

And gradually my own voice grew weaker as that of my tormentor grew stronger, till all at once I would strip the clothes from off myself and lie in my nightshirt, shivering and muttering, 'So I haven't the stuff in me, haven't I?' Then I would go downstairs before my parents were awake, strip and wash in the bucket, ice or no ice, and when Mother came down she would cry in alarm, 'Child of Grace, what has you up at this hour? Sure, 'tis only half past seven.' She almost took it as a reproach to herself, poor woman, and I couldn't tell her the reason, and even if I could have done so, I wouldn't. How could you say to anybody 'I want to be a saint'?

Then I went to Mass and enjoyed again the mystery of the streets and lanes in the early morning; the frost which made your feet clatter off the walls at either side of you like falling masonry, and the different look that everything wore, as though, like yourself, it was all cold and scrubbed and new. In the winter the lights would still be burning red in the little cottages, and in summer they were ablaze with sunshine so that their interiors were dimmed to shadows. Then there were the different people, all of whom recognized one another, like Mrs MacEntee, who used to be a stewardess on the boats, and Macken, the tall postman, people who seemed ordinary enough when you met them during the day, but carried something of their mystery with them at Mass, as though they, too, were reborn.

I can't pretend I was ever very good at school, but even there it was a help. I might not be clever, but I had always a secret reserve of strength to call on in the fact that I had what I wanted, and that beside it I wanted nothing. People frequently gave me things, like fountain pens or pencil-sharpeners, and I would suddenly find myself becoming attached to them and immediately know I must give them away, and then feel the richer for it. Even without throwing my weight around I could help and protect kids younger than myself, and yet not become involved in their quarrels. Not to become involved, to remain detached – that was the great thing; to care for things and for people, yet not to care for them so much that your happiness became dependent on them.

It was like no other hobby, because you never really got the better of yourself, and all at once you would suddenly find yourself reverting to childish attitudes; flaring up in a wax with some fellow, or sulking when Mother asked you to go for a message, and then it all came back; the nagging of the infernal alarm clock which grew louder with every moment until it incarnated as a smooth, fat, jeering face.

'Now, that's the first time you've behaved sensible for months, boy. That was the right way to behave to your mother.'

'Well, it *was* the right way. Why can't she let me alone, once in a while? I only want to read. I suppose I'm entitled to a bit of peace some time?'

'Ah, of course you are, my dear fellow. Isn't that what I'm saying? Go on with your book! Imagine you're a cowboy, riding to the rescue of a beautiful girl in a cabin in the woods, and let that silly woman go for the messages herself. She probably hasn't long to live anyway, and when she dies you'll be able to do all the weeping you like.'

And suddenly tears of exasperation would come to my eyes and I'd heave the story book to the other side of the room and shout back at the voice that gave me no rest, 'Cripes, I might as well be dead and buried. I have no blooming life.' After that I would apologize to Mother (who, poor woman, was more embarrassed than anything else and assured me that it was all her fault), go on the message, and write another tick in my notebook against the heading of 'Bad Temper' so as to be able to confess it to Father O'Regan when I went to Confession on Saturday. Not that he was ever severe with me, no matter what I did; he thought I was the last word in holiness, and was always asking me to pray for some special intention of his own. And though I was depressed, I never lost interest, for no matter what I did I could scarcely ever reduce the total of times I had to tick off that item in my notebook.

Oh, I don't pretend it was any joke, but it did give you the feeling that your life had some meaning; that inside you, you had a real source of strength; that there was nothing you could not do without, and yet remain sweet, self-sufficient, and content. Sometimes too, there was the feeling of something more than mere content, as though your body were transparent, like a window, and light shone through it as well as on it, onto the road, the houses, and the playing children, as though it were you who was shining on them, and tears of happiness would come into my eyes, and I would hurl myself among the playing children just to forget it.

But, as I say, I had no inclination to mix with other kids who might be saints as well. The fellow who really fascinated me was a policeman's son named Dalton, who was easily the most vicious kid in the locality. The Daltons lived on the terrace above ours. Mrs Dalton was dead; there was a younger brother called Stevie, who was next door to an imbecile, and there was something about that kid's cheerful grin that was even more frightening than the malice on Charlie's broad face. Their father was a tall, melancholy man, with a big black moustache, and the nearest thing imaginable to one of the Keystone cops. Everyone was sorry for his loss in his wife, but you knew that if it hadn't been that it would have been something else – maybe the fact that he hadn't lost her. Charlie was only an additional grief. He was always getting into trouble, stealing and running away from home; and only his father's being a policeman prevented his being sent to an industrial school. One of my most vivid recollections is that of Charlie's education. I'd hear a shriek, and there would be Mr Dalton, dragging Charlie along the pavement to school, and whenever the names his son called him grew a little more obscene than usual, pausing to give Charlie a good going-over with the belt which he carried loose in his hand. It is an exceptional father who can do this without getting some pleasure out of it, but Mr Dalton looked as though even that were an additional burden. Charlie's screams could always fetch me out.

'What is it?' Mother would cry after me.

'Ah, nothing. Only Charlie Dalton again.'

'Come in! Come in!'

'I won't be seen.'

'Come in, I say. 'Tis never right.'

And even when Charlie uttered the most atrocious indecencies, she only joined her hands as if in prayer and muttered, 'The poor child! The poor unfortunate child!' I never could understand the way she felt about Charlie. He wouldn't have been Charlie if it hadn't been for the leatherings and the threats of the industrial school.

Looking back on it, the funniest thing is that I seemed to be the only fellow on the road he didn't hate. The rest were all terrified of him, and some of the kids would go a mile to avoid him. He was completely unclassed: being a policeman's son, he should have been way up the social scale, but he hated the respectable kids worse than the others. When we stood under the gas-lamp at night and saw him coming up the road, everybody fell silent. He looked suspiciously at the group, ready to spring at anyone's throat if he saw the shadow of offence; ready even when there wasn't a shadow. He fought like an animal, by instinct, without judgement, and without ever reckoning the odds, and he was terribly strong. He wasn't clever; several of the older chaps could beat him to a frazzle when it was merely a question of boxing or wrestling, but it never was that with Dalton. He was out for blood and usually got it. Yet he was never that way with me. We weren't friends. All that ever happened when we passed one another was that I smiled at him and got a cold, cagey nod in return. Sometimes we stopped and exchanged a few words, but it was an ordeal because we never had anything to say to one another.

It was like the signalling of ships, or more accurately, the courtesies of great powers. I tried, like Mother, to be sorry for him in having no proper home, and getting all those leatherings, but the feeling which came uppermost in me was never pity but respect: respect for a fellow who had done all the things I would never do: stolen money, stolen bicycles, run away from home, slept with tramps and criminals in barns and doss-houses, and ridden without a ticket on trains and on buses. It filled my imagination. I have a vivid recollection of one summer morning when I was going up the hill to Mass. Just as I reached the top and saw the low, sandstone church perched high up ahead of me, he poked his bare head round the corner of a lane to see who was coming. It startled me. He was standing with his back to the gable of a house; his face was dirty and strained; it was broad and lined, and the eyes were very small, furtive and flickering, and sometimes a sort of spasm would come over them and they flickered madly for half a minute on end.

'Hullo, Charlie,' I said. 'Where were you?'

'Out,' he replied shortly.

'All night?' I asked in astonishment.

'Yeh,' he replied with a nod.

'What are you doing now?'

He gave a short, bitter laugh.

'Waiting till my old bastard of a father goes out to work and I can go home.'

His eyes flickered again, and selfconsciously he drew his hand across them as though pretending they were tired.

'I'll be late for Mass,' I said uneasily. 'So long.'

'So long.'

That was all, but all the time at Mass, among the flowers and the candles, watching the beautiful, sad old face of Mrs MacEntee and the plump, smooth, handsome face of Macken, the postman, I was haunted by the image of that other face, wild and furtive and dirty, peering round a corner like an animal looking from its burrow. When I came out, the morning was brilliant over the valley below me; the air was punctuated with bugle calls from the cliff where the barrack stood, and Charlie Dalton was gone. No, it wasn't pity I felt for him. It wasn't even respect. It was almost like envy.

Then, one Saturday evening, an incident occurred which changed my attitude to him; indeed, changed my attitude to myself, though it wasn't until long after that I realized it. I was on my way to Confession, preparatory to Communion next morning. I always went to Confession at the parish church in town where Father O'Regan was. As I passed the tramway terminus at the Cross, I saw Charlie sitting on the low wall above the Protestant church, furtively smoking the butt-end of a cigarette which somebody had dropped getting on the tram. Another tram arrived as I reached the Cross, and a number of people alighted and went off in different directions. I crossed the road to Charlie and he gave me his most distant nod.

'Hullo.'

'Hullo, Cha. Waiting for somebody?'

'No. Where are you off to?'

'Confession.'

'Huh.' He inhaled the cigarette butt deeply and then tossed it over his shoulder into the sunken road beneath without looking where it alighted. 'You go a lot.'

'Every week,' I said modestly.

'Jesus!' he said with a short laugh. 'I wasn't there for twelve months.'

I shrugged my shoulders. As I say, I never went in much for criticizing others, and, anyway, Charlie wouldn't have been Charlie if he had gone to Confession every week.

'Why do you go so often?' he asked challengingly.

'Oh, I don't know,' I said doubtfully. 'I suppose it keeps you out of harm's way.'

'But you don't do any harm,' he growled, just as though he were defending me against someone who had been attacking me.

'Ah, we all do harm.'

'But, Jesus Christ, you don't do anything,' he said almost angrily, and his eyes flickered again in that curious nervous spasm, and almost as if they put him into a rage, he drove his knuckles into them.

'We all do things,' I said. 'Different things.'

'Well, what do you do?'

'I lose my temper a lot,' I admitted.

'Jesus!' he said again and rolled his eyes.

'It's a sin just the same,' I said obstinately.

'A sin? Losing your temper? Jesus, I want to kill people. I want to kill my bloody old father, for one. I will too, one of those days. Take a knife to him.'

'I know, I know,' I said, at a loss to explain what I meant. 'But that's just the same thing as me.'

I wished to God I could talk better. It wasn't any missionary zeal. I was excited because for the first time I knew that Charlie felt about me exactly as I felt about him, with a sort of envy, and I wanted to explain to him that he didn't have to envy me, and that he could be as much a saint as I was just as I could be as much a sinner as he was. I wanted to explain that it wasn't a matter of tuppence ha'penny worth of sanctity as opposed to tuppence worth that made the difference, that it wasn't what you did, but

29

what you lost by doing it, that mattered. The whole Cross had become a place of mystery; the grey light, drained of warmth; the trees hanging over the old crumbling walls, the tram, shaking like a boat when someone mounted it. It was the way I sometimes felt afterwards with a girl, as though everything about you melted and fused and became one with a central mystery.

'But when what you do isn't any harm?' he repeated angrily, with that flickering of the eyes I had almost come to dread.

'Look, Cha,' I said, 'you can't say a thing isn't any harm. Everything is harm. It might be losing my temper with me and murder with you, like you say, but it would only come to the same thing. If I show you something, will you promise not to tell?'

'Why would I tell?'

'But promise.'

'Oh, all right.'

Then I took out my little notebook and showed it to him. It was extraordinary, and I knew it was extraordinary. I found myself, sitting on that wall, showing a notebook I wouldn't have shown to anyone else in the world to Charlie Dalton, a fellow any kid on the road would go a long way to avoid, and yet I had the feeling that he would understand it as no one else would do. My whole life was there, under different headings – Disobedience, Bad Temper, Bad Thoughts, Selfishness, and Laziness – and he looked through quietly, studying the ticks I had placed against each count.

'You see,' I said, 'you talk about your father, but look at all the things I do against my mother. I know she's a good mother, but if she's sick or if she can't walk fast when I'm in town with her, I get mad just as you do. It doesn't matter what sort of mother or father you have. It's what you do to yourself when you do things like that.'

'What do you do to yourself?' he asked quietly.

'It's hard to explain. It's only a sort of peace you have inside yourself. And you can't be just good, no matter how hard you try. You can only do your best, and if you do your best you feel peaceful inside. It's like when I miss Mass of a morning. Things mightn't be any harder on me that day than any other day, but I'm not as well able to stand up to them. It makes things a bit different for the rest of the day. You don't mind it so much if you get a hammering. You know there's something else in the world besides the hammering.'

I knew it was a feeble description of what morning Mass really meant to me, the feeling of strangeness which lasted throughout the whole day, and reduced reality to its real proportions, but it was the best I could do. I hated leaving him.

'I'll be late for Confession,' I said regretfully, getting off the wall.

'I'll go down a bit of the way with you,' he said, giving a last glance at my notebook and handing it back to me. I knew he was being tempted to come to Confession along with me, but my pleasure had nothing to do with that. As I say, I never had any missionary zeal. It was the pleasure of understanding rather than that of conversion.

He came down the steps to the church with me and we went in together.

'I'll wait here for you,' he whispered, and sat in one of the back pews.

It was dark there; there were just a couple of small, unshaded lights in the aisles above the confessionals. There was a crowd of old women outside Father O'Regan's box, so I knew I had a long time to wait. Old women never got done with their confessions. For the first time I felt it long, but when my turn came it was all over in a couple of minutes: the usual 'Bless you, my child. Say a prayer for me, won't you?' When I came out, I saw Charlie Dalton sitting among the old women outside the confessional, waiting to go in. I felt very happy about it in a quiet way, and when I said my penance I said a special prayer for him.

It struck me that he was a long time inside, and I began to grow worried. Then he came out, and I saw by his face that it was no good. It was the expression of someone who is saying to himself with a sort of evil triumph, 'There, I told you what it was like.'

'It's all right,' he whispered, giving his belt a hitch. 'You go home.'

'I'll wait for you,' I said.

'I'll be a good while.'

I knew then Father O'Regan had given him a heavy penance, and my heart sank.

'It doesn't matter,' I said. 'I'll wait.'

And it was only long afterwards that it occurred to me that I might have taken one of the major decisions of my life without being aware of it. I sat at the back of the church in the dusk and

31

waited for him. He was kneeling up in front, before the altar, and I knew it was no good. At first I was too stunned to feel. All I knew was that my happiness had all gone. I admired Father O'Regan; I knew that Charlie must have done things that I couldn't even imagine – terrible things – but the resentment grew in me. What right had Father O'Regan or anyone to treat him like that? Because he was down, people couldn't help wanting to crush him further. For the first time in my life I knew real temptation. I wanted to go with Charlie and share his fate. For the first time I realized that the life before me would have complexities of emotion which I couldn't even imagine.

The following week he ran away from home again, took a bicycle, broke into a shop to steal cigarettes, and, after being arrested seventy-five miles from Cork in a little village on the coast, was sent to an industrial school.

(1954)

The Teacher's Mass

Father Fogarty, the curate in Crislough, used to say in his cynical way that his greatest affliction was having to serve the teacher's Mass every morning. He referred, of course, to his own Mass, the curate's Mass, which was said early so that Father Fogarty could say Mass later in Costello. Nobody ever attended it, except occasionally in summer, when there were visitors at the hotel. The schoolteacher, old Considine, served as acolyte. He had been serving the early Mass long before Fogarty came, and the curate thought he would also probably be doing it long after he had left. Every morning, you saw him coming up the village street, a pedantically attired old man with a hollow face and a big moustache that was turning grey. Everything about him was abstract and angular, even to his voice, which was harsh and without modulation, and sometimes when he and Fogarty came out of the sacristy with Considine leading, carrying the book, his pace was so slow that Fogarty wondered what effect it would have if he gave him one good kick in the behind. It was exactly as Fogarty said – as though *he* were serving Considine's Mass, and the effect of it was to turn Fogarty into a more unruly acolyte than ever he had been in the days when he himself was serving the convent Mass.

Whatever was the cause, Considine always roused a bit of the devil in Fogarty, and he knew that Considine had no great affection for him, either. The old man had been headmaster of the Crislough school until his retirement, and all his life he had kept himself apart from the country people, like a parish priest or a policeman. He was not without learning; he had a quite respectable knowledge of local history, and a very good one of the ecclesiastical history of the Early Middle Ages in its local applications, but it was all book learning, and, like his wing collar, utterly unrelated to the life about him. He had all the childish vanity of the man of dissociated scholarship, wrote occasional scurrilous letters to the local paper to correct some error in etymology, and expected everyone on that account to treat him as an oracle. As a schoolmaster he had sneered cruelly at the barefoot urchins he taught, describing them as 'illiterate peasants' who believed in the fairies and in spells, and when, twenty years later, some of them came back from Boston or Brooklyn and showed off before the neighbours, with their big American hats and high-powered cars, he still sneered at them. According to him, they went away illiterate and came home illiterate.

'I see young Carmody is home again,' he would say to the curate after Mass.

'Is that so?'

'And he has a car like a house,' Considine would add, with bitter amusement. 'A car with a grin on it. 'Twould do fine to cart home his mother's turf.'

'The blessing of God on him,' the curate would say cheerfully. 'I wish I had a decent car instead of the old yoke I have.'

'I dare say it was the fairies,' the old teacher would snarl, with an ugly smile that made his hollow, high-cheeked face look like a skull. 'It wasn't anything he ever learned here.'

'Maybe we're not giving the fairies their due, Mr Considine,' said the curate, with the private conviction that it would be easier to learn from them than from the schoolmaster.

The old man's scornful remarks irritated Fogarty because he liked the wild, barefooted, inarticulate brats from the mountainy farms, and felt that if they showed off a bit when they returned from America with a few dollars in their pockets, they were well entitled to do so. Whoever was entitled to the credit, it was nothing and nobody at home. The truth was he had periods of terrible gloom when he felt he had mistaken his vocation. Or, rather, the vocation was all right, but the conditions under which he exercised it were all wrong, and those conditions, for him, were well represented by the factitious scholarship of old Considine. It was all in the air. Religion sometimes seemed no more to him than his own dotty old housekeeper, who, whatever he said, invested herself with the authority of a bishop and decided who was to see him and about what, and settled matters on her own whenever she got half a chance. Things were so bad with her that whenever the country people wanted to see him, they bribed one of the acolytes to go and ask him to come himself to their cottages. The law was represented by Sergeant Twomey, who raided the mountain pubs half an hour after closing time, in response to the orders of some lunatic superintendent at the other side of the country, while as for culture, there was the library van every couple of months, from which Considine, who acted as librarian, selected a hundred books, mainly for his own amusement. He was partial to books dealing with voyages in the Congo or Tibet ('Tibet is a very interessting country, Father'). The books that were for general circulation he censored to make sure there were no bad words like 'navel' in them that might corrupt the ignorant 'peasantry'. And then he came to Fogarty and told him he had been reading a very 'interessting' book about bird-watching in the South Seas, or something like that.

Fogarty's own temptation was towards action and energy, just as his depression was often no more than the expression of his frustration. He was an energetic and emotional man who in other circumstances would probably have become a successful businessman. Women were less of a temptation to him than the thought of an active instinctual life. All he wanted in the way of a holiday was to get rid of his collar and take a gun or rod and stand behind the bar of a country hotel. He ran the local hurling team for what it was worth, which wasn't much, and strayed down the shore with the boatmen or up the hills with the poachers and poteen-makers, who all trusted him and never tried to conceal any of their harmless misdemeanours from him. Once, for instance, in the late evening, he came unexpectedly on a party of scared poteen-makers on top of a mountain and sat down on the edge of the hollow where they were operating their still. 'Never mind me, lads!' he said, lighting a pipe. 'I'm not here at all.' 'Sure we know damn well you're not here, Father,' one old man said, and chuckled. 'But how the hell can we offer a drink to a bloody ghost?'

These were his own people, the people he loved and admired, and it was principally the feeling that he could do little or nothing for them that plunged him into those suicidal fits of gloom in which he took to the bottle. When he heard of a dance being held in a farmhouse without the permission of the priest or the police, he said, 'The blessings of God on them', and when a girl went and got herself with child by one of the islanders, he said, 'More power to her elbow!' – though he had to say these things discreetly, for fear they should get back. But the spirit of them got back, and the acolytes would whisper, 'Father, would you ever go out to Dan Mike's when you have the time?' or young men and girls would lie in wait for his car on a country road and signal timidly to him, because the country people knew that from him they would get either a regular blasting in a language they understood or the loan of a few pounds to send a girl to hospital in England so that the neighbours wouldn't know.

Fogarty knew that in the teacher's eyes this was another black mark against him, for old Considine could not understand how any educated man could make so little of the cloth as to sit drinking with 'illiterate peasants' instead of talking to a fine, well-informed man like himself about the situation in the Far East or the relationship of the Irish dioceses to the old kingdoms of the Early Middle Ages.

Then one evening Fogarty was summoned to the teacher's house on a sick call. It only struck him when he saw it there at the end of the village – a newish, red-brick box of a house, with pebble dash on the front and a steep stairway up from the front door – that it was like the teacher himself. Maisie, the teacher's unmarried daughter, was a small, plump woman with a face that must once have been attractive, for it was still all in curves, with hair about it like Mona Lisa's, though now she had lost all her freshness, and her skin was red and hard and full of wrinkles. She had a sad smile, and Fogarty could not resist a pang of pity for her because he realized that she was probably another victim of Considine's dislike of 'illiterates'. How could an 'illiterate' boy come to a house like that, or how could the teacher's daughter go out walking with him?

She had got the old man to bed, and he lay there with the engaged look of a human being at grips with his destiny. From his narrow window there was a pleasant view of the sea road and a solitary tree by the water's edge. Beyond the bay was a mountain, with a cap on it – the sign of bad weather. Fogarty gave him the last sacraments, and he confessed and received Communion with a devotion that touched Fogarty in spite of himself. He stayed on with the daughter until the doctor arrived, in case any special medicines were needed. They sat in the tiny box of a front room with a bay window and a high mahogany bookcase that filled one whole wall. She wanted to stay and make polite conversation for the priest, though all the time she was consumed with anxiety. When the doctor left, Fogarty left with him, and pressed Maisie's hand and told her to call on him for anything, at any time.

Dr Mulloy was more offhand. He was a tall, handsome young man of about Fogarty own age. Outside, standing beside his car, he said to Fogarty, 'Ah, he might last a couple of years if he minded himself. They don't, of course. You know the way it is. A wonder that daughter of his never married.'

'How could she?' Fogarty asked in a low voice, turning to glance again at the ill-designed, pretentious little suburban house. 'He'd think her too grand for any of the boys round this place.'

'Why then, indeed, if he pops off on her, she won't be too grand at all,' said the doctor. 'A wonder an educated man like that wouldn't have more sense. Sure, he can't have anything to leave her?'

'No more than myself, I dare say,' said Fogarty, who saw that the doctor only wanted to find out how much they could pay; and he went off to summon one of the boy acolytes to take Considine's place at Mass next morning.

But the next morning when Fogarty reached the sacristy, instead of the boy he had spoken to, old Considine was waiting, with everything neatly arranged in his usual pedantic manner, and a wan old man's smile on his hollow face.

'Mr Considine!' Fogarty exclaimed indignantly. 'What's the meaning of this?'

'Ah, I'm fine this morning, Father,' said the old man, with a sort of fictitious, drunken excitement. 'I woke up as fresh as a daisy.' Then he smiled malevolently and added, 'Jimmy Leary thought he was after doing me out of a job, but Dr Mulloy was too smart for him.'

'But you know yourself what Dr Mulloy said,' Fogarty protested indignantly. 'I talked to him myself about it. He said you could live for years, but any exertion might make you go off any minute.'

'And how can man die better?' retorted the teacher, with the triumphant air he wore whenever he managed to produce an apt quotation. 'You remember Macaulay, I suppose,' he added doubtfully, and then his face took on a morose look. ''Tisn't that at all,' he said. 'But 'tis the only thing I have to look forward to. The day wouldn't be the same to me if I had to miss Mass.'

Fogarty knew that he was up against an old man's stubbornness and love of habitual things, and that he was wasting his breath advising Considine himself. Instead, he talked to the parish priest, a holy and muddleheaded old man named Whelan. Whelan shook his head mournfully over the situation, but then he was a man who shook his head over everything. He had apparently decided many years ago that any form of action was hateful, and he took to his bed if people became too pressing.

'He's very obstinate, old John, but at the same time, you wouldn't like to cross him,' Whelan said.

'If you don't do something about it, you might as well put back the Costello Mass another half an hour,' Fogarty said. He was for ever trying to induce Whelan to make up his mind. 'He's getting slower every day. One of these days he'll drop dead on me at the altar.'

'Oh, I'll mention it to him,' the parish priest said regretfully. 'But I don't know would it be wise to take too strong a line. You have to humour them when they're as old as that. I dare say we'll be the same ourselves, Father.'

Fogarty knew he was wasting his breath on Whelan as well. Whelan would no doubt be as good as his word, and talk about the weather to Considine for an hour, and then end by dropping a hint, which might be entirely lost, that the old teacher shouldn't exert himself too much, and that would be all.

A month later, the old teacher had another attack, but this time Fogarty only heard of it from his mad housekeeper, who knew everything that went on in the village.

'But why didn't he send for me?' he asked sharply.

'Ah, I suppose he wasn't bad enough,' replied the housekeeper. 'Mrs MacCarthy said he got over it with pills and a sup of whiskey. They say whiskey is the best thing.'

'You're sure he didn't send for me?' Fogarty asked. There were times when he half expected the woman, in the exercise of her authority, to refuse the Last Rites to people she didn't approve of.

'Sure, of course he didn't. It was probably nothing.'

All the same, Fogarty was not easy in his mind. He knew what it meant to old people to have the priest with them at the end, and he suspected that if Considine made light of his attack, it could only be because he was afraid Fogarty would take it as final proof that he was not fit to serve Mass. He felt vaguely guilty about it. He strode down the village street, saluting the fishermen who were sitting on the sea wall in the dusk. The teacher's cottage was dark when he reached it. The cobbler, a lively little man who lived next door, was standing outside.

'I hear the old master was sick again, Tom,' said the curate.

'Begor, he was, Father,' said the cobbler. 'I hear Maisie found him crawling to the fire on his hands and knees. Terrible cold they get when they're like that. He's a sturdy old divil, though. You needn't be afraid you'll lose your altar boy for a long time yet.'

'I hope not, Tom,' said Fogarty, who knew that the cobbler, a knowledgeable man in his own way, thought there was something funny about the old schoolmaster's serving Mass. 'And I hope we're all as good when our own time comes.'

He went home, too thoughtful to chat with the fishermen. The cobbler's words had given him a sudden glimpse of old Considine's sufferings, and he was filled with the compassion that almost revolted him at times for sick bodies and suffering minds. He was an emotional man, and he knew it was partly the cause of his own savage gloom, but he could not restrain it.

Next morning, when he went to the sacristy, there was the old teacher, with his fawning smile, the smile of a guilty small boy who has done it again and this time knows he will not escape without punishment.

'You weren't too good last night, John,' the curate said, using Considine's Christian name for the first time.

'No, Father Jeremiah,' Considine replied, pronouncing the priest's name slowly and pedantically. 'I was a bit poorly in the early evening. But those pills of Dr Mulloy's are a wonder.'

'And isn't it a hard thing to say you never sent for me?' Fogarty went on.

Considine blushed furiously, and this time he looked really guilty and scared.

'But I wasn't that bad, Father,' he protested with senile intensity, his hands beginning to shake and his eyes to sparkle. 'I wasn't as frightened yesterday as I was the first time. It's the first time it frightens you. You feel sure you'll never last it out. But after that you get to expect it.'

'Will you promise me never to do a thing like that again?' the curate asked earnestly. 'Will you give me your word that you'll send for me, any hour of the day or night?'

'Very well, Father,' Considine replied sullenly. ''Tis very good of you. I'll give you my word I'll send for you.'

And they both recognized the further, unspoken part of the compact between them. Considine would send for Fogarty, but nothing Fogarty saw or heard was to permit him again to try to deprive the old teacher of his office. Not that he any longer wished to do so. Now that he recognized the passion of will in the old man, Fogarty's profound humanity only made him anxious to second it and enable Considine to do what clearly he wished to do – die in harness. Fogarty had also begun to recognize that it was not mere obstinacy that got the old man out of his bed each morning and brought him shivering and sighing and shuffling up the village street. There was obstinacy there, and plenty of it, but there was something else, which the curate valued more; something he felt the lack of in himself. It wasn't easy to put a name on it. Faith was one name, but it was no more than a name and was used to cover too many excesses of devotion that the young priest found distasteful. This was something else, something that made him ashamed of his own human weakness and encouraged him to fight the depression, which seemed at times as if it would overwhelm him. It was more like the miracle of the Mass itself, metaphor become reality. Now when he thought of his own joke about serving the teacher's Mass, it didn't seem quite so much like a joke.

One morning in April, Fogarty noticed as he entered the sacristy that the old man was looking very ill. As he helped Fogarty, his hands shook piteously. Even his harsh voice had a quaver in it, and his lips were pale. Fogarty looked at him and wondered if he shouldn't say something, but decided against it. He went in, preceded by Considine, and noticed that though the teacher tried to hold himself erect, his walk was little more than a shuffle. He went up to the altar, but found it almost impossible to concentrate on what he was doing. He heard the labouring steps behind him, and as the old man started to raise the heavy book on to the altar, Fogarty paused for a moment and looked under his brows. Considine's face was now white as a sheet, and as he raised the book he sighed. Fogarty wanted to cry out, 'For God's sake, man, lie down!' He wanted to hold Considine's head on his knee and whisper into his ear. Yet he realized that to the strange old man behind him this would be no kindness. The only kindness he could do him was to crush down his own weak warmheartedness and continue the Sacrifice. Never had he seemed further away from the reality of the Mass. He heard the labouring steps, the panting breath, behind him, and it seemed as if they had lasted some timeless time before he heard another heavy sigh as Considine managed to kneel.

At last, Fogarty found himself waiting for a response that did not come. He looked round quickly. The old man had fallen silently forward on to the altar steps. His arm was twisted beneath him and his head was turned sideways. His jaw had fallen, and his eyes were sightless.

'John!' Fogarty called, in a voice that rang through the church. 'Can you hear me? John!'

There was no reply, and the curate placed him on his back, with one of the altar cushions beneath his head. Fogarty felt under the surplice for his buttons and unloosed them. He felt for the heart. It had stopped; there was no trace of breathing. Through the big window at the west end he saw the churchyard trees and the sea beyond them, bright in the morning light. The whole church seemed terribly still, so that the mere ticking of the clock filled it with its triumphant mocking of the machine of flesh and blood that had fallen silent.

Fogarty went quickly to the sacristy and returned with the Sacred Oils to anoint the teacher. He knew he had only to cross the road for help, to have the old man's body removed and get an acolyte to finish the Mass, but he wanted no help. He felt strangely lightheaded. Instead, when he had done, he returned to the altar and resumed the Mass where he had left off, murmuring the responses to himself. As he did so, he realized that he was imitating the harsh voice of Considine. There was something unearthly about it, for now the altar which had seemed so far away was close to him, and though he was acutely aware of every detail, of every sound, he had no feeling that he was lacking in concentration. When he turned to face the body of the church and said, '*Dominus vobiscum*', he saw as if for the first time the prostrate form with its fallen jaw and weary eyes, under the light that came in from the sea through the trees in their first leaf, and murmured, '*Et cum spiritu tuo*' for the man whose spirit had flown. Then, when he had said the prayers after Mass beside the body, he took his biretta, donned it, and walked by the body, carrying his chalice, and feeling as he walked that some figure was walking before him, slowly, saying goodbye. In his excited mind echoed the rubric: 'Then, having adored and thanked God for everything, he goes away.'

(1955)

Anchors

It was always a mystery to me how anyone as rational as myself came of parents so befuddled. Sometimes it was as if I lived on a mountain-peak away up in the sunlight while they fumbled and squabbled in a valley below. Except for a tendency to quarrel violently about politics, Father was not so bad. At least, there were things I could talk to him about, but Mother was a constant source of irritation to me as well as to him.

She was a tall, thin, mournful woman, with beautiful blue eyes and a clear complexion, but harassed by hard work and piety. She had lost her second child in childbirth, and, having married late so that she was incapable of having further children, she tended to brood over it. She had no method, and was always losing a few shillings on the horses, borrowing to make it up so that Father wouldn't know, and then taking sips of whiskey on the side to nerve her for the ordeal of confessing it to him. She was in and out of churches all day, trying to pump the sly ones who had friends in the priesthood for inside information about saints who were free of their favours. At any time a few pounds would have made her solvent again, and a favour like that would be nothing to a saint. If she worried over the souls of Father and me, that was pure kindness of heart, because she had quite enough to do, worrying about herself.

Her brand of religion really got under my skin. As I say, I was a natural rationalist. Even as a young fellow, all my sympathies were with the labour movement, and I had nothing but amused contempt for the sort of faction-fighting that Father and his contemporaries mistook for politics. I had an intensely orderly mind, and had no difficulty in working out a technique to keep myself near the head of the class in school. But nothing would convince Mother but that you passed examinations by the aid of the Infant Jesus of Prague and St Rose of Lima. She was a plain woman who regarded Heaven as a glorified extension of the Cork County Council and the saints as elected representatives whose duty it was to attend to the interests of the constituents and relatives. In religion, education, and business the principle of the open competitive examination simply did not exist for Mother. People might say what they liked, but 'pull' was the thing. Naturally, in the manner of elected representatives the world over, the saints were a mixed lot. Some were smarter or more conscientious than others; some promised more than they could perform, while others had never been any good to anyone, and it was folly to rely on them. You had to study form as though they were horses, and, apart from the racing column, the only thing that interested Mother in the evening paper was the chain of acknowledgements of 'favours received on promise of publication'. From this, anyone could see that the Infant Jesus of Prague and St Rose of Lima left the rest of the field behind. Hard work might be all right in its own place; brilliance might do some good if it didn't get you into trouble; but examinations were passed by faith rather than good works.

It was a subtle sort of insult to which I was particularly sensitive, though, of course, I never let on. I had trained myself with the foolish people in school to be silent, and the most I ever permitted myself when I was riled was a sniff or a smile. I had discovered that this made them much madder.

'You'd never imagine the saints would be so keen to get into the papers,' I said one evening when she insisted on reading it aloud.

'Musha, why wouldn't they?' she asked, showing her teeth in a smile. 'I suppose they're as glad to be told they're appreciated as the rest of us.'

'Oh, I dare say,' I said lightly, 'but you wouldn't think they'd be so mad on publicity.'

'And how would people know?' she asked timidly. 'Look at this young fellow, for instance. He passed an examination the fourth time after praying to St Rose.'

'Maybe he'd have passed it the first time without praying to anybody if he did his work,' I suggested.

'Ah,' she said, 'everybody can't be smart.'

'But why worry to be smart?' I asked, getting more supercilious than ever. 'Why worry to do anything? You ought to try out your method on someone else.'

'How do you mean, on someone else?'

'Well, working on me, you're never going to find out the truth about it. You should try it on someone who needs it. There's a fellow in my class called Mahony who could do with someone's prayers.'

'Why then, indeed, I'll pray for the poor boy if you want me to.'

'Do,' I said encouragingly. 'We'll see how it works out. But you'll have to leave me out of your prayers, or we'll never get it straight.'

'Why, then, what a thing I'd do!' she retorted with real indignation.

My father never interfered in these discussions, except for an occasional snort of amusement at some impertinence of mine, and, for all the apparent interest he took in them might as well not have been listening. He was a tall, gaunt man with a haunted look, and it seemed to me that he was haunted by the revolutionary politics of his generation. In so far as the Church had opposed the revolution and distorted its aims, he was violently anti-clerical, particularly when it was a question of Father Dempsey, the parish priest. Dempsey was a fat, coarse, jolly man, and he had made fun of Father when Father had called on him to arrange for Masses for the souls of some revolutionary friends of his. I did not think much of Father's generation or of revolutionists who didn't see that before you dealt with the British Empire you had first to put the Dempseys in their place.

By the time I went to the university I hadn't a shred of belief left in St Rose of Lima or Cathleen ni Houlihan. I thought them both fetishes of the older generation, and was seriously considering severing my relations with the Church. I was restrained partly by fear of the effect that this would have on my parents, particularly my father, and partly because I could see nothing to put in its place. I didn't have to look far to see that man was prone to evil. I knew well that for all my reasonableness I had a violent temper and brutal appetites. I knew that there was a streak of positive cruelty in me. I could not even walk through the main street without averting my eyes from the shop windows that displayed women's underclothing, and sometimes it drove me mad with rage because I knew that the owners and their staffs were supposed to be pious Catholics. I had begun walking out with a girl called Babiche, which made it even worse, because she was interested in underclothing. She thought I was a queer coon, and no wonder. Little did she know of the passions that raged in me.

But in the battle between fear of the evil in myself and sheer boredom with the superstitions of people like Mother, boredom had it, and I knew I must express this in action. It was not enough to believe something; I had to show that I believed it. Now there was nothing between myself and avowed agnosticism but fear of the effect it would have on my parents.

Father and I usually went to Mass together, not to the parish church where he might be submitted to the ordeal of listening to Father Dempsey, but to the Franciscan church in Sheares Street, where he had gone to get his Masses said and where they hadn't laughed at him. Father was not a man to forget a kindness. After Mass we usually took a walk up the tree-lined Mardyke, over Wellington Bridge, and back through the expensive suburb of Sunday's Well. There were beautiful houses along the way, and Father knew who had built them and never tired of admiring them. I enjoyed those walks, the hillside of Sunday's Well seen under the trees of the Dyke, the river by the tramstop, and the great view of the city from the top of Wyse's Hill, but mainly Father's company because these were the only occasions when we were alone together and I could talk to him.

One Sunday in spring as we went up the Dyke I decided to break the bad news to him.

'You know, Dad, there's something I wanted to tell you,' I said, and realized the moment I had said it that I had begun badly. Father started and frowned. If you wanted to get at Father you had to prepare him beforehand, as you prepare an audience in the theatre for the hero's death. Mother never prepared him for anything, seeing that she never told him anything until she had herself broken down, and as a result she nearly always provoked the wrong reaction.

'What's that?' he snapped suspiciously.

'Oh, just that I don't think I can come to Mass with you any more,' I said, trying to make myself sound casual.

'Why not?' he asked angrily.

'Well,' I said deliberately, trying to make it sound as though I were full of grief about it, 'I don't know that I believe in God any more.'

'You what?' he asked, stopping dead and looking at me out of the corner of his eye. It was the reaction I had feared, the spontaneous reaction of a man who has been told that his wife is betting again.

'I'm sorry, Dad,' I said reasonably. 'I was afraid it would upset you, but at the same time I felt you ought to be told.'

Father drew a deep breath through his nose as though to indicate that I had a very lighthearted attitude to his feelings, gave me another look out of the corner of his eye and reached for his pipe. He went behind a tree to light it and walked on again, puffing at it. Then he sucked his lips in a funny way he had and grinned at me.

'I was afraid you were going to tell me something serious,' he said.

I smiled. At the same time I was surprised and suspicious. I knew he was lacking in Mother's brand of religiosity, but I had not expected this particular tone and had no confidence in it.

'It seems serious enough to me,' I said.

'You're sure 'tis God you don't believe in?' he asked roguishly. 'Not Dempsey by any chance?'

'I can't very well pretend I don't believe in the existence of Dempsey,' I said with a smile.

'It's a very important distinction,' he said gravely. 'One is anti-clericalism, a view taken only by the most religious people – myself, for instance. The other is atheism, a view held by – ah, a lot of people who are also deeply religious. You'd want to be sure you don't get in the wrong camp.'

'You think the anti-clerical camp would be good enough for me?' I asked.

'I wouldn't get things mixed up if I were you,' he said, growing serious again. 'People are only what society makes them, you know. You might think you were against religion when all you were against was a lot of scared old women. Country towns are bad that way. Religion is something more than that.'

'I'm not sure I know what you mean by religion,' I said, trying to steer him into one of my favourite arguments, but he wasn't having any.

'Ah, 'tisn't what I mean by religion, boy,' he replied testily. 'The best brains in the world are at that for thousands of years, and you talk as if I was just after making it up.'

'Well, I've only been at it for six months,' I said reasonably, 'so I have time enough. What do you think I ought to do?'

'I think you ought to make sure what you're giving up before you do it,' he said. 'I don't want you coming to me in six months' time and telling me about some astounding discovery you could have made in a penny catechism. You know, of course, a thing like that will come against you if you're looking for a job.'

'You think it would?' I asked in some surprise. There were still a lot of things I did not know about life.

'I'm damn sure it would,' he said with a little snarl of amusement. 'If you think I'm ever likely to get a church to build you're mistaken. But that's neither here nor there. If you felt like that about it I wouldn't try to stop you.'

'I know that,' I said affectionately. 'That's why I didn't want to do anything without asking your advice.'

'Oh, my advice!' he sniffed. 'I'm not a proper person to advise you. Get hold of some intelligent young priest of about your own age and get him to advise you. And there's a few books you could read.'

Now, this was the first I had heard of religious books in the home, apart from some detestable tracts that Mother had bought. Father searched them out from a pile of old papers in the lumber-room; newspapers, pamphlets, election hand-bills, and broadsheet ballads – Father's wild oats. He squatted on the floor, sucking his pipe and enthusing over them. 'Begor, I never knew I had this. This would be valuable. Look! An account of poor Jim Tracy's trial – he was shot in Cork barrack after. You ought to read that.' He had lost all interest in the books by the time he found them – a couple of volumes of Newman, a handbook of dogmatic theology and a study of Thomas Aquinas. It was a side of Father I'd never known. It was a side that didn't seem too familiar to Father himself, either, for he raised his brows over pages he had underlined and scored along the margins. As he read the marked passages he nodded a couple of times, but it was a puzzled sort of nod. He seemed uneasy and anxious to get back to more familiar surroundings.

However, it was all I needed, and it quieted the tumult in my mind. I had fancied myself so much alone, and it was a relief to know that others I could respect had shared my doubts. Church services that had left me bored took on a new interest for me. It was pleasant to be able to explain details of the rubrics to Babiche, who knew as little of them as I had known.

The result was a new wave of fervour, different from any I had known as a kid. I had always been a bit of a busybody and enjoyed helping and protecting other people, but because I had been afraid of being thought a sissy, I had concealed it. Now that I had found another source of strength outside myself, I was able to dispense with my fears. I need no longer be ashamed of coming up the road with one raggy kid riding my neck and another swinging from my arm.

And because Mother had always been such a sore trial to me, I felt I must be especially kind to her, even to the point of taking her side against Father. I rose at seven each morning, lit the fire, and brought herself and Father their tea in bed. I stayed around the house in my free hours to keep her company and do the odd jobs that Father could never be induced to do for her. I had never realized before what a tough life she had had of it; how awkward was the kitchen where she had to work, and how few comforts there were for her. I even went to the point of making an armchair for her, since when Father was in she had none of her own.

Now, anyone would assume that a pious woman like Mother would have been delighted to see her godless son turn suddenly into a walking saint. Not a bit of it. The more virtuous I became, the gloomier she got. Only gradually did it dawn on me that she did not approve of men saving their own souls, since, like cooking and laundry, this was something that could only be done for them by their womenfolk. A man who tried to do if for himself was no man at all.

'Is there anything I can get you in town?' I would ask, and she would smile mournfully at me with her fine set of false teeth.

'Ah, no, child. What would you get?'

'Oh, I just wondered if there were any messages.'

'And if there are, can't I do them myself? I'm not too old for that, am I?'

I was studying for my final at the time and she was in a frenzy, working on St Rose. As part of my new character I let her be, contenting myself with suggesting saints who were in some way related to culture – St Finnbarr, for instance, the supposed founder of the college, or St Thomas Aquinas. She had heard of St Finnbarr as patron of the Protestant cathedral, so she refused point-blank to have anything to do with him. She didn't dispute the man's orthodoxy, but it wouldn't be lucky. She didn't like to commit herself on the subject of St Thomas, who might, for all she knew, be quite decent, but by this time she was convinced that I was only making up saints to annoy her.

'Who was he?' she asked without any great confidence.

'Well, he happened to be the greatest intellect of the Church,' I said sweetly.

'Was it he wrote that old book you were reading?'

'No, that was G. K. Chesterton – a different family altogether.'

'Wouldn't you think if he was so great that someone would hear about him?'

Father gave a snort and went out to the front door. As I passed out he gave me one of his sideways looks.

'I'd try the African Mission,' he said.

'Funny the different forms religion takes,' I said, standing beside him with my hands in my pockets.

'Religion?' he repeated. 'You don't call that religion? No woman has any religion.'

As usual I felt that he was exaggerating for the sake of effect, but I had to admit that whatever religion Mother had was not of an orthodox kind. At the time I was deeply concerned with the problem of faith as against good works, but with her the problem simply didn't arise. She was just then going through a crisis on the subject of a new apparition that had taken place in County Kerry, and had succeeded in laying hold of a bottle of water from a holy well where the Blessed Virgin and a number of saints had appeared. The half of Ireland was making pilgrimages to the spot, and what made it all more mysterious was that the newspapers were not allowed by the Church authorities to refer to it in any way. I made inquiries and discovered that the apparitions had taken place on the farm of a well-known poteen-maker whose trade had fallen on evil days; that the police had searched every electrical shop for miles around in hopes of tracing batteries for a large magic lantern, and that there was no well on the farm. At the same time she was very excited by the report that Father Dempsey had performed a miraculous cure on a child with diphtheria, though, according to Mother's brand of Catholicism, this meant he had taken the disease on himself, and she was now anxiously waiting till he succumbed to it.

I kept on preaching sound doctrine on such matters to her with no great effect. But I did not grow alarmed for her till some weeks later. As I say, she had never got over the loss of her second child. In fact, she had created a sort of fantasy life for him into which she retreated whenever the horses became more incalculable than usual. She had nursed him through various childish ailments, sent him to school, and seen him through college. He had no clear outline in her mind except the negative one of not resembling me. *He* passed his examinations entirely through the power of her prayers. Naturally, he had shown a vocation from the earliest age, and I strongly suspect that for a great part of the time he was a bishop or archbishop who put manners on the raw young priests her supercilious cronies took such pride in. I had heard about him so often that I didn't attach any great importance to the matter. It was only as a result of my own reading that I began to see its doctrinal significance and realized that Mother was a heretic. I remonstrated with her, mildly enough at first, but, for all the difference it made to her, I could have been speaking of the poteen-maker's apparitions. She had accustomed herself to the thought of my brother's waiting for her in Heaven, and she continued to see him there, regardless of anything I said. As usual, Father said nothing.

'Ah, well,' she said one evening when I was having tea, 'it won't be so long till I see your brother again, please God.'

'Father and I needn't worry much about you so,' I said.

'Wisha, what do you mean, child?' she asked in alarm.

'You'll have an awful long time to wait if you're waiting for that,' I said, pleasantly enough, as I thought. 'You'll see both of us under the sod.' Then, as I saw her gaping at me, I added, 'I only mean that he can't very well be in Heaven.'

'Musha, what nonsense you're talking!' she exclaimed roughly, though at the same time she was disturbed. 'Is it an innocent child?'

'I suppose you'll tell me next you never heard of Original Sin?' I asked.

'Ah, for all the sin my poor child had on him!' she sighed. 'Where else would he be, only in Heaven, the little angel!'

'The Church says he's in Limbo,' I said cheerfully, taking another mouthful of bacon.

'The Church does?'

'Yes.'

'In Limbo?'

'That's what we're supposed to believe.'

'Pisherogues!' she said angrily.

My father got up and strode to the front door with his hands in his trouser pockets. I controlled myself as best I could at her unmannerly reference to the doctrine of Original Sin as fairytales. It didn't come too well from a woman who had just been telling us of a priest that died suddenly after seeing the Holy Ape on the poteen-maker's property.

'That's what you may think,' I said coldly. 'Of course, you don't have to believe it unless you want to, but it is a fundamental dogma and you can't be a Catholic without it.'

'Pisherogues!' she repeated violently. 'I was a Catholic before they were. What do they know about it?'

'So you *do* claim the right to private judgement?' I said menacingly.

'Private what?' she asked in exasperation.

'Private judgement,' I repeated. 'Of course, you'll find a lot of people to agree with you, but you'd better realize that you're speaking as a Protestant.'

'Are you mad?' she asked, half rising from her chair at the implication that there was anything in common between her and the poor unenlightened souls who attended St Finnibarr's.

'Isn't it true that you won't believe anything only what suits yourself?' I asked patiently.

'Listen to him, you sweet God!' Mother moaned. 'I only believe what suits me! Me that have the knees wore off myself praying for him! You pup!' she added in what for her was a flash of real anger.

'But that's exactly what you do,' I said gently, ignoring her abuse. 'You believe things that no one ever asked you to believe. You believe in the poteen-maker's apparitions and his holy well, and Dempsey's diphtheria cure, but you won't believe the essential teaching of the Church whenever it disagrees with your own foolish notions. What sort of religion is that?'

'Ah,' she said, almost weeping with rage, 'I was practising my religion before you were born. And my mother before me. Oh, you pup, to talk like that to me!'

I sighed and shrugged and left the house. I was more upset than I let on to be. I had seen her in plenty of states before, but never so angry and bewildered. I had a date with Babiche by the bridge, and we went up the hills together in the direction of a wood that was a favourite haunt of ours. I told her the whole story, making fun of it as I did so. After all, it was funny. Here had I been on the point of cutting loose from religion altogether because of my family, and now that I had really got back the faith it was only to discover that my own home was a nest of heretics.

It struck me that Babiche was not taking it in the spirit in which I offered it. Usually, she made no attempt to follow up an argument, but caught at some name or word like 'Athanasius' or 'Predestination' and then repeated it for months with joyous inconsequence and in contexts with which it had nothing whatever to do. This evening she seemed to be angry and argumentative as well.

'That was a nice thing to say to your mother,' she snapped.

'What was wrong with it?' I asked in surprise.

'Plenty. You weren't the kid's mother. She was.'

'Now, really, Babiche,' I protested, 'what has that to do with it? I suppose I was his brother, but that's neither here nor there.'

'A dead kid is neither here nor there,' she said sullenly. 'You don't care. You're only delighted to have a brother in Limbo, or wherever the blazes it is. It's like having one in the Civil Service. If you had another you could say was in Hell you'd feel you were made for life.'

I was taken aback. I knew Babiche was unjust, and I realized that Father was right and that no woman in the world had any religion whatever, but at the same time I felt I might have gone too far. I did tend to take my own line firmly and go on without considering how other people might feel about it. We were sitting in a clearing above the wood, looking down at the river winding through the valley in the evening light. I put out my hand, but Babiche pulled her own hand away.

'I'm sorry, Babiche,' I said apologetically. 'I didn't mean to start a row.'

Then she grinned and gave me back her hand, and in no time we were embracing. Babiche was anything but a profound thinker, above all when someone was making love to her. I found myself making love to her as I'd never done before, and she enjoyed it. Then she looked away towards the city and began to laugh.

'What's the joke?' I asked.

'If I have a kid like that, and you start telling me he's in Limbo, I'll scratch your eyes out,' she said.

This time I felt really guilty towards Mother. But worse than that, the wild beast in me was in danger of breaking out again. It was horrible. You swung from instinct to judgement, and from judgement back to instinct, and nothing ever seemed to arrest the pendulum.

But next morning when I woke the sun was shining through the attic window, and I lay watching it, feeling that something very peculiar had happened to me. I didn't yet know what it was, but I realized that it was very pleasant. I felt fine. Then it all became clear. The pendulum had stopped. I had lost my faith, and this time I had lost it for good. My brother might not be in Heaven, but I was sure he wasn't in Limbo either. I didn't believe in Limbo. It was too silly. The previous months of exultation and anxiety seemed like a nightmare. Nor was I in the least afraid of the beast in myself because I knew now that whatever happened I should always care too much for Babiche to injure her. Anyone who really cared for human beings need never be afraid of either conscience or passion.

The following Sunday when Father and I reached the church door I stopped and smiled at him.

'I'll see you after Mass, Dad,' I said.

Father showed no surprise, but he paused before replying in a businesslike tone: 'I think we'll go down the Marina for a change. We weren't down there this year.'

I was heartsick at his disappointment and the brave way he kept his word. That was one thing to be said for the older generation: they knew the meaning of principle.

'You know the way I feel about it?' I said, squaring up and looking at him.

'What's that?' he asked sharply. 'Oh, yes,' he added, 'we all go through it. You have time enough . . . Tell me, who's that little black-haired girl you're knocking round with?'

'Babiche Regan?' I asked, surprised that he knew so much.

'Is she one of the Regans of Sunday's Well?'

'That's right,' I replied, a bit mystified.

'They're a very good family,' Father said approvingly. 'I used to know her father on the County Council. Is she a fancy or a regular?'

'Well,' I said, shrugging my shoulders in embarrassment, 'I suppose I'll be marrying her one of these days.'

'Good man! Good man!' he said with a nod. 'Ah, well, by the time you're settled down, you'll know your own mind better . . . Now, don't be late for that walk.'

I went up the Mardyke in its summer-morning calm, a free man for the first time. But I didn't feel free. There was something about Father's tone that had disturbed me. It was as though he expected Babiche to turn out like Mother and me like himself. It was hardly possible, of course: even he couldn't believe that Babiche would ever prove so irrational or I so weak. But all the same I was disturbed.

(1952)

The Party

Old Johnny, one of the Gas Company's watchmen, was a man with a real appreciation of his job. Most of the time, of course, it was a cold, comfortless job, with no one to talk to, and he envied his younger friend Tim Coakley, the postman. Postmen had a cushy time of it – always watched and waited for, bringing good news or bad news, often called in to advise, and (according to Tim, at least) occasionally called in for more intimate purposes. Tim, of course, was an excitable man, and he could be imagining a lot of that, though Johnny gave him the benefit of the doubt. At the same time, queer things happened to Johnny now and again that were stranger than anything Tim could tell. As it seemed to Johnny, people got it worse at night; the wild ones grew wilder, the gloomy ones gloomier. Whatever it was in them that had light in it burned more clearly, the way the stars and moon did when the sun went down. It was the darkness that did it. Johnny would be sitting in his hut for hours in the daylight and no one even gave him a second glance, but once darkness fell, people would cross the street to look at his brazier, and even stop to speak to him.

One night, for instance, in the week before Christmas, he was watching in a big Dublin square, with a railed-off park in the middle of it and doctors' and lawyers' houses on all the streets about it. That suited Johnny fine, particularly at that time of year, when there was lots of visiting and entertaining. He liked to be at the centre of things, and he always appreciated the touch of elegance: the stone steps leading up to the tall door, with the figures entering and leaving looking small in the lighted doorway, and the slight voices echoing on the great brick sounding-board of the square.

One house in particular attracted him. It was all lit up as if for a party, and the curtains were pulled back to reveal the tall, handsome rooms with decorated plaster ceilings. A boy with a basket came and rang, and a young man in evening dress leaned out of the window and told the boy to leave the stuff in the basement. As he did so, a girl came and rested her hand on his shoulder, and she was in evening dress too. Johnny liked that. He liked people with a bit of style. If he had had the good fortune to grow up in a house like that, he would have done the right thing too. And even though he hadn't, it pleased him to watch the show. Johnny, who came of a generation before trade unions, knew that in many ways it is pleasanter to observe than to participate. He only hoped there would be singing; he was very partial to a bit of music.

But this night a thing happened the like of which had never happened to Johnny before. The door of the house opened and closed, and a man in a big cloth coat like fur came across the road to him. When he came closer, Johnny saw that he was a tall, thin man with greying hair and a pale discontented face.

'Like to go home to bed for a couple of hours?' the man asked in a low voice.

'What's that?' said Johnny, in astonishment.

'I'll stay here and mind your box.'

'Oh, you would, would you?' Johnny said, under the impression that the man must have drink taken.

'I'm not joking,' said the man shortly.

The grin faded on Johnny's face, and he hoped God would direct him to say the right thing. This could be dangerous. It suggested only one thing – a check-up – though in this season of goodwill you'd think people would be a bit more charitable, even if a man had slipped away for a few minutes for a drink. But that was the way of bosses everywhere. Even Christmas wasn't sacred to them. Johnny put on an appearance of great sternness. 'Oho,' he said. 'I can't afford to do things like that. There's valuable property here belonging to the Gas Company. I could lose my job over a thing like that.'

'You won't lose your job,' the man said. 'I won't leave here till you come back. If there's any trouble about it, I'll get you another job. I suppose it's money you want.'

'I never asked you for anything,' Johnny replied indignantly. 'And I can't go home at this hour, with no bus to bring me back.'

'I suppose there's other places you can go,' the man replied. 'There's a quid, and I won't expect you till two.'

The sight of the money changed Johnny's view of the matter. If a rich man wanted to amuse himself doing Johnny's job for a while – a little weakness of rich men that Johnny had heard of in other connections – and was willing to pay for it, that was all right. Rich men had to have their little jokes. Or of course, it could be a bet.

'Oh, well,' he said, rising and giving himself a shake, 'so long as there's no harm in it!' He hadn't seen the man go into the house where they were having a party, so he must live there. 'I suppose it's a joke?' he added, looking at the man out of the corner of his eye.

'It's no joke to me,' the man said gloomily.

'Oh, I wasn't being inquisitive, of course,' Johnny said hastily. 'But I see there was to be a party in the house. I thought it might be something to do with that.'

'There's your quid,' said the man. 'You needn't be back till three unless you want to. I won't get much sleep anyway.'

Johnny thanked him profusely and left in high good humour. He foresaw that the man would probably be of great use to him some time. A man who could offer to get you a job just like that was not to be slighted. And besides he had an idea of how he was going to spend the next hour or so, at least, and a very pleasant way it was. He took a bus to Ringstead to the house of Tim Coakley, the postman. Tim, though a good deal younger, was very friendly with him, and he was an expansive man who loved any excuse for a party.

As Johnny expected, Tim, already on his way to bed, welcomed him with his two arms out and a great shout of laughter. He was bald and fat, with a high-pitched voice. Johnny showed Tim and his wife the money, and announced that he was treating them to a dozen of stout. Like the decent man he was, Tim didn't want to take the money for the stout from Johnny, but Johnny insisted. 'Wait till I tell you, man!' he said triumphantly. 'The like of it never happened before in the whole history of the Gas Company.'

As Johnny told the story, it took close on half an hour, though this included Mrs Coakley's departure and return with the dozen of stout. And then the real pleasure began, because the three of them had to discuss what it all meant. Why was the gentleman in the big coat sitting in the cold of the square looking at the lights and listening to the noise of the party in his own home? It was a real joy to Johnny to hear his friend analyse it, for Tim had a powerful intellect, full of novel ideas, and in no time what had begun as a curious incident in a watchman's life was beginning to expand into a romance, a newspaper case. Tim at once ruled out the idea of a joke. What would be the point in a joke like that? A bet was the more likely possibility. It could be that the man had bet someone he could take the watchman's place for the best part of the night without being detected, but in Tim's view there was one fatal flaw in this explanation. Why would the man wear a coat as conspicuous as the one that Johnny had described? There would be big money on a wager like that, and the man would be bound to try and disguise himself better. No, there must be another explanation, and as Tim drank more stout, his imagination played over the theme with greater audacity and logic, till Johnny himself began to feel uncomfortable. He began to perceive that it might be a more serious matter than he had thought.

'We've agreed that it isn't a joke,' said Tim, holding up one finger. 'We've agreed that it isn't a bet,' he added, holding up another finger. 'There is only one explanation that covers the whole facts,' he said, holding up his open hand. 'The man is watching the house.'

'Watching his own house?' Johnny asked incredulously.

'Exactly. Why else would he pay you good money to sit in your box? A man like that, that could go to his club and be drinking champagne and playing cards all night in the best of company? Isn't it plain that he's doing it only to have cover?'

'So 'twould seem,' said Johnny meekly, like any interlocutor of Socrates.

'Now, the next question is: who is he watching?' said Tim.

'Just so,' said Johnny with a mystified air.

'So we ask ourselves: who would a man like that be watching?' Tim went on triumphantly.

'Burglars,' said Mrs Coakley.

'Burglars?' her husband asked with quiet scorn. 'I suppose they'd walk in the front door?'

'He might be watching the cars, though,' Johnny said. 'There's a lot of them young hooligans around, breaking into cars. I seen them.'

'Ah, Johnny, will you have sense?' Tim asked wearily. 'Look, if that was all the man wanted, couldn't he give you a couple of bob to keep an eye on the cars? For the matter of that, couldn't he have a couple of plainclothesmen round the square? Not at all, man! He's watching somebody, and what I say is, the one he's watching is his own wife.'

'His wife?' Johnny exclaimed, aghast. 'What would he want to watch his wife for?'

'Because he thinks someone is going to that house tonight that should not be there. Someone that wouldn't come at all unless he knew the husband was out. So what does the husband do? He pretends to go out, but instead of that he hides in a watchman's box across the road and waits for him. What other explanation is there?'

'Now, couldn't it be someone after his daughter?' said Johnny.

'What daughter?' Tim asked, hurt at Johnny's lack of logic. 'What would a well-to-do man like that do if his daughter was going with a fellow he considered unsuitable? First, he would give the daughter a clock in the jaw, and then he would say to the maid or butler or whoever he have, "If a Mr Murphy comes to this house again looking for Miss Alice, kindly tell him she is not at home." That's all he'd do, and that would be the end of your man. No, Johnny, the one he's watching is the wife, and I can only hope it won't get you into any trouble.'

'You don't think I should tell the bobbies about it?' Johnny asked in alarm.

'What *could* you tell the bobbies, though?' Tim asked. 'That there was a man in your box that paid you a quid to let him use it? What proof have you that a crime is going to be committed? None! And this is only suspicion. There's nothing you can do now, only let things take their course till two o'clock, and then I'll go round with you and see what really happened.'

'But what could happen?' Johnny asked irritably.

'He sounds to me like a desperate man,' Tim said gravely.

'Oh, desperate entirely,' agreed his wife, who was swallowing it all like a box of creams.

'You don't mean you think he might do him in?' asked Johnny.

'Him, or the wife, Johnny,' said Tim. 'Or both. Of course, it's nothing to do with you what he does,' he added comfortingly. 'Whatever it is, you had neither hand, act, nor part in it. It is only the annoyance of seeing your name in the papers.'

'A man should never take advice from anybody,' Johnny commented bitterly, opening another bottle of stout. Johnny was not a drinking man, but he was worried. He valued his own blameless character, and he knew there were people bad enough to pretend he ought not to have left his post for a couple of hours, even at Christmas time, when everybody was visiting friends. He was not a scholar like Tim, and nobody had warned him of the desperate steps that rich men took when their wives acted flighty.

'Come on,' Tim said, putting on his coat. 'I'm coming with you.'

'Now, I don't want your name dragged into this,' Johnny protested. 'You have a family to think of, too.'

'I'm coming with you, Johnny,' Tim said in a deep voice, laying his hand on Johnny's arm. 'We're old friends, and friends stick together. Besides, as a postman, I'm more accustomed to this sort of thing than you are. You're a simple man. You might say the wrong thing. Leave it to me to answer the questions.'

Johnny was grateful and said so. He was a simple man, as Tim said, and, walking back through the sleeping town, expecting to see police cordons and dead bodies all over the place, he was relieved to have a level-headed fellow like Tim along with him. As they approached the square and their steps perceptibly slowed, Tim suggested in a low voice that Johnny should stand at the corner of the square while he himself scouted round to see if everything was all right. Johnny agreed, and stopped at the corner. Everything seemed quiet enough. There were only two cars outside the house. There were lights still burning in it, but though the windows were open, as though to clear the air, there was no sound from within. His brazier still burned bright and even in the darkness under the trees of the park. Johnny wished he had never left it.

He saw Tim cross to the other side of the road and go slowly by the brazier. Then Tim stopped and said something, but Johnny could not catch the words. After a few moments, Tim went on, turned the corner, and came back round the square. It took him close on ten minutes, and when he reached Johnny it was clear that something was wrong.

'What is it?' Johnny asked in agony.

'Nothing, Johnny,' Tim said sadly. 'But do you know who the man is?'

'Sure I told you I never saw him before,' said Johnny.

'I know him,' said Tim. 'That's Hardy that owns the big stores in George's Street. It's his house. The man must be worth hundreds of thousands.'

'But what about his wife, man?' asked Johnny.

'Ah, his wife died ten years ago. He's a most respectable man. I don't know what he's doing here, but it's nothing for you to fret about. I'm glad for everyone's sake. Goodnight, Johnny.'

'Goodnight, Tim, and thanks, thanks!' cried Johnny, his heart already lighter.

The Gas Company's property and his reputation were both secure. The strange man had not killed his wife or his wife's admirer, because the poor soul, having been dead for ten years, couldn't have an admirer for her husband or anyone else to kill. And now he could sit in peace by his brazier and watch the dawn come up over the decent city of Dublin. The relief was so sharp that he felt himself superior to Tim. It was all very well for postmen to talk about the interesting life they led, but they hadn't the same experiences as watchmen. Watchmen might seem simple to postmen, but they had a wisdom of their own, a wisdom that came of the silence and darkness when a man is left alone with his thoughts, like a sailor aboard ship. Thinking of the poor man sitting like that in the cold under the stars watching a party at his own house, Johnny wondered that he could ever have paid attention to Tim. He approached his brazier smiling.

'Everything nice and quiet for you?' he asked.

'Except for some gasbag that stopped for a chat five minutes ago,' the other replied with rancour. Johnny felt rather pleased to hear Tim described as a gasbag.

'I know the very man you mean,' he said with a nod. 'He's a nice poor fellow but he talks too much. Party all over?'

'Except for one couple,' the other man said, rising from his box. 'It's no use waiting for them. They'll probably be at it till morning.'

'I dare say,' said Johnny. 'Why wouldn't you go in and have a chat with them yourself? You could do with a drink by this time, I suppose.'

'A lot they care whether I could or not,' the man said bitterly. 'All that would happen is that they'd say, "Delighted to see you, Mr Hardy," and then wait for me to go to bed.'

'Ah, now, I wouldn't say that,' said Johnny.

'I'm not asking whether you'd say it or not,' said the other savagely. 'I know it. Here I am, that paid for the party, sitting out here all night, getting my death of cold, and did my daughter or my son as much as come to the door to look for me? Did they even notice I wasn't there?'

'Oh, no, no,' Johnny said politely, talking to him as if he were a ten-year-old in a tantrum – which, in a sense, Johnny felt he was. The man might have hundreds of thousands, as Tim said, but there was no difference in the world between him and a little boy sitting out in the back on a frosty night, deliberately trying to give himself pneumonia because his younger brother had got a penny and he hadn't. It was no use being hard on a man like that. 'Children are very selfish, of course, but what you must remember is that fathers are selfish, too.'

'Selfish?' the other exclaimed angrily. 'Do you know what those two cost me between private schools and colleges? Do you know what that one party tonight cost me? As much as you'd earn in a year!'

'Oh, I know, I know!' said Johnny, holding his hands up in distress. 'I used to feel the same myself, after the wife died. I'd look at the son putting grease on his hair in front of the mirror, and I'd say to myself, "That's my grease and that's my mirror, and he's going out to amuse himself with some little piece from the lanes, not caring whether I'm alive or dead!" And daughters are worse. You'd expect more from a daughter somehow.'

'You'd expect what you wouldn't get,' the other said gloomily. 'There's that girl inside that I gave everything to, and she'd think more of some spotty college boy that never earned a pound in his life. And if I open my mouth, my children look at me as if they didn't know was I a fool or a lunatic.'

'They think you're old-fashioned, of course,' said Johnny. 'I know. But all the same you're not being fair to them. Children can be fond enough of you, only you'd never see it till you didn't care whether they were or not. That was the mistake I made. If I might have got an old woman for myself after the missis died, I'd have enjoyed myself more and seen it sooner. That's what you should do. You're a well-to-do man. You could knock down a very good time for yourself. Get some lively little piece to spend your money on who'll make a fuss over you, and then you won't begrudge it to them so much.'

'Yes,' said the other, 'to have more of them wishing I was dead so that they could get at the rest of it.'

He strode across the street without even a goodnight, and Johnny saw the flood of light on the high steps and heard the dull thud of the big door behind him.

Sitting by his brazier, waiting for the dawn over the city square, Johnny felt very fortunate, wise, and good. If ever the man listened to what he had said, he might be very good to Johnny: he might get him a proper job as an indoor watchman; he might even give him a little pension to show his appreciation. If only he took the advice – and it might sink in after a time – it would be worth every penny of it to him. Anyway, if only the job continued for another couple of days, the man would be bound to give him a Christmas box. Five bob. Ten bob. Even a quid. It would be nothing to a man like that.

Though a realist by conviction, Johnny, too, had his dreams.

(1957)

An Out-and-Out
Free Gift

When Jimmy began to get out of hand, his father was both disturbed and bewildered. Anybody else, yes, but not Jimmy! They had always been so close! Closer, indeed, than Ned ever realized, for the perfectly correct picture he had drawn of himself as a thoughtful, considerate father who treated his son as though he were a younger brother could have been considerably expanded by his wife. Indeed, to realize how close they had been you needed to hear Celia on it, because only she knew how much of the small boy there still was in her husband.

Who, for instance, would have thought that the head of a successful business had such a passion for sugar? Yet during the war, when sugar was rationed in Ireland, Celia, who was a bit of a Jansenist, had felt herself bound to give up sugar and divide her ration between Ned and Jimmy, then quite a small boy. And, even at that, Ned continued to suffer. He did admire her self-denial, but he couldn't help feeling that so grandiose a gesture deserved a better object than Jimmy. It was a matter of scientific fact that sugar was bad for Jimmy's teeth, and anything that went wrong with Jimmy's teeth was going to cost his father money. Ned felt it unfair that in the middle of a war, with his salary frozen, Celia should inflict additional burdens on him.

Most of the time he managed to keep his dignity, though he could rarely sit down to a meal without an angry glance at Jimmy's sugar bowl. To make things harder for him, Jimmy rationed himself so that towards the end of the week he still had some sugar left, while Ned had none. As a philosopher, Ned wondered that he should resent this so deeply, but resent it he did. A couple of times, he deliberately stole a spoonful while Celia's back was turned, and the absurdity of this put him in such a frivolous frame of mind for the rest of the evening that she eventually said resignedly, 'I suppose you've been at the child's sugar again? Really, Ned, you are hopeless!' On other occasions

Ned summoned up all his paternal authority and with a polite 'You don't mind, old man?' took a spoonful from under Jimmy's nose. But that took nerve and a delicate appreciation of the precise moment when Jimmy could be relied on not to cry.

Towards the end of the war, it became a matter of brute economic strength. If Jimmy wanted a bicycle lamp, he could earn it or pay up in good sugar. As Ned said, quoting from a business manual he had studied in his own youth, 'There is no such thing in business as an out-and-out free gift.' Jimmy made good use of the lesson. 'Bicycle lamp, old man?' Ned would ask casually, poising his spoon over Jimmy's sugar bowl. 'Bicycle lamp *and* three-speed gear,' Jimmy would reply firmly. 'For a couple of spoons of sugar?' his father would cry in mock indignation. 'Are you mad, boy?' They both enjoyed the game.

They could scarcely have been other than friends. There was so much of the small boy in Ned that he was sensitive to the least thing affecting Jimmy, and Jimmy would consult him about things that most small boys keep to themselves. When he was in trouble, Ned never dismissed it lightly, no matter how unimportant it seemed. He asked a great many questions and frequently reserved his decisions. He had chosen Jimmy's school himself; it was a good one for Cork, and sometimes, without informing Jimmy, he went off to the school himself and had a chat with one of the teachers. Nearly always he managed to arrange things without embarrassment or pain, and Jimmy took it for granted that his decisions were usually right. It is a wise father who can persuade his son of anything of the sort.

But now, at sixteen, Jimmy was completely out of control, and his mother had handed him over to the secular arm, and the secular arm, for all its weight, made no impression on his sullen indifference. The first sign of the change in him was the disintegration of his normally perfect manners; now he seemed to have no deference towards or consideration for anyone. Ned caught him out in one or two minor falsehoods and quoted to him a remark of his own father's that 'a lie humiliates the man who tells it, but it humiliates the one it's told to even more'. What puzzled Ned was that, at the same time, the outbreak was linked in some ways to qualities he had always liked in the boy. Jimmy was strong, and showed his strength in protecting things younger and weaker than himself. The cat regarded him as a personal enemy because he hurled himself on her the moment he saw her with a bird. At one time there had been a notice on his door that read, 'Wounded Bird. Please Keep Out'. At school his juniors worshipped him because he would stand up for them against bullies, and though Ned, in a fatherly way, advised him not to get mixed up in other people's quarrels, he was secretly flattered. He felt Jimmy was taking after him.

But the same thing that attracted Jimmy to younger and weaker boys seemed now to attract him to wasters. Outside of school, he never associated with lads he might have to look up to, but only with those his father felt a normal boy should despise. All this was summed up in his friendship with a youngster called Hogan, who was a strange mixture of spoiling and neglect, a boy who had never been young and would never be old. He openly smoked a pipe, and let on to be an authority on brands of tobacco. Ned winced when Hogan addressed him as a contemporary and tried to discuss business with him. He replied with heavy irony – something he did only when he was at a complete loss. What went on in Hogan's house when Jimmy went there he could only guess at. He suspected that the parents went out and stayed out, leaving the boys to their own devices.

At first, Ned treated Jimmy's insubordination as he had treated other outbreaks, by talking to him as an equal. He even offered him a cigarette – Jimmy had stolen money to buy cigarettes. He told him how people grew up through admiration of others' virtues, rather than through tolerance of their weaknesses. He talked to him about sex, which he suspected was at the bottom of Jimmy's trouble, and Jimmy listened politely and said he understood. Whether he did or not, Ned decided that if Hogan talked sex to Jimmy, it was a very different kind of sex.

Finally, he forbade Hogan the house and warned Jimmy against going to Hogan's. He made no great matter of it, contenting himself with describing the scrapes he had got into himself at Jimmy's age, and Jimmy smiled, apparently pleased with this unfamiliar picture of his grave and rather stately father, but he continued to steal and lie, to get bad marks and remain out late at night. Ned was fairly satisfied that he went to Hogan's, and sat there smoking, playing cards, and talking filth. He bawled Jimmy out and called him a dirty little thief and liar, and Jimmy raised his brows and looked away with a pained air, as though asking himself how long he must endure such ill-breeding. At this, Ned gave him a cuff on the ear that brought a look of hatred into Jimmy's face and caused Celia not to talk to Ned for two days. But even she gave in at last.

'Last night was the third time he's been out late this week,' she said one afternoon in her apparently unemotional way. 'You'll really have to do something drastic with him.'

These were hard words from a soft woman, but though Ned felt sorry for her, he felt even sorrier for himself. He hated himself in the part of a sergeant-major, and he blamed her for having let things go so far.

'Any notion where he has been?' he asked stiffly.

'Oh, you can't get a word out of him,' she said with a shrug. 'Judging by his tone, I'd say Hogan's. I don't know what attraction that fellow has for him.'

'Very well,' Ned said portentously. 'I'll deal with him. But, mind, I'll deal with him in my own way.'

'Oh, I won't interfere,' she said wearily. 'I know when I'm licked.'

'I can promise you Master Jimmy will know it, too,' Ned added grimly.

At supper he said in an even tone, 'Young man, for the future you're going to be home every night at ten o'clock. This is the last time I'm going to speak to you about it.'

Jimmy, apparently under the impression that his father was talking to himself, reached for a slice of bread. Then Ned let fly with a shout that made Celia jump and paralysed the boy's hand, still clutching the bread.

'Did you hear me?'

'What's that?' gasped Jimmy.

'I said you were to be in at ten o'clock.'

'Oh, all right, all right,' said Jimmy, with a look that said he did not think any reasonable person would require him to share the house any longer with one so uncivilized. Though this look was intended to madden Ned it failed to do so, because he knew that, for all her sentimentality and high liberal principles, Celia was a woman of her word and would not interfere whenever he decided to knock that particular look off Master Jimmy's face. He knew, too, that the time was not far off; that Jimmy had not the faintest intention of obeying, and that he would be able to deal with it.

'Because I warn you, the first night you're late again I'm going to skin you alive,' he added. He was trying it out, of course. He knew that Celia hated expressions of fatherly affection like 'skin you alive', 'tan you within an inch of your life', and 'knock your head off', which, to her, were relics of a barbarous age. To his great satisfaction, she neither shuddered nor frowned. Her principles were liberal, but they were principles.

Two nights after, Jimmy was late again. Celia, while pretending to read, was watching the clock despairingly. 'Of course, he may have been delayed,' she said smoothly, but there was no conviction in her tone. It was nearly eleven when they heard Jimmy's key in the door.

'I think perhaps I'd better go to bed,' she said.

'It might be as well,' he replied pityingly. 'Send that fellow in on your way.'

He heard her in the hallway, talking with Jimmy in a level, friendly voice, not allowing her consternation to appear, and he smiled. He liked that touch of the Roman matron in her. Then there was a knock, and Jimmy came in. He was a big lad for sixteen, but he still had traces of baby fat about the rosy cheeks he occasionally scraped with Ned's razor, to Ned's annoyance. Now Ned would cheerfully have given him a whole shaving kit if it would have avoided the necessity for dealing with him firmly.

'You wanted to talk to me, Dad?' he asked, as though he could just spare a moment.

'Yes, Jimmy, I did. Shut that door.'

Jimmy gave a resigned shrug at his father's mania for privacy, but did as he was told and stood against the door, his hands joined and his chin in the air.

'When did I say you were to be in?' Ned said, looking at the clock.

'When?'

'Yes. When? At what time, if you find it so hard to understand.'

'Oh, ten,' Jimmy replied wearily.

'Ten? And what time do you make that?'

'Oh, I didn't know it was so late!' Jimmy exclaimed with an astonished look at the clock. 'I'm sorry. I didn't notice the time.'

'Really?' Ned said ironically. 'Enjoyed yourself that much?'

'Not too bad,' Jimmy replied vaguely. He was always uncomfortable with his father's irony.

'Company good?'

'Oh, all right,' Jimmy replied with another shrug.

'Where was this?'

'At a house.'

'Poor people?' his father asked in mock surprise.

'What?' exclaimed Jimmy.

'Poor people who couldn't afford a clock?'

Jimmy's indignation overflowed in stammering protest. 'I never said they hadn't a clock. None of the other fellows had to be in by ten. I didn't like saying I had to be. I didn't want them to think I was a blooming . . .' The protest expired in a heavy sigh, and Ned's heart contracted with pity and shame.

Ned, now grimly determined, pursued his inquiry. 'Neither your mother nor I want you to make a show of yourself. But you didn't answer my question. Where was this party? And don't tell me any lies, because I'm going to find out.'

Jimmy grew red and angry. 'Why would I tell you lies?'

'For the same reason you've told so many already – whatever that may be. You see, Jimmy, the trouble with people who tell lies is that you have to check everything they say. Not on your account but on theirs; otherwise, you may be unfair to them. People soon get tired of being fair, though. Now, where were you? At Hogan's?'

'You said I wasn't to go to Hogan's.'

'You see, you're still not answering my questions. Were you at Hogan's?'

'No,' Jimmy replied in a whisper.

'Word of honour?'

'Word of honour.' But the tone was not the tone of honour but of shame.

'Where were you, then?'

'Ryans'.'

The name was unfamiliar to Ned, and he wondered if Jimmy had not just invented it to frustrate any attempt at checking on his statements. He was quite prepared to hear that Jimmy didn't know where the house was. It was as bad as that.

'Ryans',' he repeated evenly. 'Do I know them?'

'You might. I don't know.'

'Where do they live?'

'Gardiner's Hill.'

'Whereabouts?'

'Near the top. Where the road comes up from Dillon's Cross, four doors down. It has a tree in the garden.' It came so pat that Ned felt sure there was such a house. He felt sure of nothing else.

'And you spent the evening there? I'm warning you for your own good. Because I'm going to find out.' There was a rasp in his voice.

'I told you I did.'

'I know,' Ned said between his teeth. 'Now you're going to come along with me and prove it.'

He rose and in silence took his hat from the hall-stand and went out. Jimmy followed him silently, a pace behind. It was a moonlit night, and as they turned up the steep hill, the trees overhung a high wall on one side of the street. On the other side there were steep gardens filled with shadows.

'Where did you say this house was?'

'At the top,' Jimmy replied sullenly.

The hill stopped, the road became level, and at either side were little new suburban houses, with tiny front gardens. Near the corner, Ned saw one with a tree in front of it and stopped. There was still a light in the front room. The family kept late hours for Cork. Suddenly he felt absurdly sorry for the boy.

'You don't want to change your mind?' he asked gently. 'You're sure this is where you were?'

'I told you so,' Jimmy replied almost in exasperation.

'Very well,' Ned said savagely. 'You needn't come in.'

'All right,' Jimmy said, and braced himself against the concrete gatepost, looking over the moonlit roofs at the clear sky. In the moonlight he looked very pale; his hands were drawn back from his sides, his lips drawn back from his teeth, and for some reason his white anguished face made Ned think of a crucifixion.

Anger had taken the place of pity in him. He felt the boy was being unjust towards him. He wouldn't have minded the injustice if he'd ever been unjust to Jimmy, but two minutes before he had again shown his fairness and given Jimmy another chance. Besides, he didn't want to make a fool of himself.

He walked up the little path to the door, whose coloured-glass panels glowed in light that seemed to leak from the sitting-room door. When he rang, a pretty girl of fifteen or sixteen came out and screwed up her eyes at him.

'I hope you'll excuse my calling at this unnatural hour,' Ned said in a bantering tone. 'It's only a question I want to ask. Do you think I could talk to your father or your mother for a moment?'

'You can, to be sure,' the girl replied in a flutter of curiosity. 'Come in, can't you? We're all in the front room.'

Ned, nerving himself for an ordeal, went in. It was a tiny front room with a fire burning in a tiled fireplace. There was a mahogany table at which a boy of twelve seemed to be doing his lessons. Round the fire sat an older girl, a small woman, and a tubby little man with a greying moustache. Ned smiled, and his tone became even more jocular.

'I hope you'll forgive my making a nuisance of myself,' he said. 'My name is Callanan. I live at St Luke's. I wonder if you've ever met my son, Jimmy?'

'Jimmy?' the mother echoed, her hand to her cheek. 'I don't know that I did.'

'I know him,' said the girl who had let him in, in a voice that squeaked with pride.

'Fine!' Ned said. 'At least, you know what I'm talking about. I wonder if you saw him this evening?'

'Jimmy?' the girl replied, taking fright. 'No. Sure, I hardly know him only to salute him. Why? Is anything wrong?'

'Nothing serious, at any rate,' said Ned with a comforting smile. 'It's just that he said he spent the evening here with you. I dare say that's an excuse for being somewhere he shouldn't have been.'

'Well, well, well!' Mrs Ryan said anxiously, joining her hands. 'Imagine saying he was here! Wisha, Mr Callanan, aren't they a caution?'

'A caution against what, though?' Ned asked cheerfully. 'That's what I'd like to know. I'm only sorry he wasn't telling the truth. I'm afraid he wasn't in such charming company. Goodnight, everybody, and thank you.'

'Goodnight, Mr Callanan,' said Mrs Ryan, laying a hand gently on his sleeve. 'And don't be too hard on him! Sure, we were wild ourselves once.'

'Once?' he exclaimed with a laugh. 'I hope we still are. We're not dead yet, Mrs Ryan.'

The same girl showed him out. She had recovered from her fright and looked as though she would almost have liked him to stay.

'Goodnight, Mr Callanan,' she called blithely from the door, and when he turned, she was silhouetted against the lighted doorway, bent half-way over, and waving. He waved back, touched by this glimpse of an interior not so unlike his own, but seen from outside, in all its innocence. It was a shock to emerge on the roadway and see Jimmy still standing where he had left him, though he no longer looked crucified. Instead, with his head down and his hands by his sides, he looked terribly weary. They walked in silence for a few minutes, till they saw the valley of the city and the lamps cascading down the hillsides and breaking below into a foaming lake of light.

'Well,' Ned said gloomily, 'the Ryans seem to be under the impression that you weren't there tonight.'

'I know,' Jimmy replied, as though this were all that might be expected from him.

Something in his tone startled Ned. It no longer seemed to breathe defiance. Instead, it hinted at something very like despair. But why, he thought in exasperation. Why the blazes did he tell me all those lies? Why didn't he tell me even outside the door? Damn it, I gave him every chance.

'Don't you think this is a nice place to live, Dad?' asked Jimmy.

'Is it?' Ned asked sternly.

'Ah, well, the air is better,' said Jimmy with a sigh. They said no more till they reached home.

'Now, go to bed,' Ned said in the hallway. 'I'll consider what to do with you tomorrow.'

Which, as he well knew, was bluff, because he had already decided to do nothing to Jimmy. Somehow he felt that, whatever the boy had done to himself, punishment would be merely an anticlimax, and perhaps a relief. Punishment, he thought, might be exactly what Jimmy would have welcomed at that moment. He went into the sitting-room and poured himself a drink, feeling that if anyone deserved it, he did. He had a curious impression of having been involved in some sort of struggle and escaped some danger to which he could not even give a name.

When he went upstairs, Celia was in bed with a book, and looked up at him with a wide-eyed stare. She proved to be no help to him. 'Jimmy usen't to be like that,' she said wistfully, and he knew she had been lying there regretting the little boy who had come to her with all his troubles.

'But why, why, why, in God's name, did he tell me all those lies?' Ned asked angrily.

'Oh, why do people ever tell lies?' she asked with a shrug.

'Because they hope they won't be found out,' Ned replied. 'Don't you see that's what's so queer about it?'

She didn't, and for hours Ned lay awake, turning it over and over in his mind. It was easy enough to see it as the story of a common falsehood persisted in through some mood of bravado, and each time he thought of it that way he grew angry again. Then, all at once, he would remember the face of Jimmy against the pillar in the moonlight, as though he were being crucified, and give a frustrated sigh.

'Go to sleep!' Celia said once, giving him a vicious nudge.

'I can't, damn it, I can't,' he said, and began all over again.

Why had the kid chosen Ryans' as an excuse? Was that merely to put him further astray, or did it really represent some dream of happiness and fulfilment? The latter explanation he rejected as too simple and sentimental, yet he knew quite well that Ryan's house *had* meant something to the boy, even if it was only an alternative to whatever house he had been in and the company he had met there. Ned could remember himself at that age, and how, when he had abandoned himself to something or somebody, an alternative image would appear. The image that had flashed up in Jimmy's mind, the image that was not one of Hogan's house, was Ryans'. But it needed more than that to explain his own feeling of danger. It was as though Jimmy had deliberately challenged him, if he were the man he appeared to be, to struggle with the demon of fantasy in him and destroy it. It was as though not he but Jimmy had been forcing the pace. At the same time, he realized that this was something he would never know. All he ever would know was that somewhere behind it all were despair and loneliness and terror, under the magic of an autumn night. And yet there were sentimental fools who told you that they would wish to be young again.

Next morning at breakfast, he was cold and aloof, more from embarrassment than hostility. Jimmy, on the other hand, seemed to be in the highest spirits, helping Celia with the breakfast things, saying, 'Excuse me, Daddy,' as he changed Ned's plate. He pushed the sugar bowl towards Ned and said with a grin, 'Daddy likes sugar.'

Ned just restrained himself from flinging the bowl at him. 'As a matter of fact, I do,' he said coldly.

He had done the same sort of thing too often himself. He knew that, with the threat of punishment over his head, Jimmy was scared, as well he might be. It is one thing to be defiant at eleven o'clock at night, another thing altogether to be defiant at eight in the morning.

All day, at intervals, he found himself brooding over it. At lunch he talked to his chief clerk about it, but MacIntyre couldn't advise him. 'God, Ned,' he said impatiently, 'every kid is different. There's no laying down rules. My one told the nuns that her mother was a religious maniac and kicked the statue of the Blessed Virgin around the floor. For God's sake, Ned, imagine Kate kicking a statue around the floor!'

'Difficult, isn't it?' replied Ned with a grin, though to himself he thought complacently that that sort of fantasy was what he would expect from Kate's daughter. Parents so rarely sympathize with one another.

That evening, when he came in, Celia said coolly, 'I don't know what you said to Jimmy, but it seems to have worked.'

Relief came over Ned like a cold shower. He longed to be able to say something calm like 'Oh, good!' or 'Glad I could help' or 'Any time I can advise you again, just let me know'. But he was too honest. He shook his head, still the schoolboy that Celia had loved such a long time ago, and his forehead wrinkled up.

'That's the awful part of it,' he said. 'I said nothing at all to him. For the first time in my life I didn't know what to say. What the hell could I say?'

'Oh, no doubt you said something and didn't notice it,' Celia said confidently. 'There's no such thing in business as an out-and-out free gift.'

(1957)

Public Opinion

Now I know what you're thinking. You're thinking how nice 'twould be to live in a little town. You could have a king's life in a house like this, with a fine garden and a car so that you could slip up to town whenever you felt in need of company. Living in Dublin, next door to the mail boat and writing things for the American papers, you imagine you could live here and write whatever you liked about MacDunphy of the County Council. Mind, I'm not saying you couldn't say a hell of a lot about him! I said a few things myself from time to time. All I mean is that you wouldn't say it for long. This town broke better men. It broke me and, believe me, I'm no chicken.

When I came here first, ten years ago, I felt exactly the way you do, the way everybody does. At that time, and the same is nearly true today, there wasn't a professional man in this town with a housekeeper under sixty, for fear of what people might say about them. In fact, you might still notice that there isn't one of them who is what you might call 'happily' married. They went at it in too much of a hurry.

Oh, of course, I wasn't going to make that mistake! When I went to choose a housekeeper I chose a girl called Bridie Casey, a handsome little girl of seventeen from a village up the coast. At the same time I took my precautions. I drove out there one day when she was at home, and I had a look at the cottage and a talk with her mother and a cup of tea, and after that I didn't need anyone to recommend her. I knew that anything Bridie fell short in, her mother would not be long in correcting. After that, there was only one inquiry I wanted to make.

'Have you a boy, Bridie?' said I.

'No, Doctor, I have not,' said she with an innocent air that didn't take me in a bit. As a doctor you soon get used to innocent airs.

'Well, you'd better hurry up and get one,' said I, 'or I'm not going to keep you.'

With that she laughed as if she thought I was only joking. I was not joking at all. A housekeeper or maid without a fellow of her own is as bad as a hen with an egg.

'It's no laughing matter,' I said. 'And when you do get a fellow, if you haven't one already, you can tell him I said he could make free with my beer, but if ever I catch you diluting my whiskey I'll sack you on the spot.'

Mind, I made no mistake in Bridie or her mother either. She mightn't be any good in the Shelbourne Hotel, but what that girl could cook she cooked well, and anything she cleaned looked as if it was clean. What's more, she could size a patient up better than I could myself. Make no mistake about it, as housekeepers or maids Irish girls are usually not worth a damn, but a girl from a good Irish home can turn her hand to anything. Of course, she was so good-looking that people who came to the house used to pass remarks about us, but that was only jealousy. They hadn't the nerve to employ a good-looking girl themselves for fear of what people would say. But I knew that as long as a girl had a man of her own to look after she'd be no bother to me.

No, what broke up my happy home was something different altogether. You mightn't understand it, but in a place like this 'tis the devil entirely to get ready money out of them. They'll give you anything else in the world only money. Here, everything is what they call 'friendship'. I suppose the shops give them the habit because a regular customer is always supposed to be in debt and if ever the debt is paid off it's war to the knife. Of course they think a solicitor or a doctor should live the same way, and instead of money what you get is presents: poultry, butter, eggs and meat that a large family could not eat, let alone a single man. Friendship is all very well, but between you and me it's a poor thing for a man to be relying on at the beginning of his career.

I had one patient in particular called Willie Joe Corcoran of Clashanaddig – I buried him last year, poor man, and my mind is easier already – and Willie Joe seemed to think I was always on the verge of starvation. One Sunday I got in from twelve-o'clock Mass and went to the whiskey cupboard to get myself a drink when I noticed the most extraordinary smell. Doctors are sensitive to smells, of course – we have to be – and I shouldn't rest easy till I located that one. I searched the room and I searched the hall and I even poked my head upstairs into the bedrooms before I tried the kitchen. Knowing Bridie, I never even associated the smell with her. When I went in, there she was in a clean white uniform, cooking the dinner, and she looked round at me.

'What the hell is that smell, Bridie?' said I.

She folded her arms and leaned against the wall, as good-looking a little girl as you'd find in five counties.

'I told you before,' says she in her thin, high voice, ''tis that side of beef Willie Joe Corcoran left on Thursday. It have the whole house ruined on me.'

'But didn't I tell you to throw that out?' I said.

'You did,' says she, as if I was the most unreasonable man in the world, 'but you didn't tell me where I was going to throw it.'

'What's wrong with the ash can?' said I.

'What's wrong with the ash can?' says she. 'There's nothing wrong with it. Only the ashmen won't be here till Tuesday.'

'Then for God's sake girl, can't you throw it over the wall into the field?'

'Into the field,' says she, pitching her voice up an octave till she sounded like a sparrow in decline. 'And what would people say?'

'Begor, I don't know, Bridie,' I said, humouring her. 'What do *you* think they'd say?'

'They're bad enough to say anything,' says she.

I declare to God I had to look at her to see was she serious. There she was, a girl of seventeen with the face of a nun, suggesting things that I could barely imagine.

'Why, Bridie?' I said, treating it as a joke. 'You don't think they'd say I was bringing corpses home from the hospital to cut up?'

'They said worse,' she said in a squeak, and I saw that she took a very poor view of my powers of imagination. Because you write books, you think you know a few things, but you should listen to the conversation of pious girls in this town.

'About me, Bridie?' said I in astonishment.

'About you and others,' said she. And then, by cripes, I lost my temper with her.

'And is it any wonder they would,' said I, 'with bloody fools like you paying attention to them?'

I have a very wicked temper when I'm roused, and for the time being it scared her more than what people might say of her.

'I'll get Kenefick's boy in the morning and let him take it away,' said she. 'Will I give him a shilling?'

'Put it in the poor box,' said I in a rage. 'I'll be going out to Dr MacMahon's for supper and I'll take it away myself. Any damage that's going to be done to anyone's character can be done to mine. It should be able to stand it. And let me tell you, Bridie Casey, if I was the sort to mind what anyone said about me, you wouldn't be where you are this minute.'

I was very vicious to her, but of course I was mad. After all, I had to take my drink and eat my dinner with that smell round the house, and Bridie in a panic, hopping about me like a hen with hydrophobia. When I went out to the pantry to get the side of beef, she gave a yelp as if I'd trodden on her foot. 'Mother of God!' says she. 'Your new suit!' 'Never mind my new suit,' said I, and I wrapped the beef in a couple of newspapers and heaved it into the back of the car. I declare, it wasn't wishing to me. I had all the windows open, but even then the smell was high, and I went through the town like a coursing match with the people on the footpaths lifting their heads like beagles to sniff after me.

I wouldn't have minded that so much only that Sunday is the one day I have. In those days before I was married I nearly always drove out to Jerry MacMahon's for supper and a game of cards. I knew poor Jerry looked forward to it because the wife was very severe with him in the matter of liquor.

I stopped the car on top of the cliffs to throw out the meat, and just as I was looking for a clear drop I saw a long galoot of a countryman coming up the road towards me. He had a long, melancholy sort of face and mad eyes. Whatever it was about his appearance, I didn't want him to see what I was up to. You might think it funny in a professional man, but that is the way I am.

'Nice evening,' says he.

'Grand evening, thank God,' says I, and not to give him an excuse for being too curious I said: 'That's a powerful view.'

'Well,' says he sourly, just giving it a glance, 'the view is all right but 'tis no good to the people that has to live in it. There is no earning in that view,' says he, and then he cocked his head and began to size me up, and I knew I'd made a great mistake, opening my mouth to him at all. 'I suppose now you'd be an artist?' says he.

You might notice about me that I'm very sensitive to inquisitiveness. It is a thing I cannot stand. Even to sign my name to a telegram is a thing I never like to do, and I hate a direct question.

'How did you guess?' said I.

'And I suppose,' said he, turning to inspect the view again, 'if you painted that, you'd find people to buy it?'

'That's what I was hoping,' said I.

So he turned to the scenery again, and this time he gave it a studied appraisal as if it was a cow at a fair.

'I dare say for a large view like that you'd get nearly five pounds?' said he.

'You would and more,' said I.

'Ten?' said he with his eyes beginning to pop.

'More,' said I.

'That beats all,' he said, shaking his head in resignation. 'Sure, the whole thing isn't worth that. No wonder the country is the way it is. Good luck!'

'Good luck,' said I, and I watched him disappear among the rocks over the road. I waited, and then I saw him peering out at me from behind a rock like some wild mountain animal, and I knew if I stayed there till nightfall I wouldn't shake him off. He was beside himself at the thought of a picture that would be worth as much as a cow, and he probably thought if he stayed long enough he might learn the knack and paint the equivalent of a whole herd of them. The man's mind didn't rise above cows. And, whatever the devil ailed me, I could not give him the satisfaction of seeing what I was really up to. You might think it shortsighted of me, but that is the sort I am.

I got into the car and away with me down to Barney Phelan's pub on the edge of the bay. Barney's pub is the best in this part of the world and Barney himself is a bit of a character; a tall excitable man with wild blue eyes and a holy terror to gossip. He kept filling my glass as fast as I could lower it, and three or four times it was on the tip of my tongue to tell him what I was doing; but I knew he'd make a story out of it for the boys that night and sooner or later it would get back to Willie Joe Corcoran. Bad as Willie Joe was, I would not like to hurt his feelings. That is another great weakness of mine. I never like hurting people's feelings.

Of course that was a mistake, for when I walked out of the pub, the first thing I saw was the cliff dweller and two other yokels peering in at the parcel in the back of my car. At that I really began to feel like murder. I cannot stand that sort of unmannerly inquisitiveness.

'Well,' I said, giving the cliff dweller a shoulder out of my way, 'I hope ye saw something good.'

At that moment Barney came out, drying his hands in his apron and showing his two front teeth like a weasel.

'Are them fellows at your car, Doctor?' says he.

'Oho!' said the cliff dweller to his two friends. 'So a docthor is what he is now!'

'And what the hell else did you think he was, you fool?' asked Barney.

'A painter is what he was when last we heard of him,' said the lunatic.

'And I suppose he was looking for a little job painting the huts ye have up in Beensheen?' asked Barney with a sneer.

'The huts may be humble but the men are true,' said the lunatic solemnly.

'Blast you, man,' said Barney, squaring up to him, 'are you saying I don't know the doctor since he was in short trousers?'

'No man knows the soul of another,' said the cliff dweller, shaking his head again.

'For God's sake, Barney, don't be bothering yourself with that misfortunate clown,' said I. ''Tis my own fault for bringing the likes of him into the world. Of all the useless occupations, that and breaking stones are the worst.'

'I would not be talking against breaking stones,' said the cliff dweller sourly. 'It might not be long till certain people here would be doing the same.'

At that I let a holy oath out of me and drove off in the direction of Jerry MacMahon's. When I glanced in the driving mirror I saw Barney standing in the middle of the road with the three yokels around him, waving their hands. It struck me that in spite of my precautions Barney would have a story for the boys that night, and it would not be about Willie Joe. It would be about me. It also struck me that I was behaving in a very uncalled-for way. If I'd been a real murderer trying to get rid of a real corpse I could hardly have behaved more suspiciously. And why? Because I did not want people discussing my business. I don't know what it is about Irish people that makes them afraid of having their business discussed. It is not that it is any worse than other people's business, only we behave as if it was.

I stopped the car at a nice convenient spot by the edge of the bay miles from anywhere. I could have got rid of the beef there and then, but something seemed to have broken in me. I walked up and down that road slowly, looking to right and left to make sure no one was watching. Even then I was perfectly safe, but I saw a farmer crossing a field a mile away up the hill and I decided to wait till he was out of sight. That was where the ferryboat left me, because, of course, the moment he glanced over his shoulder and saw a strange man with a car stopped on the road he stopped himself with his head cocked like an old setter. Mind, I'm not blaming him! I blame nobody but myself. Up to that day I had never felt a stime of sympathy with my neurotic patients, giving themselves diseases they hadn't got, but there was I, a doctor, giving myself a disease I hadn't got and with no excuse whatever.

By this time the smell was so bad I knew I wouldn't get it out of the upholstery for days. And there was Jerry MacMahon up in Cahirnamona, waiting for me with a bottle of whiskey his wife wouldn't let him touch till I got there, and I couldn't go for fear of the way he'd laugh at me. I looked again and saw that the man who'd been crossing the field had changed his mind. Instead he'd come down to the gate and was leaning over it, lighting his pipe while he admired the view of the bay and the mountains.

That was the last straw. I knew now that even if I got rid of the beef my Sunday would still be ruined. I got in the car and drove straight home. Then I went to the whiskey cupboard and poured myself a drink that seemed to be reasonably proportionate to the extent of my suffering. Just as I sat down to it Bridie walked in without knocking. This is one fault I should have told you about – all the time she was with me I never trained her to knock. I declare to God when I saw her standing in the doorway I jumped. I'd always been very careful of myself and jumping was a new thing to me.

'Did I tell you to knock before you came into a room?' I shouted.

'I forgot,' she said, letting on not to notice the state I was in. 'You didn't go to Dr MacMahon's so?'

'I did not,' I said.

'And did you throw away the beef?'

'I didn't,' I said. Then as I saw her waiting for an explanation I added: 'There were too many people around.'

'Look at that now!' she said complacently. 'I suppose we'll have to bury it in the garden after dark?'

'I suppose so,' I said, not realizing how I had handed myself over to the woman, body and bones, holus-bolus.

That evening I took a spade and dug a deep hole in the garden and Bridie heaved in the side of beef. The remarkable thing is that the whole time we were doing it we talked in whispers and glanced up at the backs of other houses in the road to see if we were being watched. But the weight off my mind when it was over! I even felt benevolent to Bridie. Then I went over to Jim Donoghue, the dentist's, and told him the whole story over a couple of drinks. We were splitting our sides over it.

When I say we were splitting our sides I do not mean that this is a funny story. It was very far from being funny for me before it was over. You wouldn't believe the scandal there was about Bridie and myself after that. You'd wonder how people could imagine such things, let alone repeat them. That day changed my whole life . . . Oh, laugh! laugh! I was laughing out the other side of my mouth before it was through. Up to that I'd never given a rap what anyone thought of me, but from that day forth I was afraid of my own shadow. With all the talk there was about us I even had to get rid of Bridie and, of course, inside of twelve months I was married like the rest of them . . . By the way, when I mentioned unhappy marriages I wasn't speaking of my own. Mrs Ryan and myself get on quite well. I only mentioned it to show what might be in store for yourself if ever you were foolish enough to come and live here. A town like this can bend iron. And if you doubt my word, that's only because you don't know what they are saying about you.

(1957)

An Act of Charity

The parish priest, Father Maginnis, did not like the second curate, Father Galvin, and Father Fogarty could see why. It was the dislike of the professional for the amateur, no matter how talented, and nobody could have said that Father Galvin had much in the way of talent. Maginnis was a professional to his fingertips. He drove the right car, knew the right people, and could suit his conversation to any company, even that of women. He even varied his accent to make people feel at home. With Deasy, the owner of the garage, he talked about 'the caw', but to Lavin, the garage hand, he said 'the cyarr', smiling benignly at the homeliness of his touch.

Galvin was thin, pale, irritable, and intense. When he should have kept a straight face he made some stupid joke that stopped the conversation dead; and when he laughed in the proper place at someone else's joke, it was with a slight air of vexation, as though he found it hard to put up with people who made him laugh at all. He worried himself over little embarrassments and what people would think of them, till Fogarty asked bluntly, 'What the hell difference does it make what they think?' Then Galvin looked away sadly and said, 'I suppose you're right.' But Fogarty didn't mind his visits so much except when he had asked other curates in for a drink and a game of cards. Then he took a glass of sherry or something equally harmless and twiddled it awkwardly for half an hour as though it were some sort of patent device for keeping his hands occupied. When one of the curates made a harmless dirty joke, Galvin pretended to be looking at a picture so that he didn't have to comment. Fogarty, who loved giving people nicknames, called him Father Mother's Boy. He called Maginnis the Old Pro, but when that nickname got back, as everything a priest says gets back, it did Fogarty no harm at all. Maginnis was glad he had a curate with so much sense.

He sometimes asked Fogarty to Sunday dinner, but he soon

gave up on asking Galvin, and again Fogarty sympathized with him. Maginnis was a professional, even to his dinners. He basted his meat with one sort of wine and his chicken with another, and he liked a guest who could tell the difference. He also liked him to drink two large whiskeys before dinner and to make sensible remarks about the wine; and when he had exhausted the secrets of his kitchen he sat back, smoked his cigar, and told funny stories. They were very good stories, mostly about priests.

'Did I ever tell you the one about Canon Murphy, Father?' he would bellow, his fat face beaming. 'Ah, that's damn good. Canon Murphy went on a pilgrimage to Rome, and when he came back he preached a sermon on it. "So I had a special audience with His Holiness, dearly beloved brethren, and he asked me, 'Canon Murphy, where are you now?' 'I'm in Dromod, Your Holiness,' said I. 'What sort of a parish is it, Canon Murphy?' says he. 'Ah, 'tis a nice, snug little parish, Your Holiness,' says I. 'Are they a good class of people?' says he. 'Well, they're not bad, Your Holiness,' says I. 'Are they good-living people?' says he. 'Well, they're as good as the next, Your Holiness,' says I. 'Except when they'd have a drop taken.' 'Tell me, Canon Murphy,' says he, 'do they pay their dues?' And like that, I was nearly struck dumb. 'There you have me, Your Holiness!' says I. 'There you have me.'"'

At heart Fogarty thought Maginnis was a bit of a sham and most of his stories were fabrications; but he never made the mistake of underestimating him, and he enjoyed the feeling Maginnis gave him of belonging to a group, and that of the best kind – well-balanced, humane, and necessary.

At meals in the curates' house, Galvin had a tendency to chatter brightly and aimlessly that irritated Fogarty. He was full of scraps of undigested knowledge, picked up from papers and magazines, about new plays and books that he would never either see or read. Fogarty was a moody young man who preferred either to keep silent or engage in long emotional discussions about local scandals that grew murkier and more romantic the more he described them. About such things he was hopelessly indiscreet. 'And that fellow notoriously killed his own father,' he said once, and Galvin looked at him in distress. 'You mean he really killed him?' he asked – as though Fogarty did not really mean everything at the moment he was saying it – and then, to make things worse, added,

'It's not something I'd care to repeat – not without evidence, I mean.'

'The Romans used eunuchs for civil servants, but we're more enlightened,' Fogarty said once to Maginnis. 'We prefer the natural ones.' Maginnis gave a hearty laugh; it was the sort of remark he liked to repeat. And when Galvin returned after lunching austerely with some maiden ladies and offered half-baked suggestions, Maginnis crushed him, and Fogarty watched with malicious amusement. He knew it was turning into persecution, but he wasn't quite sure which of the two men suffered more.

When he heard the explosion in the middle of the night, he waited for some further noise to interpret it, and then rose and put on the light. The housekeeper was standing outside her bedroom door in a raincoat, her hands joined. She was a widow woman with a history of tragedy behind her, and Fogarty did not like her; for some reason he felt she had the evil eye, and he always addressed her in his most commanding tone.

'What was that, Mary?' he asked.

I don't know, Father,' she said in a whisper. 'It sounded as if it was in Father Galvin's room.'

Fogarty listened again. There was no sound from Galvin's room, and he knocked and pushed in the door. He closed the door again immediately.

'Get Dr Carmody quick!' he said brusquely.

'What is it, Father?' she asked. 'An accident?'

'Yes, a bad one. And when you're finished, run out and ask Father Maginnis to come in.'

'Oh, that old gun!' she moaned softly. 'I dreaded it. I'll ring Dr Carmody.' She went hastily down the stairs.

Fogarty followed her and went into the living room to pick up the Sacred Oils from the cupboard where they were kept. 'I don't know, Doctor,' he heard Mary moaning. 'Father Fogarty said it was an accident.' He returned upstairs and lifted the gun from the bed before anointing the dead man. He had just concluded when the door opened and he saw the parish priest come in, wearing a blue flowered dressing-gown.

Maginnis went over to the bed and stared down at the figure on it. Then he looked at Fogarty over his glasses, his face almost expressionless. 'I was afraid of something like this,' he said knowingly. 'I knew he was a bit unstable.'

'You don't think it could be an accident?' Fogarty asked, though he knew the question sounded ridiculous.

'No,' Maginnis said, giving him a downward look through the spectacles. 'Do you?'

'But how could he bring himself to do a thing like that?' Fogarty asked incredulously.

'Oh, who knows?' said Maginnis, almost impatiently. 'With weak characters it's hard to tell. He doesn't seem to have left any message.'

'Not that I can see.'

'I'm sorry 'twas Carmody you sent for.'

'But he was Galvin's doctor.'

'I know, I know, but all the same he's young and a bit immature. I'd have preferred an older man. Make no mistake about it, Father, we have a problem on our hands,' he added with sudden resolution. 'A very serious problem.'

Fogarty did not need to have the problem spelled out for him. The worst thing a priest could do was to commit suicide, since it seemed to deny everything that gave his vocation meaning – Divine Providence and Mercy, forgiveness, Heaven, Hell. That one of God's anointed could come to such a state of despair was something the Church could not admit. It would give too much scandal. It was simply an unacceptable act.

'That's his car now, I fancy,' Maginnis said.

Carmody came quickly up the stairs with his bag in his hand and his pink pyjamas showing under his tweed jacket. He was a tall, spectacled young man with a long, humorous clown's face, and in ordinary life adopted a manner that went with his face, but Fogarty knew he was both competent and conscientious. He had worked for some years in an English hospital and developed a bluntness of speech that Fogarty found refreshing.

'Christ!' he said as he took in the scene. Then he went over and looked closely at the body. 'Poor Peter!' he added. Then he took the shotgun from the bedside table where Fogarty had put it and examined it. 'I should have kept a closer eye on him,' he said with chagrin. 'There isn't much I can do for him now.'

'On the contrary, Doctor,' Maginnis said. 'There was never a time when you could do more for him.' Then he gave Fogarty a meaningful glance. 'I wonder if you'd mind getting Jack Fitzgerald for me, Father? Talk to himself, and I needn't warn you to be careful what you say.'

'Oh, I'll be careful,' Fogarty said with gloomy determination. There was something in his nature that always responded to the touch of melodrama, and he knew Maginnis wanted to talk to Carmody alone. He telephoned to Fitzgerald, the undertaker, and then went back upstairs to dress. It was clear he wasn't going to get any more sleep that night.

He heard himself called and returned to Galvin's room. This time he really felt the full shock of it: the big bald parish priest in his dressing-gown and the gaunt young doctor with his pyjama top open under the jacket. He could see the two men had been arguing.

'Perhaps you'd talk to Dr Carmody, Father?' Maginnis suggested benignly.

'There's nothing to talk about, Father Fogarty,' Carmody said, adopting the formal title he ignored when they were among friends. 'I can't sign a certificate saying this was a natural death. You know I can't. It's too unprofessional.'

'Professional or not, Dr Carmody, someone will have to do it,' Maginnis said. 'I am the priest of this parish. In a manner of speaking I'm a professional man too, you know. And this unfortunate occurrence is something that doesn't concern only me and you. It has consequences that affect the whole parish.'

'Your profession doesn't require you to sign your name to a lie, Father,' Carmody said angrily. 'That's what you want me to do.'

'Oh, I wouldn't call that a lie, Dr Carmody,' Maginnis said with dignity. 'In considering the nature of a lie we have to take account of its good and bad effects. I can see no possible good effect that might result from a scandal about the death of this poor boy. Not one! In fact, I can see unlimited harm.'

'So can I,' Fogarty burst out. His voice sounded too loud, too confident, even to his own ears.

'I see,' Carmody said sarcastically. 'And you think we should keep on denouncing the Swedes and Danes for their suicide statistics, just because they don't fake them the way we do. Ah, for God's sake, man, I'd never be able to respect myself again.'

Fogarty saw that Maginnis was right. In some ways Carmody was too immature. 'That's all very well, Jim, but Christian charity comes before statistics,' he said appealingly. 'Forget about the damn statistics, can't you? Father Galvin wasn't only a statistic.

He was a human being – somebody we both knew. And what about his family?'

'What about his mother?' Maginnis asked with real pathos. 'I gather you have a mother yourself, Dr Carmody?'

'And you expect me to meet Mrs Galvin tomorrow and tell her her son was a suicide and can't be buried in consecrated ground?' Fogarty went on emotionally. 'Would you like us to do that to your mother if it was your case?'

'A doctor has unpleasant things to do as well, Jerry,' said Carmody.

'To tell a mother that her child is dying?' Fogarty asked. 'A priest has to do that too, remember. Not to tell her that her child is damned.'

But the very word that Fogarty knew had impressed Carmody made the parish priest uncomfortable. 'Fortunately, Father, that is in better hands than yours or mine,' he said curtly. And at once his manner changed. It was as though he was a little bit tired of them both. 'Dr Carmody,' he said, 'I think I hear Mr Fitzgerald. You'd better make up your mind quick. If you're not prepared to sign the death certificate, I'll soon find another doctor who will. That is my simple duty, and I'm going to do it. But as an elderly man who knows a little more about this town than you or Father Fogarty here, I'd advise you not to compel me to bring in another doctor. If word got around that I was forced to do such a thing, it might have very serious effects on your career.'

There was no mistaking the threat, and there was something almost admirable about the way it was made. At the same time, it roused the sleeping rebel in Fogarty. Bluff, he thought angrily. Damn bluff! If Carmody walked out on them at that moment, there was very little the parish priest or anyone else could do to him. Of course, any of the other doctors would sign the certificate, but it wouldn't do them any good either. When people really felt the need for a doctor, they didn't necessarily want the doctor the parish priest approved of. But as he looked at Carmody's sullen, resentful face, he realized that Carmody didn't know his own strength in the way that Maginnis knew his. After all, what had he behind him but a few years in a London hospital, while behind Maginnis was that whole vast, historic organization that he was rightly so proud of.

'I can't sign a certificate that death was due to natural causes,'

Carmody said stubbornly. 'Accident, maybe – I don't know. I wasn't here. I'll agree to accident.'

'Accident?' Maginnis said contemptuously, and this time he did not even trouble to use Carmody's title. It was as though he were stripping him of any little dignity he had. 'Young man, accidents with shotguns do not happen to priests at three o'clock in the morning. Try to talk sense!'

And just as Fogarty realized that the doctor had allowed himself to be crushed, they heard Mary let Fitzgerald in. He came briskly up the stairs. He was a small, spare man, built like a jockey. The parish priest nodded in the direction of the bed and Fitzgerald's brows went up mechanically. He was a man who said little, but he had a face and figure too expressive for his character. It was as though all the opinions he suppressed in life found relief in violent physical movements.

'Naturally, we don't want it talked about, Mr Fitzgerald,' said Maginnis. 'Do you think you could handle it yourself?'

The undertaker's eyes popped again, and he glanced swiftly from Maginnis to Carmody and then to Fogarty. He was a great man for efficiency, though; if you had asked him to supply the corpse as well as the coffin, he might have responded automatically, 'Male or female?'

'Dr Carmody will give the certificate, of course?' he asked shrewdly. He hadn't missed much of what was going on.

'It seems I don't have much choice,' Carmody replied bitterly.

'Oh, purely as an act of charity, of course,' Fitz said hastily. 'We all have to do this sort of thing from time to time. The poor relatives have enough to worry them without inquests and things like that. Wha was the age, Father Maginnis, do you know?' he added, taking out a notebook. A clever little man, thought Fogarty. He had put it all at once upon a normal, businesslike footing.

'Twenty-eight,' said Maginnis.

'God help us!' Fitz said perfunctorily, and made a note. After that he took out a rule.

'I'd better get ready and go to see the Bishop myself,' Maginnis said. 'We'll need his permission, of course, but I haven't much doubt about that. I know he has the reputation for being on the strict side, but I always found him very considerate. I'll send Nora over to help your housekeeper, Father. In the meantime, maybe you'd be good enough to get in touch with the family.'

'I'll see to that, Father,' Fogarty said. He and Carmody followed Maginnis downstairs. He said goodbye and left, and Fogarty's manner changed abruptly. 'Come in and have a drink, Jim,' he said.

'I'd rather not, Jerry,' Carmody said gloomily.

'Come on! Come on! You need one, man! I need one myself and I can't have it.' He shut the door of the living room behind him. 'Great God, Jim, you could have suspected it?'

'I suppose I should have,' said Carmody. 'I got hints enough if only I might have understood them.'

'But you couldn't, Jim,' Fogarty said excitedly, taking the whiskey from the big cupboard. 'Nobody could. Do you think I ever expected it, and I lived closer to him than you did.'

The front door opened and they heard the slippers of Nora, Maginnis's housekeeper, in the hall. There was a low mumble of talk outside the door, and then the clank of a bucket as the women went up the stairs. Fitzgerald was coming down at the same time, and Fogarty opened the door a little.

'Well, Jack?'

'Well, Father. I'll do the best I can.'

'You wouldn't join us for a—'

'No, Father. I'll have my hands full for the next couple of hours.'

'Goodnight, Jack. And I'm sorry for the disturbance.'

'Ah, 'twas none of your doing. Goodnight, Father.'

The doctor finished his whiskey in a gulp, and his long, battered face had a bitter smile. 'And so this is how it's done!' he said.

'This is how it's done, Jim, and believe me, it's the best way for everybody in the long run,' Fogarty replied with real gravity.

But, looking at Carmody's face, he knew the doctor did not believe it, and he wondered then if he really believed it himself.

When the doctor had gone, Fogarty got on the telephone to a provincial town fifty miles away. The exchange was closed down, so he had to give his message to the police. In ten minutes or so a guard would set out along the sleeping streets to the house where the Galvins lived. That was one responsibility he was glad to evade.

While he was speaking, he heard the parish priest's car set off and knew he was on his way to the Bishop's palace. Then he shaved, and, about eight, Fitzgerald drove up with the coffin in his van. Silently they carried it between them up the stairs. The body was lying decently composed with a simple bandage about the head. Between them they lifted it into the coffin. Fitzgerald looked questioningly at Fogarty and went on his knees. As he said the brief prayer, Fogarty found his voice unsteady and his eyes full of tears. Fitzgerald gave him a pitying look and then rose and dusted his knees.

'All the same there'll be talk, Father,' he said.

'Maybe not as much as there should be, Jack,' Fogarty said moodily.

'We'll take him to the chapel, of course?' Fitzgerald went on.

'Everything in order, Jack. Father Maginnis is a smart man. You saw him?'

'I saw him.'

'No nerves, no hysterics. I saw other people in the same situation. "Oh, Mr Fitzgerald, what am I going to do?" His mind on essential things the whole time. He's an object lesson to us all, Father.'

'You're right, Jack, he is,' Fogarty said despondently.

Suddenly the undertaker's hand shot out and caught him by the upper arm. 'Forget about it, boy! Forget about it! What else can you do? Why the hell should you break your heart over it?'

Fogarty still had to meet the family. Later that morning, they drove up to the curates' house. The mother was an actressy type and wept a good deal. She wanted somebody to give her a last message, which Fogarty couldn't think up. The sister, a pretty, intense girl, wept a little too, but quietly with her back turned, while the brother, a young man with a great resemblance to Galvin, said little. Mother and brother accepted without protest the ruling that the coffin was not to be opened, but the sister looked at Fogarty and asked, 'You don't think I could see him? Alone? I wouldn't be afraid.' When he said the doctor had forbidden it, she turned her back again, and he had an impression that there was a closer link between her and Galvin than between the others and him.

That evening they brought the body to lie before the altar of the church, and Maginnis received it and said the prayers. The church was crowded, and Fogarty knew with a strange mixture of rejoicing and mortification that the worst was over. Maginnis's master stroke was the new curate, Rowlands, who had arrived within a couple of hours after his own return. He was a tall, thin

91

ascetic-looking young man, slow-moving and slow-speaking, and Fogarty knew that all eyes were on him.

Everything went in perfect propriety at the Requiem Mass next morning, and after the funeral Fogarty attended the lunch given by Maginnis to the visiting clergy. He almost laughed out loud when he heard Maginnis ask in a low voice, 'Father Healy, did I ever tell you the story of Canon Murphy and the Pope?' All that would follow would be the mourning card with the picture of Galvin and the Gothic lettering that said, '*Ecce Sacerdos Magnus*'. There was no danger of scandal any longer. Carmody would not talk. Fitzgerald would not talk either. None of the five people involved would. Father Galvin might have spared himself the trouble.

As they returned from the church together, Fogarty tried to talk to the new curate about what had happened, but he soon realized that the whole significance of it had escaped Rowlands, and that Rowlands thought he was only over-dramatizing it all. Anybody would think he was over-dramatizing it, except Carmody. After his supper he would go to the doctor's house, and they would talk about it. Only Carmody would really understand what it was they had done between them. No one else would.

What lonely lives we live, he thought unhappily.

(1967)

A Great Man

Once when I was visiting a famous London hospital, I met the matron, Miss Fitzgerald, a small, good-looking woman of fifty. She was Irish, and we discussed acquaintances in common until I mentioned Dermot O'Malley, and then I realized that somehow or other I had said the wrong thing. The matron frowned and went away. A few minutes later she returned, smiling, and asked me to lunch, in a way that, for some reason, reminded me of a girl asking a young fellow for the first time to her home. 'You know, Dr O'Malley was a great friend of my father,' she said abruptly and then frowned again.

'Begor, I was,' said O'Malley when I reported this to him later. 'And I'll tell you a story about it, what's more.' O'Malley is tall and gentle, and has a wife who is a pain in the neck, though he treats her with a consideration that I can only describe as angelic. 'It was when I was a young doctor in Dublin, and my old professor, Dwyer, advised me to apply for a job in the hospital in Dooras. Now, you never heard of Dooras, but we all knew about it then, because that was in the days of Margaret's father, old Jim Fitzgerald, and he was known, all right.

'I met him a couple of nights later in a hotel in Kildare Street. He had come up to Dublin to attend a meeting of doctors. He was a man with piercing eyes and a long, hard face – more the face of a soldier than a doctor. The funny thing was his voice, which was rather high and piping and didn't seem to go at all with his manner.

'"Dooras is no place for a young man who likes entertainment," he said.

'"Ah, I'm a country boy myself," said I, "So that wouldn't worry me. And of course, I know the hospital has a great reputation."

'"So I understand," he said grimly. "You see, O'Malley, I don't believe in all this centralization that's going on. I know it's all for the sake of equipment, and equipment is a good thing, too, but it's taking medicine away from where it belongs. One of these days, when their centralization breaks down, they'll find they haven't hospitals, doctors, or anything else."

'By the time I'd left him, I'd as good as accepted the job, and it wasn't the job that interested me so much as the man. It could be that, my own father having been a bit of a waster, I'm attracted to men of strong character, and Fitzgerald was a fanatic. I liked that about him.

'Now, Dwyer had warned me that I'd find Dooras queer, and Dwyer knew that Dublin hospitals weren't up to much, but Dooras was dotty. It was an old hospital for infectious diseases that must have dated from about the time of the Famine, and Fitzgerald had got a small local committee to take it over. The first couple of days in it gave me the horrors, and it was weeks before I even began to see what Fitzgerald meant by it all. Then I did begin to see that in spite of all the drawbacks, it worked in a way bigger hospitals didn't work, and it was happy in a way that bigger hospitals are never happy. Everybody knew everybody else, and everybody was madly curious about everybody else, and if anybody ever gave a party, it wasn't something devised by the staff to entertain the patients; it was more likely to be the patients entertaining the staff.

'Partly this was because Margaret Fitzgerald, the woman you met in London, was the head nurse. I don't know what she's like now, and from all I can hear she's a bit of a Tartar, but in those days she was a pretty little thing with an air of being more efficient than anybody ever was. Whenever you spoke to Margaret, she practically sprang to attention and clicked her heels, and if you were misguided enough to ask her for anything she hadn't handy, she gave you a demonstration of greyhound racing. And, of course, as you can see from the job she has now, she was a damn great nurse.

'But mainly the place worked because of Fitzgerald and his colleagues, the local doctors. Apart from him, none of them struck me as very brilliant, though he himself had a real respect for an old doctor called Pat Duane, a small, round, red-faced man with an old-fashioned choker collar and a wonderful soupy bedside manner. Pat looked as though some kind soul had left him to mature in a sherry cask till all the crude alcohol was drawn out of him. But they were all conscientious; they all listened to advice, even from me – and God knows I hadn't much to offer – and they all deferred in the most extraordinary way to Fitzgerald. Dwyer had described him to me as a remarkable man, and I was beginning to understand the full force of that, because I knew Irish small towns the way only a country boy knows them, and if those men weren't at one another's throats, fighting for every five-bob fee that could be picked up, it was due to his influence. I asked a doctor called MacCarthy about it one night he invited me in for a drink. MacCarthy was a tall old poseur with a terrible passion for local history.

"'Has it occurred to you that Fitzgerald may have given us back our self-respect, young man?" he asked in his pompous way.

"'Your what?" I asked in genuine surprise. In those days it hadn't once occurred to me that a man could at the same time be a show-box and be lacking in self-respect.

"'Oh, come, O'Malley, come!" he said, sounding like the last Duke of Dooras. "As a medical man you are more observant than you pretend. I presume you have met Dr Duane?"

"'I have. Yes," said I.

"'And it didn't occur to you that Dr Duane was ever a victim of alcohol?" he went on portentously. "You understand, of course, that I am not criticizing him. It isn't easy for the professional man in Ireland to maintain his standards of behaviour. Fitzgerald has a considerable respect for Dr Duane's judgement – quite justified, I may add, quite justified. But at any rate, in a very short time Pat eased off on the drink, and even began to read the medical journals again. Now Fitzgerald has him in the hollow of his hand. We all like to feel we are of some use to humanity – even the poor general practitioner . . . But you saw it all for yourself, of course. You are merely trying to pump a poor country doctor."

'Fitzgerald was not pretentious. He liked me to drop in on him when I had an hour to spare, and I went to his house every week for dinner. He lived in an old, uncomfortable family house a couple of miles out on the bay. Normally he was cold, concentrated, and irritable, but when he had a few drinks in he got melancholy, and this for some reason caused him to be indiscreet and say dirty things about his committee and even about the other doctors. "The most interesting thing about MacCarthy," he said to me once, "is that he's the seventh son of a seventh son, and so he can diagnose a case without seeing the patient at all. It leaves him a lot of spare time for local history." I suspected he made the same sort of dirty remarks about me, and that secretly the man had no faith in anyone but himself. I told him so, and I think he enjoyed it. Like all shy men he liked to be insulted in a broad masculine way, and one night when

I called him a flaming egotist he grunted like an old dog when you tickle him and said, "Drink makes you very offensive, O'Malley. Have some more!"

'It wasn't so much that he was an egotist (though he was) as that he had a pernickety sense of responsibility, and whenever he hadn't a case to worry over, he could always find some equivalent of a fatal disease in the hospital – a porter who was too cheeky or a nurse who made too free with the men patients – and he took it all personally and on a very high level of suffering. He would sulk and snap at Margaret for days over some trifle that didn't matter to anyone, and finally reduce her to tears. At the same time, I suppose it was part of the atmosphere of seriousness he had created about the makeshift hospital, and it kept us all on our toes. Medicine was his life, and his gossip was shop. Duane or MacCarthy or some other local doctor would drop in of an evening to discuss a case – which by some process I never was able to fathom had become Fitzgerald's case – and over the drinks he would grow gloomier and gloomier about our ignorance, till at last, without a word to any of us, he got up and telephoned some Dublin specialist he knew. It was part of the man's shyness that he only did it when he was partly drunk and could pretend that instead of asking a favour he was conferring one. Several times I watched that scene with amusement. It was all carefully calculated, because if he hadn't had enough to drink he lacked the brass and became apologetic, whereas if he had had one drink too much he could not describe what it was about the case that really worried him. Not that he rated a specialist's knowledge any higher than ours, but it seemed the best he could do, and if that didn't satisfy him, he ordered the specialist down, even when it meant footing the bill himself. It was only then I began to realize the respect that Dublin specialists had for him, because Dwyer, who was a terrified little man and hated to leave home for fear of what might happen to him in out-of-the-way places like Cork and Belfast, would only give out a gentle moan about coming to Dooras. No wonder Duane and MacCarthy swore by him, even if for so much of the time they, like myself, thought him a nuisance.

'Margaret was a second edition of himself, though in her the sense of responsibility conflicted with everything feminine in her till it became a joke. She was small. She was pretty, with one of those miniature faces that seem to have been reduced until every coarse line has been refined in them. She moved at twice the normal speed and was for ever fussing and bossing and wheedling, till one of the nurses would lose her temper and say, "Ah, Margaret, will you for God's sake give us time to breathe!" That sort of impertinence would make Margaret scowl, shrug, and go off somewhere else, but her sulks never lasted, as her father's did. The feminine side of her wouldn't sustain them.

'I remember one night when all hell broke loose in the wards, as it usually does in any hospital once a month. Half a dozen patients decided to die all together, and I was called out of bed. Margaret and the other nurse on night duty, Joan Henderson, had brewed themselves a pot of tea in the kitchen, and they were scurrying round with a mug or a bit of seedcake in their hands. I was giving an injection to one of my patients, who should have been ready for discharge. In the next bed was a dying old mountainy man who had nothing in particular wrong with him except old age and a broken heart. I suddenly looked up from what I was doing and saw he had come out of coma and was staring at Margaret, who was standing at the other side of the bed from me, nibbling the bit of cake over which she had been interrupted. She started when she saw him staring at the cake, because she knew what her father would say if ever he heard that she was eating in the wards. Then she gave a broad grin and said in a country accent, "Johnny, would 'oo like a bit of seedcake?" and held it to his lips. He hesitated and then began to nibble too, and then his tongue came out and licked round his mouth, and somehow I knew he was saved. "Tay, Johnny," she said mockingly. "Thot's what 'oo wants now, isn't it?" And that morning as I went through the wards, my own patient was dead, but old Johnny was sitting up, ready for another ten years of the world's hardship. That's nursing.

'Margaret lived at such a pitch of nervous energy that every few weeks she fell ill. "I keep telling that damn girl to take it easy," her father would say with a scowl at me, but any time there was the least indication that Margaret was taking it easy, he started to air his sufferings with the anguish of an elephant. She was a girl with a real sense of service and at one time had tried to join a nursing order in Africa, but dropped it because of his hatred of all nursing orders. In itself this was funny because Margaret was a liberal Catholic who, like St Teresa, was "for the Moors, and martyrdom", but never worried her head about human weaknesses and made no more of an illegitimate baby than if she had them herself every Wednesday, while he was an old-fashioned Catholic and full of obscure prejudices. At the same time, he felt that the religious orders were leaving Ireland without nurses – not that he thought so much of nurses!

'"And I suppose nuns can't be nurses?" Margaret would ask with a contemptuous shrug.

'"How can they?" he would say, in his shrillest voice. 'The business of religion is with the soul, not the body. My business is with the body. When I'm done with it, the nuns can have it – or anyone else, for that matter."

'"And why not the soul and the body?" Margaret would ask in her pertest tone.

'"Because you can't serve two masters, girl."

'"Pooh!" Margaret would say with another shrug. "You can't serve one Siamese twin, either."

'As often as I went to dinner in that house, there was hardly a meal without an argument. Sometimes it was about no more than the amount of whiskey he drank. Margaret hated drink, and watched every drop he poured in his glass, so that often, just to spite her, he went on to knock himself out. I used to think that she might have known her father was a man who couldn't resist a challenge. She was as censorious as he was, but she had a pertness and awkwardness that a man rarely had, and suddenly, out of the blue, would come some piece of impertinence that plunged him into gloom and made her cringe away to her bedroom, ready for tears. He and I would go into the big front room, overlooking Dooras Bay, and without a glance at the view he would splash enormous tasheens of whiskey into our glasses, just to indicate how little he cared for her, and say in a shrill complaining voice, "I ruined that girl, O'Malley. I know I did. If her mother was alive, she wouldn't talk to me that way."

'Generally, they gave the impression of two people who hated one another with a passionate intensity, but I knew well that he was crazy about her. He always brought her back something from his trips to Dublin or Cork, and once, when I was with him, he casually wasted my whole afternoon looking for something nice for her. It never occurred to him that I might have anything else to do. But he could also be thoughtful; for once when for a full week he had been so intolerable that I could scarcely bring myself to answer him he grinned and said, "I know exactly what you think of me, O'Malley. You think I'm an old slave driver."

'"Not exactly," I said, giving him tit for tat. "Just an old whoor!"

'At this, he gave a great guffaw and handed me a silver cigarette case, which I knew he must have bought for me in town the previous day, and added sneeringly, "Now, don't you be going round saying your work is quite unappreciated."

'"Did I really say that?" I asked, still keeping my end up, even though there was something familiar about the sentiment.

'"Or if you do, say it over the loudspeaker. Remember, O'Malley, I hear *everything*." And the worst of it was, he did!

'Then, one night, when my year's engagement was nearly ended, I went to his house for dinner. That night there was no quarrelling, and he and I sat on in the front room, drinking and admiring the view. I should have known there was something wrong, because for once he didn't talk shop. He talked about almost everything else, and all the time he was knocking back whiskey in a way I knew I could never keep pace with. When it grew dark, he said with an air of surprise, "O'Malley, I'm a bit tight. I think we'd better go for a stroll and clear our heads."

'We strolled up the avenue of rhododendrons to the gate and turned left up the hill. It was a wild, rocky bit of country, stopped dead by the roadway and then cascading merrily down the little fields to the bay. There was still a coppery light in the sky, and the reflection of a bonfire on one of the islands, like a pendulum, in the water. The road fell again, between demesne walls and ruined gateways where the last of the old gentry lived, and I was touched – partly, I suppose, by all the whiskey, but partly by the place itself.

'"I'll regret this place when I leave it," I said.

'"Oh, no, you won't," he snapped back at me. "This is no place for young people."

'"I fancy it might be a very pleasant memory if you were in the East End of London," said I.

'"It might," said Fitzgerald, "if you were quite sure you wouldn't have to go back to it. That's what worries me about Margaret."

'I had never noticed him worrying very much about Margaret – or anyone else, for that matter – so I took it as merely a matter of form.

'"Margaret seems to do very well in it," I said.

'"It's no place for Margaret," he said sharply. "People need friends of their own age and ideas old men like myself can't supply. It's largely my fault for letting her come back here at

99

all. I made this place too much of my life, and that's all right for a man, but it's not good enough for a high-spirited girl like that."

'"But doesn't Margaret have friends here?" I asked, trying to comfort him.

'"She has friends enough, but not of her own age," he said. "She's too mature for the girls here that are her own age. Not that I ever cared much for her friends from Dublin," he added shortly. "They struck me as a lot of show-boxes. I don't like those intellectual Catholics, talking to me about St Thomas Aquinas. I never read St Thomas Aquinas, and from all I can hear I haven't missed much. But young people have to make their own mistakes. All the men around here seem to want is some good-natured cow who'll agree to everything they say, and because she argues with them they think she's pert and knowing. Well, she is pert, and she is knowing – I realize that as well as anybody. But there's more than that to her. They'd have said the same about me, only I proved to them that I knew what I was doing."

'Suddenly I began to realize what he was saying, and I was frightened out of my wits. I said to myself that it was impossible, that a man like Fitzgerald could never mean a thing like that, but at the same time I felt that he did mean it, and that it had been in his mind from the first night he met me. I muttered something about her having more chances in Dublin.

'"That's the trouble," he said. "She didn't know what she was letting herself in for when she came back here, and no more did I. Now she won't leave, because I'd be here on my own. Well, I would be on my own, and I know I wouldn't like it, but still I have my work to do, and for a man that's enough. I like pitting my wits against parish priests and county councillors and nuns. Besides, when you reach my age you realize that you could have worse, and they'll let me have my own way for the time I have left me. But I haven't so long to live, and when I die, they'll have some champion footballer running the place, and Margaret will be taking orders from the nuns. She thinks now that she won't mind, but she won't do it for long. I know the girl. She ought to marry, and then she'd have to go wherever her husband took her."

'"But you don't really think the hospital will go to pieces like that?" I asked, pretending to be deeply concerned, but really only trying to head Fitzgerald off the subject he seemed to have on his mind. "I mean, don't you think Duane and MacCarthy will hold it together?"

'"How can they?" he asked querulously. "It's not their life, the way it's been mine. I don't mean they won't do their best, but the place will go to pieces just the same. It's a queer feeling, Dermot, when you realize that nothing in the world outlasts the man that made it."

'That sentence was almost snapped at me, out of the side of his mouth, and yet it sounded like a cry of pain – maybe because he'd used my Christian name for the first time. He was not a man to use Christian names. I didn't know what to say.

'"Of course, I should have had a son to pass on my responsibilities to," he added wonderingly. "I'm not any good with girls. I dare say that was why I liked you, the first time we met – because I might have had a son like you."

'Then I couldn't bear it any longer, and it broke from me. "And it wasn't all on one side!"

'"I guessed that. In certain ways we're not so unlike. And that's what I really wanted to say to you before you go. If ever you and Margaret got to care for one another, it would mean a lot to me. She won't have much, but she'll never be a burden on anybody, and if ever she marries, she'll make a good wife."

'It was the most embarrassing moment of my life – and mind, it wasn't embarrassing just because I was being asked to marry a nice girl I'd never given a thought to. I'm a country boy, and I knew all about "made" matches by the time I was seventeen, and I never had anything but contempt for the snobs that pretend to despise them. Damn good matches the most of them are, and a thousand times better than the sort you see nowadays that seem to be made up out of novelettes or moving pictures! Still and all, it's different when it comes to your own turn. I suppose it's only at a moment like that you realize you're just as silly as any little servant girl. But it wasn't only that. It was because I was being proposed to by a great man, a fellow I'd looked up to in a way I never looked up to my own father, and I couldn't do the little thing he wanted me to do. I muttered some nonsense about never having been able to think about marriage – as if there ever was a young fellow that hadn't thought about it every night of his life! – and he saw how upset I was and squeezed my arm.

'"What did I tell you?" he said. "I knew I was drunk, and if she ever gets to hear what I said to you, she'll cut me in little bits."

'And that tone of his broke my heart. I don't even know if you'll understand what I mean, but all I felt was grief to think a great man who'd brought life to a place where life never was before would have to ask a favour of me, and me not to be able to grant it. Because all the time I wanted to be cool and suave and say of course I'd marry his daughter, just to show the way I felt about himself, and I was too much of a coward to do it. In one way, it seemed so impossible, and in another it seemed such a small thing.

'Of course, we never resumed the conversation, but that didn't make it any easier, because it wasn't only between myself and him; it was between me and Margaret. The moment I had time to think of it, I knew Fitzgerald was too much of a gentleman to have said anything to me without first making sure that she'd have me.

'Well, you know the rest yourself. When he died, things happened exactly the way he'd prophesied; a local footballer got his job, and the nuns took over the nursing, and there isn't a Dublin doctor under fifty that could even tell you where Dooras is. Fitzgerald was right. Nothing in the world outlasts a man. Margaret, of course, has a great reputation, and I'm told on the best authority that there isn't a doctor in St Dorothy's she hasn't put the fear of God into, so I suppose it's just as well that she never got the opportunity to put it into me. Or don't you agree?'

I didn't, of course, as O'Malley well knew. Anyway, he could hardly have done much worse for himself. And I had met Margaret, and I had seen her autocratic airs, but they hadn't disturbed me much. She was just doing it on temperament, rather than technique – a very Irish way, and probably not so unlike her father's. I knew I didn't have to tell O'Malley that. He was a gentleman himself, and his only reason for telling me the story was that already, with the wisdom that comes of age, he had begun to wonder whether he had not missed something in missing Margaret Fitzgerald. I knew that he had.

(1958)

A Story by
Maupassant

People who have not grown up in a provincial town won't know what
I mean when I say what Terry Coughlan meant to me. People who
have won't need to know.

As kids we lived a few doors from each other on the same terrace,
and his sister, Tess, was a friend of my sister, Nan. There was a time
when I was rather keen on Tess myself. She was a small, plump, gay
little thing, with rosy cheeks like apples, and she played the piano
very well. In those days I sang a bit, though I hadn't much of a
voice. When I sang Mozart, Beethoven, or even Wagner, Terry
would listen with brooding approval. When I sang commonplace
stuff, Terry would make a face and walk out. He was a good-looking
lad with a big brow and curly black hair, a long, pale face and a pair
of intent dark eyes. He was always well spoken and smart in his
appearance. There was nothing sloppy about him.

When he could not learn something by night he got up at five in
the morning to do it, and whatever he took up he mastered. Even
as a boy he was always looking forward to the day when he'd have
money enough to travel, and he taught himself French and German
in the time it took me to find out I could not learn Irish. He was
cross with me for wanting to learn it; according to him it had 'no
cultural significance', but he was crosser still with me because I
couldn't learn it. 'The first thing you should learn to do is to work,'
he would say gloomily. 'What's going to become of you if you don't?'
He had read somewhere that when Keats was depressed, he had a
wash and brush-up. Keats was his god. Poetry was never much in
my line, except Shelley, and Terry didn't think much of him.

We argued about it on our evening walks. Maybe you don't
remember the sort of arguments you had when you were young.
Lots of people prefer not to remember, but I like thinking of them.
A man is never more himself than when he talks nonsense about

God, Eternity, prostitution, and the necessity for having mistresses. I argued with Terry that the day of poetry was over, and that the big boys of modern literature were the fiction writers – the ones we'd heard of in Cork at that time, I mean – the Russians and Maupassant.

'The Russians are all right,' he said to me once. 'Maupassant you can forget.'

'But why, Terry?' I asked.

'Because whatever you say about the Russians, they're noble,' he said. 'Noble' was a great word of his at the time: Shakespeare was 'noble', Turgenev was 'noble', Beethoven was 'noble'. 'They are a religious people, like Greeks, or the English of Shakespeare's time. But Maupassant is slick and coarse and commonplace. Are his stories literature?'

'Ah, to hell with literature!' I said. 'It's life.'

'Life in this country?'

'Life in his own country, then.'

'But how do you know?' Terry asked, stopping and staring at me. 'Humanity is the same here as anywhere else. If he's not true of the life we know, he's not true of any sort of life.'

Then he got the job in the monks' school and I got the job in Carmody's and we began to drift apart. There was no quarrel. It was just that I liked company and Terry didn't. I got in with a wild group – Marshall and Redmond and Donnelan, the solicitor – and we sat up until morning, drinking and settling the future of humanity. Terry came with us once, but he didn't talk, and when Donnelan began to hold forth on Shaw and the Life Force I could see his face getting dark. You know Donnelan's line – 'But what I mean – what I want to say – Jasus, will somebody let me talk? I have something important to say.' We all knew that Donnelan was a bit of a joke, but when I said goodnight to Terry in the hall he turned on me with an angry look.

'Do those friends of yours do anything but talk?' he asked.

'Never mind, Terry,' I said. 'The Revolution is coming.'

'Not if they have anything to say to it,' Terry said, and walked away from me. I stood there for a while, feeling sorry for myself, as you do when you know that the end of a friendship is in sight. It didn't make me happier when I went back to the room and Donnelan looked at me as if he didn't believe his eyes.

'Magner,' he asked, 'am I dreaming or was there someone with you?'

Suddenly, for no particular reason, I lost my temper.

'Yes, Donnelan,' I said. 'But somebody I wouldn't expect you to recognize.'

That, I suppose, was the last flash of the old love, and after that it was bogged down in argument. Donnelan said that Terry lacked flexibility – flexibility!

Occasionally I met Tess with her little shopping basket and her round rosy cheeks, and she would say reproachfully, 'Ah, Ted, aren't you becoming a great stranger? What did we do to you at all?' And a couple of times I dropped round to sing a song and borrow a book, and Terry told me about his work as a teacher. He was a bit disillusioned with his job, and you wouldn't wonder. Some of the monks kept a mackintosh and muffler handy so that they could drop out to the pictures after dark with some doll. And then there was a thundering row when Terry discovered that a couple of his brightest boys were being sent up for public examinations under the names of notorious ignoramuses, so as to bolster up the record. When Brother Dunphy, the headmaster, argued with Terry that it was only a simple act of charity, Terry replied sourly that it seemed to him more like a criminal offence. After that he got the reputation of being impossible and was not consulted when Patrick Dempsey, the boy he really liked, was put up for examination as Mike MacNamara, the County Councillor's son – Mike the Moke, as Terry called him.

Now, Donnelan is a gasbag, and, speaking charitably, a bit of a fool, but there were certain things he learned in his Barrack Street slum. One night he said to me, 'Ted, does that fellow Coughlan drink?' 'Drink?' I said, laughing outright at him. 'Himself and a sparrow would have about the same consumption of liquor.' Nothing ever embarrassed Donnelan, who had the hide of a rhinoceros.

'Well, you might be right,' he said reasonably, 'but, begor, I never saw a sparrow that couldn't hold it.'

I thought myself that Donnelan was dreaming, but next time I met Tess I sounded her. 'How's that brother of yours keeping?' I asked. 'Ah, fine, Ted, why?' she asked, as though she was really surprised. 'Oh, nothing,' I said. 'Somebody was telling me that he wasn't looking well.'

'Ah, he's that way this long time, Ted,' she replied, 'and 'tis nothing only the want of sleep. He studies too hard at night, and then he goes wandering all over the country, trying to work off the excitement. Sure, I'm always at him!'

That satisfied me. I knew Tess couldn't tell me a lie. But then, one moonlight night about six months later, three or four of us were standing outside the hotel – the night porter had kicked us out in the middle of an argument, and we were finishing it there. Two was striking from Shandon when I saw Terry coming up the pavement towards us. I never knew whether he recognized me or not, but all at once he crossed the street, and even I could see that the man was drunk.

'Tell me,' said Donnelan, peering across at him, 'is that a sparrow I see at this hour of night?' All at once he spun round on his heels, splitting his sides with laughing. 'Magner's sparrow!' he said. 'Magner's sparrow!' I hope in comparing Donnelan with a rhinoceros I haven't done injustice to either party.

I saw then what was happening. Terry was drinking all right, but he was drinking unknown to his mother and sister. You might almost say he was drinking unknown to himself. Other people could be drunkards, but not he. So he sat at home reading, or pretending to read, until late at night, and then slunk off to some low pub on the quays where he hoped people wouldn't recognize him, and came home only when he knew his family was in bed.

For a long time I debated with myself about whether I shouldn't talk to him. If I made up my mind to do it once, I did it twenty times. But when I ran into him in town, striding slowly along, and saw the dark, handsome face with the slightly ironic smile, I lost courage. His mind was as keen as ever – it may even have been a shade too keen. He was becoming slightly irritable and arrogant. The manners were as careful and the voice was as pleasant as ever – a little too much so. The way he raised his hat high in the air to some woman who passed and whipped the big handkerchief from his breast pocket reminded me of an old actor going down in the world. The farther down he went the worse the acting got. He wouldn't join me for a drink; no, he had this job that simply must be finished tonight. How could I say to him, 'Terry, for God's sake, give up trying to pretend you have work to do. I know you're an impostor and you're drinking yourself to death.' You couldn't talk like that to a man of his kind. People like him are all of a piece; they have to stand or fall by something inside themselves.

He was forty when his mother died, and by that time it looked as though he'd have Tess on his hands for life as well. I went back to the house with him after the funeral. He was cruelly broken up. I discovered that he had spent his first few weeks abroad that summer and he was full of it. He had stayed in Paris and visited the cathedrals round, and they had made a deep impression on him. He had never seen real architecture before. I had a vague hope that it might have jolted him out of the rut he had been getting into, but I was wrong. It was worse he was getting.

Then, a couple of years later I was at home one evening, finishing up some work, when a knock came to the door. I opened it myself and saw old Pa Hourigan, the policeman, outside. Pa had a schoolgirl complexion and a white moustache, china-blue eyes and a sour elderly mouth, like a baby who has learned the facts of life too soon. It surprised me because we never did more than pass the time of day.

'May I speak to you for a moment, Mr Magner?' he asked modestly. ''Tis on a rather private matter.'

'You can to be sure, Sergeant,' I said, joking him. 'I'm not a bit afraid. 'Tis years since I played ball on the public street. Have a drink.'

'I never touch it, going on night duty,' he said, coming into the front room. 'I hope you will pardon my calling, but you know I am not a man to interfere in anyone else's private affairs.'

By this time he had me puzzled and a bit anxious. I knew him for an exceptionally retiring man, and he was clearly upset.

'Ah, of course you're not,' I said. 'No one would accuse you of it. Sit down and tell me what the trouble is.'

'Aren't you a friend of Mr Coughlan, the teacher?' he asked.

'I am,' I said.

'Mr Magner,' he said, exploding on me, 'can you do nothing with the man?'

I looked at him for a moment and had a premonition of disaster.

'Is it as bad as that?' I asked.

'It cannot go on, Mr Magner,' he said, shaking his head. 'It cannot go on. I saved him before. Not because he was anything to me, because I hardly knew the man. Not even because of his poor decent sister, though I pity her with my whole heart and soul. It was for the respect I have for education. And you know that, Mr Magner,' he added earnestly, meaning (which was true enough) that I owed it to him that I had never paid a fine for drinking during prohibited hours.

'We all know it, Sergeant,' I said. 'And I assure you, we appreciate it.'

'No one knows, Mr Magner,' he went on, 'what sacrifices Mrs Hourigan and myself made to put that boy of ours through college, and I would not give it to say to him that an educated man could sink so low. But there are others at the barrack who don't think the way I do. I name no names, Mr Magner, but there are those who would be glad to see an educated man humiliated.'

'What is it, Sergeant?' I asked. 'Drink?'

'Mr Magner,' he said indignantly, 'when did I ever interfere with an educated man for drinking? I know when a man has a lot on his mind he cannot always do without stimulants.'

'You don't mean drugs?' I asked. The idea had crossed my mind once or twice.

'No, Mr Magner, I do not,' he said, quivering with indignation. 'I mean those low, loose, abandoned women that I would have whipped and transported.'

If he had told me that Terry had turned into a common thief, I couldn't have been more astonished and horrified. Horrified is the word.

'You don't mind my saying that I find that very hard to believe, Sergeant?' I asked.

'Mr Magner,' he said with great dignity, 'in my calling a man does not use words lightly.'

'I know Terry Coughlan since we were boys together, and I never as much as heard an unseemly word from him,' I said.

'Then all I can say, Mr Magner, is that I'm glad, very glad that you've never seen him as I have, in a condition I would not compare to the beasts.' There were real tears in the old man's eyes. 'I spoke to him myself about it. At four o'clock this morning I separated him from two of those vile creatures that I knew well were robbing him. I pleaded with him as if he was my own brother. "Mr Coughlan," I said, "what will your soul do at the Judgement?" and Mr Magner, in decent society I would not repeat the disgusting reply he made me.'

'*Corruptio optimi pessima*,' I said to myself.

'That is Latin, Mr Magner,' the old policeman said with real pleasure.

'And it means "Lilies that fester smell far worse than weeds," Sergeant,' I said. 'I don't know if I can do anything. I suppose I'll have to try. If he goes on like this he'll destroy himself, body and soul.'

'Do what you can for his soul, Mr Magner,' whispered the old man, making for the door. 'As for his body, I wouldn't like to answer.' At the door he turned with a mad stare in his blue eyes. 'I would not like to answer,' he repeated, shaking his grey pate again.

It gave me a nasty turn. Pa Hourigan was happy. He had done his duty but mine still remained to be done. I sat for an hour, thinking about it, and the more I thought the more hopeless it seemed. Then I put on my hat and went out.

Terry lived at that time in a nice little house on College Road; a little red-brick villa with a bow window. He answered the door himself, a slow, brooding, black-haired man with a long pale face. He didn't let on to be either surprised or pleased.

'Come in,' he said with a crooked smile. 'You're a great stranger, aren't you?'

'You're a bit of a stranger yourself, Terry,' I said jokingly. Then Tess came out, drying her hands in her apron. Her little cheeks were as rosy as ever, but the gloss was gone. I had the feeling that now there was nothing much she didn't know about her brother. Even the nervous smile suggested that she knew what I had come for – of course, old Hourigan must have brought him home.

'Ah, Ted, 'tis a cure for sore eyes to see you,' she said. 'You'll have a cup? You will, to be sure.'

'You'll have a drink,' Terry said.

'Do you know, I think I will, Terry,' I said, seeing a nice natural opening for the sort of talk I had in mind.

'Ah, you may as well have both,' said Tess, and a few minutes later she brought in the tea and cake. It was like old times until she left us, and then it wasn't. Terry poured out the whiskey for me and the tea for himself, though his hand was shaking so badly that he could scarcely lift his cup. It was not all pretence; he didn't want to give me an opening, that was all. There was a fine print over his head – I think it was a Constable of Salisbury Cathedral. He talked about the monastery school, the usual clever, bitter, contemptuous stuff about monks, inspectors and pupils. The whole thing was too carefully staged, the lifting of the cup and the wiping of the moustache, but it hypnotized me. There was something there you couldn't do violence to. I finished my drink and got up to go.

'What hurry is on you?' he asked irritably.

I mumbled something about it's getting late.

'Nonsense!' he said. 'You're not a boy any longer.'

Was he just showing off his strength of will or hoping to put off the evil hour when he would go slinking down the quays again?

'Ah, they'll be expecting me,' I said, and then, as I used to do when we were younger, I turned to the bookcase. 'I see you have a lot of Maupassant at last,' I said.

'I bought them last time I was in Paris,' he said, standing beside me and looking at the books as though he were seeing them for the first time.

'A death-bed repentance?' I asked lightly, but he ignored me.

'I met another great admirer of his there,' he said sourly. 'A lady you should meet some time.'

'I'd love to if I ever get there,' I said.

'Her address is the Rue de Grenelle,' he said, and then with a wild burst of mockery, 'the left-hand pavement.'

At last his guard was down, and it was Maupassant's name that had done it. And still I couldn't say anything. An angry blush mounted his pale dark face and made it sinister in its violence.

'I suppose you didn't know I indulged in that hideous vice?' he snarled.

'I heard something,' I said. 'I'm sorry, Terry.'

The angry flush died out of his face and the old brooding look came back.

'A funny thing about those books,' he said. 'This woman I was speaking about, I thought she was bringing me to a hotel. I suppose I was a bit muddled with drink, but after dark one of these places is much like another. "This isn't a hotel," I said when we got upstairs. "No," she said, "it's my room."'

As he told it, I could see that he was living it all over again, something he could tell nobody but myself.

'There was a screen in the corner. I suppose it's the result of reading too much romantic fiction, but I thought there might be somebody hidden behind it. There was. You'd never guess what?'

'No.'

'A baby,' he said, his eyes boring through me. 'A child of maybe eighteen months. I wouldn't know. While I was looking, she changed him. He didn't wake.'

'What was it?' I asked, searching for the message that he obviously thought the incident contained. 'A dodge?'

'No,' he said almost grudgingly. 'A country girl in trouble, trying to support her child, that's all. We went to bed and she fell asleep.

I couldn't. It's many years now since I've been able to sleep like that. So I put on the light and began to read one of the books that I carried round in my pocket. "Oh, Maupassant," she said. "He's a great writer." "Is he?" I said. I thought she might be repeating something she'd picked up from one of her customers. She wasn't. She began to talk about *Boule de Suif*. It reminded me of the arguments we used to have in our young days.' Suddenly he gave me a curious boyish smile. 'You remember, when we used to walk up the river together.'

'Oh, I remember,' I said with a sigh.

'We were terrible young idiots, the pair of us,' he said sadly. 'Then she began to talk about *The Tellier Household*. I said it had poetry. "Oh, if it's poetry you want, you don't go to Maupassant. You go to Vigny, you go to Musset, but Maupassant is life, and life isn't poetry. It's only when you see what life can do to you that you realize what a great writer Maupassant is." . . . Wasn't that an extraordinary thing to happen?' he asked fiercely, and again the angry colour mounted his cheeks.

'Extraordinary,' I said, wondering if Terry himself knew how extraordinary it was. But it was exactly as if he were reading the thoughts as they crossed my mind.

'A prostitute from some French village, a drunken old waster from an Irish provincial town, lying awake in the dawn in Paris, discussing Maupassant. And the baby, of course. Maupassant would have made a lot of the baby.'

'I declare to God, I think if I'd been in your shoes, I'd have brought them back with me,' I said. I knew when I said it that I was talking nonsense, but it was a sort of release for all the bitterness inside me.

'What?' he asked, mocking me. 'A prostitute and her baby? My dear Mr Magner, you're becoming positively romantic in your old age.'

'A man like you should have a wife and children,' I said.

'Ah, but that's a different story,' he said malevolently. 'Maupassant would never have ended a story like that.'

And he looked at me almost triumphantly with those mad, dark eyes. I knew how Maupassant would have ended that story all right. Maupassant, as the girl said, was life, and life was pretty nearly through with Terry Coughlan.

(1945–1968)

Lost Fatherlands

One spring day, Father Felix in the monastery sent word down to Spike Ward, the motor-driver, to pick up a gentleman for the four-fifteen train. Spike had no notion of who the gentleman was. All sorts came and went to that lonesome monastery up the mountain: people on pilgrimage, drunks going in for a cure, cures coming out for a drunk, men joining the novitiate, and others leaving it, some of them within twenty-four hours – they just took one good look at the place and bolted. One of the novices stole a suit of overalls left behind by a house painter and vanished across the mountain. As Spike often said, if it was him he wouldn't have waited to steal the overalls.

It lay across the mountainside, a gaunt, Victorian barracks. Spike drove up to the guesthouse, which stood away in by the end of the chapel. Father Felix, the Guestmaster, was waiting on the steps with the passenger – a tall, well-built, middle-aged man with greying hair. Father Felix himself inclined to fat; he wore big, shiny glasses, and his beard cascaded over his chest. Spike and the passenger loaded the trunk and bag, and Spike noticed that they were labelled for Canada. The liner was due at Cobh two days later.

'Goodbye now,' Father Felix said, shaking the passenger's hand. 'And mind and don't lead Spike into bad ways on me. He's a fellow I have my eye on this long time. When are you coming up to us for good, Spike?' he asked gravely.

'When ye take a few women into the order, Father,' Spike replied in his thin drawl. 'What this place needs is a woman's hand.'

The passenger sat in front with Spike, and they chatted as they drove down the hill, glancing back at the monks working in the fields behind the monastery. You could see them from a long way off, like magpies.

'Was it on a holiday you were?' asked Spike, not meaning to be inquisitive, only to make conversation.

'A long holiday,' said the passenger, with a nod and a smile.

'Ah, well, everyone to his taste,' Spike said tolerantly. 'I suppose a lot depends on what you're used to. I prefer a bit of a change myself, like Father Felix's dipsos.'

'He has a few of them up there now,' said the passenger, with a quiet amusement that told Spike he wasn't one of them.

'Well, I'm sure I hope the poor souls are enjoying it,' said Spike with unction.

'They weren't enjoying it much at three this morning,' said the passenger in the same tone. 'One of them was calling for his mother. Father Felix was with him for over an hour, trying to calm him.'

'Not criticizing the good man, 'tisn't the same thing at all,' Spike said joyously.

'Except for the feeding bottle,' said the passenger. And then, as though he were slightly ashamed of his own straight-faced humour: 'He does a wonderful job on them.'

'Well, they seem to have great faith in him,' Spike said, without undue credulity. 'He gets them from England and all parts – a decent little man.'

'And a saintly little man,' the passenger said, almost reproachfully.

'I dare say,' Spike said, without enthusiasm. 'He'd want to be, judging by the specimens I see.'

They reached town with about three-quarters of an hour to spare, and put the trunk and bag in the stationmaster's office. Old Mick Hurley, the stationmaster, was inside, and looked at the bags over his glasses. Even on a warm day, in his own office, he wore his braided frock-coat and uniform cap.

'This is a gent from the monastery, Mick,' said Spike. 'He's travelling by the four-fifteen. Would he have time for the pictures?'

But Spike might have known the joke would be lost on Mick, who gave a hasty glance at the clock behind him and looked alarmed. 'He'd hardly have time for that,' he said. 'She's only about twenty-five minutes late.'

'You have over an hour to put in,' said Spike as they left the office. 'You don't want to be sitting round there the whole time. Hanagan's lounge is comfortable enough, if you like a drink.'

'Will you have one with me?' asked the passenger.

'I don't know will I have the time,' Spike said. 'I have another call at four. I'll have one drink with you, anyway.'

They went into the bar, which was all done up in chromium, with concealed lighting. Tommy Hanagan, the Yank, was behind the bar himself. He was a tall, fresh-faced, rather handsome man, with fair hair of a dirty colour and smoke-blue eyes. His hat was perched far back on his head. Spike often said Tommy Hanagan was the only man he knew who could make a hat speak. He had earned the price of his public house working in Boston and, according to him, had never ceased to regret his return. Tommy looked as though he lived in hopes that some day, when he did something as it should be done, it would turn out to be a convenience to somebody. So far, it had earned him nothing but mockery, and sometimes his blue eyes had a slightly bewildered expression, as though he were wondering what he was doing in that place at all.

Spike loved rousing him. All you had to do was give him one poke about America and the man was off, good for an hour's argument. America was the finest goddam country on the face of the earth, and the people that criticized it didn't know what they were talking about. In America, even the priests were friends: 'Tommy, where the hell am I going to get a hundred dollars?' 'I'll get it for you, Father Joe.' In Ireland, it was '*Mister* Hanagan, don't you consider five pounds is a bit on the small side?' 'And I don't,' the Yank would say, pulling up his shirtsleeves. 'I'd sooner give a hundred dollars to a friend than fifteen to a bastard like that.' The same with the women. Over there, an Irishman would say, 'I'll do the washing up, Mary.' Here it was 'Where's that bloody tea, woman?' And then bawling her out for it! Not, as Spike noticed, that this ever prevented the Yank from bawling out his own wife twenty times a day. And Spike suspected that however he might enjoy rousing the Yank, the Yank enjoyed it more. It probably gave the poor man the illusion of being alive.

'What are you drinking?' the passenger asked in his low voice.

'Whiskey,' said Spike. 'I have to take whiskey every time I go up to that monastery. It's to restore the circulation.'

'Beer for me, please,' said the passenger.

'Your circulation is easily damaged, Spike,' said Hanagan as he turned to the whiskey bottle.

'If you knew as much about that place as I do, you'd be looking for whiskey, too.'

'Who said I don't know about it?' blustered Hanagan. 'I know as much about it as you do; maybe more.'

'You do,' Spike said mockingly. 'Yourself and the kids went up there two years ago, picking primroses. I heard about it. Ye brought the flask and had tea up the mountain two miles away. "Oh, what a lovely place the monks have! Oh, what a wonderful life they have up here!" Damn all you care about the poor unfortunates, getting up at half past one of a winter's morning and waiting till half five for a bit of breakfast.'

The Yank sprawled across the counter, pushing his hat back a shade farther. It was set for reasonable discussion. 'But what's that, only habit?' he asked.

'Habit!'

'What else is it?' the Yank asked appealingly. 'I have to get up at half past six every morning, winter and summer, and I have to worry about a wife and kids, and education and doctors for them, and paying income tax, which is more than the monks have to do.'

'Give me the income tax every time!' said Spike. 'Even the wife!'

'The remarkable thing about this country,' said Hanagan, 'is that they'll only get up in the morning when no one asks them to. I never asked the monks to get up at half past one. All I ask is that the people in this blooming town will get up at half past eight and open their shops by nine o'clock. And how many of them will do it?'

'And what the hell has that to do with the argument?' asked Spike, not that he thought it had anything to do with it. He knew only too well the Yank's capacity for getting carried away on a tide of his own eloquence.

'Well, what after all does the argument boil down to?' retorted Hanagan. 'The argument is that no one in this blooming country is respected for doing what he ought to do – only for doing what no one ever asked him to do.'

'Are people to sit down and wait for someone to ask them to love God?' the passenger growled suddenly. Spike noticed that even though he mentioned God, he looked a nasty customer to cross in a discussion.

'I didn't say that,' Hanagan replied peaceably. 'But do you know this town?'

'No.'

'I do,' said Hanagan. 'I know it since I was a kid. I spent eighteen years out of it, and for all the difference it made to the town, I might have been out of it for a week. It's dead. The people are dead. They're no use to God or man.'

'You didn't answer my question.'

'You're talking about one sort of responsibility,' said Hanagan. 'I'm only saying there are other responsibilities. Why can't the people here see that they have a responsibility to the unfortunate women they marry? Why can't they see their responsibility to their own country?'

'What Tommy means is that people shouldn't be making pilgrimages to the monastery at all,' said Spike drily. 'He thinks they should be making pilgrimages to him. He lights candles to himself every night – all because he doesn't beat his wife. Good luck to you now, and don't let him make you miss your train with his old guff.'

Spike and the passenger shook hands, and after that Spike put him out of his head completely. Meeting strangers like that, every day of the week, he couldn't remember the half of them. But three evenings later he was waiting in the car outside the station, hoping to pick up a fare from the four-fifteen, when Mick Hurley came flopping out to him with his spectacles down his nose.

'What am I going to do with them bags you left on Tuesday, Spike?' he asked.

What was he to do with the bags? Spike looked at him without comprehension. 'What bags, Mick?'

'Them bags for Canada.'

'Holy God!' exclaimed Spike, getting slowly out of the car. 'Do you mean he forgot his bags?'

'Forgot them?' Mick Hurley repeated indignantly. 'He never travelled at all, man.'

'Holy God!' repeated Spike. 'And the liner gone since yesterday! That's a nice state of affairs.'

'Why?' asked Mick. 'Who was it?'

'A man from the monastery.'

'One of Father Felix's drunks?'

'What the hell would a drunk be coming from Canada for?'

asked Spike in exasperation.

'You'd never know,' said Mick. 'Where did you leave him?'

'Over in Tommy Hanagan's bar.'

'Then we'd better ask Tommy.'

Hanagan came out to them in his shirtsleeves, his cuffs rolled up and his hat well back.

'Tommy,' said Spike, 'you remember that passenger I left in your place on Tuesday?'

Tommy's eyes narrowed. 'The big, grey-haired bloke?' he said. 'What about him?'

'Mick Hurley, here, says he never took that train. You wouldn't know what happened to him?'

Tommy rested one bare, powerful arm against the jamb of the door, leaned his head against it, and delicately tilted the hat forward over his eyes. 'That sounds bad,' he said. 'You're sure he didn't go off unknown to you?'

'How could he, man?' asked Mick excitedly, feeling that some slight on the railway company was implied. 'His bags are still there. No one but locals travelled on that train.'

'The man had a lot of money on him,' Hanagan said, looking at the ground.

'You're sure of that, Tommy?' Spike asked, in alarm. It was bad enough for a motor-driver to be mixed up in a mysterious disappearance without a murder coming into it as well.

'Up to a hundred pounds,' Hanagan said, giving a sharp glance up the street. 'I saw it when he paid for the drinks. I noticed Linehan, of the guards, going in to his dinner. We might as well go over and ask him did he hear anything.'

They strode briskly in the direction of the policeman's house. Linehan came shuffling out, buttoning up his tunic – a fat, black-haired man who looked like something out of a butcher's shop.

'I didn't hear a word of it,' he said, looking from one to another, as though they might be concealing evidence. 'We'll ring up a few of the local stations. Some of them might have word of him.'

Hanagan went to get his coat. Mick Hurley had to leave them, to look after the four-fifteen, and at last Spike, Hanagan, and Linehan went to the police station, where the others waited while Linehan had long, confidential chats about football and the weather with other policemen for ten miles around. Guards are lonely souls; they cannot trust their nearest and dearest, and can communicate only with one another, like mountaineers with signal fires. Hanagan sat on the table, pretending to read a paper, though every look and gesture betrayed impatience and disgust. Spike just sat, reflecting mournfully on the loss of his good time and money.

'We'll have to find out what his name was,' Linehan said, at last. 'The best thing we can do is drive up to the monastery and get more particulars.'

'The devil fly away with Mick Hurley!' Spike said bitterly. 'Wouldn't you think he'd tell us what happened without waiting three days? If he was after losing an express train, he'd wait a week to see would it turn up.'

The three of them got into Spike's car, and he drove off up the mountain road, wondering how he was to get his fare out of it and from whom. The monks were holy enough, but they expected you to run a car on holy water, and a policeman thought he was doing you a favour if he was seen in the car with you. The veiled sunlight went out; they ran into thick mist, and before they reached the mountain-top, it had turned to rain. They could see it driving in for miles from the sea. The lights were on in the chapel; there was some service on. Spike noticed the Yank pause under the traceried window and look away down the valley. Within the church, the choir wailed, '*Et exspecto resurrectionem mortuorum. Et vitam venturi saeculi.*'

Father Felix came out and beckoned them in from the rain. His face was very grave. 'You needn't tell me what you came about, lads,' he said.

'You knew he was missing so, Father?' said Linehan.

'We saw him,' said the priest.

'Where, Father?' asked Spike.

'Out there,' Father Felix said, with a nod.

'On the mountain?'

'I dare say he's there still.'

'But what is he doing?'

'Oh, nothing. Nothing only staring. Staring at the monastery and the monks working in the fields. Poor fellow! Poor fellow!'

'But who is it?'

'One of our own men. One of the old monks. He's here these fifteen years.'

'Fifteen years!' exclaimed Linehan. 'But what came over him after all that time?'

'Some nervous trouble, I suppose,' said Father Felix in the tone of a healthy man who has heard of nerves as a well-recognized ailment of quite respectable people. 'A sort of mental blackout, I heard them saying. He wouldn't know where he'd be for a few minutes at a time.'

'Ah, poor soul! Poor soul!' sighed Linehan, with a similar blankness of expression.

'But what was taking him to Canada?' asked Hanagan.

'Ah, well, we had to send him somewhere he wouldn't be known,' explained Father Felix sadly. 'He wanted to settle down in his own place in Kilkenny, but, of course, he couldn't.'

'Why not?' asked Hanagan.

'Oh, he couldn't, he couldn't,' Linehan said, with a sharp intake of breath as he strode to the window. 'Not after leaving the monastery. 'Twould cause terrible scandal.'

'That's why I hope you can get him away quietly,' Father Felix said. 'We did everything we could for him. Now the less talk there is, the better.'

'In that bleddy mist you might be searching the mountain for a week,' sighed Linehan, who had often shot it. 'If we knew where to look itself! We'll go up the road and see would any of Sullivan's boys have word of him.'

Sullivan's was the nearest farmhouse. The three men got into the car again and drove slowly down under the trees past the monastery. There was an iron railing, which seemed strangely out of place, and then a field, and then the bare mountain again. It was coming on to dark, and it struck Spike that they would find no one that night. He was sorry for that poor devil, and could not get over the casualness of Mick Hurley. A stationmaster! God, wouldn't you think he'd have some sense?

'It isn't Mick Hurley I blame at all,' Hanagan said angrily.

'Ah, well, Tommy, you can't be too hard on the poor monks,' Linehan said reasonably. 'I suppose they were hoping he'd go away and not cause any scandal.'

'A poor bloody loony!' snapped the Yank, his emotion bringing out a strong Boston accent. 'Gahd, you wouldn't do it to a dawg!'

'How sure you are he was a loony!' Spike said, with a sneer. 'He didn't seem so very loony to me.'

'But you heard what Father Felix said!' Hanagan cried. 'Mental blackouts. That poor devil is somewhere out on that goddam mountain with his memory gone.'

'Ah, I'll believe all I hear when I eat all I get,' Spike said in the same tone.

It wasn't that he really disbelieved in the blackouts so much as that he had trained himself to take things lightly, and the Yank was getting on his nerves. At that moment he spotted the passenger out of the corner of his eye. The rain seemed to have caught him somewhere on top of a peak, and he was running, looking for shelter, from rock to rock. Without looking round, Spike stopped the car quietly and lit a cigarette.

'Don't turn round now, boys!' he said. 'He's just over there on our right.'

'What do you think we should do, Spike?' Linehan asked.

'Get out of the car quietly and break up, so that we can come round him from different directions,' said Spike.

'Then you'd scare him properly,' said Hanagan. 'Let me go and talk to him!'

Before they could hinder him, he was out of the car and running up the slope from the road. Spike swore. He knew if the monk took to his heels now, they might never catch him. Hanagan shouted and the monk halted, stared, then walked towards him.

'It looks as if he might come quietly,' said Linehan. He and Spike followed Hanagan slowly.

Hanagan stopped on a little hillock, hatless, his hands in his trouser pockets. The monk came up to him. He, too, was hatless; his raincoat was covered with mud; and he wore what looked like a week's growth of beard. He had a sullen, frightened look, like an old dog called to heel after doing something wrong.

'That's a bad evening now,' Hanagan said, with an awkward smile, which made him look unexpectedly boyish.

'I hope you're not taking all this trouble for me,' the monk said, looking first at Hanagan, then at Spike and the policeman, who stood a little apart from him.

'Ah, what trouble?' Hanagan said, with fictitious lightness. 'We were afraid you might be caught in the mist. It's bad enough even for those that know the mountain. You'd want to get those wet things off you quick.'

'I suppose so,' the monk said, looking down at his drenched clothes as though he were seeing them for the first time. Spike could now believe in the mental blackout, the man looked so stunned, like a sleepwalker.

'We'll stop at the pub and Spike can bring over whatever bags you want,' said Hanagan.

The public-house hotel looked uncannily bright after the loneliness of the mountain. Hanagan was at his most obnoxiously efficient. Linehan wanted to take a statement from the monk, but Hanagan stopped him. 'Is it a man in that state? How could he give you a statement?' He rushed in and out, his hat on the back of his head, producing hot whiskeys for them all, sending Spike to the station for the bag, and driving his wife and the maid mad seeing that there was hot water and shaving tackle in the bathroom and that a hot meal was prepared.

When the monk came down, shaved and in dry clothes, Hanagan sat opposite him, his legs spread and his hands on his thighs.

'What you'll do,' he said, with a commanding air, 'is rest here for a couple of days.'

'No, thanks,' the monk said, shaking his head.

'It won't cost you anything,' Hanagan said, with a smile.

'It's not that,' said the monk in a low voice. 'I'd better get away from this.'

'But you can't, man. You'll have to see about getting your tickets changed. We can see to that for you. You might get pneumonia after being out so long.'

'I'll have to go on,' the monk said stubbornly. 'I have to get away.'

'You mean you're afraid you might do the same thing again?' Hanagan said in a disappointed tone. 'Maybe you're right. Though what anyone wants to go back to that place for beats me.'

'What do people want to go back anywhere for?' the monk asked in a dull tone.

Spike thought it was as close as he'd ever seen anyone get to knocking the Yank off his perch. Hanagan grew red, then rose and went in the direction of the door, suddenly changed his mind, and turned to grasp the monk's left hand in his own two. 'I'm a good one to talk,' he said in a thick voice. 'Eighteen years, and never a day without thinking of this place. You mightn't believe it, but there were nights I cried myself to sleep. And for what, I ask you? What did I expect?'

He had changed suddenly; no longer the big-hearted, officious ward boss looking after someone in trouble, he had become humble and almost deferential. When they were leaving, he half opened the front door and halted. 'You're sure you won't stay?' he snapped over his shoulder.

'Sure,' said the monk, with a nod.

Hanagan waved his left arm, and they went out across the dark square to the station.

Spike and he saw the last of the monk, who waved to them till the train disappeared in the darkness. Hanagan followed it, waving, with a mawkish smile, as though he were seeing off a girl. Spike could see that he was deeply moved, but what it was all about was beyond him. Spike had never stood on the deck of a liner and watched his fatherland drop away behind him. He didn't know the sort of hurt it can leave in a boy's mind, a hurt that doesn't heal even when you try to conjure away the pain by returning. Nor did he realize, as Hanagan did at that moment, that there are other fatherlands, whose loss can hurt even more deeply.

(1954)

The Mass Island

When Father Jackson drove up to the curates' house, it was already drawing on to dusk, the early dusk of late December. The curates' house was a red-brick building on a terrace at one side of the ugly church in Asragh. Father Hamilton seemed to have been waiting for him and opened the front door himself, looking white and strained. He was a tall young man with a long, melancholy face that you would have taken for weak till you noticed the cut of the jaw.

'Oh, come in, Jim,' he said with his mournful smile. ''Tisn't much of a welcome we have for you, God knows. I suppose you'd like to see poor Jerry before the undertaker comes.'

'I might as well,' Father Jackson replied briskly. There was nothing melancholy about Jackson, but he affected an air of surprise and shock. ''Twas very sudden, wasn't it?'

'Well, it was and it wasn't, Jim,' Father Hamilton said, closing the front door behind him. 'He was going downhill since he got the first heart attack, and he wouldn't look after himself. Sure, you know yourself what he was like.'

Jackson knew. Father Fogarty and himself had been friends, of a sort, for years. An impractical man, excitable and vehement, Fogarty could have lived for twenty years with his ailment, but instead of that, he allowed himself to become depressed and indifferent. If he couldn't live as he had always lived, he would prefer not to live at all.

They went upstairs and into the bedroom where he was. The character was still plain on the stern, dead face, though, drained of vitality, it had the look of a studio portrait. That bone structure was something you'd have picked out of a thousand faces as Irish, with its odd impression of bluntness and asymmetry, its jutting brow and craggy chin, and the snub nose that looked as though it had probably been broken twenty years before in a public house row.

123

When they came downstairs again, Father Hamilton produced half a bottle of whiskey.

'Not for me, thanks,' Jackson said hastily. 'Unless you have a drop of sherry there?'

'Well, there is some Burgundy,' Father Hamilton said. 'I don't know is it any good, though.'

''Twill do me fine,' Jackson replied cheerfully, reflecting that Ireland was the country where nobody knew whether Burgundy was good or not. 'You're coming with us tomorrow, I suppose?'

'Well, the way it is, Jim,' Father Hamilton replied, 'I'm afraid neither of us is going. You see, they're burying poor Jerry here.'

'They're what?' Jackson asked incredulously.

'Now, I didn't know for sure when I rang you, Jim, but that's what the brother decided, and that's what Father Hanafey decided as well.'

'But he told you he wanted to be buried on the Mass Island, didn't he?'

'He told everybody, Jim,' Father Hamilton replied with growing excitement and emotion. 'That was the sort he was. If he told one, he told five hundred. Only a half an hour ago I had a girl on the telephone from the Island, asking when they could expect us. You see, the old parish priest of the place let Jerry mark out the grave for himself, and they want to know should they open it. But now the old parish priest is dead as well, and, of course, Jerry left nothing in writing.'

'Didn't he leave a will, even?' Jackson asked in surprise.

'Well, he did and he didn't, Jim,' Father Hamilton said, looking as if he were on the point of tears. 'Actually, he did make a will about five or six years ago, and he gave it to Clancy, the other curate, but Clancy went off on the Foreign Mission and God alone knows where he is now. After that, Jerry never bothered his head about it. I mean, you have to admit the man had nothing to leave. Every damn thing he had he gave away – even the old car, after he got the first attack. If there was any loose cash around, I suppose the brother has that.'

Jackson sipped his Burgundy, which was even more Australian than he had feared, and wondered at his own irritation. He had been irritated enough before that, with the prospect of two days' motoring in the middle of winter, and a night in a godforsaken pub in the mountains, a hundred and fifty miles away at the other side of Ireland. There, in one of the lakes, was an island where in Cromwell's time, before the causeway and the little oratory were built, Mass was said in secret, and it was here that Father Fogarty had wanted to be buried. It struck Jackson as sheer sentimentality; it wasn't even as if it was Fogarty's native place. Jackson had once allowed Fogarty to lure him there, and had hated every moment of it. It wasn't only the discomfort of the public house, where meals erupted at any hour of the day or night as the spirit took the proprietor, or the rain that kept them confined to the cold dining and sitting room that looked out on the gloomy mountainside, with its couple of whitewashed cabins on the shore of the lake. It was the over-intimacy of it all, and this was the thing that Father Fogarty apparently loved. He liked to stand in his shirt-sleeves behind the bar, taking turns with the proprietor, who was one of his many friends, serving big pints of porter to rough mountainy men, or to sit in their cottages, shaking in all his fat whenever they told broad stories or sang risky folk songs. 'God, Jim, isn't it grand?' he would say in his deep voice, and Jackson would look at him over his spectacles with what Fogarty called his 'Jesuitical look', and say, 'Well, I suppose it all depends on what you really like, Jerry.' He wasn't even certain that the locals cared for Father Fogarty's intimacy; on the contrary, he had a strong impression that they much preferred their own reserved old parish priest, whom they never saw except twice a year, when he came up the valley to collect his dues. That had made Jackson twice as stiff. And yet now when he found out that the plans that had meant so much inconvenience to him had fallen through, he was as disappointed as though they had been his own.

'Oh, well,' he said with a shrug that was intended to conceal his perturbation, 'I suppose it doesn't make much difference where they chuck us when our time comes.'

'The point is, it mattered to Jerry, Jim,' Father Hamilton said with his curious shy obstinacy. 'God knows, it's not anything that will ever worry me, but it haunted him, and somehow, you know, I don't feel it's right to flout a dead man's wishes.'

'Oh, I know, I know,' Jackson said lightly, 'I suppose I'd better talk to old Hanafey about it. Knowing I'm a friend of the Bishop's he might pay more attention to me.'

'He might, Jim,' Father Hamilton replied sadly, looking away over Jackson's head. 'As you say, knowing you're a friend of the

Bishop's, he might. But I wouldn't depend too much on it. I talked to him till I was black in the face, and all I got out of him was the law and the rubrics. It's the brother Hanafey is afraid of. You'll see him this evening, and, between ourselves, he's a tough customer. Of course, himself and Jerry never had much to say to one another, and he'd be the last man in the world that Jerry would talk to about his funeral, so now he doesn't want the expense and inconvenience. You wouldn't blame him, of course. I'd probably be the same myself. By the way,' Father Hamilton added, lowering his voice, 'before he does come, I'd like you to take a look round Jerry's room and see is there any little memento you'd care to have – a photo or a book or anything.'

They went into Father Fogarty's sitting room, and Jackson looked at it with a new interest. He knew of old the rather handsome library – Fogarty had been a man of many enthusiasms, though none of long duration – the picture of the Virgin and Child in Irish country costume over the mantelpiece, which some of his colleagues had thought irreverent, and the couple of fine old prints. There was a newer picture that Jackson had not seen – a charcoal drawing of the Crucifixion from a fifteenth-century Irish tomb, which was brutal but impressive.

'Good Lord,' Jackson exclaimed with a sudden feeling of loss. 'He really had taste, hadn't he?'

'He had, Jim,' Father Hamilton said, sticking his long nose into the picture. 'This goes to a young couple called Keneally, outside the town, that he was fond of. I think they were very kind to him. Since he had the attack, he was pretty lonely, I'd say.'

'Oh, aren't we all, attack or no attack,' Jackson said almost irritably.

Father Hanafey, the parish priest of Asragh, was a round, red, cherubic-looking old man with a bald head and big round glasses. His house was on the same terrace as the curates'. He, too, insisted on producing the whiskey Jackson so heartily detested, when the two priests came in to consult him, but Jackson had decided that this time diplomacy required he should show proper appreciation of the dreadful stuff. He felt sure he was going to be very sick next day. He affected great astonishment at the quality of Father Hanafey's whiskey, and first the old parish priest grew shy, like a schoolgirl whose good looks are being praised, then he looked self-satisfied, and finally he became almost emotional. It was a great pleasure, he said, to meet a young priest with a proper understanding of whiskey. Priests no longer seemed to have the same taste, and as far as most of them were concerned, they might as well be drinking poteen. It was only when it was seven years old that Irish began to be interesting, and that was when you had to catch it and store it in sherry casks to draw off what remained of crude alcohol in it, and give it that beautiful roundness that Father Jackson had spotted. But it shouldn't be kept too long, for somewhere along the line the spirit of a whiskey was broken. At ten, or maybe twelve, years old it was just right. But people were losing their palates. He solemnly assured the two priests that of every dozen clerics who came to his house not more than one would realize what he was drinking. Poor Hamilton grew red and began to stutter, but the parish priest's reproofs were not directed at him.

'It isn't you I'm talking about, Father Hamilton, but elderly priests, parish priests, and even canons, that you would think would know better, and I give you my word, I put the two whiskeys side by side in front of them, the shop stuff and my own, and they could not tell the difference.'

But though the priest was mollified by Father Jackson's maturity of judgement, he was not prepared to interfere in the arrangements of the funeral of his curate. 'It is the wish of the next-of-kin, Father,' he said stubbornly, 'and that is something I have no control over. Now that you tell me the same thing as Father Hamilton, I accept it that this was Father Fogarty's wish, and a man's wishes regarding his own interment are always to be respected. I assure you, if I had even one line in Father Fogarty's writing to go on, I would wait for no man's advice. I would take the responsibility on myself. Something on paper, Father, is all I want.'

'On the other hand, Father,' Jackson said mildly, drawing on his pipe, 'if Father Fogarty was the sort to leave written instructions, he'd hardly be the sort to leave such unusual ones. I mean, after all, it isn't even the family burying ground, is it?'

'Well, now, that is true, Father,' replied the parish priest and it was clear that he had been deeply impressed by this rather doubtful logic. 'You have a very good point there, and it is one I did not think of myself, and I have given the matter a great deal of thought. You might mention it to his brother. Father Fogarty, God rest him, was *not* a usual type of man. I think you might even go so far as to say that he was a rather *unusual* type of man, and not orderly, as you say – not by any means orderly. I would certainly mention that to the brother and see what he says.'

But the brother was not at all impressed by Father Jackson's argument when he turned up at the church in Asragh that evening. He was a good-looking man with a weak and pleasant face and a cold shrewdness in his eyes that had been lacking in his brother's.

'But why, Father?' he asked, turning to Father Hanafey. 'I'm a busy man, and I'm being asked to leave my business for a couple of days in the middle of winter, and for what? That is all I ask. What use is it?'

'It is only out of respect for the wishes of the deceased, Mr Fogarty,' said Father Hanafey, who clearly was a little bit afraid of him.

'And where did he express those wishes?' the brother asked. 'I'm his only living relative, and it is queer he would not mention a thing like that to me.'

'He mentioned it to Father Jackson and Father Hamilton.'

'But when, Father?' Mr Fogarty asked. 'You knew Father Jerry, and he was always expressing wishes about something. He was an excitable sort of man, God rest him, and the thing he'd say today might not be the thing he'd say tomorrow. After all, after close on forty years, I think I have the right to say I knew him,' he added with a triumphant air that left the two young priests without a leg to stand on.

Over bacon and eggs in the curates' house, Father Hamilton was very despondent. 'Well, I suppose we did what we could, Jim,' he said.

'I'm not too sure of that,' Jackson said with his 'Jesuitical air', looking at Father Hamilton sidewise over his spectacles. 'I'm wondering if we couldn't do something with that family you say he intended the drawing for.'

'The Keneallys,' said Father Hamilton in a worried voice. 'Actually, I saw the wife in the church this evening. You might have noticed her crying.'

'Don't you think we should see if they have anything in writing?'

'Well, if they have, it would be about the picture,' said Father Hamilton. 'How I know about it is she came to me at the time to ask if I couldn't do something for him. Poor man, he was crying himself that day, according to what she told me.'

'Oh dear!' Jackson said politely, but his mind was elsewhere. 'I'm not really interested in knowing what would be in a letter like that. It's none of my business. But I would like to make sure that they haven't something in writing. What did Hanafey call it – "something on paper"?'

'I dare say we should inquire, anyway,' said Father Hamilton, and after supper they drove out to the Keneallys', a typical small red-brick villa with a decent garden in front. The family also was eating bacon and eggs, and Jackson shuddered when they asked him to join them. Keneally himself, a tall, gaunt, cadaverous man, poured out more whiskey for them, and again Jackson felt he must make a formal attempt to drink it. At the same time, he thought he saw what attraction the house had for Father Fogarty. Keneally was tough and with no suggestion of lay servility towards the priesthood, and his wife was beautiful and scatterbrained, and talked to herself, the cat, and the children simultaneously. 'Rosaleen!' she cried determinedly. 'Out! Out I say! I told you if you didn't stop meowing you'd have to go out . . . Angela Keneally, the stick! . . . You do not want to go to the bathroom, Angela. It's only five minutes since you were there before. I will not let Father Hamilton come up to you at all unless you go to bed at once.'

In the children's bedroom, Jackson gave a finger to a stolid-looking infant, who instantly stuffed it into his mouth and began to chew it, apparently under the impression that he would be bound to reach sugar at last.

Later, they sat over their drinks in the sitting room, only interrupted by Angela Keneally, in a fever of curiosity, dropping in every five minutes to ask for a biscuit or a glass of water.

'You see, Father Fogarty left no will,' Jackson explained to Keneally. 'Consequently, he'll be buried here tomorrow unless something turns up. I suppose he told you where he wanted to be buried?'

'On the Island? Twenty times, if he told us once. I thought he took it too far. Didn't you, Father?'

'And me not to be able to go!' Mrs Keneally said, beginning to cry. 'Isn't it awful, Father?'

'He didn't leave anything in writing with you?' He saw in Keneally's eyes that the letter was really only about the picture, and raised a warning hand. 'Mind, if he did, I don't want to know what's in it! In fact, it would be highly improper for anyone to be told before the parish priest and the next-of-kin were consulted. All I do want to know is whether' – he waited a moment to see that Keneally was following him – 'he did leave any written instructions, of any kind, with you.'

Mrs Keneally, drying her tears, suddenly broke into rapid speech. 'Sure, that was the day poor Father Jerry was so down in himself because we were his friends and he had nothing to leave us, and—'

'Shut up, woman!' her husband shouted with a glare at her, and then Jackson saw him purse his lips in quiet amusement. He was a man after Jackson's heart. 'As you say, Father, we have a letter from him.'

'Addressed to anybody in particular?'

'Yes, to the parish priest, to be delivered after his death.'

'Did he use those words?' Jackson asked, touched in spite of himself.

'Those very words.'

'God help us!' said Father Hamilton.

'But you had not time to deliver it?'

'I only heard of Father Fogarty's death when I got in. Esther was at the church, of course.'

'And you're a bit tired, so you wouldn't want to walk all the way over to the presbytery with it. I take it that, in the normal way, you'd post it.'

'But the post would be gone,' Keneally said with a secret smile. 'So that Father Hanafey wouldn't get it until maybe the day after tomorrow. That's what you were afraid of, Father, isn't it?'

'I see we understand one another, Mr Keneally,' Jackson said politely.

'You wouldn't, of course, wish to say anything that wasn't strictly true,' said Keneally, who was clearly enjoying himself enormously, though his wife had not the faintest idea of what was afoot. 'So perhaps it would be better if the letter was posted now, and not after you leave the house.'

'Fine!' said Jackson, and Keneally nodded and went out. When he returned, a few minutes later, the priest rose to go.

'I'll see you at the Mass tomorrow,' Keneally said. 'Good luck, now.'

Jackson felt they'd probably need it. But when Father Hanafey met them in the hall, with the wet snow falling outside, and they explained about the letter, his mood had clearly changed. Jackson's logic might have worked some sort of spell on him, or perhaps it was just that he felt they were three clergymen opposed to a layman.

'It was very unforeseen of Mr Keneally not to have brought that letter to me at once,' he grumbled, 'but I must say I was expecting something of the sort. It would have been very peculiar if Father Fogarty had left no instructions at all for me, and I see that we can't just sit round and wait to find out what they were, since the burial is tomorrow. Under the circumstances, Father, I think we'd be justified in arranging for the funeral according to Father Fogarty's known wishes.'

'Thanks be to God,' Father Hamilton murmured as he and Father Jackson returned to the curates' house. 'I never thought we'd get away with that.'

'We haven't got away with it yet,' said Jackson. 'And even if we do get away with it, the real trouble will be later.'

All the arrangements had still to be made. When Mr Fogarty was informed, he slammed down the receiver without comment. Then a phone call had to be made to a police station twelve miles from the Island, and the police sergeant promised to send a man out on a bicycle to have the grave opened. Then the local parish priest and several old friends had to be informed, and a notice inserted in the nearest daily. As Jackson said wearily, romantic men always left their more worldly friends to carry out their romantic intentions.

The scene at the curates' house next morning after Mass scared even Jackson. While the hearse and the funeral car waited in front of the door, Mr Fogarty sat, white with anger, and let the priests talk. To Jackson's surprise Father Hanafey put up a stern fight for Father Fogarty's wishes.

'You have to realize, Mr Fogarty, that to a priest like your brother the Mass is a very solemn thing indeed, and a place where the poor people had to fly in the Penal Days to hear Mass would be one of particular sanctity.'

'Father Hanafey,' said Mr Fogarty in a cold, even tone, 'I am a simple businessman, and I have no time for sentiment.'

'I would not go so far as to call the veneration for sanctified ground mere sentiment, Mr Fogarty,' the old priest said severely. 'At any rate, it is now clear that Father Fogarty left instructions to be delivered to me after his death, and if those instructions are what we think them, I would have a serious responsibility for not having paid attention to them.'

'I do not think that letter is anything of the kind, Father Hanafey,' said Mr Fogarty. 'That's a matter I'm going to inquire into when I get back, and if it turns out to be a hoax, I am going to take it further.'

'Oh, Mr Fogarty, I'm sure it's not a hoax,' said the parish priest, with a shocked air, but Mr Fogarty was not convinced.

'For everybody's sake, we'll hope not,' he said grimly.

The funeral procession set off. Mr Fogarty sat in the front of the car by the driver, sulking. Jackson and Hamilton sat behind and opened their breviaries. When they stopped at a hotel for lunch, Mr Fogarty said he was not hungry and stayed outside in the cold. And when he did get hungry and came into the dining room, the priests drifted into the lounge to wait for him. They both realized that he might prove a dangerous enemy.

Then, as they drove on in the dusk, they saw the mountain country ahead of them in a cold, watery light, a light that seemed to fall dead from the ragged edge of a cloud. The towns and villages they passed through were dirtier and more derelict. They drew up at a crossroads, behind the hearse, and heard someone talking to the driver of the hearse. Then a car fell into line behind them. 'Someone joining us,' Father Hamilton said, but Mr Fogarty, lost in his own dream of martyrdom, did not reply. Half a dozen times within the next twenty minutes, the same thing happened, though sometimes the cars were waiting in lanes and by-roads with their lights on, and each time Jackson saw a heavily coated figure standing in the roadway shouting to the hearse driver: 'Is it Father Fogarty ye have there?' At last they came to a village where the local parish priest's car was waiting outside the church, with a little group about it. Their headlights caught a public house, isolated at the other side of the street, glaring with whitewash, while about it was the vague space of a distant mountainside.

Suddenly Mr Fogarty spoke. 'He seems to have been fairly well known,' he said with something approaching politeness.

The road went on, with a noisy stream at the right-hand side of it falling from group to group of rocks. They left it for a by-road, which bent to the right heading towards the stream, and then began to mount, broken by ledges of naked rock, over which hearse and cars seemed to heave themselves like animals. On the left-hand side of the road was a little whitewashed cottage, all lit up, with a big turf fire burning in the open hearth and an oil lamp with an orange glow on the wall above it. There was a man standing by the door, and as they approached he began to pick his way over the rocks towards them, carrying a lantern. Only then did Jackson notice the other lanterns and flashlights, coming down the mountain or crossing the stream, and realize that they represented people, young men and girls and an occasional sturdy old man, all moving in the direction of the Mass Island. Suddenly it hit him, almost like a blow. He told himself not to be a fool, that this was no more than the desire for novelty one should expect to find in out-of-the-way places, mixed perhaps with vanity. It was all that, of course, and he knew it, but he knew, too, it was something more. He had thought when he was here with Fogarty that those people had not respected Fogarty as they respected him and the local parish priest, but he knew that for him, or even for their own parish priest, they would never turn out in midwinter, across the treacherous mountain bogs and wicked rocks. He and the parish priest would never earn more from the people of the mountains than respect; what they gave to the fat, unclerical young man who had served them with pints in the bar and egged them on to tell their old stories and bullied and ragged and even fought them was something infinitely greater.

The funeral procession stopped in a lane that ran along the edge of a lake. The surface of the lake was rough, and they could hear the splash of the water upon the stones. The two priests got out of the car and began to vest themselves, and then Mr Fogarty got out, too. He was very nervous and hesitant.

'It's very inconvenient, and all the rest of it,' he said, 'but I don't want you gentlemen to think that I didn't know you were acting from the best motives.'

'That's very kind of you, Mr Fogarty,' Jackson said. 'Maybe we made mistakes as well.'

'Thank you, Father Jackson,' Mr Fogarty said, and held out his hand. The two priests shook hands with him and he went off, raising his hat.

'Well, that's one trouble over,' Father Hamilton said wryly as an old man plunged through the mud towards the car.

'Lights is what we're looking for!' he shouted. 'Let ye turn her sidewise, and throw the headlights on the causeway the way we'll see what we're doing.'

Their driver swore, but he reversed and turned the front of the car till it almost faced the lake. Then he turned on his headlights. Somewhere farther up the road the parish priest's car did the same. One by one, the ranked headlights blazed up, and at every moment the scene before them grew more vivid – the gateway and the stile, and beyond it the causeway that ran towards the little brown stone oratory with its mock Romanesque doorway. As the lights strengthened and steadied, the whole island became like a vast piece of theatre scenery cut out against the gloomy wall of the mountain with the tiny whitewashed cottages at its base. Far above, caught in a stray flash of moonlight, Jackson saw the snow on its summit. 'I'll be after you,' he said to Father Hamilton, and watched him, a little perturbed and looking behind him, join the parish priest by the gate. Jackson resented being seen by them because he was weeping, and he was a man who despised tears – his own and others'. It was like a miracle, and Father Jackson didn't really believe in miracles. Standing back by the fence to let the last of the mourners pass, he saw the coffin, like gold in the brilliant light, and heard the steadying voices of the four huge mountainy men who carried it. He saw it sway above the heads, shawled and bare, glittering between the little stunted holly bushes and hazels.

(1959)

The Mad
Lomasneys

Contents

Guests of the Nation

1

At dusk the big Englishman, Belcher, would shift his long legs out of the ashes and say, 'Well, chums, what about it?' and Noble or myself would say, 'All right, chum' (for we had picked up some of their curious expressions), and the little Englishman, Hawkins, would light the lamp and bring out the cards. Sometimes Jeremiah Donovan would come up and supervise the game, and get excited over Hawkins' cards, which he always played badly, and shout at him as if he was one of our own, 'Ah, you divil, why didn't you play the tray?'

But ordinarily Jeremiah was a sober and contented poor devil like the big Englishman, Belcher, and was looked up to only because he was a fair hand at documents, though he was slow even with them. He wore a small cloth hat and big gaiters over his long pants, and you seldom saw him with his hands out of his pockets. He reddened when you talked to him, tilting from toe to heel and back, and looking down all the time at his big farmer's feet. Noble and myself used to make fun of his broad accent, because we were both from the town.

I could not at the time see the point of myself and Noble guarding Belcher and Hawkins at all, for it was my belief that you could have planted that pair down anywhere from this to Claregalway and they'd have taken root there like a native weed. I never in my short experience saw two men take to the country as they did.

They were passed on to us by the Second Battalion when the search for them became too hot, and Noble and myself, being young, took them over with a natural feeling of responsibility, but Hawkins made us look like fools when he showed that he knew the country better than we did.

'You're the bloke they call Bonaparte,' he says to me. 'Mary Brigid O'Connell told me to ask what you'd done with the pair of her brother's socks you borrowed.'

For it seemed, as they explained it, that the Second had little evenings, and some of the girls of the neighbourhood turned up, and, seeing they were such decent chaps, our fellows could not leave the two Englishmen out. Hawkins learned to dance *The Walls of Limerick, The Siege of Ennis* and *The Waves of Tory* as well as any of them, though he could not return the compliment, because our lads at that time did not dance foreign dances on principle.

So whatever privileges Belcher and Hawkins had with the Second they just took naturally with us, and after the first couple of days we gave up all pretence of keeping an eye on them. Not that they could have got far, because they had accents you could cut with a knife, and wore khaki tunics and overcoats with civilian pants and boots, but I believe myself they never had any idea of escaping and were quite content to be where they were.

It was a treat to see how Belcher got off with the old woman in the house where we were staying. She was a great warrant to scold, and cranky even with us, but before ever she had a chance of giving our guests, as I may call them, a lick of her tongue, Belcher had made her his friend for life. She was breaking sticks, and Belcher, who had not been more than ten minutes in the house, jumped up and went over to her.

'Allow me, madam,' he said, smiling his queer little smile. 'Please allow me,' and he took the hatchet from her. She was too surprised to speak, and after that, Belcher would be at her heels, carrying a bucket, a basket or a load of turf. As Noble said, he got into looking before she leapt, and hot water, or any little thing she wanted, Belcher would have ready for her. For such a huge man (and though I am five foot ten myself I had to look up at him) he had an uncommon lack of speech. It took us a little while to get used to him, walking in and out like a ghost, without speaking. Especially because Hawkins talked enough for a platoon it was strange to hear Belcher with his toes in the ashes come out with a solitary 'Excuse me, chum,' or 'That's right, chum.' His one and only passion was cards, and he was a remarkably good card player. He could have skinned myself and Noble, but whatever we lost to him, Hawkins lost to us, and Hawkins only played with the money Belcher gave him.

Hawkins lost to us because he had too much old gab, and we probably lost to Belcher for the same reason. Hawkins and Noble argued about religion into the early hours of the morning, and Hawkins worried the life out of Noble, who had a brother a priest, with a string of questions that would puzzle a cardinal. Even in treating of holy subjects, Hawkins had a deplorable tongue. I never met a man who could mix such a variety of cursing and bad language into any argument. He was a terrible man, and a fright to argue. He never did a stroke of work, and when he had no one else to argue with, he got stuck in the old woman.

He met his match in her, for when he tried to get her to complain profanely of the drought she gave him a great come-down by blaming it entirely on Jupiter Pluvius (a deity neither Hawkins nor I had ever heard of, though Noble said that among the pagans it was believed that he had something to do with the rain). Another day he was swearing at the capitalists for starting the German war when the old lady laid down her iron, puckered up her little crab's mouth and said: 'Mr Hawkins, you can say what you like about the war, and think you'll deceive me because I'm only a simple poor countrywoman, but I know what started the war. It was the Italian Count that stole the heathen divinity out of the temple in Japan. Believe me, Mr Hawkins, nothing but sorrow and want can follow people who disturb the hidden powers.'

A queer old girl, all right.

2

One evening we had our tea and Hawkins lit the lamp and we all sat into cards. Jeremiah Donovan came in too, and sat and watched us for a while, and it suddenly struck me that he had no great love for the two Englishmen. It came as a surprise to me because I had noticed nothing of it before.

Late in the evening a really terrible argument blew up between Hawkins and Noble about capitalists and priests and love of country.

'The capitalists pay the priests to tell you about the next world so that you won't notice what the bastards are up to in this,' said Hawkins.

'Nonsense, man!' said Noble, losing his temper. 'Before ever a capitalist was thought of people believed in the next world.'

Hawkins stood up as though he was preaching.

'Oh, they did, did they?' he said with a sneer. 'They believed all the things you believe – isn't that what you mean? And you believe

God created Adam, and Adam created Shem, and Shem created Jehoshophat. You believe all that silly old fairytale about Eve and Eden and the apple. Well listen to me, chum! If you're entitled to a silly belief like that, I'm entitled to my own silly belief – which is that the first thing your God created was a bleeding capitalist, with morality and Rolls-Royce complete. Am I right, chum?' he says to Belcher.

'You're right, chum,' says Belcher with a smile, and he got up from the table to stretch his long legs into the fire and stroke his moustache. So, seeing that Jeremiah Donovan was going, and that there was no knowing when the argument about religion would be over, I went out with him. We strolled down to the village together, and then he stopped, blushing and mumbling, and said I should be behind, keeping guard. I didn't like the tone he took with me, and anyway I was bored with life in the cottage, so I replied by asking what the hell we wanted to guard them for at all.

He looked at me in surprise and said: 'I thought you knew we were keeping them as hostages.'

'Hostages?' I said.

'The enemy have prisoners belonging to us, and now they're talking of shooting them,' he said. 'If they shoot our prisoners, we'll shoot theirs.'

'Shoot Belcher and Hawkins?' I said.

'What else did you think we were keeping them for?' he said.

'Wasn't it very unforeseen of you not to warn Noble and myself of that in the beginning?' I said.

'How was it?' he said. 'You might have known that much.'

'We could not know it, Jeremiah Donovan,' I said. 'How could we when they were on our hands so long?'

'The enemy have our prisoners as long and longer,' he said.

'That's not the same thing at all,' said I.

'What difference is there?' said he.

I couldn't tell him, because I knew he wouldn't understand. If it was only an old dog that you had to take to the vet's, you'd try and not get too fond of him, but Jeremiah Donovan was not a man who would ever be in danger of that.

'And when is this to be decided?' I said.

'We might hear tonight,' he said. 'Or tomorrow or the next day at latest. So if it's only hanging round that's a trouble to you, you'll be free soon enough.'

It was not the hanging round that was a trouble to me at all by this time. I had worse things to worry about. When I got back to the cottage the argument was still on. Hawkins was holding forth in his best style, maintaining that there was no next world, and Noble saying that there was; but I could see that Hawkins had had the best of it.

'Do you know what, chum?' he was saying with a saucy smile. 'I think you're just as big a bleeding unbeliever as I am. You say you believe in the next world, and you know just as much about the next world as I do, which is sweet damn-all. What's heaven? You don't know. Where's heaven? You don't know. You know sweet damn-all! I ask you again, do they wear wings?'

'Very well, then,' said Noble. 'They do. Is that enough for you? They do wear wings.'

'Where do they get them then? Who makes them? Have they a factory for wings? Have they a sort of store where you hand in your chit and take your bleeding wings?'

'You're an impossible man to argue with,' said Noble. 'Now, listen to me—' And they were off again.

It was long after midnight when we locked up and went to bed. As I blew out the candle I told Noble. He took it very quietly. When we'd been in bed about an hour he asked if I thought we should tell the Englishmen. I didn't, because I doubted if the English would shoot our men. Even if they did, the Brigade officers, who were always up and down to the Second Battalion and knew the Englishmen well, would hardly want to see them plugged. 'I think so too,' said Noble. 'It would be great cruelty to put the wind up them now.'

'It was very unforeseen of Jeremiah Donovan, anyhow,' said I.

It was next morning that we found it so hard to face Belcher and Hawkins. We went about the house all day, scarcely saying a word. Belcher didn't seem to notice; he was stretched into the ashes as usual, with his usual look of waiting in quietness for something unforeseen to happen, but Hawkins noticed it and put it down to Noble's being beaten in the argument of the night before.

'Why can't you take the discussion in the proper spirit?' he said severely. 'You and your Adam and Eve! I'm a Communist, that's what I am. Communist or Anarchist, it all comes to much the same thing.' And he went round the house, muttering when the fit took

143

him: 'Adam and Eve! Adam and Eve! Nothing better to do with their time than pick bleeding apples!'

3

I don't know how we got through that day, but I was very glad when it was over, the tea things were cleared away, and Belcher said in his peaceable way: 'Well, chums, what about it?' We sat round the table and Hawkins took out the cards, and just then I heard Jeremiah Donovan's footsteps on the path and a dark presentiment crossed my mind. I rose from the table and caught him before he reached the door.

'What do you want?' I asked.

'I want those two soldier friends of yours,' he said, getting red.

'Is that the way, Jeremiah Donovan?' I asked.

'That's the way. There were four of our lads shot this morning, one of them a boy of sixteen.'

'That's bad,' I said.

At that moment Noble followed me out, and the three of us walked down the path together, talking in whispers. Feeney, the local intelligence officer, was standing by the gate.

'What are you going to do about it?' I asked Jeremiah Donovan.

'I want you and Noble to get them out; tell them they're being shifted again; that'll be the quietest way.'

'Leave me out of that,' said Noble under his breath.

Jeremiah Donovan looked at him hard.

'All right,' he says. 'You and Feeney get a few tools from the shed and dig a hole by the far end of the bog. Bonaparte and myself will be after you. Don't let anyone see you with the tools. I wouldn't like it to go beyond ourselves.'

We saw Feeney and Noble go round to the shed and went in ourselves. I left Jeremiah Donovan to do the explanations. He told them that he had orders to send them back to the Second Battalion. Hawkins let out a mouthful of curses, and you could see that though Belcher didn't say anything, he was a bit upset too. The old woman was for having them stay in spite of us, and she didn't stop advising them until Jeremiah Donovan lost his temper and turned on her. He had a nasty temper, I noticed. It was pitch-dark in the cottage by this time, but no one thought of lighting the lamp, and in the darkness the two Englishmen fetched their topcoats and said goodbye to the old woman.

'Just as a man makes a home of a bleeding place, some bastard at headquarters thinks you're too cushy and shunts you off,' said Hawkins, shaking her hand.

'A thousand thanks, madam,' said Belcher. 'A thousand thanks for everything' – as though he'd made it up.

We went round to the back of the house and down towards the bog. It was only then that Jeremiah Donovan told them. He was shaking with excitement.

'There were four of our fellows shot in Cork this morning and now you're to be shot as a reprisal.'

'What are you talking about?' snaps Hawkins. 'It's bad enough being mucked about as we are without having to put up with your funny jokes.'

'It isn't a joke,' says Donovan. 'I'm sorry, Hawkins, but it's true,' and begins on the usual rigmarole about duty and how unpleasant it is. I never noticed that people who talk a lot about duty find it much of a trouble to them.

'Oh, cut it out!' said Hawkins.

'Ask Bonaparte,' said Donovan, seeing that Hawkins wasn't taking him seriously. 'Isn't it true, Bonaparte?'

'It is,' I said, and Hawkins stopped.

'Ah, for Christ's sake, chum!'

'I mean it, chum,' I said.

'You don't sound as if you meant it.'

'If he doesn't mean it, I do,' said Donovan, working himself up.

'What have you against me, Jeremiah Donovan?'

'I never said I had anything against you. But why did your people take out four of your prisoners and shoot them in cold blood?'

He took Hawkins by the arm and dragged him on, but it was impossible to make him understand that we were in earnest. I had the Smith and Wesson in my pocket and I kept fingering it and wondering what I'd do if they put up a fight for it or ran, and wishing to God they'd do one or the other. I knew if they did run for it, that I'd never fire on them. Hawkins wanted to know was Noble in it, and when we said yes he asked us why Noble wanted to plug him. Why did any of us want to plug him? What had he done to us? Weren't we all chums? Didn't we understand him and didn't he understand us? Did we imagine for an instant that he'd shoot us for all the so-and-so officers in the so-and-so British Army?

By this time we'd reached the bog, and I was so sick I couldn't even answer him. We walked along the edge of it in the darkness, and every now and then Hawkins would call a halt and begin all over again, as if he was wound up, about our being chums, and I knew that nothing but the sight of the grave would convince him that we had to do it. And all the time I was hoping that something would happen; that they'd run for it or that Noble would take over the responsibility from me. I had the feeling that it was worse on Noble than on me.

4

At last we saw the lantern in the distance and made towards it. Noble was carrying it, and Feeney was standing somewhere in the darkness behind him, and the picture of them so still and silent in the bogland brought it home to me that we were in earnest, and banished the last bit of hope I had.

Belcher, on recognizing Noble, said: 'Hallo, chum,' in his quiet way, but Hawkins flew at him at once, and the argument began all over again, only this time Noble had nothing to say for himself and stood with his head down, holding the lantern between his legs.

It was Jeremiah Donovan who did the answering. For the twentieth time, as though it was haunting his mind, Hawkins asked if anybody thought he'd shoot Noble.

'Yes, you would,' said Jeremiah Donovan.

'No, I wouldn't, damn you!'

'You would, because you'd know you'd be shot for not doing it.'

'I wouldn't, not if I was to be shot twenty times over. I wouldn't shoot a pal. And Belcher wouldn't – isn't that right, Belcher?'

'That's right, chum,' Belcher said, but more by way of answering the question than of joining in the argument. Belcher sounded as though whatever unforeseen thing he'd always been waiting for had come at last.

'Anyway, who says Noble would be shot if I wasn't? What do you think I'd do if I was in his place, out in the middle of a blasted bog?'

'What would you do?' asked Donovan.

'I'd go with him wherever he was going, of course. Share my

last bob with him and stick by him through thick and thin. No one can ever say of me that I let down a pal.'

'We've had enough of this,' said Jeremiah Donovan, cocking his revolver. 'Is there any message you want to send?'

'No, there isn't.'

'Do you want to say your prayers?'

Hawkins came out with a cold-blooded remark that even shocked me and turned on Noble again.

'Listen to me, Noble,' he said. 'You and me are chums. You can't come over to my side, so I'll come over to your side. That show you I mean what I say? Give me a rifle and I'll go along with you and the other lads.'

Nobody answered him. We knew that was no way out.

'Hear what I'm saying?' he said. 'I'm through with it. I'm a deserter or anything else you like. I don't believe in your stuff, but it's no worse than mine. That satisfy you?'

Noble raised his head, but Donovan began to speak and he lowered it again without replying.

'For the last time, have you any messages to send?' said Donovan in a cold, excited sort of voice.

'Shut up, Donovan! You don't understand me, but these lads do. They're not the sort to make a pal and kill a pal. They're not the tools of any capitalist.'

I alone of the crowd saw Donovan raise his Webley to the back of Hawkins' neck, and as he did so I shut my eyes and tried to pray. Hawkins had begun to say something else when Donovan fired, and as I opened my eyes at the bang, I saw Hawkins stagger at the knees and lie out flat at Noble's feet, slowly and as quiet as a kid falling asleep, with the lantern-light on his lean legs and bright farmer's boots. We all stood very still, watching him settle out in the last agony.

Then Belcher took out a handkerchief and began to tie it about his own eyes (in our excitement we'd forgotten to do the same for Hawkins), and, seeing it wasn't big enough, turned and asked for the loan of mine. I gave it to him and he knotted the two together and pointed with his foot at Hawkins.

'He's not quite dead,' he said. 'Better give him another.'

Sure enough, Hawkins' left knee was beginning to rise. I bent down and put my gun to his head; then, recollecting myself, I got up again. Belcher understood what was in my mind.

'Give him his first,' he said. 'I don't mind. Poor bastard, we don't know what's happening to him now.'

I knelt and fired. By this time I didn't seem to know what I was doing. Belcher, who was fumbling a bit awkwardly with the handkerchiefs, came out with a laugh as he heard the shot. It was the first time I had heard him laugh and it sent a shudder down my back; it sounded so unnatural.

'Poor bugger!' he said quietly. 'And last night he was so curious about it all. It's very queer, chums, I always think. Now he knows as much about it as they'll ever let him know, and last night he was all in the dark.'

Donovan helped him to tie the handkerchiefs about his eyes. 'Thanks, chum,' he said. Donovan asked if there were any messages he wanted sent.

'No, chum,' he said. 'Not for me. If any of you would like to write to Hawkins' mother, you'll find a letter from her in his pocket. He and his mother were great chums. But my missus left me eight years ago. Went away with another fellow and took the kid with her. I like the feeling of a home, as you may have noticed, but I couldn't start another again after that.'

It was an extraordinary thing, but in those few minutes Belcher said more than in all the weeks before. It was just as if the sound of the shot had started a flood of talk in him and he could go on the whole night like that, quite happily, talking about himself. We stood around like fools now that he couldn't see us any longer. Donovan looked at Noble, and Noble shook his head. Then Donovan raised his Webley, and at that moment Belcher gave his queer laugh again. He may have thought we were talking about him, or perhaps he noticed the same thing I'd noticed and couldn't understand it.

'Excuse me, chums,' he said. 'I feel I'm talking the hell of a lot, and so silly, about my being so handy about a house and things like that. But this thing came on me suddenly. You'll forgive me, I'm sure.'

'You don't want to say a prayer?' asked Donovan.

'No, chum,' he said. 'I don't think it would help. I'm ready, and you boys want to get it over.'

'You understand that we're only doing our duty?' said Donovan.

Belcher's head was raised like a blind man's, so that you could only see his chin and the top of his nose in the lantern-light.

'I never could make out what duty was myself,' he said. 'I think you're all good lads, if that's what you mean. I'm not complaining.'

Noble, just as if he couldn't bear any more of it, raised his fist at Donovan, and in a flash Donovan raised his gun and fired. The big man went over like a sack of meal, and this time there was no need of a second shot.

I don't remember much about the burying, but that it was worse than all the rest because we had to carry them to the grave. It was all mad lonely with nothing but a patch of lantern-light between ourselves and the dark, and birds hooting and screeching all round, disturbed by the guns. Noble went through Hawkins' belongings to find the letter from his mother, and then joined his hands together. He did the same with Belcher. Then, when we'd filled in the grave, we separated from Jeremiah Donovan and Feeney and took our tools back to the shed. All the way we didn't speak a word. The kitchen was dark and cold as we'd left it, and the old woman was sitting over the hearth, saying her beads. We walked past her into the room, and Noble struck a match to light the lamp. She rose quietly and came to the doorway with all her cantankerousness gone.

'What did ye do with them?' she asked in a whisper, and Noble started so that the match went out in his hand.

'What's that?' he asked without turning round.

'I heard ye,' she said.

'What did you hear?' asked Noble.

'I heard ye. Do ye think I didn't hear ye, putting the spade back in the houseen?'

Noble struck another match and this time the lamp lit for him.

'Was that what ye did to them?' she asked.

Then, by God, in the very doorway, she fell on her knees and began praying, and after looking at her for a minute or two Noble did the same by the fireplace. I pushed my way out past her and left them at it. I stood at the door, watching the stars and listening to the shrieking of the birds dying out over the bogs. It is so strange what you feel at times like that that you can't describe it. Noble says he saw everything ten times the size, as though there were nothing in the whole world but that little patch of bog with the two Englishmen stiffening into it, but with me it was as if the patch of bog where the Englishmen were was a million miles away, and even Noble and the old woman, mumbling behind me, and the birds and the bloody stars were all far away, and I was somehow very small and very lost and lonely like a child astray in the snow. And anything that happened to me afterwards, I never felt the same about again.

Guests of the Nation (1931)

The Procession
of Life

One night Andy Coleman came home and found the front door locked against him. It was not the first time it had happened. Ever since his mother died six months before Andy's father had made a dead set at him. It was an extraordinary thing, just as though his mother's death had released in his father a flood of malice and jealousy that until then had been dammed up. Jealousy was the only way Andy could describe it to himself, though when he tried to think what his father had to be jealous about he couldn't put his finger on it. He had a miserable little job on the railway, few friends and no girl; but that was how things were. Watching Andy put on a tie, light a cigarette, or even brush his hair before going for his evening walk, his father seemed like a man distracted with envy. Andy knocked again, a little bit louder.

'Who's that?' his father asked from upstairs – as if he didn't know, the old bastard!

'It's me, father,' Andy replied in a low, appealing voice.

'This house is locked at ten o'clock,' his father snarled.

'Ah, for God's sake, let us in, can't you?' Andy begged.

'This house is locked at ten, I say.'

Despairingly Andy began to knock again. It was easily seen that his mother was dead. She wouldn't have lain there and left him outside, not for twenty men like his father. Now, they were both of them out. Andy was a finely-strung young fellow with a long, keen face, quick to mirth and quick to misery. Suddenly he put his hands before his eyes and began to sob, as much for his mother as himself – all her years of misery and toil, and nothing to show for it but this. A neighbour's door opened discreetly and a woman's voice whispered: 'Is anything wrong, Andy?'

'No, thanks, Mrs Walsh,' he said hastily, shaking off the boy in him. But he could not reach for a man quickly enough. He knew that now he had roused the neighbours he would only have to knock a little longer to shame his brute of a father into opening the door, but he was too sensitive to face it and the storm of abuse that would follow. He turned on his heel and went quickly down the lane. He had begun to weep again. On the road people were returning home in the early night, mellow and lingering. Only he had no home to go to.

He walked quickly in the shadow where people would be unlikely to identify him and ask the cause of his tears. One of them would have brought him home all right; he was a popular boy, well-liked because he had the friendly word for everybody, but he could not face explaining to them what a hell his life had become. His mind was full of wild schemes for running away, joining the army or taking a ship.

It was only when the storm of tears had passed over that he could consider his own plight with any reasonableness. It was obvious that he could not wander round and round the city the whole night. Some policeman would be bound to pick him up and bring him to the Bridewell, and that, in his imagination, was all bound up with courts and things in the newspapers. The only place that seemed to promise safety was the river bank. At that hour of the night it was usually deserted, and there were frequently bales of merchandise or piles of timber that a fellow could lie down between. At least, it wasn't raining.

With a sinking heart he crossed the New Bridge and faced the murk and blackness of the ill-lit quay. There were only two small boats at the jetties, and they, too, seemed deserted. He passed them, and then some storehouses and mills before he saw the gleam of a fire ahead. It was a watchman's brazier, and the watchman himself was sitting in his little sentry-box. He was a man in his late fifties or early sixties, with grey hair cropped close, a small grey moustache, a fresh childish complexion and blue, innocent red-rimmed eyes as though the brazier smoke hurt them. He looked suspiciously at Andy.

'Goodnight, sir,' Andy said with what he always thought of as a winning smile.

The watchman looked him over again and his jaw set in an obstinate look. Andy, who was accustomed to summing up people rapidly, decided he was an obstinate old brute.

'Goodnight,' he said with finality.

'I suppose you wouldn't be able to tell me where there's any place round I could doss down for the night?' Andy asked lightly, not making too much of his trouble.

'What do you want to sleep out for, boy?' the watchman asked sternly.

'Because I'm after being locked out – that's why,' Andy replied.

'Why were you locked out?'

'I only wish I knew,' Andy said with a touch of bitterness. 'My father wouldn't give you many reasons.'

'What school do you go to?' the watchman asked, and Andy knew he was trying to find out what class of boy he was.

'Ah, I'm left school, sir,' Andy said. 'I used to go to the Monastery but I had to leave after my mother died. I'm working on the railway now.'

'This is no hour for a boy of your age to be out,' the watchman said severely.

'Oh, but I wasn't out till this hour,' Andy protested quickly. He was a boy who tended to lose his head and fly into tempers, but up to the final moment he tried to keep up a reasonable tone. 'As a matter of fact, it was hardly half past ten.'

'Half past ten is late enough,' the watchman said, refusing to yield an inch. 'Young fellows do be only getting into trouble, stopping out till all hours.'

'Well, I never got into much trouble anyhow,' Andy said with his candid, almost grown-up air. If Andy were ever to be hanged in the wrong, he would be trying to explain his innocence even with the rope round his neck. 'I mean, you know yourself the way it is. You get talking to a man at his door about one thing or another, and the time passes.'

'There is a place further down the river where you could stop,' the watchman said.

'Is that down opposite Tivoli, sir?' Andy asked.

'Yes, that is where the tramps go.'

Andy knew it well, though only from fine Sunday afternoons when his mother had taken him there; a bandstand on the river bank with trees about it; a lonesome place at that hour of night.

'You wouldn't mind me stopping here by the fire, would you, sir?' he asked gently.

'I would mind it,' the watchman replied sourly. 'I cannot have people making a rendezvous of this place. I have too much valuable property to protect.'

'You needn't worry about the property, sir,' said Andy with an affected laugh. ''Twould be there a long time before I'd touch it. 'Tis only while I get warm.'

'You can warm yourself, but you cannot stay,' the watchman said. 'You are a very foolish boy. It would be wiser for you to obey your father. He knows what is good for you, better than you do. But things are made too easy for young people nowadays; they expect too much. When I was your age I worked from seven in the morning till seven at night – twelve hours, and no such thing as half days either, and sixpence a week was all my father allowed me. That is the truth. Four and sixpence I had to give my mother; five shillings was all I got. Things are made too easy nowadays – pictures, cigarettes and everything.'

'To tell the truth, I never bother my head with the pictures,' Andy said, conscious at the same time that he had put a cigarette in his mouth. 'Have one of these, sir.'

'I do not smoke them,' the watchman said, shaking his head severely.

'But I don't see any harm in them, do you?' Andy asked.

'I do see harm in them. I see great harm in them. Young fellows cannot afford them at the cruel price they are sold at. A young fellow should be steady and do without things he cannot afford. I saw clever men that never learned that and I saw what happened to them. Drink, horses, women – once they start there is no end to it. I saw one professor from the college here one night, and the conduct and language of that man, there is no describing it.'

He began to tell of other characters he had known, a doctor on Patrick's Hill, a stockbroker, even a priest, all of whom had succumbed to temptation the way Andy was succumbing to it now, and had ended up bad. Andy listened deferentially, but all the same it struck him as queer that a man as well able to mind himself as the watchman wouldn't have done a bit better for himself in life. His conversation seemed to be one long moan, like a Good Friday service: all the same, it passed the time, and listening to Shandon strike the hours Andy was aware of the night's passing.

At last the watchman rose stiffly.

'Now you have to be going, boy,' he said. 'I have duties to attend to.'

'Ah, I'll go now, in a minute,' said Andy.

'You will go at once, boy,' the watchman said, his voice rising to a wail. 'People come round here – policemen and inspectors – and I have to mind my reputation. A man's reputation is everything.'

'Ah, for God's sake, I'm not going to do any harm to your reputation,' said Andy. He had heard the footsteps coming down the quay and hoped for better company.

'I will have no back answers from you,' the watchman said fiercely. 'Go on now where you were going, boy!'

'Oh, I'll go, I'll go,' Andy said coolly, but he had no intention of going. He moved slowly in the direction of the footsteps, and when he saw it was a woman he smiled and raised his cap.

'Is that you, Mac?' she asked in surprise.

'No, miss,' he replied with an easy laugh. 'My name is Andy Coleman. I just happened to be taking a heat at the fire.'

'Jesus!' she said. 'You gave me a start. Who are you anyway?'

'Never mind who he is or what he is,' cried the watchman. 'Leave him go back where he came from.'

'Ah, give us a breeze, Mac!' she said reproachfully. 'Can't we even pass the time of day? What are you doing here?'

'I was locked out,' Andy said with a shrug, but he noticed himself the way his tone had changed. It was more light-hearted, as if being locked out were an everyday occurrence with him.

'Sit down and tell us about it,' she said. 'Mac, are we going to get that cup of tea?'

'Ah, I have something better to do than be making tea for night-walkers like that,' the watchman said with an indignant quaver in his voice.

The woman collapsed on to a box by the brazier.

'God, am I not to be allowed to talk to the boy for two minutes?' she cried. 'Or what sort of old fool are you at all? Will you put that billy can on for the love of God, and give us less of your old gab.'

She was a big, blowsy woman with the remains of her good looks still about her, and something pleasant and musical in her loud, hoarse, scolding voice. The watchman looked at her, trembling with rage, his blue eyes with their raw surrounds looking as though at any moment he might burst into tears. Then he shook his head at no one in particular and put the billy can on to boil.

'Sit down and tell us about yourself,' she said, making room for Andy.

'Ah, there isn't much to tell,' Andy said. 'I came home at half ten, and my old fellow had the house locked up and wouldn't let me in.'

'And wasn't there anyone to open the door for you?'

'Ah, no. I'm an only child.'

'And what about your mother?'

'She died a few months ago. I had to leave school, and 'tis since then all the trouble started.'

'I suppose he can do what he likes now,' she said bitterly.

'He might have his reasons,' the watchman said, addressing nobody in particular.

'Ah, 'tis easy the talk comes to you,' she said shrilly. ''Tis a hard day for a child when he leaves his mother in the graveyard and comes back to live with his father. Bloody misfortunate brutes! I seen too much of them.'

'You know nothing about it,' the watchman said violently.

'Don't I? I suppose I don't know what happened to the houseful of us after we left my poor mother up in the Botanics? It wasn't long before she had company either.'

'I say it's not fair to judge a man you do not know,' said the watchman. 'Men have great responsibilities that women know nothing about.'

'They have, I hear!' she retorted mockingly. 'Like my old fellow. The only responsibility he ever had was to see that his kids wouldn't have enough to eat for fear the publicans would go short, and he done that like a right true Christian. Bloody old brute! God forgive me!'

'It is not right to talk like that,' the watchman said as he poured a paper of tea into the can.

'What's wrong about it?'

'Encouraging young fellows to talk like that about their fathers. Little enough respect they have.'

'And what respect could they have and the way they're treated? If that child got his death of cold, I'll guarantee his father wouldn't care much.'

'Even so, even so,' the watchman said sourly. 'My own father was a severe man, but I never talked against him like that.'

'Your own sons weren't so obliging, though.'

'That is what I mean,' he said with sudden dignity.

'And what the hell do you expect? Wanting to marry again at your age with an old floosie like Mollie Anderson?'

'Whatever I might do, I am entitled to respect,' the watchman said in a bigoted tone. 'You do not raise your hand to your father without paying for it sooner or later.'

'Send us word when pay day comes round,' she said with sudden pity. 'Don't you believe it, Mac. They'll be warming their ass in corporation jobs when you're dying in the workhouse . . . Ah, Christ, sure I'm only talking,' she added with sudden despair. ''Tis a hard bloody old life, whatever way you look at it. When you're young you're walked on, and when you're old you're in the way. You might as well enjoy it while you can . . . What are you going to do?' she asked Andy in a whisper, almost without moving her lips. 'Never mind Mac. He's as deaf as a post.'

'To tell you the God's truth I don't know,' Andy replied in the same way. 'If I could stop here for another hour or so, I'd be all right.'

'Would you like to come home with me?'

'That'd be grand,' he said with a shy smile.

'God knows, 'tisn't much, but 'tis better than this,' she said sadly. The watchman filled three jam jars with tea and passed them round.

'Was Guard Dunphy round at all, Mac?' she asked.

'No,' the watchman said sourly, 'I didn't see him these ten days.'

'With the help of God he might be shifted,' she said piously. 'He'd be a small loss . . . This is a policeman,' she said to Andy. 'He goes on his holidays to the Cistercians. He'd have you demented with Father Prissy and Father Prossy. Biggest old ram in Cork, and he's never out of churches and chapels. He'd cure you of religion.'

They drank their tea while the woman chattered on. The city bells sounded clearer as the darkness began to thin away beyond the cliffs at the farther side of the river. At last the woman rose.

'Come on, child,' she said, giving Andy her hand. 'I may as well get you back to the old doss or you'll be on my hands tomorrow.'

'What's that?' the watchman asked incredulously, raising his head.

157

'The boy,' she said shortly. 'I'm taking him back to let him have a few hours' sleep before he goes to work.'

'To corrupt him, you mean?' the watchman said, raising his voice.

'What the hell do you mean, corrupt him?' she shouted. 'At least, I'm not trying to throw him into the gutter the way you are. You and your dirty old mind!'

He rose, staring at her, and his head began to shake again.

'Very well!' he said in a low voice, pointing dramatically up the quay. 'Go! But don't ever come back here again! Don't turn to me for anything again, the longest day you live!'

'Ah, what ails you, you old fool?' she asked.

'Not the longest day you live,' he said in a heart-broken voice. 'It is my own fault. I knew what you were the first day I met you. I put myself out to oblige you, and this is my thanks.'

'Ah, Mac,' she said in a wail, 'don't be going on like that, for the love of God. You'll only upset yourself.'

'Go away, woman, go away!' he said.

Andy saw with interest that there were real tears in the old man's eyes. A new feeling of confidence and excitement welled up in him. He took the woman's arm and squeezed it to his side.

'Come on if you're coming,' he said. He was astonished by her whispered reply.

'Ah, for God's sake!' she said impatiently. 'Can't you see the poor divil is lonely?'

At the same moment they heard heavy footsteps, approaching from the river walk.

'Christ, come on!' she said, but she was too late. The light of the brazier caught the buttons on a policeman's uniform as he moved towards them at a comfortable stride, his cap slightly to one side of his head.

'The bloody bastard I'm trying to dodge the whole time!' she whispered despairingly, and then in a terrible voice: 'Bad luck and end to you, you sanctimonious ould ram!'

'God bless all here,' the policeman said piously.

'Ah, and you too, Guard Dunphy,' she replied.

'What's going on here?' the policeman asked, looking first at the watchman and then at Andy.

'Ah, nothing, guard,' she replied. 'Only a young fellow I was trying to get an old doss for.'

'What hurry is there?' the policeman asked as he took a packet of cigarettes from the pocket of his tunic. 'Isn't the night long? Who is it?'

'Just a friend of mine, guard.'

'If he's a friend of yours he's all right,' the policeman said. 'What did you say his name was?'

'Coleman, guard,' Andy chipped in uneasily. 'Andy Coleman.'

'And tell me, Andy, what has you out to this hour of night?'

'He was locked out,' the woman said shortly.

'Locked out?' the policeman said in surprise. 'Who locked him out?'

'Who the hell do you think only his father?' she asked. 'The poor unfortunate boy have to be at work in the morning, and I was going to get him a bed somewhere.'

'Time enough! Time enough! Take a fag and sit down for a minute.' As she did so, he turned on Andy again. 'What did he lock you out for?'

'Nothing, guard,' said Andy, his new confidence beginning to ebb. He wasn't really afraid of the guard; he didn't think the guard was a bad man, but he had a strong notion that the guard had a warm welcome for himself.

'Was it drink, tell me?'

'No, guard,' Andy said with a watchful smile. 'I never drink.'

'Horses?'

'No. I don't bet.'

'Then it could only be one other thing,' said the policeman. 'And that is something I would most strongly advise you against.'

'You'd be the one that would be well able to advise him,' the woman said curtly.

'I would. It is a thing I would advise any young fellow against. Do you know what I was doing for the last week, Lena?'

'Ah, I do not.'

'You wouldn't believe me. I was at a retreat.'

'Was this the Cistercians again?'

'It was not the Cistercians. The Cistercians do not give retreats here. What sort of old heretic are you? This was the Redemptorists. They're the boys to put the fear of God into you. I wouldn't say anything against the other orders, but when it comes to hellfire they're only like "I roved out".'

'Well, I hope the hellfire did you good.'

'It did me great good. There is nothing in the world I like better than a good sermon. Except a hurling match . . . Not comparing them, of course . . . I didn't see you at the match on Sunday, Mac.'

'No, guard,' said the watchman. 'I was not there. What sort of match was it?'

'Rotten.'

'So I heard.'

'The rottenest match I saw in years. That team of the Barrs was not fit to send against a girls' school . . . Well, Lena, what about that little walk we were going to take?'

'And what would the holy fathers say about that?' the woman asked with ill-concealed acerbity. It was lost on the policeman though.

'Ah, the holy fathers are men like ourselves,' he replied complacently. '"Sins against Faith are serious, sins against morals, sure we all commit them." Some great Corkman said that, if only I could remember his name. Don't you agree with me, Mac?'

'I knew that fellow's father well,' said the watchman.

'Look, guard, I'll be back to you,' the woman said desperately. 'I only want to get the kid settled for the night. I won't be more than ten minutes.'

'Ah, Andy here is all right,' said the policeman in the same jovial authoritative tone, which, for some reason, reminded Andy of a priest's. 'Andy and Mac will be company for one another . . . I wouldn't be down here too often, young fellow,' he added gaily to Andy. 'There's bad company round here. Goodnight, Mac.'

'Goodnight, Guard Dunphy,' the watchman said.

With a wry face, the woman took his arm, and soon the pair of them were lost in the darkness. Andy sat on for a few minutes, but the watchman did not speak.

'I think I might as well be going home,' Andy said at last.

'You might as well stop as you're here,' the watchman said despondently. 'One of them might be back.'

'I doubt it,' said Andy. 'I might as well be making for home. Goodnight and – thanks.'

The watchman did not reply, and Andy set off slowly in the direction of the city. The dawn was breaking over the cliffs to his right across the river, and buildings and ships began to emerge from the shadows. Soon a single spot of light reached out and struck the sleeping city, and in a curious way Andy's heart felt lighter. He knew he wasn't as good a boy as he had been when he came down but he felt better prepared to deal with his father and the rest that life might have in store for him. His life had been too sheltered, too much under the wing of a woman who was now under the ground. Now, the world stretched ahead of him, different from what he had imagined it, different from what it seemed by daylight, lit up with the spectral intensity of the night.

Guests of the Nation (1931)

'The Star that Bids
the Shepherd Fold'

Father Whelan, the parish priest, called on his curate, Father Devine, one evening in autumn. Father Whelan was a tall, stout man with a broad chest, a head that did not detach itself too clearly from the rest of his body, bushes of wild hair in his ears, and the rosy, innocent, good-natured face of a pious old countrywoman who made a living by selling eggs.

Devine was pale and worn-looking, with a gentle, dreamy face that had the soft gleam of an old piano keyboard, and he wore pince-nez perched on his unhappy, insignificant nose. He and Whelan got on all right considering – well, considering that Devine, who didn't know when he was well-off, had fathered a dramatic society and an annual festival on Whelan, and that, whenever his curate's name was mentioned, the parish priest – a charitable old man who never said an unkind word about anybody – tapped his head and said poor Devine's poor father was just the same. 'A national teacher – sure, I knew him well, poor man!'

What Devine said about Whelan in that crucified drawl of his mainly consisted of the old man's own words, with just the faintest inflection to underline their fatuity. 'I know some of the clergy are very opposed to books, but I like a book myself. I am very fond of Zane Grey. Zane Grey is an author I would recommend to anybody, Father. Even poetry I like. Some of the poems you see on advertisements are very clever.' Devine was clever; he was lonely; he had a few good original water-colours and a bookcase full of works that were a constant source of wonder to the parish priest. Whelan stood in front of them now, his hat in his hands, his glasses raised, lifting his warty old nose while his eyes were as blank and hopeless as his charity.

'Nothing there in your line, I'm afraid,' Devine said with his maddeningly respectful, deprecating air, as if he really put the parish priest's taste on a level with his own.

162

"Tisn't that at all,' Whelan said in a mournful, faraway voice. 'Only you have a lot of foreign books. I suppose you know the languages well.'

"Well enough to read,' Devine said wearily, his handsome head on one side. 'Why?'

'That foreign boat at the jetties,' Whelan said without looking round. 'What is it? French or German or something. There's terrible scandal about it.'

'Is that so?' drawled Devine. 'I didn't hear.'

'Oh, terrible,' Whelan said mournfully, turning on him the full battery of his round, rosy old face and shining spectacles. 'There's girls on it every night. I told Sullivan I'd go round and hunt them out. It occurred to me we might want someone to speak the language.'

'I'm afraid my French would hardly rise to that,' Devine said drily, but he made no further objection, for, except for his old-womanly fits of virtue, Whelan was all right as parish priests go. Devine had had sad experience of how they could go. He put on his faded old coat and clamped his battered hat down over his pince-nez, and the two priests went down Main Street to the post office corner. It was deserted, but for two out-of-works supporting either side of the door like ornaments, and a few others hanging hypnotized over the bridge while they studied the foaming waters of the weir. Devine had taken up carpentry in an attempt to lure them into the technical school classes, but it hadn't worked too well.

'The dear knows, you'd hardly wonder where those girls would go,' he said thoughtfully.

'Ah, what do they want to go anywhere for?' asked the parish priest, holding his head as though it were a flowerpot that might fall and break. 'They're mad on pleasure. That girl, Nora Fitzpatrick, is one of them, and her mother dying at home.'

'That might be her reason,' said Devine, who, unlike the parish priest, called at the Fitzpatricks and knew what their home was like, with six children and a mother dying of cancer.

'Ah, her place is at home, Father,' Whelan said without rancour.

They went past the Technical School to the quays, deserted but for a coal boat and the big foreign grain boat which rose high and dark above the edge of the jetty on a full tide. The

town was historically reputed to have been a great place, and
had masses of grey stone warehouses, all staring with sightless
eyes across the river. Two men who had been standing against
the wall, looking up at the grain boat, came to join them. One
was a tall, gaunt man with a long, sour, melancholy face which
looked particularly hideous because he had a youthful pink and
white complexion, and it made him resemble an old hag, heavily
made up. He wore a wig and carried a rolled-up umbrella behind
his back. His name was Sullivan; he was manager of a shop in
town and a man Devine loathed. The other man, Joe Sheridan,
was small, fat, and Jewish-looking with dark skin and an excitable
manner. He was the inevitable local windbag, who lived in a
perpetual hang-over from his own bouts of self-importance. As
the four men met, Devine looked up and saw two young foreign
faces, propped on their hands, peering over the edge of the boat.

'Well, boys?' Whelan asked boldly.

'There's two of them on board at present, father,' Sullivan said
in a shrill, scolding voice. 'Nora Fitzpatrick and Phillie O'Malley.
They're the worst of the lot.'

'Well, I think you'd better go on board and tell them to come
out here to me,' said Whelan.

'I was wondering what our legal position was, father?' Sheridan
said with mock thoughtfulness. 'I mean, have we any sort of *locus
standi*?'

'Oh, if they stabbed you, or cut your throat, I think they could
be tried for it,' Devine replied with bland malice. 'Of course, I
don't know if your family would be entitled to compensation.'

The malice was lost on Whelan, who laid one hairy paw on
Devine's shoulder, and the other on Sheridan's to soothe their
fears. He exuded pious confidence. It was the eggs all over again.
God would look after His hens!

'Never mind about the legal position,' he said paternally. 'I'll
be answerable for that.'

'That's enough for me, father,' said Sheridan, straightening
himself proudly, and then he pulled his hat down over his eyes
and joined his hands behind his back before striding up the
gangway, with the air of a detective in a bad American film.
Sullivan, clutching his umbrella comfortingly against his back-
bone, strutted after him, head in air. A lovely pair, Devine
thought. They went up to the two sailors.

'Two girls,' Sullivan said in his shrill voice. 'We're looking for the two girls who came on board half an hour ago.'

Neither of the sailors stirred. One turned his eyes lazily and looked Sullivan up and down.

'Not this boat,' he said insolently. 'The other. There are always girls on that.'

Then Sheridan, who had glanced down a companionway, gave tongue.

'Phillie O'Malley!' he shouted. 'Come out here to Father Whelan! He wants to talk to you.'

Nothing happened for a minute or two. Then a tall girl with a consumptive face emerged on deck with a handkerchief pressed to her eyes. Devine couldn't help feeling sick at the sight of her wretched finery, her cheap hat and bead necklace. He was angry and ashamed, and a cold fury of sarcasm rose in him. The Good Shepherd, indeed!

'Come on, lads!' shouted Whelan encouragingly. 'What about the other one?'

Sheridan, flushed with triumph, was about to disappear down the companionway when one of the sailors gave him a heave that threw him to the edge of the ship. Then the sailor stood nonchalantly in the doorway, blocking the way. Whelan grew red with anger, and he only waited for the girl to leave the gangway before he went up himself. Devine paused to whisper to her.

'Get off home as quick as you can, Phillie,' he said. 'And don't be upsetting yourself about it.'

At the real tenderness in his voice she took the handkerchief from her face and began to weep in earnest, tossing her silly little head from side to side. Devine went slowly after the others. It was a ridiculous scene; the fat old priest, his head in the air, trembling with senile astonishment and anger at being blocked.

'Get out of my way, you lout!' he said.

'Don't be a fool, man!' Devine whispered with quiet ferocity. 'They're not accustomed to being spoken to like that. If you got a knife in your ribs, it would be your own fault. We want to talk to the captain.' And then, bending forward with his eyebrows raised, he asked politely: 'Would you be good enough to tell the captain we'd like to see him.'

The sailor who was blocking the way looked at him for a moment and then nodded in the direction of the upper deck.

Taking Whelan's arm and telling the others to stay behind, Devine went up the ship. The second sailor passed them out, knocked at a door and said something Devine couldn't catch. Then with a scowl he held the door open.

The captain was a middle-aged man with a heavily-lined, sallow face, close-cropped hair and a black moustache. There was something Mediterranean about his air.

'*Bonsoir, messieurs,*' he said in a loud, businesslike tone that did not conceal a certain anxiety.

'*Bonsoir, monsieur le capitaine,*' Devine said with the same plaintive, ingratiating air as he bowed and raised his battered old hat. '*Est-ce que nous vous dérangeons?*'

'*Mais, pas du tout; entrez, je vous prie,*' the captain said heartily, clearly relieved by Devine's amiability. '*Vous parlez français, alors?*'

'*Un peu, monsieur le capitaine,*' Devine said modestly. '*Vous savez, ici en Irlande on n'a pas souvent l'occasion.*'

'Ah, well, I speak English good enough,' the captain said cheerfully. 'Won't you sit down?'

'I wish my French were anything as good as your English,' Devine said as he sat down.

'One travels a good deal,' said the captain with a shrug, but he was pleased just the same. 'You'll have a drink. Some brandy, eh?'

'I'd be delighted, of course, but we have a favour to ask you first.'

'A favour?' the captain said enthusiastically. 'Certainly, certainly. Anything I can do. Have a cigar?'

'Never smoke them,' Whelan said sullenly, and to mask his rudeness, Devine, who never smoked cigars, took one and lit it.

'I'd better explain who we are,' he said, sitting back, his head on one side, his long delicate hands hanging over the arms of the chair. 'This is Father Whelan, the parish priest. My name is Devine: I'm the curate.'

'And mine is Platon Demarrais,' the captain said proudly. 'I bet you never before heard of someone called Platon?'

'A relation of the philosopher, I presume,' said Devine.

'And I have two brothers, Zenon and Plotin!'

'Quite an intellectual family.'

'Pagans, of course,' the captain explained complacently. 'Greeks. My father was a schoolteacher. He called us that to annoy the priest. He was anti-clerical.'

'That isn't confined to schoolteachers in France,' Devine said drily. 'My father was a schoolteacher too, but he never got round to calling me Aristotle. Which might be as well,' he added with a chuckle. 'At any rate, there's a girl called Fitzpatrick on the ship, with some sailor, I suppose. She's one of Father Whelan's parishioners, and we'd be grateful if you'd have her put off.'

'Speak for yourself, father,' said Whelan, raising his stubborn old peasant head and quelling fraternization with a glance. 'I wouldn't be grateful to anyone for doing what 'tis his simple duty to do.'

'Then perhaps you'd better explain your errand yourself, Father Whelan,' Devine said with an abnegation that wasn't far removed from positive waspishness.

'I think so, father,' said Whelan, unaware of the rebuke. 'That girl, Captain Whatever-your-name-is, has no business to be on your ship at all. It is no place for a young unmarried girl to be at this hour of night.'

'I don't understand,' the captain said uneasily, with a sideway glance at Devine that begged for an interpreter. 'This girl is a relative of yours?'

'No, sir,' Whelan said emphatically. 'She's nothing whatever to me.'

'Then I don't see what you want with her,' said the captain.

'That's only as I'd expect, sir,' Whelan replied boorishly.

'Oh, for Heaven's sake!' Devine interrupted impatiently. 'We'll be here all night at this rate . . . You see, captain,' he said patiently, bending forward with his anxious air, his head tilted back so that the pince-nez wouldn't fall off, 'this girl is one of Father Whelan's parishioners. She's not a very good girl – I don't mean there's any harm in her,' he added hastily, catching the censoriousness in the words and feeling ashamed of himself. 'It's just that she's a bit wild. It's Father Whelan's duty to keep her out of temptation so far as he can. He is a shepherd, and she is one of his sheep,' he added with a faint smile at his own eloquence.

The captain bent forward and touched him lightly on the knee.

'You're a funny race,' he said with interest. 'All over the world I meet Englishmen, and you are all the same, and I will never understand you. Never!'

'We're not Englishmen,' Whelan said with the first trace of animation he had shown. 'Don't you know what country you're in? This is Ireland.'

'Same thing,' said the captain.

'It is not the same thing,' said Whelan.

'Pooh!' snorted the captain.

'Surely, captain,' Devine protested gently, 'we admit some distinction.'

'Distinction?' the captain said. 'What distinction?'

'At the Battle of the Boyne you fought for us,' Devine said persuasively. 'We fought for you at Fontenoy and Ramillies.

> *When on Ramillies' bloody field*
> *The baffled French were forced to yield,*
> *The victor Saxons backward reeled*
> *Before the shock of Clare's Dragoons.'*

He recited the lines with the same apologetic smile he had worn when speaking of sheep and shepherds, but they seemed to have no effect on the captain.

'No, no, no,' he cried. 'There is no difference. No difference at all. You call yourselves Irish, the others call themselves Scotch, but you are all English. It is always the same: always women, always hypocrisy, always excuses. *Toujours des excuses!* Who is this girl? The *curé*'s daughter?'

'The *curé*'s daughter?' Devine repeated in surprise.

'Whose dau.....r?' Whelan asked with his mouth hanging open.

'Yours, I gather,' Devine said drily.

'Well, well, well!' the old man said, blushing. 'What sort of up-bringing do they have? Does he even know we can't get married?'

'That, I should say, he takes for granted,' replied Devine over his shoulder. '*Elle n'est pas sa fille,*' he added with amusement to the captain.

'*C'est sûr?*'

'*C'est certain.*'

'*Sa maîtresse alors?*'

'*Ni cela non plus,*' Devine replied evenly with only the faintest of smiles on the worn shell of his face.

'*Ah, bon, bon, bon!*' the captain said excitedly, springing from his seat and striding about the cabin, scowling and waving his arms. '*Vous vous moquez de moi, monsieur le curé. Comprenez donc, c'est seulement par politesse que j'ai voulu faire croire que c'était sa fille. On voit bien que le vieux est jaloux. Est-ce que je n'ai pas vu les flics qui surveillent mon bateau toute la semaine? Mais croyez-moi, monsieur, je me fiche de lui et de ses agents.*'

'He seems very excited about something,' Whelan said with distaste. 'What's he saying?'

'I'm trying to persuade him that she's not your mistress now,' Devine could not refrain from saying with quiet malice.

'My what?'

'Your mistress. The woman he thinks you live with. He says you're jealous and that you've had detectives watching his ship for a week.'

The blush which had risen to the old man's face now began to spread to his neck and ears, and when he spoke, his voice quavered with real emotion.

'We'd better go home, father,' he said. ''Tis useless talking to that man. He's either mad or bad.'

'He seems to think exactly the same of us,' said Devine as he rose. '*Venez manger demain soir et je vous expliquerai tout,*' he added to the captain.

'*Je vous remercie, monsieur,*' the captain replied with a shrug. '*Mais je n'ai pas besoin d'explications. Il n'y a rien d'inattendu, mais vous en faites toute une histoire.*' He clapped his hand jovially on Devine's shoulder and almost embraced him. '*Naturellement – je vous rends la fille, parce que vous la demandez, mais comprenez bien que je fais à cause de vous, et non pas à cause de monsieur et de ses agents.*' He drew himself up to his full height and glared at the parish priest, who stood in a dumb stupor like a cow just fallen from a cliff.

'*Oh, quant à moi, vous feriez mieux en l'emmenant où vous allez,*' Devine said with weary humour. '*Moi-même, aussi, parbleu!*'

'*Quoi? Vous l'aimez aussi?*' shouted the captain in desperation.

'No, no, no, no,' Devine said good-humouredly, patting him on the arm. 'It's all too complicated. I wouldn't try to understand it if I were you.'

'What's he saying now?' Whelan asked with some suspicion.

'Oh, it seems he thinks she's my mistress as well,' Devine replied pleasantly. 'He thinks we're sharing her.'

'Come on, come on!'Whelan said despairingly. 'My goodness, even I never thought they were as bad as that. And we sending missions to the blacks!'

Meanwhile, the captain had rushed aft and shouted down the companionway. A second girl appeared, also weeping, and the captain, quite moved, slapped her encouragingly on the shoulder and said something in a gruff voice which Devine didn't hear. Either he was telling her to choose younger lovers for the future or advising her to come back when the coast was clear. Devine hoped it was the latter. Then the captain went up bristling to Sullivan, who stood by the gangway, leaning on his rolled-up umbrella, and ordered him rudely off the vessel.

'*Allez-vous-en!*' he said curtly. '*Allez, allez, allez!*'

Sullivan and Sheridan went first. Dusk had crept suddenly along the quay and lay heaped there coloured like blown sand. Over the bright river mouth, shining under a bank of cloud, one lonely star twinkled. 'The star that bids the shepherd fold,' Devine thought with mournful humour. He felt hopeless and lost. Whelan preceded him down the gangway with his old woman's dull face sunk in his broad barrel chest. At the foot he stopped and looked back at the captain, who was scowling fiercely over the ship's side.

'Anyway, thanks be to the almighty God that your accursed race is withering off the face of the earth,' he said heavily.

Devine, with a rueful smile, raised his battered old hat and pulled the skirts of his coat about him as he stepped down the gangway.

'*Vous viendrez demain, monsieur le capitaine?*' he asked gently.

'*Avec plaisir. A demain, Monsieur le berger,*' replied the captain with a knowing look.

Crab Apple Jelly (1944)

The Mad Lomasneys

1

Ned Lowry and Rita Lomasney had, one might say, been lovers from childhood. The first time they had met was when he was fourteen and she a year or two younger. It was on the North Mall on a Saturday afternoon, and she was sitting on a bench by the river under the trees; a tall, bony string of a girl with a long, obstinate jaw. Ned was a studious-looking young fellow in a blue and white college cap – thin, pale and spectacled. As he passed he looked at her owlishly, and she gave him back an impudent stare. This upset him – he had no experience of girls – so he blushed and raised his cap. At this she seemed to relent.

'Hullo,' she said experimentally.

'Good afternoon,' he replied with a pale, prissy smile.

'Where are you off to?' she asked.

'Oh, just up the Dyke for a walk.'

'Sit down,' she said in a sharp voice, laying her hand on the bench beside her, and he did as he was told. It was a summer evening, and the white quay walls and tall, crazy, claret-coloured tenements under a blue and white sky were reflected in the lazy water, which wrinkled only at the edges and seemed like a painted carpet.

'It's very pleasant here,' he said complacently.

'Is it?' she asked with a truculence that startled him. 'I don't see anything very pleasant about it.'

'Oh, it's very nice and quiet,' he said in mild surprise as he raised his fair eyebrows and looked up and down the Mall. 'My name is Lowry,' he added politely.

'Are ye the ones that have the jeweller's shop on the Parade?' she asked.

'That's right,' he replied with modest pride.

'We have a clock we got from ye,' she said. ''Tisn't much good of an old clock either,' she added with quiet malice.

'You should bring it back to the shop,' he said with concern. 'It probably needs overhauling.'

'I'm going down the river in a boat with a couple of fellows,' she said, going off at a tangent. 'Will you come?'

'Couldn't,' he said with a smile.

'Why not?'

'I'm only left go up the Dyke for a walk,' he replied complacently. 'On Saturdays I go to Confession at St Peter and Paul's; then I go up the Dyke and come back the Western Road. Sometimes you see very good cricket matches. Do you like cricket?'

'A lot of old sissies pucking a ball!' she said shortly. 'I do not.'

'I like it,' he said firmly. 'I go up there every Saturday when it's fine. Of course, I'm not supposed to talk to anyone,' he added with mild amusement at his own audacity.

'Why not?'

'My mother doesn't like me to.'

'Why doesn't she?'

'She comes of an awfully good family,' he answered mildly, and but for his gentle smile she might have thought he was deliberately insulting her. 'You see,' he went on gravely in his thin, pleasant voice, ticking things off on his fingers and then glancing at each finger individually as he ticked it off – a tidy sort of boy – 'there are three main branches of the Hourigan family: the Neddy Neds, the Neddy Jerrys, and the Neddy Thomases. The Neddy Neds are the Hayfield Hourigans. They are the oldest branch. My mother is a Hayfield Hourigan, and she'd have been a rich woman only for her father backing a bill for a Neddy Jerry. He defaulted and ran away to Australia,' he concluded with a contemptuous sniff.

'Cripes!' said the girl. 'And had she to pay?'

'She had. But of course,' he went on with as close as he ever seemed likely to get to a burst of real enthusiasm, 'my grandfather was a very well-behaved man. When he was eating his dinner the boys from the National School in Bantry used to be brought up to watch him, he had such beautiful table manners. Once he caught my uncle eating cabbage with a knife, and he struck him with a poker. They had to put four stitches in him after,' he added with a joyous chuckle.

'Cripes!' said the girl again. 'What did he do that for?'

'To teach him manners,' Ned said earnestly.

'That's a queer way to teach him manners. He must have been dotty.'

'Oh, I wouldn't say that,' Ned said, a bit ruffled. Everything this girl said seemed to come as a shock to him. 'But that's why my mother won't let us mix with other children. On the other hand, we read a good deal. Are you fond of reading, Miss – I didn't catch the name.'

'You weren't told it,' she said quietly, showing her claws. 'But, if you want to know, it's Rita Lomasney.'

'Do you read much, Miss Lomasney?'

'I couldn't be bothered.'

'I read everything,' he said enthusiastically. 'And as well as that, I'm learning the violin from Miss Maude on the Parade. Of course, it's very difficult, because it's all classical music.'

'What's that?'

'*Maritana* is classical music,' he said eagerly. He was a bit of a puzzle to Rita. She had never before met anyone who had such a passion for teaching. 'Were you at *Maritana* in the Opera House, Miss Lomasney?'

'I was never there at all,' she said curtly, humiliated.

'And *Alice Where Art Thou* is classical music,' he added. 'It's harder than plain music. It has signs like this on it' – he began to draw things on the air – 'and when you see the signs, you know it's after turning into a different tune, though it has the same name. Irish music is all the same tune and that's why my mother won't let us learn it.'

'Were you ever at the Opera in Paris?' she asked suddenly.

'No,' said Ned with regret. 'I was never in Paris. Were you?'

'That's where you ought to go,' she said with airy enthusiasm. 'You couldn't hear any operas here. The staircase alone is bigger than the whole Opera House here.'

It seemed as if they were in for a really informative conversation when two fellows came down Wyse's Hill. Rita got up to meet them. Ned looked up at them for a moment and then rose too, lifting his college cap politely.

'Well, good afternoon,' he said cheerfully. 'I enjoyed the talk. I hope we meet again.'

'Some other Saturday,' said Rita with regret. By this time she would readily have gone up the Dyke and even watched cricket with him if he asked her.

'Oh, good evening, old man,' one of the fellows said in an affected English accent, pretending to raise a top hat. 'Do come and see us soon again.'

'Shut up, Foster, or I'll give you a puck in the gob!' Rita said sharply.

'Oh, by the way,' Ned said, returning to hand her a number of the *Gem*, which he took from his jacket pocket, 'you might like to look at this. It's not bad.'

'I'd love to,' she said insincerely, and he smiled and touched his cap again. Then with a polite and almost deferential air he went up to Foster. 'Did you say something?' he asked.

Foster looked as astonished as though a kitten had suddenly got up on his hind legs and challenged him to fight.

'I did not,' he said, and backed away.

'I'm glad,' Ned said, almost purring. 'I was afraid you might be looking for trouble.'

It astonished Rita. 'There's a queer one for you!' she said when Ned had gone. But she was curiously pleased to see that he was no sissy. She didn't like sissies.

2

The Lomasneys lived on Sunday's Well in a small house with a long sloping garden and a fine view of the river and the city. Harry Lomasney, the builder, was a small man who wore grey tweed suits and soft collars several sizes too big for him. He had a ravaged brick-red face with keen blue eyes, and a sandy straggling moustache with one side going up and the other down, and the workmen said you could tell what humour he was in by the side he pulled. He was nicknamed 'Hasty Harry'. 'Great God!' he fumed when his wife was having her first baby. 'Nine months over a little job like that! I'd do it in three weeks if I could get started.'

His wife was tall and matronly and very pious, but her piety never got much in her way. A woman who had survived Hasty would have survived anything. Their eldest daughter, Kitty, was loud-voiced and gay, and had been expelled from school for writing indecent letters to a boy. She had failed to tell the nuns that she had copied the letters out of a French novel and didn't know what they meant. Nellie was placider than her sister and took more after her mother; besides, she didn't read French novels.

Rita was the exception among the girls. She seemed to have no softness, never had a favourite saint or a favourite nun, and said it was soppy. For the same reason she never had flirtations. Her friendship with Ned Lowry was the nearest she got to that, and though Ned came regularly to the house and took her to the pictures every week, her sisters would have found it hard to say if she ever did anything with him she wouldn't do with a girl. There was something tongue-tied, twisted, and unhappy in her. She had a curious, raw, almost timid smile as though she thought people only intended to hurt her. At home she was reserved, watchful, mocking. She could listen for hours to her mother and sisters without opening her mouth, and then suddenly mystify them by dropping a well-aimed jaw-breaker – about classical music, for instance – before relapsing into sulky silence, as though she had merely drawn back the veil for a moment on depths in herself she would not permit them to explore. This annoyed her sisters, because they knew there weren't any depths; it was all swank.

After taking her degree, she got a job in a convent school in a provincial town in the west of Ireland. She and Ned corresponded, and he even went to see her there. At home he reported that she seemed quite happy.

But it didn't last. A few months later, the Lomasneys were at supper when they heard a car stop; the gate squeaked, and steps came up the long path to the front door. Then came the bell and a cheerful voice from the hall.

'Hullo, Paschal, I suppose ye weren't expecting me?'

''Tis never Rita!' said her mother, meaning that it was but shouldn't be.

'As true as God, that one is after getting into trouble,' said Kitty prophetically.

The door opened and Rita slouched in; a long, stringy girl with a dark, glowing face. She kissed her father and mother lightly.

'What happened to you at all, child?' her mother asked placidly.

'Nothing,' replied Rita, an octave up the scale. 'I just got the sack.'

'The sack?' said her father, beginning to pull the wrong side of his moustache. 'What did you get the sack for?' Hasty would sack a man three times in a day, but nobody paid any attention.

'Give us a chance to get something to eat first, can't you?' Rita said laughingly. She took off her hat and smiled at herself in the mirror above the mantelpiece. It was a curious smile as though she were amused by what she saw. Then she smoothed back her thick black hair. 'I told Paschal to bring in whatever was going. I'm on the train since ten. The heating was off as usual. I'm frizzled.'

'A wonder you wouldn't send us a wire,' said Mrs Lomasney as Rita sat down and grabbed some bread and butter.

'Hadn't the cash,' said Rita.

'But what happened, Rita?' Kitty asked brightly.

'You'll hear it all in due course. Reverend Mother is bound to write and tell ye how I lost my character.'

'Wisha, what did you do to her, child?' asked her mother with amusement. She had been through all this before, with Hasty and Kitty, and she knew that God was very good and nothing much ever happened.

'Fellow that wanted to marry me,' said Rita. 'He was in his last year at college, and his mother didn't like me, so she got Reverend Mother to give me the push.'

'But what business is it of hers?' asked Nellie.

'None whatever, girl,' said Rita.

But Kitty looked suspiciously at her. Rita wasn't natural: there was something about her that was not in control. After all, this was her first real love affair, and Kitty could not believe that she had gone about it like anyone else.

'Still, you worked pretty fast,' she said.

'You'd have to work fast in that place,' said Rita. 'There was only one possible man in the whole place – the bank clerk. We used to call him "The One". I wasn't there a week when a nun ticked me off for riding on the pillion of his motor-bike.'

'And did you?' Kitty asked innocently.

'Fat chance I got!' said Rita. 'They did that to every teacher to give her the idea that she was well-watched. The unfortunates were scared out of their wits. I only met Tony Donoghue a fortnight ago. He was home with a breakdown.'

'Well, well, well!' said her mother without rancour. 'No wonder his poor mother was upset. A boy that's not left college yet! Couldn't ye wait till he was qualified anyway?'

'Not very well,' said Rita. 'He's going to be a priest.'

Kitty sat back with a superior grin. She had known it all the time. Of course, Rita couldn't do anything like other people. If it hadn't been a priest it would have been a married man or a Negro, and Rita would have shown off about it just the same.

'What's that you say?' her father asked, springing to his feet.

'All right, don't blame me!' Rita said hastily, beaming at him. 'It wasn't my fault. He said he didn't want to be a priest. His mother was driving him into it. That's why he had the breakdown.'

'Let me out of this before I have a breakdown myself,' said Hasty. 'I'm the one that should be the priest. If I was I wouldn't be saddled with a mad, distracted family the way I am.'

He stamped out of the room, and the girls laughed. The idea of their father as a priest appealed to them almost as much as the idea of him as a mother. But Mrs Lomasney did not laugh.

'Reverend Mother was perfectly right,' she said severely. 'As if it wasn't hard enough on the poor boys without girls like you throwing temptation in their way. I think you behaved very badly, Rita.'

'All right, if you say so,' Rita said shortly with a boyish shrug, and refused to talk any more about it.

After supper, she said she was tired and went to bed, and her mother and sisters sat on in the front room, discussing the scandal. Someone rang and Nellie opened the door.

'Hullo, Ned,' she said. 'I suppose you came up to congratulate us.'

'Hullo,' Ned said, smiling primly with closed lips. With a sort of automatic movement he took off his overcoat and hat and hung them on the rack. Then he emptied the pockets with the same thoroughness. He had not changed much. He was thin and pale, spectacled and clever, with the same precise and tranquil manner – 'like an old Persian cat', as Nellie said. He read too many books. In the last year or two something seemed to have happened to him. He did not go to Mass any longer. Not going to Mass struck all the Lomasneys as too damn clever. 'On what?' he added, having avoided any unnecessary precipitation.

'You didn't know who was here?'

'No,' he said, raising his brows mildly.

'Rita!'

'Oh!' The same tone. It was part of his cleverness not to be surprised at anything. It was as though he regarded any attempt to surprise him as an invasion of his privacy.

'She's after getting the sack for trying to run off with a priest,' said Nellie.

If she thought that would shake him she was badly mistaken. He tossed his head with a silent chuckle and went into the room, adjusting his pince-nez. For a fellow who was supposed to be in love with her, this was very peculiar behaviour, Nellie thought. He put his hands in his trousers pockets and stood on the hearth with his legs well apart.

'Isn't it awful, Ned?' Mrs Lomasney asked in her deep voice.

'Is it?' Ned purred, smiling.

'With a priest!' cried Nellie.

'Now, he wasn't a priest, Nellie,' Mrs Lomasney said severely. 'Don't be trying to make it worse.'

'Suppose you tell me what happened,' suggested Ned.

'But sure, when we don't know, Ned,' cried Mrs Lomasney. 'You know what that one is like in one of her sulky fits. Maybe she'll tell you. She's up in bed.'

'I may as well try,' said Ned.

Still with his hands in his pockets, he rolled after Mrs Lomasney up the thickly carpeted stairs to Rita's little bedroom at the top of the house. While Mrs Lomasney went in to see that her daughter was decent he paused to look out over the river and the lighted city behind it. Rita, wearing a pink dressing jacket, was lying with one arm under her head. By the bed was a table with a packet of cigarettes she had been using as an ashtray. He smiled and shook his head reprovingly.

'Hullo, Ned,' she said, reaching him a bare arm. 'Give us a kiss. I'm quite kissable now.'

He didn't need to be told that. He was astonished at the change in her. Her whole bony, boyish face seemed to have gone soft and mawkish and to be lit up from inside. He sat on an armchair by the bed, carefully pulling up the bottoms of his trousers, then put his hands in the pockets again and sat back with crossed legs.

'I suppose they're hopping downstairs,' said Rita.

'They seem a little excited,' Ned replied, with bowed head cocked sideways, looking like some wise old bird.

'Wait till they hear the details!' Rita said grimly.

'Are there details?' he asked mildly.

'Masses of them,' said Rita. 'Honest to God, Ned, I used to laugh at the glamour girls in the convent. I never knew you could get like that about a fellow. It's like something busting inside you. Cripes, I'm as soppy as a kid!'

'And what's the fellow like?' Ned asked curiously.

'Tony? How the hell do I know? He's decent enough, I suppose. His mother has a shop in the Main Street. He kissed me one night coming home and I was so furious I cut the socks off him. Next evening, he came round to apologize, and I never got up or asked him to sit down or anything. I suppose I was still mad with him. He said he never slept a wink. "Didn't you?" said I. "It didn't trouble me much." Bloody lies, of course; I was twisting and turning the whole night. "I only did it because I was so fond of you," says he. "Is that what you told the last one, too?" said I. That got him into a wax as well, and he said I was calling him a liar. "And aren't you?" said I. Then I waited for him to hit me, but instead he began to cry, and then I began to cry – imagine me crying, Ned! – and the next thing I was sitting on his knee. Talk about the Babes in the Wood. First time he ever had a girl on his knee, he said, and you know how much of it I did.'

There was a discreet knock and Mrs Lomasney smiled benevolently at them round the door.

'I suppose 'tis tea Ned is having?' she asked in her deep voice.

'No, I'm having the tea,' Rita said lightly, throwing him a cigarette. 'Ned says he'd sooner a drop of the hard tack.'

'Oh, isn't that a great change, Ned?' cried Mrs Lomasney.

''Tis the shock,' said Rita. 'He didn't think I was that sort of girl.'

'He mustn't know much about girls,' said Mrs Lomasney.

'He's learning now,' said Rita.

When Paschal brought up the tray, Rita poured out tea for Ned and whiskey for herself. He made no comment: things like that were a commonplace in the Lomasney household.

'Anyway,' she went on, pulling at her cigarette, 'he told his old one he wanted to chuck the Church and marry me. There was ructions. The people in the shop at the other side of the street had a son a priest, and she wanted to be as good as them. Away with her up to Reverend Mother, and Reverend Mother sends for me. Did I want to destroy the young man and he on the threshold of a great calling? I told her 'twas his mother wanted to destroy him, and I asked her what sort of a priest did she think Tony would make. Oh, he'd be twice the man, after a sacrifice like that. Honest to God, Ned, the way that woman went on, you'd think she was talking of doctoring an old tom-cat. I think this damn country must be full of female vets. After that, she dropped the Holy Willie stuff and told me his mother was after getting into debt to put him in for the priesthood, and if he chucked it now, she'd never be able to pay it back. Wouldn't they kill you with style?'

'And what did you do then?'

'I went to see his mother, of course.'

'You didn't!'

'I told you I was off my head. I thought I might work it with the personal touch.'

'You don't seem to have been successful.'

'I'd as soon try the personal touch on a traction engine, Ned,' Rita said ruefully. 'That woman was twice my weight. I told her I wanted to marry Tony. "I'm sorry, you can't," she said. "What's to stop me?" says I. "He's gone too far," says she. "If he was gone further it wouldn't stop me," says I. I told her then what Reverend Mother said about the three hundred pounds and offered to pay it back for her if she let me marry him.'

'And had you the three hundred?' Ned asked in surprise.

'Ah, where would I get three hundred? And she knew it, the old jade! She didn't believe a word I said. I saw Tony afterwards, and he was crying. He said he didn't want to break her heart. I declare to God, Ned, that woman has as much heart as a traction engine.'

'Well, you seem to have done it in style,' said Ned as he put away his teacup.

'That wasn't the half of it. When I heard the difficulties his mother was making, I offered to live with him instead.'

'Live with him!' said Ned. That startled even him.

'Well, go away on holidays with him. Lots of girls do it. I know they do. And, God Almighty, isn't it only natural?'

'And what did he say to that?' Ned asked curiously.

'He was scared stiff.'

'He would be,' said Ned, giving his superior little sniff as he took out a packet of cigarettes.

'Oh, it's all very well for you,' cried Rita, bridling up. 'You may think you're a great fellow, all because you read Tolstoy and don't go to Mass, but you'd be just as scared if a doll offered to go to bed with you.'

'Try me,' he said sedately as he lit her cigarette, but somehow the idea of suggesting such a thing to Ned only made her laugh.

He stayed till quite late, and when he went downstairs Mrs Lomasney and the girls fell on him and dragged him into the sitting room.

'Well, doctor, how's the patient?' asked Mrs Lomasney.

'Oh, I think the patient is coming round nicely,' said Ned with a smile.

'But would you ever believe it, Ned?' she cried. 'A girl that wouldn't look at the side of the road a fellow was on, unless 'twas to go robbing orchards with him. You'll have another drop of whiskey?'

'I won't.'

'And is that all you're going to tell us?'

'You'll hear it all from herself.'

'We won't.'

'I dare say not,' he said with a hearty chuckle, and went for his coat.

'Wisha, Ned, what will your mother say when she hears it?' asked Mrs Lomasney, and Ned put his nose in the air and gave an exaggerated version of what Mrs Lomasney called 'his Hayfield sniff'.

'"All *quite* mad",' he said.

'The dear knows, she might be right,' she said with resignation, helping him on with his coat. 'I hope your mother doesn't notice the smell of whiskey from your breath,' she added drily just to show him that she missed nothing, and then stood at the door, looking up and down, while she waited for him to wave from the gate.

'Ah, with the help of God it might be all for the best,' she said as she closed the door behind him.

'If you think he's going to marry her, you're mistaken,' said Kitty. 'Merciful God, I'd like to see myself telling Bill O'Donnell a thing like that. He'd have my sacred life. That fellow positively enjoys it.'

'Ah, God is good,' her mother said cheerfully, kicking a mat into place. 'Some men might like that.'

*

3

Ned apparently did, but he was the only one. Within a week, Kitty and Nellie were sick to death of Rita round the house. She was bad enough at the best of times – or so they said – but now she brooded and mooned and quarrelled. Most afternoons she strolled down the Dyke to Ned's little shop where she sat on the counter, swinging her legs and smoking, while Ned leaned against the window, tinkering with some delicate instrument at the insides of a watch. Nothing seemed to rattle Ned, not even Rita doing what no customer would dare to do. When he finished work he changed his coat and they went out to tea. He sat in a corner at the back of the teashop, pulled up the bottoms of his trousers, and took out a packet of cigarettes and a box of matches, which he placed on the table before him with a look that commanded them to stay there and not get lost. His face was pale and clear and bright, like an evening sky when the last light has drained from it.

'Anything wrong?' he asked one evening when she was moodier than usual.

'Oh, just fed up,' she said thrusting out her jaw.

'Still fretting?' he asked in surprise.

'Ah, no. I can get over that. It's Kitty and Nellie. They're bitches, Ned; proper bitches. And all because I don't wear my heart on my sleeve. If one of them got dumped by a fellow she'd take two aspirins and go to bed with the other one. They'd have a lovely talk – can't you imagine? "And was it then he said he loved you?" That sort of balls! I can't do it. And it's all because they're not sincere, Ned. They couldn't be sincere.'

'Remember, they have a long start on you,' Ned said.

'Is that it?' she asked without interest. 'They think I'm batty. Do you, Ned?'

'Not altogether,' he said with a tight-lipped smile. 'I've no doubt that Mrs Donoghue, if that's her name, thought something of the sort.'

'And wasn't she right?' Rita asked tensely. 'Suppose she'd agreed to take the three hundred quid, wouldn't I be properly shown up? I wake in a sweat whenever I think of it. I'm just a bloody chancer, Ned. Where would I get three hundred quid?'

'Oh, I dare say someone would have lent it to you,' he said with a shrug.

'They would like hell. Would you?'

'Probably,' he said gravely after a moment's thought. 'I think I could raise it.'

'Are you serious?' she whispered earnestly.

'Quite,' he said in the same tone.

'Cripes, you must be very fond of me,' she gasped.

'Looks like it,' said Ned, and this time he laughed with real heartiness; a boy's laugh of sheer delight at her astonishment. Of course, it was just like Rita to regard a lifetime's friendship as sport, and the offer of three hundred pounds as the real thing.

'Would you marry me?' she asked with a frown. 'I'm not proposing to you, mind, only asking,' she added hastily.

'Certainly, whenever you like,' he said, spreading his hands.

'Honest to God?'

'Cut my throat,' he replied, making the schoolboy gesture.

'My God, why didn't you ask me before I went down to that kip? I'd have married you like a shot. Was it the way you weren't keen on me?' she added, wondering if there wasn't really something queer about him, as her sisters said.

'No,' he replied matter-of-factly, drawing himself together like an old clock preparing to strike. 'I think I've been keen on you since the first day I met you.'

'It's easily seen you're a Neddy Ned,' she said. 'I go after mine with a scalping knife.'

'I stalk mine,' he said smugly.

'Cripes, Ned,' she said with real regret, 'I wish you'd told me sooner. I couldn't marry you now.'

'Couldn't you? Why not?'

'Because it wouldn't be fair to you.'

'You think I can't look after myself?'

'I have to look after you now.' She glanced round the restaurant to make sure that no one was listening, and then went on in a dry, dispassionate voice, leaning one elbow wearily on the table. 'I suppose you'll think this is all cod, but it's not. Honest to God, I think you're the finest bloody man I ever met – even though you do think you're an atheist or something,' she interjected maliciously with a characteristic Lomasney flourish in the cause of Faith and Fatherland. 'There's no one in the world I have more respect for. I think I'd nearly cut my throat if I did something you really disapproved of – I don't mean telling lies or going on a skite,' she added hastily. 'That's only gas. I mean something that really shocked you. I think if I was tempted I'd ask myself: "How the hell would I face Lowry afterwards?"'

For a moment she thought from his smile that he was going to cry. Then he squelched the butt of his cigarette on a plate and spoke in an extraordinarily quiet voice.

'That'll do me grand for a beginning,' he said.

'It wouldn't, Ned,' she said sadly. 'That's why I say I have to look after you now. You couldn't understand it unless it happened to yourself and you fell in love with a doll the way I fell in love with Tony. Tony is a scut, and a cowardly scut at that, but I was cracked about him. If he came in here now and asked me to go off to Killarney on a weekend with him, I'd buy a nightdress and a toothbrush and go. And I wouldn't give a damn what you or anybody thought. I might chuck myself in the lake afterwards, but I'd go. Christ, Ned,' she exclaimed, flushing and looking as though she might burst into tears, 'he couldn't come into a room but I went all mushy inside. That's what the real thing is like.'

'Well,' said Ned, apparently not in the least put out – in fact, looking rather pleased with himself, Rita thought – 'I'm in no hurry. In case you get tired of scalping them, the offer will still be open.'

'Thanks, Ned,' she said absent-mindedly, as though she weren't listening.

While he paid the bill, she stood in the porch, doing her face in the big mirror that flanked it, and paying no attention to the crowds who were hurrying homeward through lighted streets. As she emerged from the shop she turned on him suddenly.

'About that matter, Ned,' she said. 'Will you ask me again, or do I have to ask you?'

He just managed to refrain from laughing outright.

'As you like,' he said with quiet amusement. 'Suppose I repeat the proposal every six months.'

'That would be a hell of a time to wait if I changed my mind,' she said with a scowl. 'All right,' she added, taking his arm. 'I know you well enough to ask you. If you don't want me by that time, you can always say so. I won't mind. I'm used to it now.'

4

Ned's proposal came as a considerable support to Rita. It buttressed her self-esteem, which was always in danger of collapsing. She might be ugly and uneducated and a bit of a chancer, but the best man in Cork – the best in Ireland, she sometimes thought – wanted to marry her, even when she had been let down by another man. That was a queer one for her enemies! So while Kitty and Nellie made fun of her, she bided her time, waiting till she could really rock them. Since her childhood she had never given anything away without squeezing the last ounce of theatrical effect from it. She would tell her sisters, but not till she could make them feel properly sick.

It was a pity she didn't because Ned was not the only one. There was also Justin Sullivan, the lawyer, who had once been by way of being engaged to Nellie. He had not become engaged to her because Nellie was as slippery as an eel, and had her cap set all the time at a solicitor called Fahy whom Justin despised with his whole heart and soul as a lightheaded, butterfly sort of man. But Justin continued to come to the house. There happened to be no other that suited him half as well, and besides, he knew that sooner or later Nellie would make a mess of her life with Fahy, and his services would be required.

Justin, in fact, was a sticker. He was a good deal older than Rita; a tall, burly man with a broad face, a brow that was rising from baldness as well as brains, and a slow, watchful, ironic air. Like many lawyers he tended to conduct a conversation as though the person he was speaking to was a hostile witness who had to be coaxed into an admission of perjury or bullied into one of mental deficiency.

When Justin began to talk Fahy simply clutched his head and retired to sit on the stairs. 'Can no one shut that fellow up?' he would moan with a martyred air. No one could. The girls shot their little darts at him, but he only brushed them aside. Ned was the only one who could even stand up to him, and when the two of them argued about religion, the room became a desert. Justin, of course, was all for the Church. 'Imagine for a moment that I am Pope,' he would declaim in a throaty, rounded voice that turned easily to pompousness. 'Easiest thing in the world, Justin,' Kitty assured him once. He drank whiskey like water, and the more he drank, the more massive and logical and piously Catholic he became.

But for all his truculent airs he was exceedingly gentle, patient and understanding, and disliked the way her sisters ragged Rita.

'Tell me, Nellie,' he asked one night in his lazy, amiable way, 'do you talk like that to Rita because you like it, or out of a sense of duty?'

'How soft you have it!' cried Nellie. 'We have to live with her. You haven't.'

'That may be my misfortune, Nellie,' said Justin.

'Is that a proposal, Justin?' Kitty asked shrewdly.

'Scarcely, Kitty,' said Justin. 'You're not what I might call a good jury.'

'Better be careful or you'll have her calling on your mother, Justin,' Kitty said maliciously.

'I hope my mother has sufficient sense to realize it would be an honour, Kitty,' Justin said severely.

When he rose to go, Rita accompanied him to the hall.

'Thanks for the moral support, Justin,' she said in a low voice and threw an overcoat over her shoulders to accompany him to the gate. When he opened the door they both stood and gazed round them. It was a moonlit night: the garden, patterned in black and silver, sloped to the quiet suburban roadway where the gas lamps burned with a dim green light. Beyond this gateways shaded by black trees led to flights of steps or steep-sloping avenues behind the moonlit houses on the river's edge.

'God, isn't it lovely?' said Rita.

'Oh, by the way, Rita, that was a proposal,' he said, slipping his arm through hers.

'Janey Mack, they're falling,' she said, and gave his arm a squeeze.

'What are?'

'Proposals. I never knew I was so popular.'

'Why? Have you had others?'

'I had one anyway.'

'And did you accept it?'

'No,' Rita said doubtfully. 'Not quite. At least, I don't think I did.'

'You might consider this one,' Justin said with unusual humility. 'You know, of course, that I was very fond of Nellie. At one time I was very fond of her, indeed. You don't mind that, I hope. It's all over and done with now, and no regrets on either side.'

'No, Justin, of course I don't mind. If I felt like marrying you I wouldn't give it a second thought. But I was very much in love with Tony too, and that's not all over and done with yet.'

'I know that, Rita,' he said gently. 'I know exactly what you feel. We've all been through it.' He might as well have left it there, but, being a lawyer, Justin liked to see his case properly set out. 'That won't last forever. In a month or two you'll be over it, and then you'll wonder what you saw in that fellow.'

'I don't think so, Justin,' she said with a crooked smile, not altogether displeased to be able to enlighten him about the utter hopelessness of her position. 'I think it will take a great deal longer than that.'

'Well, say six months even,' Justin went on, prepared to yield a point to the defence. 'All I ask is that in one month or six, when you've got over your regrets for this – this amiable young man,' (momentarily his voice took on its familiar ironic tone) 'you'll give me a thought. I'm old enough not to make any more mistakes. I know I'm fond of you, and I feel sure I could make a success of my end of it.'

'What you really mean is that I wasn't in love with Tony at all,' Rita said, keeping her temper with the greatest difficulty. 'Isn't that it?'

'Not quite,' Justin replied judiciously. Even if he had had a serenade as well as moonlight and a girl, Justin could not have resisted correcting what he considered a false deduction. 'I've no doubt you were very much attracted by this – this clerical Adonis; this Mr Whatever-his-name-is, or that at any rate you thought you were, which in practice comes to the same thing, but I also know that that sort of thing, though it's painful enough while it lasts, doesn't last very long.'

'You mean yours didn't, Justin,' Rita said tartly. By this time she was flaming.

'I mean mine or anyone else's,' said Justin. 'Because love – the only sort of thing you can really call love – is something that comes with experience. You're probably too young yet to know what the real thing is.'

As Rita had only recently told Ned that he didn't yet know what the real thing was, she found this very hard to stomach.

'How old would you say you'd have to be,' she asked viciously. 'Thirty-five?'

'You'll know soon enough – when it hits you,' said Justin.

'Honest to God, Justin,' she said withdrawing her arm and looking at him furiously, 'I think you're the thickest man I ever met.'

'Goodnight, my dear,' said Justin with perfect good humour, and he took the few steps to the gate at a run.

Rita stood gazing after him with folded arms. At the age of twenty to be told that there is anything you don't know about love is like a knife in your heart.

5

Kitty and Nellie persuaded Mrs Lomasney that the best way of distracting Rita's mind was to find her a new job. As a new environment was also supposed to be good for her complaint, Mrs Lomasney wrote to her sister, who was a nun in England, and the sister found her work in a convent there. Rita let on to be indifferent though she complained bitterly enough to Ned.

'But why England?' he asked in surprise.

'Why not?'

'Wouldn't any place nearer do you?'

'I suppose I wouldn't be far enough away.'

'But why not make up your own mind?'

'I'll probably do that too,' she said with a short laugh. 'I'd like to see what's in theirs first though. I might have a surprise for them.'

She certainly had that. She was to leave for England on Friday, and on Wednesday the girls gave a farewell party. Wednesday was the weekly half-holiday, and it rained steadily all day. The girls' friends all turned up. Most of these were men: Bill O'Donnell of the bank, who was engaged to Kitty; Fahy, the solicitor, who was Justin's successful rival for Nellie; Justin himself, who simply could not be kept out of the house by anything short of an injunction, Ned Lowry and a few others. Hasty soon retired with his wife to the dining room to read the evening paper. He said all his daughters' young men looked exactly alike and he never knew which of them he was talking to.

Bill O'Donnell was acting as barman. He was a big man, bigger even than Justin, with a battered boxer's face and a Negro smile that seemed to well up from the depths of good humour with life rather than from anything that happened in it. He carried out loud conversations with everyone he poured out a drink for, and his voice overrode every intervening tête-à-tête, and even challenged the piano, on which Nellie was vamping music-hall songs.

'Who's this one for, Rita?' he asked. 'A bottle of Bass for Paddy. Ah, the stout man! Remember the New Year's Night in Bandon, Paddy? Remember how you had to carry me up to the bank in evening dress and jack me up between the two wings of the desk? Kitty, did I ever tell you about that night in Bandon?'

'Once a week for the past five years, Bill,' Kitty sang out cheerfully.

'Nellie,' said Rita. 'I think it's time for Bill to sing his song. *Let Me Like a Soldier Fall*, Bill!'

'My one little song!' Bill said with a roar of laughter. 'The only song I know, but I sing it grand. Don't I, Nellie? Don't I sing it fine?'

'Fine!' agreed Nellie, looking up at his big moon-face beaming at her over the piano. 'As the man said to my mother, "Finest bloody soprano I ever heard."'

'He did not, Nellie,' Bill said sadly. 'You're making that up . . . Silence, please!' he shouted, clapping his hands. 'Ladies and gentlemen, I must apologize. I ought to sing something like Tosti's *Goodbye* but the fact is, ladies and gentlemen, that I don't know Tosti's *Goodbye*.'

'Recite it, Bill,' suggested Justin amiably.

'I don't know the words of it either, Justin,' said Bill. 'In fact, I'm not sure if there is any such song, but if there is, I ought to sing it.'

'Why, Bill?' asked Rita innocently. She was wearing a long black dress that threw up the unusual brightness of her dark, bony face. She looked more cheerful than she had looked for months. All the evening it was as though she were laughing to herself at something.

'Because 'twould be only right, Rita,' Bill said with great melancholy, putting his arm round her and drawing her closer. 'You know I'm very fond of you, don't you, Rita?'

'And I'm mad about you, Bill,' Rita said candidly.

'I know that, Rita,' he said mournfully, pulling at his collar as though to give himself air. 'I only wish you weren't going, Rita. This place isn't the same without you. Kitty won't mind my saying that,' he added with a nervous glance at Kitty, who was flirting with Justin on the sofa.

'Are you going to sing your blooming old song or not?' Nellie asked impatiently, running her fingers over the keys.

'I'm going to sing now in one minute, Nellie,' Bill replied ecstatically, stroking Rita fondly under the chin. 'I only want Rita to know we'll miss her.'

'Damn it, Bill,' Rita said, snuggling up to him, 'if you go on like that I won't go at all. Would you sooner I didn't go?'

'I would sooner it, Rita,' he said, stroking her cheeks and eyes. 'You're too good for the fellows there.'

'Oh, go on doing that, Bill,' she said. 'It's gorgeous, and you're making Kitty mad jealous.'

'Kitty isn't jealous,' Bill said mawkishly. 'Kitty is a lovely girl and you're a lovely girl. I hate to see you go, Rita.'

'That settles it, Bill,' she said, pulling herself free of him with a mock-determined air. 'As you feel that way about it, I won't go at all.'

'Won't you though!' said Kitty sweetly.

'Don't worry your head about it, Bill,' said Rita briskly. 'It's all off.'

Justin, who had been quietly getting through large whiskies, looked up lazily.

'Perhaps I should have mentioned that the young lady has just done me the honour of proposing to me, and I've accepted her,' he boomed.

Ned, who had been enjoying the little scene between Bill and Rita, looked at Justin in surprise.

'Bravo! Bravo!' cried Bill, clapping his hands with delight. 'A marriage has been arranged and all the rest of it – what? I must give you a kiss, Rita. Justin, you don't mind if I give Rita a kiss?'

'Not at all, not at all,' said Justin with a lordly wave of the hand. 'Anything that's mine is yours.'

'You're not serious, Justin, are you?' Kitty asked incredulously.

'Oh, I'm serious all right,' said Justin, and then he gave Rita a puzzled look. 'I'm not quite certain whether your sister is. Are you, Rita?'

'What?' Rita asked, as though she were listening to something else.

'Why? Are you trying to give me the push already?' asked Justin with amusement.

'We're much obliged for the information,' Nellie said angrily as she rose from the piano. 'I wonder did you tell Father?'

'Hardly,' said Rita coolly. 'It was only settled an hour ago.'

'Maybe 'twill do with some more settling by the time Father is done with you,' Nellie said furiously. 'The impudence of you! Go in at once and tell him.'

'Keep your hair on, girl,' Rita said with cool malice and then went jauntily out of the room. Kitty and Nellie began to squabble viciously with Justin. They were convinced that the whole scene had been arranged by Rita to make them look ridiculous, and in this they weren't very far out. Justin sat back and began to enjoy the sport. Then Ned struck a match and lit another cigarette, and something about the slow, careful way he did it drew everyone's attention. Just because he was not the sort to make a fuss, anything unusual about him stuck out, and a feeling of awkwardness ensued. Ned was too old a friend for the girls not to feel that way about him.

Rita returned, laughing.

'Consent refused,' she growled, bowing her head and tugging the wrong side of an imaginary moustache.

'What did I tell you?' Nellie said without rancour.

'You don't think it makes any difference?' asked Rita drily.

'What did he say?' asked Kitty.

'Oh, he hadn't a notion who I was talking about,' Rita said lightly. '"Justin who?"' she mimicked. '"How the hell do you think I can remember all the young scuts ye bring to the house?"'

'Was he mad?' asked Kitty.

'Hopping. The poor man can't even settle down to read his *Echo* without one of his daughters interrupting him to announce her engagement.'

'He didn't call us scuts?' Bill asked in a tone of genuine grief.

'Oh, begor, that was the very word he used, Bill.'

'Did you tell him he was very fond of me the day I gave him the tip for Golden Boy at the Park Races?' asked Justin.

'I did,' said Rita. 'I told him you were the stout block of a fellow with the brown hair that he said had the fine intelligence, and he said he never gave a damn about intelligence. Character was all that mattered. He wanted me to marry the thin fellow with the specs. "Only bloody gentleman that comes to this house."'

'Is it Ned?' asked Nellie.

'Of course. I asked him why he didn't tell me that before and he nearly ate the head off me. "Jesus Christ, girl, don't I feed and clothe ye? Isn't that enough without having to coort for ye as well. Next thing is ye'll be asking me to have a couple of babies for ye." Anyway, Ned,' she added with a crooked, almost malicious smile, 'there's no doubt about who was Pa's favourite.'

Once more the attention was directed on Ned. He put his cigarette down with care and rose, holding out his hand.

'I wish you all the luck in the world, Justin,' he said.

'I know that well, Ned,' boomed Justin, catching Ned's hand. 'And I'd feel the same if it was you.'

'And you too, Miss Lomasney,' Ned said gaily.

'Thanks, Mr Lowry,' she replied with the same crooked smile.

And they all felt afterwards as though they had been attending a funeral.

6

Justin and Rita married, and Ned, like all the Hayfield Hourigans, behaved in a decorous and sensible manner. He did not take to drink or violence or do any of the things people are expected to do under the circumstances. He gave them an expensive clock as a wedding present, went a couple of times to visit them, permitted Justin to try and convert him back to Catholicism, and took Rita to the pictures when Justin was on circuit. At the same time he began to walk out with an assistant in Halpin's; a gentle, humorous girl with a great mass of jet-black hair, a snub nose and a long, melancholy face. You saw them everywhere together. He also went regularly to Sunday's Well to see the old couple and Nellie, who wasn't married yet. One evening when he called, Mr and Mrs Lomasney were down at the church, but Rita was there, Justin being again away. It was months since she and Ned had met; she was having a baby and very near her time, and it made her self-conscious and rude. She said it made her feel like a yacht that had been turned into a cargo-boat. Three or four times she said things to Ned that would have maddened anyone else, but he took them in his usual way, without resentment.

'And how's little Miss Bitch?' she asked insolently.

'Little Miss who?' he asked.

'Miss – how the hell can I remember the names of all your dolls? The Spanish-looking one who sells the knickers at Halpin's.'

'Oh, she's very well, thanks.'

'What you might call a prudent marriage,' Rita went on, all on edge.

'How's that?'

'You'll have the ring and the trousseau at cost price.'

'Aren't you very interested in her?' Nellie asked suspiciously.

'I don't give a damn about her,' Rita said contemptuously. 'Would Senorita What's-her-name ever let you stand godfather to my footballer, Ned?'

'Why not?' Ned asked mildly. 'I'd be delighted, of course.'

'You have the devil's own neck to ask him after the way you treated him,' said Nellie.

Nellie was fascinated. She knew that Rita was in one of her emotional states and longed to know what it all meant. Ordinarily Rita would have delighted in thwarting her, but now it was as though she actually wanted an audience.

'What did I do to him?' she asked with interest.

'Codding him along like that for years, and then marrying a man that was twice your age. What sort of conduct is that?'

'Well, how did he expect me to know the difference?'

Ned rose, and took out a packet of cigarettes. Like Nellie, he knew that Rita had deliberately staged the scene for some purpose of her own. She was leaning far back in her chair and laughed up at him while she took a cigarette and waited for him to light it.

'Come on, Rita,' he said encouragingly. 'As you've said so much you may as well tell us the rest.'

'What else is there to tell?'

'What had you against me,' he said, growing pale.

'Who said I had anything against you?'

'Didn't you?'

'Not a damn thing. Just that I didn't love you. Didn't I tell you distinctly when you asked me to marry you that I didn't love you? I suppose you thought I didn't mean it?'

He paused for a moment and then raised his eyebrows.

'I did,' he said quietly.

She laughed. Nellie did not laugh.

'The conceit of some people!' Rita said lightly: then, with a change of tone: 'I had nothing against you, Ned. This was the one I had the needle in. Herself and Kitty forcing me into it.'

'Well, the impudence of you!' cried Nellie.

'And isn't it true for me? Weren't you both trying to get me out of the house?'

'We were not,' Nellie replied hotly. 'And even if we were, that has nothing to do with it. We didn't want you to marry Justin if you wanted to marry Ned.'

'I didn't want to marry Ned. I didn't want to marry at all.'

'What made you change your mind, so?'

'Nothing made me change my mind. I didn't care about anyone only Tony, only I didn't want to go to that damn place, and I had no alternative. I had to marry one of them, so I made up my mind that I'd marry the first one that called.'

It was directed to Nellie, but every word was aimed straight at Ned, and Nellie was wise enough to realize it.

'My God, you must have been mad!' she said.

'I felt it,' Rita said with a shrug. 'I sat at the window the whole afternoon, looking out at the rain. Remember that day, Ned?'

He nodded.

'Blame the rain if you want to blame something. I think I half hoped you'd come first. Justin came instead – an old aunt of his was sick and he came to supper. I saw him at the gate and he waved to me with his old brolly. I ran downstairs to open the door for him. "Justin, if you still want to marry me, I'm ready," I said, and I grabbed him by the coat. He gave me a dirty look – you know Justin! "Young woman, there's a time and place for everything," he said, and off with him to the lavatory. Talk about romantic engagements! Damn the old kiss did I get off him, even!'

'I declare to God!' Nellie said in stupefaction. 'You're not natural, Rita.'

'I know,' Rita said, laughing again at her own irresponsibility. 'Cripes, when I knew what I'd done I nearly dropped dead!'

'Oh, so you did come to your senses, for once?' Nellie asked.

'Of course I did. That's the trouble with Justin. He's always right. That fellow knew I wouldn't be married a week before I'd forgotten Tony. And there was I, sure that my life was over and that it was marriage or the river. Women!' she cried, shaking her head in a frenzy. 'Good God. The idiots we make of ourselves about men!'

'And I suppose it was then that you found out you'd married the wrong man?' Nellie asked, but not inquisitively this time. She knew.

'Who said I married the wrong man?' Rita asked hotly.

'It sounds damn like it, Rita,' Nellie said wearily.

'You get things all wrong, Nellie,' Rita said, her teeth on edge again. 'You jump to conclusions too much. If I married the wrong man, I wouldn't be likely to tell you – or Ned either.'

She looked mockingly at Ned, but her look belied her. It was plain enough now why she needed Nellie as audience. It kept her from saying more than she had to say, from saying things that once said, might make her own life unbearable. We all do it. Once let her say 'Ned, I love you', which was all she was saying, and he would have to do something about it, and then everything would fall in ruin about them.

He rose and flicked his cigarette ash into the fire. Then he stood with his back to it, his hands behind his back, his feet spread out on the hearth, exactly as he had stood on that night when he had defended her against her family.

'You mean, if I'd come earlier you'd have married me?' he asked quietly.

'If you'd come earlier, I'd probably be asking Justin to stand godfather to your brat,' said Rita. 'And how do you know but Justin would be walking out the Senorita, Ned?'

'And you wouldn't be quite so interested whether he was or not,' Nellie said, but she didn't say it maliciously. It was only too plain what Rita meant, and Nellie was sorry for her. She had a long lifetime yet to go through. 'Dear God,' she added ingenuously, 'isn't life awful?'

Ned turned and lashed his cigarette savagely into the fire. Rita looked up at him mockingly.

'Go on' she taunted him. 'Say it, blast you!'

'I couldn't,' he said bitterly.

A month later, he married the Senorita.

Crab Apple Jelly (1944)

The Custom
of the Country

1

It is remarkable the difference that even one foreigner can make in a community when he is not yet accustomed to its ways, the way he can isolate its customs and hold them up for your inspection. Things that had been as natural to you as bread suddenly need to be explained, and the really maddening thing is that you can't explain them. After a while you begin to wonder if they're real at all. Sometimes you doubt if you're real yourself.

We saw that with the new factory when they brought over an English foreman named Ernest Thompson to teach the local workers the job. It was not that people didn't like Ernie. They did. He was a thoroughly obliging chap, more particularly in confidential matters that our people wouldn't like to discuss among themselves, and a number of respectable married couples, as well as some that were neither married nor respectable, were under obligations to him which they would have found it dangerous to admit. Nor was it that he was stand-offish, because, in fact, he wanted to be in on everything, from the way you made love to your wife to the way the mountainy men made poteen, and he was never without ideas for improving the one or the other. There wasn't much he didn't know something about, and quite a lot of things he let on to know everything about. But for all that he could give you useful tips about mending a car or building a house, he put you off at the same time by the feeling that if he was natural, then there must be something wrong with you.

Take, for instance, the time when he started walking out with Anna Martin. Anna was a really nice girl even if she was a bit innocent. That is never much harm in a girl you care for. Anna's innocence showed even in her face, plump, dark, childish, and all in smooth curves from the bulging boyish forehead to the big, dimpled chin, with the features nesting in the hollows as if only waiting for a patch of sunlight to emerge.

Her mother, a widow woman of good family who had had the misfortune to marry one Willie Martin, a man of no class, kept a tiny huckster shop at a corner of the Cross. She was a nice, well-preserved, well-spoken little roly-poly of a woman with bad feet which gave her a waddle, and piles, which made her sit on a high hard chair, and she sat for the greater part of the day in the kitchen behind the shop with her hands joined in her lap and an air of regret for putting the world to the trouble of knowing her, though all the time she was thinking complacently of the past glories of her family, the Henebry-Hayeses of Coolnaleama. Mrs Martin had a sallow face that looked very innocent down the middle and full of guile round the edges, like a badly ironed pillowcase, and appeared so refined and ethereal that you thought her soul must be made of shot silk. Anna knew her mother's soul was made of stouter stuff. She was a woman of great principle, and if Anna bought a dress in a fashionable Protestant shop, she had to pretend it was bought in a Catholic one. It was not that her mother would create scenes; she was not a woman for scenes, but back the Protestant frock would go if she had to bring it herself. The coffee they drank tasted mouldy, but it was Catholic coffee. She didn't believe in digging with the wrong foot; it was linked somewhere in her mind with family pride and keeping to your own class, and until the last maid left, having smashed the last bit of family china off the kitchen wall, and denounced 'the Hungry Hayeses' as she called them, to the seventh generation of horse-stealers and land-grabbers, Mrs Martin had never ceased in her humble deprecating way to persuade them to wear cap and apron, serve from the left, and call Anna 'miss'.

That she had failed was entirely the doing of the Mahoneys, two mad sisters who kept another small shop farther up towards the chapel and corrupted their maids with tea and scandal. They were two tall, excitable women, one with the face of a cow and the other with the face of a greyhound, and the greyhound had a son who was going in for the priesthood. The madness of the Mahoneys took a peculiar form which made them think themselves as good as the Henebry-Hayeses of Coolnaleama; a harmless enough illusion in itself if only they didn't act as though it were true. When Mrs Martin had Anna taught to play the violin, they had Jerry taught to play the piano (the scandal was dreadful, because the piano wouldn't go through their front door and up the stairs, and had to be hoisted aboard like a cow on a hooker). When Anna and Jerry were both to have played at a concert in the convent, the Mahoneys, by a diabolical intrigue, succeeded in getting her name omitted from the programme, and Mrs Martin refused to let Anna play at all and dragged her from the hall by the hand. Sister Angela, Mrs Martin's friend, agreed that she was perfectly right, but Anna bawled the whole night through and said her mother had made a show of her. Even at that age Anna had no sense of what was fitting.

Then Jeremiah Henebry-Hayes, Mrs Martin's brother, came home from the States and stayed with her, driving off each day to Killarney, Blarney, or Glengariff in a big car with the Stars and Stripes flying from the bonnet, and the madness of the Mahoneys reached such a pitch that they brought home a dissolute brother of their own from Liverpool and hired a car for him to drive round in. They couldn't get rid of him after, and it was Mrs Martin who gave him the couple of cigarettes on tick. She was never paid, but it was worth it to her.

It was no easy life she had of it at all, with the Mahoneys sending in their spies to see if she was selling proprietary stuff at cut prices, but it must be said for the commercial travellers that they knew a lady when they saw one, and tipped her off about the Mahoneys' manoeuvres.

Finally Ernest Thompson made the shop his home. Mrs Martin's cooking was good, and he returned the compliment in scores of ways from mending the electric light to finding cures for her piles. She couldn't get over his referring to the piles, but, of course, he wasn't Irish. She was very amiable with him, and waddled round after Anna, correcting her constantly over her shoulder in a refined and humorous way; not, as Anna well knew, in any hope of improving her, but just to show Ernest that she knew what was becoming.

'Well, well!' she exclaimed in mock alarm at one of Anna's outbursts of commonness. 'Where on earth do you pick up those horrible expressions Anna? I wonder do young ladies in England talk like that, Mr Thompson?'

'I should say there aren't many young ladies anywhere who can talk like Anna,' Ernest said fondly.

'Oh, my!' cried Mrs Martin, deliberately misunderstanding him and throwing up her hands in affected fright. 'You don't mean she's as bad as that, Mr Thompson?'

'Anna is a very exceptional girl, Mrs Martin,' he replied gravely.

'Ah, I don't know,' sighed Mrs Martin, looking doubtfully at Anna as though she were some sort of beast she wouldn't like to pass off on a friend. 'Of course, she should be all right,' she added, ironing out another crease or two in the middle of her face. 'She comes of good stock, on one side anyway. I don't suppose you'd have heard of the Henebry-Hayeses?' she added with quivering modesty. 'You wouldn't, to be sure – how could you?'

Ernest skirted this question, which seemed to involve a social gaffe of the first order, like not knowing who the Habsburgs were.

'Of course,' Mrs Martin went on, almost going in convulsions of abnegation, 'I believe people nowadays don't think as much of breeding as they used to, but I'm afraid I'm terribly old-fashioned.'

'You're not old-fashioned at all, Ma,' said Anna, who knew all the vanity that her mother concealed behind her girlish modesty. 'You're antediluvian.'

'Of course, her father's people were what we in Ireland call self-made,' added Mrs Martin, revenging herself in a ladylike way. 'I suppose you can see it breaking out in her sometimes.'

On the whole, though Mrs Martin wasn't an enthusiastic woman, she was inclined to approve of Ernest. At any rate he was socially more presentable than an Irishman of the same class. Only a woman as refined as herself would be likely to notice that he wasn't quite the thing. That showed how little Mrs Martin really knew about people; Ernest wasn't the thing at all for even while he was listening deferentially to her account of the Henebry-Hayeses, he was plotting in connection with Anna things that would have made the Henebry-Hayeses turn in their graves. Ernest was lonely, he was accustomed to having women; he knew all the approaches. He took Anna for drives, filled her with gin, talked to her in the most intimate fashion of his experiences with other women, but he found that he was really getting nowhere with her. Anna's innocence would have stopped a cavalry charge.

She didn't even understand what he was getting at until one night when the two of them were walking in a lane up the hill with the valley of the city far below them. Ernest felt if Anna had any romance in her at all that this should touch her. He suggested that they go away for a weekend together.

'But what do you want to go away for a weekend for, Ernie?' drawled Anna in an accent which her mother said was like the wind up a flue.

'Because I want to make love to you, Anna,' he replied in a voice that throbbed like an organ.

'And what do you think you're doing now?' Anna asked gaily.

'Don't you want me to make love to you?' he asked earnestly, seizing her by the wrists and looking deep into her eyes. 'We love one another, don't we? What more do we need?'

'Ah, merciful God, Ernie,' she cried in panic, understanding him at last. 'I couldn't do that. I couldn't.'

'Why not, Anna?' He was almost sobbing.

'Because 'twould be a sin.'

'Is love like ours a sin?'

'What the hell has love to do with it? 'Tis always a sin unless people are married.'

'Always?'

'Always.'

He looked at her doubtfully for a few moments as though he were trying to hypnotize her and then dropped her hands mournfully and with finality.

'Oh, well, if you feel like that about it!'

She saw he had expected something different and that he was now disappointed and hurt. She took out her cigarettes and offered him one, more by way of peace-offering than anything else. By way of peace-offering, he also refused it. She saw then he was really mad with her. He stood against the wall, his hands by his sides, looking up at the sky, and the match-flame showed his plump, dark, handsome face with the injured expression of a child who has been told he can't have an apple. Anna felt terrible about it.

'I suppose you think I'm not fond of you now?' she drawled miserably, turning up her face to let out a column of smoke.

'I don't go by what people think,' Ernest said stiffly without even looking at her. 'I can only go by how they behave.'

'Because I am, in case you want to know,' she said, trying to keep back her tears. 'And God knows, I wouldn't tell you a lie.'

'I suppose it's not altogether your fault,' Ernest said in the same stiff judicial tone. 'I dare say you're inhibited.'

'I dare say I am,' agreed Anna, who did not know what he was talking about, but was prepared to plead guilty to anything if only it made him happy. 'I suppose 'tis only the custom of the country. Would an English girl do it?'

'If she loved a man,' Ernest said hollowly, studying the Milky Way.

'And what would her family say?'

'They wouldn't be consulted,' Ernest said. 'A woman's life is her own, isn't it?'

It was as well for Mrs Martin that she couldn't hear that question. It was as well for Ernest that the dead generations of Henebry-Hayeses in Coolnaleama couldn't hear it, because men had died at their hands for less.

2

In spite of this rebuff Ernest continued to call and see Anna. He borrowed a car and took her and her mother for long drives through the country. By this time Mrs Martin had become quite reconciled to the thought of him as a husband for Anna. So few Irishmen of good family would look at a girl without money; and if Anna had to marry outside what Mrs Martin regarded as her class, it was as well for her to marry a foreigner whose origins would be obscured by his manners.

'Of course, he's not what I'd call a gentleman,' she said with resignation. 'But then, I suppose we can't have everything.'

'Well, I'm not a lady either, so we suit one another fine,' retorted Anna.

'It's nice to hear it from your own lips anyway,' giggled her mother in that genteel way she had of bridling up.

'Well, I'm not and that's the holy bloody all of it,' said Anna, being deliberately coarse so as to persuade her mother that everything was fine. 'I'm not a lady, and I couldn't be a lady, and it's no use trying to make me a lady.'

'The language is absolutely delightful,' her mother said with the affected lightness that always drove Anna mad. 'I hope you talk to them like that in England. They're sure to love it.'

'Who said I was going to England anyway?' bawled Anna, growing commoner under the provocation. 'He didn't ask me yet.'

'Well, I hope when he does that you won't forget you're supposed to be a Catholic as well as a lady,' said her mother, moving off as though to bed.

'A Catholic?' Anna cried in alarm. 'What difference does that make?'

'Oh, none in the world, child,' her mother said cheerfully over her shoulder. 'Only that you can't marry him unless he turns.'

'Oh, Christ!' moaned Anna.

'I beg your pardon, Anna,' her mother said, huffing up in the doorway, a picture of martyred gentility. 'Did I hear you say something?'

'I said I might as well stuff my head in the gas oven,' said Anna.

'Ah, well, I dare say he'll turn,' her mother said complacently. 'Most men do.'

But Anna, lying awake, could not treat it so lightly. Every morning she was up at seven, gave her mother tea in bed before going to early Mass, did the shopping, and minded the shop three nights a week, and a girl does not behave like that unless she has a man so much on her mind that whatever she does seems done under his eye, for his approval, as though she were living in a glasshouse. 'I have it bad all right,' she thought in her common way, but even her commonness seemed different when Ernest was there. She had been brought up to look on it as a liability, but Ernest made it seem like a talent.

Besides, she already had a bad conscience about the weekend she had denied him. Anna might be inhibited, but her maternal instinct was very strong, and she was haunted by the memory of Ernest, looking up at the stars on the point of tears, and all because of her; and she felt that, no matter what the priest said, it could never, never be right to deprive a man you cared for of any little pleasure he valued. To suggest now that she should refuse to marry him unless he became a Catholic seemed to her the end.

He did propose to her a fortnight later, when they were in the sitting room that overlooked the Cross – a stuffy little room with all the Henebry-Hayes treasures round them. Her heart sank. She got up hastily and looked in the glass; then lit a cigarette and threw herself into an armchair with her legs crossed – a boyish pose that her mother would certainly have denounced as vile, only Anna had gone too far even to bother imagining what her mother would have said.

'Cripes, I'd love to, Ernie, but I don't know that I can,' she said.

'What's the difficulty?' asked Ernest, leaning forward with his pudgy hands clasped and a look of fresh anxiety on his face.

'It's hard to explain, Ernie,' she said, taking a puff of her cigarette and managing to look as brassy as three film stars.

'Is there another man?' he asked, growing pale.

'Ah, not at all!' she said impatiently, wishing to God he wouldn't always be trying to keep three jumps ahead so as to maintain his pose of omniscience.

'You needn't be afraid to tell me, you know,' he said in a manly tone. 'I don't mind if there is another man. I don't even mind if you've got a kid already.'

'A what?' she asked with a start.

'A kid. Lots of girls do.'

'They don't here,' she said, growing red and thinking that girls in England must have great nerve. 'It isn't that at all, only that I'm a Catholic.'

'Are you really, Anna?' Ernest asked with interest and real pleasure. 'I always thought you were an RC.'

'That's the same thing, surely,' she said.

'Is it?' he asked doubtfully. He hated to be caught out on a matter of fact.

'Oh, I'm sure it is. And anyway it seems I can't marry a Protestant.'

'But why not, Anna? I don't mind.'

'Other people do, though. I don't understand the half of it myself. It's Ma – she's dotty on religion. You could ask her.'

'I will,' Ernest said grimly. She could see from the battle-light in his eyes that he was looking forward to the scene. He loved scenes.

Mrs Martin was sitting by the fire in the kitchen, and when they came in, she fluttered in great concern about Ernest, but for once he was too angry for ceremony. He took a kitchen chair and rested one knee on it, smiling crookedly like a sunset in a stormy sky.

'Mrs Martin, Anna says she can't marry me because of my religion,' he said in a low, complaining tone. 'Is that true?'

'Oh, are ye going to be married, Ernest?' Mrs Martin cried joyously, not forgetting her own manners in spite of his bad ones. 'Well, well, this is a great surprise! I think she's very lucky, Ernest; indeed, I do, and I hope you'll be very happy.'

Ernest again gave her a wry smile, but refused to let go of the chair and embrace her tenderly the way she expected.

'I don't see how we can be,' he said.

'Ah, that's nothing,' Mrs Martin said with a shrug and a giggle. 'Where there's a will there's a way, Ernest. We'll soon get round that. Of course,' she added, just to show him how simple it was, 'if you were a Catholic, you could be married in the morning.'

'No doubt, but you see, I'm not,' Ernest went on remorselessly. 'I was brought up Church of England, and I see nothing wrong with it.'

'And why would you?' cried Mrs Martin. 'I had some very dear friends who were Church of England. Indeed, they were better than a good many of our own. You might even be able to get a dispensation,' she added, going on her knees with the poker, a tactical position that enabled her to look at him or not as it suited her.

'A dispensation?' repeated Ernest. 'What's that?'

'It's really permission from the Pope.' She gave him a quick glance over her shoulder. 'You understand, of course I needn't tell you that – the children would have to be brought up Catholics.'

'It's nothing to me how they're brought up,' said Ernest. 'That's Anna's look-out.'

'We could try it,' Mrs Martin said doubtfully, and Anna knew from her tone that she didn't mean a word of it. Ernest, poor lamb, was not smart enough to see how he was being outflanked by the old witch. He had given too much ground, and now that he was shaken, Mrs Martin was not going to be satisfied with a compromise like a dispensation. A son-in-law who dug with the wrong foot, indeed! She was out to make a convert of him, and Anna knew he hadn't a chance against her. 'Wouldn't that fire melt you?' Mrs Martin added wearily. 'Of course,' she went on, hoisting herself back into her chair, ''twouldn't be much of a marriage.'

'Why not?' asked Ernest. 'What would be wrong with it?'

'You'd have to be married out of the diocese,' Mrs Martin said cheerfully, not concealing the fact that she looked on a marriage that the Mahoneys couldn't see as not much better than open scandal. 'Wales, I believe is the nearest place. You can imagine what the neighbours would say about that. Wisha, do ye have people like that in England, Ernest?' she asked in amusement.

'God Almighty, wouldn't you think mixed marriages were catching?' Anna said, chagrined to see him so helpless. 'A wonder they wouldn't put us up in the Fever Hospital as they're at it.'

Her mother promptly saw her abandoning the cause of religion through human weakness and adopted the meek air she wore when she was really piqued.

'Of course, if that's how Anna feels, I don't see why ye wouldn't get married in a register office,' she said. 'I suppose 'tis as good as anything else.'

'Mrs Martin,' Ernest said with great dignity, dominating her, or at any rate imagining he was doing so. 'I don't expect Anna to do anything she doesn't think right, but I have principles too, remember. My religion means as much to me as hers to her.'

'I hope it means a good deal more, Ernest,' she said abjectly, getting in an extra poke at Anna under his guard. 'I'd be long sorry to think that was all it meant to you . . . But you see, Ernest, there is a difference,' she added with great humility. 'We look on ourselves as the One True Church.'

'And what do you think we look on ourselves as?' Ernest asked sharply. 'Mrs Martin,' he went on appealingly with a throb of manly pathos in his voice, 'why should you despise a man merely because he worships at a different altar?'

'Oh, I wouldn't say we despise anybody, Ernest,' Mrs Martin said in alarm, fearing she might have gone too far. Then her tone grew grave again. 'But 'tisn't alike, you know.'

'Isn't it?'

'No, Ernest. The Catholic Church was founded by Our Blessed Lord when he appointed St Peter to be His vicar on earth. St Peter is not quite the same thing as Henry VIII, Ernest.'

She looked at Ernest with a triumphant little smile, but it was revealed to her that Ernest did not know the first thing about Henry VIII – the history of his own country at that! Indeed, he seemed to take her remark as some sort of reflection on royalty.

'And what is the difference, Mrs Martin?' he asked.

'And all the wives, Ernest?' she replied meekly.

'Doesn't that depend on the wives, Mrs Martin?' Ernest said, refusing to be put down. 'Some men are luckier than others in the women they marry. He may have been one of the unlucky ones.' At this he really began to get into his stride. 'You know, Mrs Martin, I don't think you should judge a man's conduct unless you know all about his circumstances. People are sometimes nothing like so bad as they're made out to be. Often they're very good people who find themselves in circumstances beyond their own control . . . Anyhow, I'm marrying Anna, even if I have to become a Mohammedan, but at the same time I must say that I consider it unnecessary and unfair. I shouldn't be honest with myself or you unless I made that clear.'

'Ah, well, maybe you'll think differently when you know us a bit better,' Mrs Martin said without rancour as she spread the tablecloth for supper. 'Though indeed, Ernest,' she added with a wounded giggle that showed what she thought of Ernest's bad taste, 'I hope you'll find we're a cut above Mohammedans.'

Anna had to butt in to prevent Ernest from glorifying Mohammedans. That was one of the troubles about a man who knew everything like Ernest: he was so confoundedly tolerant that he was always picking quarrels with those who were not.

3

Next evening Anna brought Ernest to the convent, a large hospital on a hill overlooking the town. This was where the nuns gave instructions to would-be converts. There was a statue of the Sacred Heart on the lawn, a statue of the Blessed Virgin in the hall, and a coloured statue of St Joseph at the end of the corridor. Ernest tried to walk with a careless, masculine swing but skated on the polished floor, got red, and swore. When they entered a parlour with open windows, a bookcase and a picture of the Holy Family, he looked so sorry for himself that Anna's heart was wrung.

'And you won't forget to call her "Sister", Ernie, will you?' she whispered appealingly.

'I'll try, Anna,' Ernest said wearily, slumped in his chair with his head hanging. 'I can't guarantee anything.'

The door opened and in bounced Mrs Martin's friend, Sister Angela, beaming at them with an array of prominent teeth. She had a rather good-looking, emaciated face with a big-boned nose, and an intensely excitable manner exacerbated by deafness. Mrs

Martin said in her modest way that quite a lot of people looked on Sister Angela as one of the three great intellects of Europe, which she seemed to think was the same thing as her other favourite remark, that 'poor Sister Angela was very simple and childish'. She had been for years the bosom friend of the old parish priest who had visions, and she was now collecting evidence to have him beatified. She had cut up and distributed his nightshirts among the poor as relics, and one of his trousers, used as a belt, was supposed to have turned one of the city drunkards into a model husband.

She wrung both their hands simultaneously, beaming sharply from one to the other with a birdlike cock of her head. Like all deaf people she relied as much on expression as speech.

'Anna, dear!' she said breathlessly. 'So delighted when your mother told me. And this is your fiancé? Quite a handsome man! What's his name? Speak up!'

Anna shouted.

'Thompson?' Sister Angela cried as though this were a most delightful and unexpected coincidence. 'He's not one of us, your mother says,' she added, lowering her voice. 'What persuasion is he?'

'Church of England,' said Anna.

'Not a bit,' said Sister Angela, shaking her head vigorously.

'I said he was Church of England,' bawled Anna.

'Oooh! Church of England?' hooted Sister Angela, her face lighting up. Anna noticed she had really lovely eyes. 'So near and yet so far,' she said. 'But we never have any difficulty,' she added firmly. 'Last month,' she said to Ernest, 'we had a sun-worshipper.'

'You didn't!' said Anna. 'And did he turn?'

'I didn't like him,' Sister Angela said, clamping her lips and shaking her head as she stared into the fireplace. She had a tendency to drop out of conversations as unexpectedly as she burst in on them. 'He was a mechanic. You'd think he'd know better. So silly!' She entered the conversation again with a smile in Anna's direction. 'I wouldn't say he was sincere, would you?'

'I'll leave ye to it,' Anna said in a panic, knowing well that at any moment Ernest was liable to break into an impassioned defence of sun-worshippers. In fact, he had told her already that it was a religion that appealed to him a lot. He would not like to hear it described as silly. When she turned at the door to smile at him she failed to catch his eye, and it grieved her to see the trapped look on his handsome, sulky face.

She waited for him in a little paper-shop opposite the convent. When he came out she knew at once that things had gone wrong because he kept his head down and failed to raise his hat to her.

'Well?' she asked gaily. 'How did you get on?'

'It's hard to say,' he said moodily, striding on without looking at her. 'I've listened to some tall stories in my life, but she takes the biscuit.'

'But what did she say?' wailed Anna.

'She had nothing to say,' Ernest replied with gloomy triumph. 'I refuted her on every single point.'

'She must have loved that,' said Anna ironically.

'She didn't,' said Ernest. 'Women never appreciate clear, logical discussion. You'd think if Catholicism meant so much to them, they'd have men to teach it.'

'And did you call her "Sister"?'

'No, she didn't sound much like a sister to me. She said, "I thought you were Church of England," and I said, "I was brought up Church of England, but for many years I've been a disciple of Abou Ben Adhem." She hadn't even heard of Abou Ben Adhem!'

'Go on!' Anna said despairingly. 'And who was he when he was at home?'

'Abou Ben Adhem?' Ernest said. 'He was the man who said to the angel: "Write me as one who loved his fellow men." Abou Ben Adhem has been the great religious inspiration of my life,' he added reverently.

'Well, I hope he inspires you now,' said Anna. 'That one will be after you with a carving knife.'

Knowledgeable and all as he was, Ernest simply had no idea how serious the situation had become. Seeing Anna so depressed, he cheered up, and told her that he would make things all right next day: it was just that he hadn't been feeling well, and women were so illogical anyway. For the future he'd swallow everything that Sister Angela said. Anna told him that he didn't know what he was talking about. For a man to suggest doubts of the Bleeding Statues of Templemore or the Apparitions of Annaghishin was to go looking for trouble. For once her mother agreed with her. Mrs Martin, who had been married to one of them, knew only too well the harm men with loose tongues could do themselves with neighbours like the Mahoneys around. She treated it as a major crisis; put on her best things and went off to the convent herself.

When she returned she looked more apologetic than ever and fluttered about the house, fussing over trifles with a crucified air till she got on Anna's nerves.

'Well?' Anna bawled when she could bear it no longer. 'Aren't you going to tell us what she said?'

'Sister Angela?' Mrs Martin breathed lightly. 'She's not seeing anybody.'

'Go on!' Anna said with a cold hand on her heart. 'What ails her?'

'She's too upset,' Mrs Martin said almost joyously. 'She won't be able to go on with the instruction. She's afraid he'll upset her faith. He wasn't Church of England at all, but some religion they'd never heard of.'

'I know; an Abou Ben Something,' said Anna.

'Ah, well, if 'twas any decent sort of religion they'd know about it,' her mother said with resignation. 'They think it's probably something like the Dippers. Of course, I knew he wasn't a gentleman. Church of England people are well brought up. Reverend Mother gave me the name of a Dominican theologian, but she thinks herself you'd better have no more to do with him.'

'How soft she has it!' blazed Anna. 'To suit her, I suppose.'

'Maybe you'd better instruct him yourself,' giggled her mother.

'I will,' said Anna. 'And make a better job of it than them.'

She put on her coat and strode blindly out without a notion of where she was going. It was dark night by this time, and she walked up the hill past the Mahoneys' shop and said as she did so: 'Blast ye, anyway! Ye're just as bad.' Then she found herself beside the church, a plain, low, towerless church which lay on top of the hill with its soft lights burning like the ark left high on top of Mount Ararat. The thought that she might never come down the steps of it in wreath and veil gave her courage. She knew there was a new curate in the presbytery, and that he was young like herself.

When the housekeeper showed her in, he was sitting before the fire, listening to the wireless, a handsome young man with a knobby face. He got up, smiling, one hand in his trousers pocket, the other outstretched.

'I'm Anna Martin,' Anna said, plunging straight into her business, 'and I'm engaged to an English bloke that's over here at the new factory. He wants to turn, but he can't make head or tail of what the nuns tell him.'

'Sit down and tell me about him,' said the curate amiably, turning off the wireless. 'Will you have a fag?'

'I will,' said Anna, crossing her legs and opening her coat. 'As true as God,' she said, her lip beginning to quiver, 'I'm nearly dotty with it.'

'What religion is he?' asked the curate, holding out a lighted match to her.

'An Abou Ben Something,' replied Anna, screwing up her eyes from the smoke. 'You never heard of it?'

'I did not,' said the curate. 'I thought you said he was English.'

'He is, too,' said Anna. 'I don't know much about it. 'Tis something about loving your neighbour – the usual stuff! And damn little love there is when you start looking for it,' she added bitterly.

'Do you take a drink?' asked the curate.

'I do,' said Anna, who thought he was a pet.

'Don't worry any more about it,' he advised, pouring her out a glass of sherry. 'We'll make him all right for you.'

'You'll have no trouble as long as you don't mind what he says,' Anna said eagerly. 'He's the best fellow in the world only he likes to hear himself talk.'

''Tis a good man's fault,' said the curate.

Next evening, outside the presbytery gate, Anna gave Ernest his final instructions. Desperation had changed her. She was now masterful and precise to the point of vindictiveness, and Ernest was unusually subdued.

'And mind you call him "Father",' she said sharply.

'All right, all right,' said Ernest sulkily. 'I won't forget.'

'And whatever the hell you do, don't contradict him,' said Anna. 'There's nothing they hate like being contradicted.'

Then feeling she had done everything in her power, she went into the little church to say a prayer. Afterwards she met Ernest outside, and had every reason to feel gratified. He and the curate had got on like a house afire.

'Isn't he a delightful fellow?' Ernest chuckled enthusiastically. 'And what a brain! It's positively a pleasure to argue with him.'

Ernest was himself again, his face shining, his eyes popping. 'You see, Anna, I told you that woman had no brains.'

After that it was almost impossible to keep him away from the presbytery, instruction or no instruction. He courted the curate with considerably more warmth than he courted Anna. He repaired the curate's shotgun and practically rewired the whole presbytery, and in return the curate told him all the things he wanted to know about clerical life. Ernest even began to see himself as a priest; celibacy, which to him might have been a major obstacle, was explained when you realized how free it left you to deal with other people's sex life, and Ernest enjoyed other people's sex life almost more than he did his own. Ernest was nothing if not broad-minded.

One Saturday afternoon, six weeks later, he made his profession of faith and renounced all his previous heresies, including Abou Ben Adhemism, made his first confession, was baptised and received absolution for all the sins of his past life. Unfortunately, the Mahoneys had got hold of the convent version of it and were putting it about that he was a Turk. Mrs Martin countered this by exaggerating, in her deprecating way, his wealth, rank, and education – of course, his family was only upper middle class and his salary only a thousand a year, but then, you couldn't expect everything.

He cut a splendid figure coming from the altar with Anna, in a new suit specially bought for the occasion, his hands joined and a look of childish beatitude on his big, fat, good-natured face.

4

It was too good to be true, of course. It all became clear to Anna on the boat off Holyhead when Ernest disappeared into the saloon and only emerged half-seas-over. She had never seen him drunk before and she didn't like it. He was hysterical, jubilant, swaggering, and there was a wild look in his eyes.

'What's wrong, Ernie?' she said impatiently, staring hard at him.

'Wrong?' replied Ernest with a shrill laugh. 'What could be wrong?'

'That's what I want to know,' Anna said quietly. 'And I'm not going any farther with you till I do know.'

'Why?' he asked in the same wild tone. 'Do I look like someone there was something wrong with?'

'You look as if you were scared out of your wits,' Anna said candidly.

That sobered him. He leaned over the side of the boat, flushed and wry-faced as though he were going to be sick. The sunlit water was reflected up on to his big, heavy-jowled face, and he no longer looked handsome. He scarcely looked human.

'You didn't pinch anything, did you?' she asked anxiously.

'No, Anna,' he replied, beginning to sob, 'it's not that.'

'I suppose you're going to tell me that you're married already?'

He nodded a couple of times, too full for speech.

'That's grand,' she said with bitter restraint, already hearing the comments of the Mahoneys. 'And kids, I suppose?'

'Two,' sobbed Ernest, and buried his head in his arms.

'Sweet of you to tell me,' she said, growing white.

'Well, can you blame me?' he asked wildly, drawing himself up with what was almost dignity. 'I loved you. I knew from the first moment that you were the only woman in the world for me. I had to have you.'

'Oh, you had me all right, Ernie,' said Anna, unable, even at this most solemn moment of her life, to be anything but common.

But in spite of all his pleadings she refused to go beyond Holyhead with him. Her childhood training had been too strong, and though she might be common, she wouldn't deliberately do anything she thought really wrong. She felt sure she was going to have a baby: that was the only thing lacking to her degradation. And it all came of going with foreigners.

In the weeks that followed, she almost came to admire her mother. It was bad enough for Anna, but for her mother it was unredeemed catastrophe. Unless Father Jeremiah Mahoney not only left the Church but left it to live with a married woman or a Negress – a thing Mrs Martin was too conscientious even to desire – the war between herself and the Mahoneys was over. But she wasn't going to let herself be dislodged on that account. Under all the convent-school fatuity was the stout, sensible peasant stuff. She even approved of Anna's decision to give no information to the police, who were after Ernest. Even the prospect of a baby she accepted as the will of God – anything that couldn't be concealed from the Mahoneys seemed to be her definition of the will of God.

But Anna couldn't take things in that spirit. The whole neighbourhood was humming with spite. When she went into town she ran the gauntlet of malicious eyes and tongues. 'She knew, she knew! Sure, of course, she knew! Didn't Sister Angela warn them what he was? All grandeur and false pride. She wanted to say she could get a husband – a pasty-faced thing like that.' But it wasn't only the spite. Every second day she got some heart-rending appeal from Ernest not to let him down and threatening to kill himself. She knew she shouldn't open his letters, but she couldn't keep off them. She read and re-read them. That is what I mean by the influence of a foreigner. Things that had been as natural as breathing to Anna suddenly began to seem queer. She didn't know why she was doing them or why anyone else expected her to do them. Under the strain her character began to change. She grew explosive.

One night she had been sitting in the back kitchen, listening to her mother and a neighbour whispering in the shop, and when the neighbour left, Anna came to the inner door and leaned against the jamb with folded arms, blowsy and resentful.

'Who was the "poor Anna" ye were talking about?' she asked casually.

'Ah, indeed, Anna, you may well ask,' sighed her mother.

'But why "poor"?' Anna went on reasonably. 'I didn't marry a boozer that knocked me about like that old one did. I'm going to have a kid, which is more than a lot of the old serpents will ever have.'

'I'm glad you appreciate it,' her mother said waspishly. 'I hope you tell everyone. They'll be all delighted you're not down-hearted about it.'

'Why?' asked Anna. 'Am I supposed to be down-hearted?'

'Why should you be?' said her mother. 'Haven't you every reason for being cheerful?'

'That's exactly what I was thinking,' Anna said in a heart-breaking drawl. 'It just crossed my mind that I wasn't suited to this place at all.' Then, as she heard her own voice speaking, she was aghast. 'Cripes!' she thought in her common way. 'There goes the blooming china.' She was exactly like the last maid giving notice after breaking the last of the Henebry-Hayes china off the kitchen wall. She realized that at that moment there was not a drop of Henebry-Hayes blood left in her veins; from head to foot she was pure Martin; a woman of no class. 'I'm not grand enough for this place,' she went on recklessly. 'I think I'll have to go somewhere I'm better suited.'

She was suddenly filled with a great sense of liberation and joy. The strain of being a real Henebry-Hayes is something you cannot appreciate until it is lifted. Then she went upstairs and wrote to Ernest, telling him when to expect her.

Under the circumstances, it was perhaps the best thing she could have done. Once those foreign notions have found their way into your mind, it is impossible ever to expel them entirely afterwards.

The Common Chord (1947)

Judas

'Sure you won't be late, Jerry?' the mother said and I going out.

'Am I ever late?' I said, and I laughed.

That was all we said, but it stuck in my mind. As I was going down the road I was thinking it was months since I'd taken her to the pictures. Of course, you might think that funny, but after the father's death we were thrown together a lot. And I knew she hated being alone in the house after dark.

At the same time I had my own troubles. You see, being an only child I never knocked round the way other fellows did. All the fellows in the office went with girls, or at any rate let on that they did. They said: 'Who was the old doll I saw you with the other night, Jerry? You'd better mind yourself, or you'll be getting into trouble.' To hear them talk, you'd imagine there was no sport in the world only girls, and that they'd always be getting you into trouble. Paddy Kinnane, for instance, always talked like that, and he never saw how it upset me. I think he thought it a great compliment. It wasn't until years after that I began to suspect that Paddy's acquaintance with girls was about of one kind with my own.

Then I met Kitty Doherty. Kitty was a hospital nurse, and all the chaps in the office said a fellow should never go with hospital nurses. Ordinary girls were bad enough, but nurses were a fright – they knew too much. When I met Kitty Doherty I knew that this was a lie. She was a well-educated, superior girl; she lived up the river in a posh locality, and her mother was on all sorts of councils and committees. Kitty was small and wiry; a good-looking girl, always in good humour, and when she talked, she hopped from one subject to another like a robin on a frosty morning. I used to meet her in the evening up the river road, as though I were walking there by accident and very surprised to see her. 'Fancy meeting you!' I'd say or, 'Well, well, isn't this a great surprise!' Mind you, it usually was, because no matter how much I was expecting her, I was never prepared for the shock of her presence. Then we'd stand talking for half an hour and I'd see her home. Several times she asked me in, but I was too nervous. I knew I'd lose my head, break the china, use some dirty word, and then go home and cut my throat. Of course, I never asked her to come to the pictures or anything of the sort. She was above all that. My only hope was that if I waited long enough I might be able to save her from drowning or the white slavers or something else dramatic, that would show in a modest and dignified way how I felt about her. At the same time I had a bad conscience because I knew I should stay at home more with the mother, but the very thought that I might be missing an opportunity of fishing Kitty out of the river would spoil a whole evening for me.

That night in particular I was nearly distracted. I had not seen Kitty for three weeks. I was sure that, at the very least, she was dying and asking for me, but that no one knew my address. A week before, I had felt I simply couldn't bear it any longer and made an excuse to go down to the post office. I rang up the hospital and asked for Kitty. I fully expected them to say in gloomy tones that Kitty had died half an hour before, and had the shock of my life when the girl at the other end asked my name. I lost my head. 'I'm afraid I'm a stranger to Miss Doherty,' I said with an embarrassed laugh. 'But I have a message for her from a friend.'

Then I became completely panic-stricken. What could a girl like Kitty make of a damned, deliberate lie like that? What else was it but a trap laid by an old and cunning hand? I held the receiver out and looked at it as if it were someone whose neck I was just going to wring. 'Moynihan,' I said to it, 'you're mad. An asylum, Moynihan, is the only place for you.'

I heard Kitty's voice, not in my ear at all, but in the telephone booth as though she were standing there with me, and I nearly dropped the receiver in terror. Then I raised it and asked in what I thought of as a French accent: 'Who is dat speaking, please?' 'This is Kitty Doherty,' she replied impatiently. 'Who are you?'

That was exactly what I was wondering myself. Who the blazes was I? 'I am Monsieur Bertrand,' I said cautiously. 'I am afraid I have the wrong number. I am so sorry.' Then I put down the receiver and thought how nice it would be if only I had a penknife handy to cut my throat. It's funny, but from the moment I met Kitty I was always coveting sharp things like razors and penknives. It didn't seem to me that there were enough of them in the world at all.

After that an awful idea dawned on me. Of course, I should have thought of it sooner, but, as you can see, I was not exactly knowledgeable where girls were concerned. I began to see that I was not meeting Kitty for the very good reason that Kitty did not want to meet me. What her objection was I could only imagine, but then imagination was my strong point. I examined my conscience to see what I might have said to upset her. I remembered every single remark I had made without exception, and unfortunately it was only too clear what her objection was because every single one was either brutal, indecent or disgusting. I had talked of Paddy Kinnane as a fellow who 'went with dolls'. What could a pure-minded girl think of a chap who naturally used such an expression except – what unfortunately was quite true – that he had a mind like a cesspit.

But this evening I felt more confident. It was a lovely summer evening with views of hillsides and fields between the gaps in the houses, and it raised my spirits. Perhaps I was wrong; perhaps she had not noticed or understood my filthy conversation; perhaps we might meet and walk home together. I walked the full length of the river road and back, and then started to walk it again. The crowds were thinning out as fellows and girls slipped off up the lanes or down the river-bank, courting. As the streets went out like lamps about me my hopes sank lower. I saw clearly that she was avoiding me because she knew that I was not the quiet, good-natured fellow I let on to be but a volcano of brutality and lust. 'Lust! lust! lust!' I hissed to myself, clenching my fists. I could have forgiven myself anything but the lust.

Then I glanced up and saw her on top of a tram. I instantly forgot about the lust and smiled and waved my cap at her, but she was looking ahead and did not see me. At least, I hoped she didn't see me. I raced after the tram, intending to jump on to it, sit in one of the back seats on top where she would not notice me, and then say in astonishment as she got off: 'Fancy meeting you here.' But as if the driver knew exactly what was in my mind, he put on speed, and the old tram went bucketing and screeching down the one straight bit of road in the whole town, and I stood panting in the roadway, smiling as though missing a tram were the best joke in the world, and wishing all the time that I had a penknife and the courage to use it. My position was hopeless!

Then I must have gone a bit mad – really mad, I mean – because I started to race the tram. There were still a lot of people out walking, and they stared after me in an incredulous way, so I lifted my fists to my chest in the attitude of a professional runner and dropped into what I hoped would look like a comfortable stride and delude them into the belief that I was training for a big race. By the time I was finished, I *was* a runner, and full of indignation against the people who still continued to stare at me.

Between my running and the tram's halts I just managed to keep it in view as far as the other side of town. When I saw Kitty get off and go up a hilly street I collapsed and was only able to drag myself after her. When she went into a house on the terrace above the road I sat on the high curb with my head between my knees till the panting stopped. At least, I had run her to earth. I could afford to rest and walk up and down before the house till she came out and then say with an innocent smile: 'Fancy meeting you!'

But my luck was dead out that night. As I walked up and down, close enough to the house to keep it in view but not close enough to be seen from the windows, I saw a tall man strolling up at the opposite side of the road and my heart sank. It was Paddy Kinnane.

'Hallo, Jerry,' he chuckled with that knowing grin he put on whenever he wanted to compliment you on being discovered in a compromising situation. 'What are you doing here?'

'Just waiting for a chap I had a date with, Paddy,' I said trying to sound casual.

'Looks more to me as if you were waiting for an old doll,' Paddy said flatteringly. 'Still waters run deep. When were you supposed to meet him?'

Cripes, I didn't even know what the time was!

'Half eight,' I said at random.

'Half eight?' said Paddy. ''Tis nearly nine now.'

'Ah, he's a most unpunctual fellow,' I said angrily. 'He's always the same. He'll turn up all right.'

'I may as well wait with you,' said Paddy, leaning against the wall and taking out a packet of cigarettes. 'You might find yourself stuck at the end of the evening. There's people in this town who have no consideration for anyone.'

That was Paddy all out – a heart of gold, no trouble too much for him if he could do you a good turn – I'd have loved to strangle him. I knew there was nothing for it but to make a fresh start.

'Ah, to hell with him!' I said impatiently. 'I won't bother waiting any longer. It only struck me this minute that I have another appointment – up the Western Road. You'll excuse me now, Paddy. I'll tell you about it another time.'

And back I went to the tramline. I caught a tram and went on to the farther terminus, near Kitty's house. There, at least, Paddy Kinnane could not get at me. I sat on the river wall in the dusk. The moon was rising, and every fifteen minutes a tram came grunting and squeaking over the old bridge and went black-out as the conductor switched his trolley. Each time I got off the wall and stood on the kerb in the moonlight, searching for Kitty among the passengers. Then a policeman came along, and, as he seemed suspicious of me, I slunk slowly off up the hill and stood against a wall in shadow. There was a high wall at the other side of the road, and behind it the roof of a house was cut out of the sky in moonlight. Every now and then a tram came in and people passed, and the snatches of conversation I caught were like the warmth from an open door to the heart of a homeless man. It was quite clear now that my position was hopeless. If Kitty had walked or been driven she would have reached home from the opposite direction. She could be at home in bed by now. The last tram came and went, and still there was no Kitty, and still I hung on despairingly. While one glimmer of a chance remained I could not go home.

Then I heard a woman's step. I could not even pretend to myself that it might be Kitty till she suddenly shuffled past me with that hasty little stride. I started and called her name. She glanced quickly over her shoulder and, seeing a man emerge from the shadow, took fright and ran. I ran too, but she put on speed and began to leave me behind. At this I despaired and shouted after her at the top of my voice.

'Kitty! Kitty! For God's sake, wait!'

She ran a few steps further and then halted incredulously. She looked back, and then turned and slowly retraced her steps.

'Jerry Moynihan!' she whispered in astonishment. 'What are you doing here?'

I was summoning strength to tell her that I had happened to

be taking a stroll in that direction and was surprised to see her
when I realized the improbability of it and began to cry instead.
Then I laughed. It was hysteria, I suppose. But Kitty had had
a bad fright, and, now that she was getting over it, she was as
cross as two sticks.

'Are you out of your mind or what?' she snapped.

'But I didn't see you for weeks,' I said.

'What about it?' she asked. 'I wasn't out.'

'I thought it might be something I said to you,' I said
desperately.

'What did you say?' she asked, but I could not repeat any of the
hideous things I knew I had said. I might, by accident, repeat one
she hadn't noticed.

'Oh, anything,' I said.

'Oh, it's not that,' she said impatiently. 'It's just Mother.'

'Why, is there something wrong with her?' I asked almost
joyously. A nice fatal or near-fatal illness might just provide me
with the opportunity I needed for rushing to her rescue.

'No, but she made such a fuss of it, I felt it wasn't worth it.'

'A fuss? A fuss about what?'

'About you, of course,' Kitty said in exasperation.

This was worse than anything I had imagined. A woman I had
never met in my life making a fuss about me. This was really
terrible!

'But what did I do?' I asked.

'You didn't *do* anything, but people were talking about us just
the same. And you wouldn't come in and meet her like anyone
else. I know she's a bit of a fool, and her head is stuffed with
old nonsense about her family. I could never see that they were
different to anybody else, and anyway, she married a commercial
traveller herself, so she has nothing much to talk about. Still, you
needn't be so superior.'

I began to shiver all over. I had thought of Kitty as a secret
between God, herself and me, and assumed that she only knew
the half of it. Now it seemed that I didn't even know the half.
People were talking about us! I was superior! What next?

'But what has she against me?' I asked, wondering if she had a
spy in the office, reporting on things I said and did.

'She thinks we're doing a big tangle, of course,' snapped Kitty
as though she were surprised at my stupidity. 'I suppose she

imagines you're not grand enough for a great-great-grandniece of Daniel O'Connell. I told her you were above that sort of thing, but she wouldn't believe me. She said I was a deep, callous, crafty little intriguer and that I hadn't a drop of Daniel O'Connell's blood in my veins.' Kitty giggled at the thought of herself as an intriguer, and no wonder.

'That's all she knows,' I said despairingly.

'I know,' Kitty agreed sadly. 'The woman has no sense. And anyway she has no reason to think I'd tell her lies. Cissy and I always had fellows, and we spooned with them all over the shop under her very nose, so I don't see why she thinks I'm trying to conceal anything now.'

At this I laughed like an idiot. This was worse than appalling. This was nightmare. Kitty, whom I had thought so angelic, talking in cold blood of 'spooning'. Even the bad women in the bad books I had read didn't talk about love-making in that cold-blooded way. Madame Bovary herself had the decency to pretend that she didn't like it. It was another door opening on an outside world, but Kitty thought I was laughing at her and began to apologize.

'Of course, I had no sense,' she said. 'You were the first fellow that treated me properly. The others only wanted to fool around, and now, because I don't like it, Mother is convinced I've got into something really ghastly. I can see her looking at me sideways to see is my figure all right. She really is a bit dotty. I told her I liked you better than any other fellow I knew, but that I'd grown out of that sort of thing.'

'And what did she say to that?' I asked. I was beginning to see that imagination was not enough. All round me there was an objective reality that was a thousand times more nightmarish than any fantasy of my own, and I wanted to know about it, though at the same time it turned my stomach.

'Ah, I told you she was silly,' Kitty said in embarrassment.

'Go on!' I said desperately.

'Well,' said Kitty with a demure grin, 'she said you were a deep, designing guttersnipe who knew exactly how to get round feather-pated little idiots like me . . . I suppose I'm not clever, but I'm not as stupid as all that . . . But you see, it's quite hopeless. I think she's a bit common. She doesn't understand.'

'Oh, God!' I said, almost in tears. 'I only wish I was.'

'You wish you were what?' she asked.

'A deep, designing whatever she called me. Because then I might have some chance with you.'

Kitty looked at me for a moment, and I could see she was wondering about something.

'To tell the truth, I thought you were a bit keen on me at first, but then I wasn't sure. I mean, you didn't give any indication.'

'God, when I think what I've been through in the past few weeks!' I said bitterly.

'I know,' said Kitty. 'I was a bit fed up myself. You get used to people, I suppose.'

Then we said nothing for a few moments. It didn't seem to me there was much more to be said.

'You're sure now you mean it?' she asked.

'But I tell you I was on the point of committing suicide,' I said angrily.

'Ah, what good would that be?' she asked with another shrug, and this time she looked at me and laughed outright – the little jade!

I insisted on telling her about my prospects. She didn't want to hear about my prospects; she wanted me to kiss her, but that seemed to me a very sissy sort of occupation, so I told her just the same, in the intervals. It was as if a stone had been lifted off my heart, and I went home in the moonlight, singing. Then I heard the clock strike, and the singing stopped. I remembered the mother's 'Sure you won't be late?' and my own 'Am I ever late?' This was desperation too, but of a different sort.

The door was ajar and the kitchen in darkness. I saw her sitting before the fire by herself, and just as I was about to throw my arms round her, I smelt Kitty's perfume and was afraid to go near her. God help us, as though that would have told her anything!

'Hullo, Mum,' I said with a nervous laugh, rubbing my hands. 'You're all in darkness.'

'You'll have a cup of tea?' she said.

'I might as well.'

'What time is it?' she said, lighting the gas. 'You're very late.'

'I met a fellow from the office,' I said, but at the same time I was stung by the complaint in her tone.

'You frightened me,' she said with a little whimper. 'I didn't know what happened to you. What kept you at all?'

'Oh, what do you think?' I said, goaded by my own sense of guilt. 'Drinking and blackguarding as usual.'

I could have bitten my tongue off as I said it; it sounded so cruel, as if some stranger had said it instead of me. She turned to me with a frightened stare as if she were seeing the stranger too, and somehow I couldn't bear it.

'God Almighty!' I said. A fellow can have no life in his own house.'

I went hastily upstairs, lit the candle, undressed, and got into bed. A chap could be a drunkard and blackguard and not be made to suffer what I was being made to suffer for being out late one single night. This, I felt, was what you got for being a good son.

'Jerry,' she called from the foot of the stairs, 'will I bring you up your cup?'

'I don't want it now, thanks,' I said.

I heard her sigh and turn away. Then she locked the doors, front and back. She didn't wash up, and I knew that my cup of tea was standing on the table with a saucer on top in case I changed my mind. She came slowly upstairs and her walk was that of an old woman. I blew out the candle before she reached the landing, in case she came in to ask if I wanted anything else, and the moonlight came in the attic window and brought me memories of Kitty. But every time I tried to imagine her face as she grinned up at me, waiting for me to kiss her, it was the mother's face that came up instead, with that look like a child's when you strike him for the first time – as if he suddenly saw the stranger in you. I remembered all our life together from the night my father died; our early Mass on Sunday; our visits to the pictures, and our plans for the future, and Christ! it was as if I was inside her mind while she sat by the fire waiting for the blow to fall. And now it had fallen, and I was a stranger to her, and nothing I could ever do would make us the same to one another again. There was something like a cannon-ball stuck in my chest, and I lay awake till the cocks started crowing. Then I could bear it no longer. I went out on the landing and listened.

'Are you awake, Mother?' I asked in a whisper.

'What is it, Jerry?' she replied in alarm, and I knew that she hadn't slept any more than I had.

'I only came to say I was sorry,' I said, opening the door of her room, and then as I saw her sitting up in bed under the Sacred

Heart lamp, the cannon-ball burst inside me and I began to cry like a kid.

'Oh, child, child, child,' she exclaimed; 'what are you crying for at all, my little boy?' She spread out her arms to me. I went to her and she hugged me and rocked me as she did when I was only a nipper. 'Oh, oh, oh,' she was saying to herself in a whisper, 'my storeen bawn, my little man!' – all the names she hadn't called me in years. That was all we said. I couldn't bring myself to tell her what I had done, nor could she confess to me that she was jealous: all she could do was to try and comfort me for the way I'd hurt her, to make up to me for the nature she had given me. 'My storeen bawn!' she said. 'My little man!'

The Common Chord (1947)

The Miracle

Vanity, according to the Bishop, was the Canon's great weakness, and there might be some truth in that. He was a tall, good-looking man with a big chin and a manner of deceptive humility. He deplored the fact that so many of the young priests came from poor homes where good manners were not taught, and looked back regretfully to the old days when, according to him, every parish priest read his Virgil. He gave himself out for an authority on food and wine, and ground and brewed his own coffee. He refused to live in the ramshackle old presbytery that had served generations of priests, and had built himself a residence second only to the Bishop's palace and furnished with considerably more taste and expense. There he ate his meals with the right wines, brewed his coffee and sipped his green chartreuse, and occasionally dipped into ecclesiastical history. He liked to read about days when the clergy were really well off.

It was distasteful to the Canon that the lower classes should be creeping into the Church and gaining high office in it, but it was a real heartbreak to him that its functions and privileges were being usurped by new men and methods, and that miracles were now being performed out of bottles and syringes. He would have preferred surgeons to remain tradesmen and barbers as they had been in the good old days and, though he would have been astonished to hear it himself, was as jealous as a prima donna at the interference of Bobby Healy, the doctor, with his flock.

There was certainly some truth in the Bishop's criticism. The Canon hated competition; he liked young Dr Devaney, who affected to believe that medicine was all hocus-pocus, and took a grave view of Bobby Healy, who didn't. This caused Bobby's practice to go down quite a bit. When the Canon visited a dying man he took care to ask who the doctor was. If it was Bobby Healy he nodded and looked grave, and everyone knew Bobby had killed the unfortunate patient as usual. When the two men met the

225

Canon was courteous and condescending, Bobby respectful and obliging, and nobody could ever have told from the doctor's face whether or not he knew what was going on. But there was very little Bobby didn't know. There is a certain sort of guile that goes deeper than any cleric's – the peasant's guile. Dr Healy had that.

But there was one person in his parish whom the Canon disliked even more than he disliked the doctor. That was a man called Bill Enright. Nominally, Bill was a farmer and breeder of greyhounds; really, he was the last of a family of bandits who had terrorized the countryside for generations. He was a tall, gaunt man with fair hair and a small golden moustache; perfectly rosy skin like a baby's, and a pair of bright blue eyes that seemed to expand into a wide, unwinking, animal glare. His cheekbones were so high that they gave the impression of cutting his skin, and gave his eyes an oriental slant. With its low, sharp-sloping forehead, his whole face seemed to point outward to the sharp tip of his nose and then retreat again in a pair of high teeth, very sharp and very white, a drooping lower lip, and a small, weak feminine chin.

Now, Bill, as he would be the first to tell you, was not a bad man. He was a traditionalist and did as his father and grandfather had done before him. He had gone to Mass and the sacraments and even paid his dues, and been in every way prepared to treat the Canon as a bandit of similar dignity to himself, but the Canon had merely been outraged by his presumption. Bill was notoriously living in sin with his housekeeper, Nellie Mahony from Doonamon, and the Canon had ordered her to leave the house. When she didn't, he went to her brothers and demanded that they should bring her home, but her brothers had too much experience of the Enrights to try such a risky experiment, and Nellie remained on, while Bill, declaring loudly that religion was all his eye, ceased going to Mass. People agreed that it wasn't altogether Bill's fault, and that the Canon could not brook another authority than his own – a hasty man!

To Bobby Healy, on the other hand, Bill was bound by the strongest tie that could bind an Enright, because the doctor had once cured a greyhound for him, the mother of King Kong. Four or five times a year the doctor was summoned to treat Bill for an overdose of whiskey; Bill owed him just as much money as was fitting to owe a friend, and all Bill's companions knew that when they were in trouble themselves, Dr Healy was the man.

Whatever the Canon might think, Bill was one it paid to stand in well with.

One spring day Bobby got one of his usual summonses to the presence. Bill lived in a fine Georgian house a mile outside the town. It had once belonged to the Rowes, but Bill had got them out by making their lives a hell. The avenue was overgrown, and the house with its fine Ionic portico looked dirty and dilapidated. Two dogs got up and barked at him in a neighbourly way. They hated it when Bill was sick and they knew that Bobby had a knack of putting him on his feet again.

Nellie Mahony opened the door. She was a small, fat country girl with a rosy complexion and mass of jet-black hair that shone almost as brilliantly as her eyes. The doctor, who was sometimes seized with such fits of amiable idiocy, gave her a squeeze and she replied with a shriek of laughter that broke off suddenly.

'Wisha, Dr Healy, oughtn't you to be ashamed, and the state we're in?' she asked complainingly.

'How's that, Nellie?' he asked. 'Isn't it the usual thing?'

'The usual thing?' she shrieked. She had a trick of snatching up and repeating someone's final words in a brilliant tone, a full octave higher, like a fiddle repeating a phrase from the double bass. Then with dramatic abruptness she let her voice drop to a whisper and dabbed her eyes with her apron. 'He's dying, doctor,' she said.

'For God's sake!' whispered the doctor. Life had rubbed down his principles considerably, and the fact that Bill was suspected of a share in at least one murder did not prejudice him in the least. 'Sure, I saw him in town on Monday and he never looked better.'

'Never looked better?' echoed the fiddle, while Nellie's beautiful black eyes filled with a tragic emotion not far removed from joy. 'And then didn't he go out on the Tuesday morning on me, in the pouring rain, with three men and two dogs, and not come back till Friday night, with the result' – this was a boss phrase of Nellie's, always followed by a dramatic pause and change of key – 'that he caught a chill up through him and never left the bed since.'

'What are you saying to Bobby Healy?' a man's voice called from upstairs. It was nearly as high-pitched as Nellie's but with a wild, nervous tremolo in it.

'What am I saying to Bobby Healy?' she echoed mechanically. 'I'm saying nothing at all to him.'

'Well, don't be keeping him down there, after I waiting all day for him.'

'There's nothing wrong with his lungs anyway,' the doctor said professionally and went up the stairs. They were bare and damp. It was a lifelong grievance of Bill Enright's that the Rowes had been mean enough to take the furniture to England with them.

He was sitting up in an iron bed, and the grey afternoon light and the white pillows threw up the brilliance of his colouring, already heightened by a touch of fever.

'What was she telling you?' he asked in his high-pitched voice – the sort of keen and unsentimental voice one would attribute in fancy to some cunning and swift-footed animal, like a fox.

'What was I telling him?' Nellie echoed boldly, feeling the doctor's authority behind her. 'I was telling him you went out with three men and two dogs and never came back to me till Friday night.'

'Ah, Bill, how often did I tell you to stick to women and cats?' the doctor said. 'What ails you now?'

'I'm bloody bad, doctor,' whinnied Bill.

'You look it,' said Bobby candidly. 'That's all right, Nellie,' he added, seeing that Nellie was proposing to examine the patient with him.

'And make a lot of noise downstairs,' said Bill after her.

Bobby gave Bill a thorough examination. So far as he could see there was nothing wrong with him but a chill, though he realized from the way Bill's mad blue eyes followed him that the man was in a panic. He wondered whether, as he sometimes did, he shouldn't give him a worse one. It was unprofessional, of course, but it was the only treatment that ever worked, and with most of his men patients he had to choose a time, before it was too late and had not yet passed from fiction to fact, when the threat of heart disease or cirrhosis might reduce their drinking to reasonable proportions. Then the inspiration came to him like heaven opening to sinners, and he sat for some moments in silence, thinking it out. Even threats would be lost on Bill Enright. What Bill needed was a miracle, and miracles are not things to be undertaken lightly. Properly performed, a miracle might do as much good for the doctor as for Bill.

'Well, Bobby?' Bill asked, on edge with nerves.

'You're bad enough,' the doctor said gravely. 'Tell me, how long is it since you were at confession?'

Bill's rosy face turned the colour of wax, and Bobby, a kindly man, felt almost ashamed of himself.

'Is that the way it is, Bobby?' Bill asked.

'I didn't mean it like that,' the doctor said, beginning already to relent. 'But I should have a second opinion.'

'Your opinion is good enough for me, Bobby,' Bill said loyally, pouring coals of fire on Bobby. He sat up in bed and drew the clothes round him. 'Take a fag and light one for me. What the hell difference does it make? I lived my life and bred the best greyhound bitches in Europe.'

'You'll breed more,' the doctor said firmly. 'It's just that after a certain point I don't like my patients not to see a priest. It gets me a bad name. Will I go to the Canon for you?'

'The Half-Gent?' Bill said indignantly. 'You will not.'

'I know he has an unfortunate manner,' the doctor admitted sadly. 'But I can easy bring you someone else.'

'Ah, what the hell do I want with any of them?' Bill asked angrily. 'They're all the same. Money, money, money! They never think of anything else.'

'Ah, I wouldn't say that, Bill,' the doctor said, thoughtfully pacing the room, his wrinkled old face as grey as his homespun suit. 'I hope you won't think I'm intruding. I'm talking as a friend.'

'I know you mean it well, Bobby,' Bill said with a sturdiness that went to the doctor's heart.

'But you see, Bill, I feel you need a different sort of priest altogether. Of course, I'm not criticizing the Canon, but after all, he's only a secular. I suppose you never had a chat with a Jesuit?'

He asked this with an innocent air as though he didn't know that the one thing a secular priest dreads after the Devil himself is a Jesuit, and that Jesuits were particularly hateful to the Canon, who considered that as much intellect and authority as his flock required were centred in himself.

'Never,' said Bill.

'They're a very cultured order,' said the doctor.

'What the hell do I want with a Jesuit?' Bill cried. 'A drop of drink and bit of skirt – what harm is there in that?'

'Oh, none in the world, Bill,' agreed Bobby. ''Tisn't as if you were ever a bad-living man.'

'I wasn't,' Bill said with unexpected self-pity. 'I was a good friend to anyone I liked.'

'And you know the Canon would take it as a personal favour if anything happened you? You won't repeat what I'm saying – I'm speaking as a friend.'

'You are, Bobby,' said Bill, his voice hardening under the injustice of it. 'You're speaking like a Christian. Nothing would please that fellow better than to say I was down in hell. I see that clearly now. You're right. That's the way to thwart him. I could even leave the Jesuits a few pounds for Masses, Bobby,' he went on with childlike enthusiasm. 'That would really break his heart.'

'Ah, I wouldn't go as far as that, Bill,' the doctor said with some alarm. His was a delicate undertaking, and Bill was altogether too apt a pupil for his taste.

'No, but that's what you mean, Bobby,' Bill said, showing his teeth. 'And you're right as usual. Bring whoever you like and I'll let him talk. What the hell harm can it do me anyway?'

The doctor went downstairs and found Nellie waiting for him.

'I'm running over to Aharna for a priest, Nellie,' he whispered. 'You might get things ready for him while I'm away.'

'And is that the way it is?' she asked, growing pale.

'Ah, he'll be all right now. Just leave him to me,' the doctor said, squeezing her arm.

He drove off to Aharna where an ancient bishop called McGinty, whose name was remembered in clerical circles only with sorrow, had permitted the Jesuits to establish a house. There he had a friend called Father Finnegan, a stocky, middle-aged man with a tight mouth and clumps of white hair in his ears. It is not to be supposed that the doctor told him all that was in his mind, or that Father Finnegan believed he did, but they were old friends, and Father Finnegan knew that this was an occasion.

As they drove up the avenue, Nellie rushed out to meet them.

'What is it, Nellie?' the doctor asked anxiously. He could not help dreading that at the last moment Bill would play a trick on him and die of shock.

'He's gone mad, doctor,' she replied reproachfully, as though she hadn't thought Bobby would do a thing like that to her.

'When did he go mad?' Bobby asked.

'When he saw me putting up the altar in the room. He thrown a glass at me. Now he's after barricading the door and says he'll shoot the first one that tries to get in.'

'That's quite all right, my dear young lady,' Father Finnegan said comfortingly. 'Sick people often take turns like that.'

'Has he a gun, Nellie?' Bobby asked cautiously.

'Did you ever know him without one?' retorted Nellie.

The doctor, who was of a timid disposition, was impressed by the Jesuit's quiet courage. While Bobby knocked on the bedroom door, Father Finnegan stood beside it, his hands behind his back and his head bowed in meditation.

'Who's there?' cried Bill.

'It's me, Bill,' the doctor said soothingly.

'I'm not seeing anyone,' shouted Bill. 'I'm too sick.'

'One moment, doctor,' Father Finnegan said, putting his shoulder to the door. The barricade gave way and they went in. One glance was enough to show the doctor that Bill had had time to panic. He hadn't a gun, but this was the only thing lacking to remind Bobby of Two-Gun Joe's last stand. He was sitting well up in bed, supported on his elbows, his head craned forward, while his blue eyes flashed unseeingly from the priest to Bobby and from Bobby to the improvised altar. Bobby was sadly afraid that Bill was going to disappoint him. He felt he had been too optimistic. You might as well have tried to convert something in the zoo.

'I'm Father Finnegan, Mr Enright,' the Jesuit said, holding out his hand.

'I didn't send for you,' snapped Bill.

'I appreciate that, Mr Enright,' said the priest. 'But any friend of Dr Healy is a friend of mine. Won't you shake hands?'

'I don't mind,' whinnied Bill, letting him partake slightly of a limp paw but without looking at him. 'I warn you I'm not a religious sort of bloke, though. Anyone that thinks I'm not a hard nut to crack is in for a surprise.'

'If I went in for cracking nuts I'd say the same,' Father Finnegan said gamely. 'You look well able to protect yourself.'

Bill gave a harsh snort, indicating how much he could say on that score if he felt like it, and his eyes continued to wander sightlessly like a mirror in a child's hand, but Bobby felt the priest had said the right thing. He closed the door softly behind him and went down to the drawing room. The six windows opened on three landscapes. The lowing of distant cows pleased him. Then he swore and threw open the door to the hall. Nellie was sitting snugly on the stairs with her ear cocked. He beckoned her down.

'What is it, doctor?' she asked in surprise.

'Bring in a lamp. And don't forget the priest will want his supper.'

''Tisn't listening you thought I was?' she cried indignantly.

'No,' said Bobby drily. 'You looked as if you were joining in the devotions.'

'Joining in the devotions,' she cried. 'I'm up since six, waiting hand and foot on him, with the result that I dropped down in a dead weakness on the stairs. Would you believe that now?'

'I would not,' said Bobby.

'You would not?' she said. 'Jesus!' she added after a moment. 'I'll bring you the lamp,' she said in a tone of defeat.

Nearly an hour passed before there was any sound from upstairs. Then Father Finnegan came down, rubbing his hands briskly and saying the nights were turning cold. Bobby found a lamp lit in the bedroom and the patient lying with one arm under his head.

'How are you feeling now, Bill?' the doctor asked.

'Fine, Bobby,' said Bill in a tone of great satisfaction. 'I'm feeling grand. You were right about the priest, Bobby. You're always right. I'll say that for you. I was a fool to bother my head with the other fellow. He's not educated at all, Bobby, not compared with this man.'

'I thought you'd like him,' said Bobby.

'Damn it, I like a fellow to know his job, Bobby,' Bill said in the tone of one expert appraising another. 'There's nothing like the bit of education. I should have had more of it myself. I wish I met that priest sooner.' The wild blue eyes came to rest hauntingly on the doctor's face. 'I feel the better of it already, Bobby. I feel like a new man. What sign would that be?'

'I dare say it's the excitement,' Bobby said, giving nothing away. 'I'll have another look at you.'

'What's that she's frying, Bobby? Sausages and bacon?'

'I suppose so,' said the doctor, who suffered from dyspepsia and knew what the rural cookery ran to.

'There's nothing I'm so fond of,' Bill said wistfully. 'Bobby, could I have just a mouthful? My stomach feels as if it was sandpapered.'

'I suppose you could,' the doctor said grudgingly. 'But tea is all you can have with it.'

'Hah!' Bill crowed bitterly. 'That's all I'm ever going to be let have if I live to be as old as Methuselah. But I'm not complaining, Bobby. I'm a man of my word. Oh, God, yes.'

'Don't tell me you took the pledge, Bill!' the doctor said doubtfully.

'Christ, Bobby,' said the patient, giving a wild heave in the bed, 'I took the whole bloody book, cover and all . . . God forgive me for swearing!' he added piously. 'He made me promise to marry the Screech,' he said with a look that challenged the doctor to laugh if he didn't value his life.

'And why wouldn't you if you wanted to?' asked the doctor.

'How sure he is I'll have him!' Nellie bawled cheerfully, showing her moony face at the door.

'That's why, Bobby,' Bill said without rancour. 'It have my nerves on edge. I'm a man that likes to keep his mind to himself.'

'Go on, Nellie!' said the doctor. 'I'm having a look at Bill . . . You had a trying day of it,' he added as she went out. He sat on the bed and took Bill's wrist. Then he stuck a thermometer in his throat, flashed a torch in his eyes and examined his throat while Bill looked at him with a hypnotized glare.

'Begor, Bill, I wouldn't say but you were right,' the doctor said with a laugh that might have suggested surprise and embarrassment. 'I'd almost say you were a shade better.'

'A shade?' said Bill, beginning to do physical exercises for him. 'Look at that, Bobby! I couldn't do that before. That's not what I call a shade. It came over me while he was talking. I call that a blooming miracle.'

'When you've seen as much as I have, you won't believe so much in miracles,' the doctor said sourly. At this stage he did not want Bill to go out and get double pneumonia on him, all to prove that a Jesuit had cured him when a doctor had given him up. 'Take a couple of these tablets, and I'll have another look at you in the morning.'

He was almost depressed as he went downstairs. It was too easy altogether. The most up-to-date treatments were wasted on

Bobby's patients. What they all secretly wanted was to be rubbed with three pebbles from a Holy Well.

'Well, on the whole, Dr Healy,' Father Finnegan said as they drove off, 'that was a very satisfactory evening.'

'I'd say it was,' Bobby said guardedly. He had no intention of telling his friend exactly how satisfactory it was.

'And people do make the most extraordinary rallies after the sacraments,' Father Finnegan went on, and Bobby saw that it wasn't even necessary to explain to him. Educated men can understand one another without such embarrassing admissions. His own conscience was quite clear. A little religion wouldn't do Bill the least bit of harm. He felt that the priest's conscience wasn't troubling him much either. He wasn't especially required to love seculars, and, even without a miracle, Bill's conversion would throw the parish wide open to the order. *With* a miracle, testified to by a medical man, every old woman, male and female, for miles around, would be calling for a Jesuit.

'They do,' Bobby said wonderingly. ''Tis a thing you'd often notice.'

'But I'm afraid, Dr Healy, that the Canon won't like it,' the Jesuit added candidly.

'He won't,' the doctor said as though the idea had only just occurred to him. 'I'm afraid he won't like it at all.'

He was an honest man who gave credit where credit was due, and he knew it wasn't only the money – a couple of hundred a year at least – that would upset the Canon. It was the thought that under his very nose a miracle had been worked on one of his own parishioners by a member of the hated Jesuit order. Clerics, he knew, are as cruel as small boys. The Canon would not be allowed to forget the Jesuit miracle the longest day he lived.

But for the future he'd let Bobby alone.

The Common Chord (1947)

The Frying Pan

Father Fogarty's only friends in Kilmulpeter were the Whittons. Whitton, the schoolteacher, had been to the seminary with Fogarty, and like him, intended to be a priest, but when the time came for him to take the vow of celibacy, he had contracted scruples of conscience and married the most important of them. Fogarty, who had known her too, had agreed that there was justification for that particular scruple, and now, in this lonely place where chance had thrown them together again, she formed the real centre of what little social life he had.

With Tom Whitton he had a quiet friendship based on exchanges of opinion about books and wireless talks, but he felt that Whitton didn't really like him. When they went to the races together, Fogarty felt that Whitton disapproved of having to put on bets for him and believed that priests should not bet at all. Like other outsiders, he knew perfectly what priests should do, without the necessity for doing it himself. He was sometimes savage in the things he said about the parish priest, old Father Whelan. On the other hand, he had a ready wit, and Fogarty enjoyed retelling his cracks against the cloth. Men as intelligent as Whitton were rare in country schools, and soon he, too, would grow stupid and wild for lack of educated society.

One evening Father Fogarty invited the Whittons to dinner to see some films he had taken at the races. Films were his latest hobby. Before that it had been fishing and shooting. Like all bachelors he had a mania for adding to his possessions, and his lumber-room was piled high with every sort of junk from chest-developers to field-glasses (these belonged to his bird-watching phase), and his library cluttered with text-books on everything from Irish history to Freudian psychology. He passed from craze to craze, each the key to the universe.

He sprang up at the knock, and found Una at the door, all in furs, her shoulders about her ears, her big, bony, masculine face blue with cold. She had an amiable monkey-grin. Tom, a handsome man, was tall and self-conscious. He had greying hair, brown eyes, a prominent jaw, and was quiet-spoken in a way that concealed passion. He and Una disagreed a lot about how the children should be brought up. He thought she spoiled them.

'Come in, let ye, come in!' cried Fogarty, showing the way into his warm study, with its roaring turf-fire, deep leather chairs, and the Raphael print over the mantelpiece – a typical bachelor's room. 'You're perished, Una!' he said with concern, holding her hand a moment longer than was necessary. 'What'll you have to drink?'

'Whi-hi-hi—' stammered Una excitedly, her eyes beginning to pop. 'I can't say the bloody word.'

'Call it malt,' said Fogarty, spinning on his heel towards the sideboard.

'That's enough! That's enough!' she cried laughingly, snatching the glass from him. 'You'll send me home on my ear, and then I'll hear about it from this fellow.'

'Whiskey, Tom?'

'Whiskey, Jerry,' Whitton said quietly with a quick friendly glance. He kept his head very still and used his eyes a lot instead.

Meanwhile Una, unabashedly inquisitive, was making the tour of the room with the glass in her hand, to see if there wasn't something new in it. There usually was.

'Is this new, father?' she asked, halting before a pleasant eighteenth-century print.

'Ten bob,' the priest said promptly. 'Wasn't it a bargain?'

'I couldn't say. What is it?'

'The old courthouse in town.'

'Go on!' said Una.

Whitton walked over and studied the print closely. 'That place is gone these fifty years and I never saw a picture of it,' he said. 'This is a bargain all right.'

'I'd say so,' Fogarty said with quiet pride.

'And what's the sheet for?' asked Una, poking at a tablecloth pinned between the windows.

'That's not a sheet, woman!' Fogarty exclaimed. 'For God's sake don't be displaying your ignorance.'

'Oh, I know,' she cried girlishly. 'For the pictures. I'd forgotten about them. That's grand!'

Then Bella, a coarse, good-looking country girl, announced dinner, and the curate, with a self-conscious, boyish swagger, led them into the dining room, which was even more ponderous than the study. Everything in it was large, heavy and dark.

'And now, what'll ye drink?' he asked over his shoulder, studying his array of bottles. 'There's some damn good Burgundy – 'pon my soul, 'tis great!'

'How much did it cost?' Whitton asked with poker-faced humour. 'The only way I have of identifying wine is by the price.'

'Eight bob a bottle,' Fogarty replied at once, without perceiving the joke.

'That's a very good price,' said Whitton with a nod. 'We'll have some of that.'

'You can take a couple of bottles home with you,' said Fogarty, who, in the warmth of his heart, was always wanting to give his treasures away. 'The last two dozen he had – wasn't I lucky?'

'You have the appetite of a canon on the income of a curate,' Whitton said in the same tone of grave humour, but Fogarty caught the scarcely perceptible note of criticism in it. He did not allow it to worry him.

'Please God, we won't always be curates,' he said sunnily.

'Bella looks after you well,' said Una when the meal was nearly over. The compliment was deserved so far as it went, though it was a man's meal rather than a woman's.

'Doesn't she though?' Fogarty exclaimed with pleasure. 'Isn't she damn good for a country girl?'

'How does she get on with Stasia?' asked Una. Stasia, Father Whelan's old housekeeper, was an affliction to the whole community.

'They don't talk. Stasia says she's an immoral woman.'

'And is she?' asked Una hopefully.

'If she's not, she's wasting her own time and my whiskey,' said Fogarty. 'She entertains Paddy Coakley in the kitchen every Saturday night while I'm hearing confessions. I told her I wouldn't keep her unless she got a boy. Aren't I right? One Stasia is enough for any parish. Father Whelan tells me I'm going too far.'

'And did you tell him to mind his own business?' Whitton asked with a penetrating look.

'I did, to be sure,' said Fogarty, who had done nothing of the kind. It was hardly the sort of thing you could say to a parish priest.

'Ignorant, interfering old fool!' Whitton said quietly, the ferocity of his sentiments belied by the mildness of his manner.

'That's only because you'd like to do the interfering yourself, love,' said Una, who frequently had to act as peace-maker between the parish priest and her husband.

'And a robber as well,' Whitton added, ignoring her. 'He's been collecting for new seats for the church for the last ten years. I'd like to know where that money is going.'

'He had a collection for repairing my roof and 'tis leaking still,' said Fogarty. 'He must be worth twenty thousand.'

'Now, that's not fair,' Una said flatly. 'You know yourself there's no harm in Father Whelan. It's only that he's sure he's going to die in the poorhouse. It's just like Bella and her boy – he has nothing more serious to worry about, and he worries about that.'

Fogarty knew there was a certain amount of truth in what Una said, and that Whelan's miserliness was more symbolic than real, but at the same time he felt in her words criticism of a different kind. Though she wasn't aware of it herself, she was implying that the priest's office made him an object of pity. He wasn't a man like anybody else, and this made her sorry for him, and, by implication, for Fogarty himself. This had to be put down.

'Still, Tom is right, Una,' he said gravely. 'It's not a question of what harm Father Whelan intends but what harm he does. Scandal is scandal, whatever the cause may be.'

Tom grunted approval, but he said no more on the subject, as though refusing to enter into argument with his wife about things she didn't understand.

They returned to the study for coffee, and Fogarty brought out the film projector. At once the censoriousness of Tom Whitton's manner dropped away, and he behaved with the new toy like a pleasant and intelligent boy of seventeen. Una, sitting by the fire with her legs crossed, watched them with amusement. Whenever they came to the priest's house, the same sort of thing was liable to happen. Once it had been a microscope, another time a chest-developer, and now they were kidding themselves that their real interest in the cinema was educational. Within a month the projector, like the microscope, would be lying in the lumber-room with the rest of the junk.

Fogarty switched off the light and showed some films he had taken at the races. They were very patchy, mostly out of focus, and had to be interpreted by a running commentary, which was always a shot or two behind.

'I suppose ye wouldn't know who that is?' he asked as the film showed Una, eating a sandwich and talking excitedly and demonstratively to a couple of wild-looking country boys.

'It looks like someone from the County Club,' her husband said drily.

'But wasn't it good?' Fogarty asked innocently, switching on the light again. 'Now, wasn't it very interesting?' He was exactly like a small boy who has performed a conjuring trick and is waiting for the applause.

'Marvellous, father,' Una said with a sly and affectionate grin.

He blushed and turned away to pour out more whiskey for them. He saw that she had noticed the pictures of herself and wasn't displeased with them. When he drove them home, she held his hand and said they had had the best evening for years – a piece of flattery so gross and uncalled for that it made her husband more tongue-tied than ever.

'Thursday, Jerry?' he said with a quick glance.

'Thursday, Tom,' said the priest.

The room looked terribly desolate after Una; the crumpled cushions, the glasses, the screen and the film projector. Everything had become frighteningly inert, while outside his window the desolate countryside had taken on even more of its supernatural animation – bogs, hills and fields, full of ghosts and shadows. He sat by the fire, wondering what his life might have been with a girl like that, all furs and scent and laughter, and two bawling, irrepressible brats upstairs. When he tiptoed up to his bedroom he remembered that there never would be children there to wake, and it seemed to him that with all the things he bought to fill his home, he was merely trying desperately to stuff the yawning holes in his own big, empty heart.

On Thursday, when he went to their house, Ita and Brendan were in bed, but refusing to sleep till he said goodnight to them – a regular ritual. While he was taking off his coat the two of them rushed to the banisters and screamed: 'We want Father Fogey.' When he went upstairs they were sitting bolt-upright in their cots, unnaturally clean, a little fat, fair-haired rowdy boy and a solemn baby girl.

'Father, will I be your alboy when I grow up?' Brendan began at once. To be an acolyte was now his great ambition.

'You will to be sure, son,' said Fogarty. 'I wouldn't have anyone else.'

'Ladies first! Ladies first!' the baby shrieked in a frenzy. 'Will I be your alboy, father?'

'Go on!' Brendan said scornfully. 'Little girls can't be alboys, sure they can't, father?'

'I can, I can,' shrieked Ita, who in her excitement exactly resembled her mother. 'Can't I, father?'

'Ah, we'll get a dispensation for you,' Fogarty said soothingly. 'In a pair of trousers, who'd know?'

He was in a wistful frame of mind when he came downstairs again. Children would always be a worse temptation to him than women. Children were the devil, the way they got under your guard.

The house was gay and spotless. The Whittons had no fine mahogany suite like his, but Una managed to make the few coloured odds and ends seem deliberate. The ashtrays were polished, the cushions puffed up. Tom, standing before the fireplace (not to disturb the cushions, thought Fogarty), looked as though someone had held his head under a tap, and was very self-consciously wearing a new brown tie. With his greying hair plastered flat, he looked schoolboyish, sulky and resentful, as though he was contemplating ways of restoring his authority over a mutinous household. The thought crossed Fogarty's mind that he and Una had probably quarrelled over the tie. It went altogether too well with his suit.

'We want Father Fogey,' the children began to chant monotonously from the bedroom.

'Shut up!' Tom shouted back, as though glad to find an enemy to hit back at.

'We want Father Fogey,' the chant went on, but with a groan in it somewhere.

'Well, you're not going to get him. Go to sleep!'

The chant stopped. The old man was clearly in a bad humour.

'You don't mind if I drop down to a meeting tonight, Jerry?' Tom asked in his anxious, quiet way. 'I won't be much more than half an hour.'

'Not at all, Tom,' said Fogarty. 'Sure, I'll drive you.'

'No, thanks,' Whitton said with a quick smile. 'It won't take me ten minutes to get there.'

It was clear that a lot of trouble had gone into the supper, but out of sheer perversity, Whitton let on not to recognize any of the dishes. When they had drunk their coffee he rose and glanced at his watch.

'See you later, Jerry,' he said.

'Tom, you're *not* going to that meeting?' Una asked appealingly.

'I tell you I have to.'

'And I met Mick Mahoney this afternoon, and he said there was no need for you to come.'

'A fat lot Mick Mahoney knows about it!'

'I told him to say that Father Fogarty would be here and you wouldn't come,' she went on desperately, fighting for the success of her evening.

'Then you had no business to do it,' Whitton said angrily, and even Fogarty realized that she had gone the wrong way about it. He began to feel uncomfortable. 'If they come to some damn fool decision when I'm not there, I'll have to take the responsibility for it.'

'If you're late you'd better knock,' she sang out gaily to cover his rudeness. 'Will we go into the sitting room, father?' she asked over-eagerly. 'I'll be with you in two minutes. There are fags on the mantelpiece, and you know where to find the whi-hi-hi—blast that word!'

Fogarty lit a cigarette and sat down. He was feeling very uncomfortable. Whitton was an uncouth and irritable bastard and always had been. He heard Una upstairs and someone turned on the tap in the bathroom. 'Bloody brute!' he thought indignantly. There had been no call for Whitton to insult her before a guest. Why couldn't he have finished his quarrelling while they were alone? The tap stopped and he waited, listening. You could hear everything in that cheap modern house. He was a warm-hearted man and he could not bear the thought of her alone and miserable upstairs. He went quietly up the stairs and stood on the landing. 'Una!' he called softly, afraid of waking the children. There was a light in the bedroom; the door was ajar and he pushed it in. Una was sitting at the end of the bed with a handkerchief in her hand and grinned up dolefully at him.

'Sorry for the whine, father,' she said, making an attempt to smile. Then, with the street-urchin's humour he found so attractive – 'Can I have a loan of your shoulder, please?'

'What the blazes ails Tom?' he asked, sitting beside her.

'He – he's jealous,' she stammered, and began to weep again with her head on his chest. He put his arm about her and patted her awkwardly.

'Jealous?' he asked incredulously, turning over in his mind the half dozen men Una could meet at the best of times. 'Who is he jealous of?'

'He's jealous of you,' she said, sobbing.

'Me?' Fogarty exclaimed, and grew red, thinking of how he had given himself away with his pictures. 'He must be mad! I never gave him any cause for jealousy.'

'Oh, I know he's completely unreasonable,' she said. 'He always was.'

'But you didn't say anything to him, did you?' Fogarty asked anxiously. 'About me, I mean?'

'Oh, he doesn't know about that,' Una replied frantically. 'That's not what he's jealous about. He doesn't give a snap of his fingers about me that way.'

And Fogarty realized that in the simplest way in the world he had been brought to admit to a married woman that he was in love with her and she to imply that she didn't mind, without an indelicate word on either side. Clearly, these things sometimes happened more innocently than he had ever imagined. That made him more embarrassed than ever.

'But what is he jealous of, so?' he asked.

'He's jealous of you because you're a priest,' she said, laughing through her tears. 'Surely, you saw that.'

'I certainly didn't. It never even crossed my mind. It's rather a queer thing for a man to be jealous about.'

Yet at the same time Fogarty wondered if this might not be the reason for the censoriousness he sometimes felt in Whitton against his harmless extravagances.

'But he's hardly ever out of your house, and he's always borrowing your religious books, and talking theology and Church

history to you,' she said, shaking her head at him wonderingly.
'And he has shelves of them already here – look, will you? Look
at that bookcase! In my bedroom! That's why he hates Father
Whelan. Don't you see, Jerry,' she said, calling him by his
Christian name for the first time, 'you have all the things he
wants.'

'I have?' Fogarty asked incredulously. 'What things?'

'Oh, how do I know?' she replied contemptuously, relegating
them to the same class as Father Whelan's bank balance and his
own film camera. 'Respect and responsibility and freedom from
family worries, I suppose.'

'He's welcome to them,' Fogarty said with a wry laugh. 'What's
that the advertisements say? – owner having no further use for
same. I'd say he was the one who had everything.'

'Oh, I know,' she said with another shrug, and he saw that
from the beginning she had realized how he felt about her,
and liked him too, and been sorry. He was sure there was
some contradiction here between her almost inordinate piety
and her calm acceptance of his feeling for her – something that
was exclusively feminine.

'It's a change to be with a man who likes you,' she added with
a mawkish smile.

'Ah, now, Una, that's not true,' he protested gravely, the
priest in him getting the upper hand of the lover, who still had
a considerable amount to learn. 'You only fancy that.'

'I don't, Jerry,' she said with bitter emphasis. 'It's always been
the same from the first month we were married – always, always,
always! I was a bloody fool to marry him at all.'

'Even so, you know he's still fond of you,' Fogarty said
manfully, doing his duty by his friend with schoolboy gravity.
'That's only his way.'

'It's not, Jerry,' she said obstinately. 'He wanted to be a priest
and I stopped him.'

'But you didn't.'

'That's how he looks at it. He thinks I tempted him. Maybe I
did. I paid dear for it.'

'And damn glad he was to fall!'

'But he *did* fall, Jerry, and that's what he'll never forgive me
for. In his heart he despises me, and he despises himself for not
being able to do without me.'

'But what does he despise himself for?' cried Fogarty. 'That's what I can't understand.'

'Because he despises all women, and he wants to be independent of us all. He has to teach to keep a home for me, and he doesn't want to teach. He wants to say Mass and hear confessions, and be God Almighty for seven days of the week.'

Fogarty couldn't grasp it, but he realized that there was something in what she said, and that Whitton was probably a lonely frustrated man who felt he was forever excluded from the only world that interested him.

'I don't understand it,' he said explosively. 'Damn it, it's unnatural.'

'It's unnatural to you because you have it, Jerry,' she said. 'I used to think Tom was unnatural too, but now I'm beginning to think there are more spoiled priests in the world than ever went into seminaries. I don't mean people like you. You're different. You could never be as inhuman as that. But you see, Jerry, I'm a constant reproach to him. He wants to make love to me once a month, and even then, he's ashamed of it . . . I can talk like this to you because you're a priest.'

'You can,' Fogarty said, though he wished she wouldn't. Anybody else but she! But she was so full of her grievance that she didn't even notice the pain she caused him.

'And even when he does, he manages to make me feel that I'm doing it all.'

'And why shouldn't you?' asked Fogarty angrily.

'Because it's a sin!' she said tempestuously.

'Who says it's a sin?'

'He thinks it's a sin. He's like a bear with a sore head for days after it. Don't you see, Jerry, to him it's never anything only adultery, and he goes away and curses himself because he hasn't the strength to resist it.'

'Adultery?' repeated Fogarty, the familiar word knocking at his conscience as though it were Tom Whitton himself at the door.

'Whatever you call it,' Una rushed on. 'It's always adultery, adultery, and I'm always a bad woman and he always wants to show God it wasn't him but me, and I'm sick to death of it. I want to get a bit of fun out of going to bed with a man, and feel like a respectable married woman after it. I feel respectable with you, though I suppose I shouldn't.' She looked in the mirror of the dressing table and her face fell. 'Oh, Lord!' she sighed. 'I don't look very respectable, do I? . . . I'll be down in two minutes now, Jerry,' she said eagerly.

'You're grand,' he muttered thickly.

As he went downstairs he was very thoughtful. He heard Tom's key in the latch and looked at himself in the mirror over the fireplace. He heard Tom's step in the hall, and it sounded in his ears as it had never sounded before, like that of a man carrying a burden too great for him. He realized that he had never before seen Whitton as he really was, a man at war with his animal nature, longing for some high, solitary existence of the intellect and imagination. And he knew that the three of them, Whitton, Una and himself, would die as they had lived, their desires unsatisfied.

The Common Chord (1947)

The Man
of the House

As a kid I was as good as gold so long as I could concentrate.
Concentration, that was always my weakness, in school and
everywhere else. Once I was diverted from whatever I was doing,
I was lost.

It was like that when Mother got ill. I remember it well;
how I waked that morning and heard the strange cough in
the kitchen below. From that very moment I knew something
was wrong. I dressed and went down. She was sitting in a
little wickerwork chair before the fire, holding her side. She
had made an attempt to light the fire but it had gone against
her.

'What's wrong, Mum?' I said.

'The sticks were wet and the fire started me coughing,' she
said, trying to smile, though I could see she was doubled up with
pain.

'I'll light the fire and you go back to bed,' I said.

'Ah, how can I, child?' she said. 'Sure, I have to go to work.'

'You couldn't work like that,' I said. 'Go on up to bed now and
I'll bring up your breakfast.'

It's funny about women, the way they'll take orders from
anything in trousers, even if it is only ten.

'If you could make a cup of tea for yourself I'd be all right
in an hour or two,' she said, and shuffled feebly upstairs. I
went with her, supporting her arm, and when she reached the
bed she collapsed. I knew then she must be feeling bad. I got
more sticks – she was so economical that she never used enough
– and I soon had the fire roaring and the kettle on. I made
her toast as well: I was always a great believer in buttered
toast.

I thought she looked at the cup of tea rather doubtfully.

'Is that all right?' I asked.

'You wouldn't have a sup of boiling water left?' she asked.

"'Tis too strong,' I said, trying to keep the disappointment out of my voice. 'I'll pour half of it away. I can never remember about tea.'

'I hope you won't be late for school,' she said anxiously.

'I'm not going to school,' I said. 'I'll get you your tea now and do the messages after.'

She didn't complain at my not going to school. It was just as I said: orders were all she wanted. I washed up the breakfast things, then I washed myself and went up to her with the shopping basket, a piece of paper, and a lead pencil.

'I'll do the messages if you'll write them down,' I said. I suppose I'll go to Mrs Slattery first.'

'Tell her I'll be in tomorrow, without fail.'

'Write down Mrs Slattery,' I said firmly. 'Would I get the doctor?'

'Indeed, you'll do nothing of the kind,' Mother said anxiously. 'He'd only want to send me to hospital. They're all alike. You could ask the chemist to give you a good strong cough bottle.'

'Write it down,' I said, remembering my own weakness. 'If I haven't it written down I might forget it. And put "strong" in big letters. What will I get for the dinner? Eggs?'

That was really only swank, because eggs were the only thing I could cook, but the mother told me to get sausages as well in case she was able to get up.

It was a lovely sunny morning. I called first on Mrs Slattery, whom my mother worked for, to tell her she wouldn't be in. Mrs Slattery was a woman I didn't like much. She had a big broad face that needed big broad features, but all she had was narrow little eyes and a thin, pointed nose that seemed to get lost in the width of her face.

'She said she'll try to get in tomorrow, but I don't know will I let her up,' I said airily.

'I wouldn't if she wasn't well, Gus,' she said, and gave me a penny.

By this time pride was going a little to my head. That is another weakness of mine, pride. I went by the school and stood opposite it for a full ten minutes, staring. The school-house and the sloping yard were like a picture, except for the chorus of poor sufferers through the open windows, and a glimpse of Danny Delaney's bald pate as he did sentry-go before the front door with his cane wriggling like a tail behind his back. That was nice. It was nice too to be chatting to the assistants in the shops and telling them about Mother's cough. I made it out a bit worse to make a better story of it, but all the time I had a hope that when I reached home she'd be up so that we could have sausages for dinner. I hated boiled eggs, and, anyway, I was beginning to feel the strain of my responsibilities.

But when I got home it was to find Minnie Ryan with her. Minnie was an old maid, gossipy and pious, but very knowledgeable.

'How are you feeling now, Mum?' I asked.

'Oh, I'm grand,' she said with a smile.

'She won't be able to get up today, though,' Minnie said firmly.

'I'll pour you out your cough-bottle so, and make you a cup of tea,' I said, concealing my disappointment and a certain resentment of Minnie Ryan, who could have minded her own business.

'Wisha, I'll do that for you, child,' she said meekly, getting up.

'Ah, you needn't mind, Miss Ryan,' I said nobly. 'I can manage all right.'

'Isn't he great?' I heard Minnie say in a low, wondering voice as I went downstairs. She expressed my own sentiments exactly.

'Minnie, he's the best a woman ever reared,' whispered my mother.

'Why, then, there aren't many like him,' Minnie said bleakly. 'The most of the children that's going are more like savages than Christians.'

In the afternoon Mother wanted me to go out and play, but remembering my weakness, I didn't go far. I knew if I once went a certain distance I should drift towards the Glen, with the barrack drill-field perched on a cliff above it; the rifle-range below, and below that again, the mill-pond and mill-stream running through a wooded gorge – the Rockies, Himalayas, or Highlands, according to your mood. If I once went in that direction, the Lord alone knew when I should come back, and then I should be among the children Minnie Ryan disapproved of who were more like savages than Christians.

Evening came; the street lamps were lit, and the paper boy went crying up the road. I bought a paper, lit the lamp in the kitchen and the candle in the bedroom, and read the police court news to Mother. I knew it was the piece she liked best. I wasn't very quick about it, because I was only at words of one syllable, but she didn't seem to mind.

Later Minnie Ryan came again, and as she left I went to the front door with her. She looked grave.

'If she's not better in the morning I think I'd get a doctor to her, Gus,' she said quietly.

'Why?' I asked in alarm. 'Is she worse?'

'Ah, no, only I'd be frightened of the old pneumonia,' she said, giving her shawl a nervous tug.

'But wouldn't he send her to hospital, Miss Ryan?' I asked. To us, of course, the hospital almost meant the end.

'Ah, he mighn't,' she said without conviction. 'He could give her a good bottle. And even if he did send her to hospital, God between us and all harm, 'twould be better than neglecting it . . . If you had a drop of whiskey you could give it to her hot with a squeeze of lemon.'

'I'll get it,' I said at once.

Mother did not want the whiskey; she said we couldn't afford it, but I felt it might cost less than hospital and all its horrors, and I wouldn't let her put me off.

I had never been in a public house before, and the crowd inside frightened me.

'Hullo, my old flower,' said one tall man, grinning diabolically at me. 'It must be ten years since I saw you last. One minute now – wasn't it in South Africa?'

I was never in South Africa, so I knew the man must be drunk. My pal, Bob Connell, boasted to me once how he had asked a drunk man like that for a half-crown and the man gave it to him. I was always trying to work up courage to do the same, but even then I hadn't the nerve.

'It was not,' I said. 'I want half a glass of whiskey for my mother.'

'Oh, the thundering ruffian!' the man said, clapping his hands and looking at me with astonished eyes. 'Pretending 'tis for his mother, and he the most notorious boozer in Cape Town!'

'I am not,' I said, on the verge of tears. 'And 'tis for my mother. She's sick.'

'Leave the child alone, Johnny!' the barmaid said. 'Don't you hear him say his mother is sick?'

Mother fell asleep after the hot whiskey, but I couldn't rest, wondering how the man in the public house could think I was in South Africa, and blaming myself a lot for not asking him for the half-crown. A half-crown would come in very handy if the mother was really sick, because we never had more than a couple of shillings in the house. When I did fall asleep I was wakened again by her coughing, and when I went in, she was rambling in her speech, and didn't recognize me at first. That frightened me more than anything else.

When she was no better next morning in spite of the whiskey, I was bitterly disappointed. After I had given her her breakfast I went to see Minnie Ryan, and she came and talked to Mother for a few minutes.

'I'd get the doctor at once, Gus,' she said when she came downstairs. 'I'll stop with her while you're out.'

To get the doctor I had first to go to the house of an undertaker who was a Poor Law Guardian to get a ticket to show we couldn't pay. The Poor Law Guardian was very good about that, because afterwards he was sure of the funeral. Then I had to rush back to get the house ready, and prepare a basin of water, soap and a towel for the doctor to wash his hands.

He didn't come until after dinner. He was a fat, slow-moving, loud-voiced man with a grey moustache and the reputation of being 'the cleverest doctor in Cork if only he'd mind himself'. From the way he looked, he hadn't been minding himself much that morning.

'How are you going to get this?' he growled, sitting on the edge of the bed with his prescription pad. 'The only place open now is the North Dispensary.'

'I'll go, doctor,' I said at once.

"Tis a long way,' he said doubtfully. 'Do you think you'll be able to find it?'

'Oh, I'll find it,' I said confidently.

'Isn't he a great help to you?' he said to Mother.

'The best in the world, doctor,' she sighed with a long look at me.

'That's right,' he told me cunningly. 'Look after your mother while you can. She'll be the best for you in the long run . . . We don't mind them when we have them,' he said to Mother, and I could have sworn he was crying. 'Then we spend the rest of our lives regretting them.'

I didn't think he could be a very good doctor, because, after all my trouble, he never washed his hands, but I was prepared to overlook that because he had said nothing about the hospital.

The road to the dispensary led uphill through a poor and thickly-populated neighbourhood to the military barrack, which was perched on the hilltop, and then descended between high walls till it suddenly almost disappeared over the edge of the hill and degenerated into a stony pathway flanked on one side by red-brick council houses and on the other by a wide common with an astounding view of the city. From this the city looked more like the backcloth of a theatre than a real place. The pathway dropped away to the bank of a stream where a brewery stood; and from the brewery, far beneath, the opposite hillside, a murmuring honeycomb of factory chimneys and houses, where noises came to you, dissociated and ghostlike, rose steeply to the gently-rounded hilltop from which a limestone spire and a purple sandstone tower mounted into the clouds. It was so wide and bewildering a view that it was never all lit up at the same time. Sunlight wandered across it as across a prairie, picking out a line of roofs with a brightness like snow, or delving into the depth of some tunnel-like street and outlining in shadow the figures of carts and straining horses.

I felt exalted, a voyager, a heroic figure. I made up my mind to spend the penny Mrs Slattery had given me on a candle to the Blessed Virgin in the cathedral on the hilltop for my mother's recovery. A fellow couldn't expect much attention lighting candles in a small parish church.

The dispensary was a squalid hallway with a bench to one side and a window like a ticket office at the end. There was a little girl with a green plaid shawl about her shoulders sitting on the bench. She gave me a quick look and I saw that her eyes were green as well. For years after, whenever a girl looked at me like that, I hid. I knew by that time what it meant. I knocked at the office and a seedy, angry-looking man banged up the wooden screen. Without waiting to hear what I was trying to say he grabbed bottle and prescription and banged the shutter down again. I waited a minute and then lifted my hand to knock again.

'You'll have to wait, little boy,' the girl said hastily.

'Why will I have to wait?' I asked.

'He have to make it up,' she explained. 'He might be half an hour at it. You might as well sit down.'

As she obviously knew how to behave in a place like that, I did what she had told me.

'Where are you from?' she asked, dropping the shawl, which she held in front of her mouth exactly the way I'd seen old women hold it. 'I live in Blarney Lane.'

'I live beyond the barrack,' I said.

'And who's the bottle for?'

'My mother.'

'What's wrong with your mother?'

'She have a cough.'

'She might have consumption,' the girl said cheerfully. 'That's what my sister that died last year had. My other sister has to have tonics. That's what I'm waiting for. Is it nice up where ye live?'

I told her about the Glen, and she told me about the river up Sunday's Well way. It seemed a nicer place altogether than ours, as she described it. She was a pleasant, talkative little girl, and I never noticed the time passing. Suddenly the shutter went up and a bottle was banged on the counter.

'Dooley!' said the man, and the shutter went down again.

'That's mine,' said the little girl. 'My name is Nora Dooley. Yours won't be ready for a long time yet. Is it red or black?'

'I don't know,' I said. 'I never got it before.'

'Black ones is better,' she said. 'Red is more for hacking coughs.'

'I have a penny,' I said. 'I'm going to get sweets.'

I had decided that after all I didn't need to light a candle. I felt sure Mother would be all right soon, anyway, and it seemed a pity to waste the money like that.

When I got the bottle, it was black. The little girl and I sat on the steps of the infirmary and ate the sweets I had bought. At the end of the Lane was the limestone spire of Shandon; all along it young trees overhung the high, hot walls, and the sun, when it came out in hot, golden blasts behind us, threw our linked shadows on to the road.

'Give us a taste of your bottle, little boy,' said the girl.

'Can't you have a taste of your own?' I said.

'Ah, you couldn't drink mine,' she said. 'Tonics is all awful. Try it and see.'

I did, and I spat it out hastily. It was awful, all right. But after that, I couldn't do less than let her taste mine. She took a long drink out of it, and this alarmed me.

'That's beautiful,' she said. 'That's like my sister that died used to get. I love cough bottles.'

I tried it, and saw she was right in a way. It was very sweet and sticky, like treacle.

'Give us another slug,' she said.

'I will not,' I said in alarm. 'What am I going to do with it now?'

'All you have to do is put water in it out of a pump. That's what I used to do, and nobody ever noticed.'

I couldn't refuse her. Mother was far away, and I was swept from anchorage into an unfamiliar world of spires, towers, trees, steps and little girls who liked cough bottles. Then I began to panic. I saw that even if you put water into it, you could not conceal the fact that it wasn't the same.

'What am I going to do now?' I said miserably.

'Ah, finish it and say the cork fell out,' she said lightly, as if surprised at my innocence. I believed her, but as I put down the empty bottle I remembered my mother sick and the Blessed Virgin slighted, and I knew I could never tell a lie the way she could. I knew, too, that she didn't care. She was through with me now. It was my cough bottle she had been after all the time. I began to weep despairingly.

'What ails you?' she said impatiently.

'My mother is sick, and you're after drinking her medicine, and now, if she dies, 'twill be my fault,' I said.

'Ah, what old nonsense you have!' she said contemptuously. 'No one ever died of a cough. All you have to say is that the cork fell out – 'tis a thing that might happen to anyone.'

'And I promised to light a candle to the Blessed Virgin, and I spent it on sweets for you,' I cried, and went away up the road, sobbing and clutching my empty bottle. She looked after me curiously, I noticed, but she didn't even follow me. I was well paid out for my folly. Now I had only one hope – a miracle. I went into the cathedral to the shrine of the Blessed Virgin, and promised her a candle with the next penny I got if only she made Mother better by the time I got home. Then I went miserably home. All the light had gone out of the day, and the echoing hillside had

253

become a vast, alien, cruel world. Besides, I felt terribly sick. It struck me that I might even die myself. In one way that would be a great ease to me.

When I reached home, the silence of the kitchen and the sight of the empty grate told me at once that my prayers had not been heard: Mother was still sick and in bed. I began to howl.

'Wisha, what is it at all, child?' Mother cried anxiously from upstairs.

'I lost the medicine,' I bellowed from the foot of the stairs, and then dashed blindly up to bury my face in the bedclothes.

'Ah, wisha, wisha, if that's all that's a trouble to you, you poor misfortunate child!' she cried in relief, running her hand through my hair. 'I was afraid you were lost. Is anything the matter?' she added anxiously. 'You feel hot.'

'I drank the medicine,' I bawled, and buried my face again.

'And if you did itself, what harm?' she murmured. 'You poor child, going all that way by yourself, without a proper dinner or anything! Why wouldn't you? Take off your clothes and lie down now, till you're better.'

She rose, put on her slippers and overcoat, and unlaced my shoes. Even before she finished I was asleep. Whatever was in the medicine, I couldn't keep my eyes open. I didn't hear her go out, but some time later I felt a cool hand on my forehead, and saw Minnie Ryan peering down at me.

'Ah, 'tis nothing, woman,' she said, more in amusement than anything else. 'He'll sleep it off by morning. Well, aren't they the devil! God knows, you'd never be up to them! And, indeed and indeed, Mrs Sullivan, you're the one that should be in bed.'

I knew all that. I knew it was her judgement on me. I was only another of those who were more like savages than Christians; I was no good as a nurse, no good to anyone at all. I accepted it meekly. But when Mother came up to the bedroom with her evening paper, and sat reading by the bed, I knew the miracle had happened all right. Somebody had cured her.

Travellers' Samples (1951)

My First Protestant

It was when I was doing a line with Maire Daly that I first came to know Winifred Jackson. She was my first Protestant. There were a number of them in our locality, but they kept to themselves. The Jacksons were no exception. Winifred's father was a bank manager, a tall, thin, weary-looking man, and her mother a chubby, pious woman who had a lot to do with religious bazaars. They had one son, Ernest, a medical student who was forever trying to get engaged to whatever trollop he was going with at the time – a spoiled pup, I thought him.

I had never noticed before how lovingly and carefully the two sects were kept apart. That was probably why Winifred caused her parents more concern than Ernest did. She and Maire were both learning the piano from old Streichl, and they became great friends. The Dalys' was a great house in those days. Mick Daly was a builder; a tall, thin, sardonic man who, after long and bitter experience, had come to the conclusion that the whole town was in a conspiracy against him, and that his family – all but his wife, whom he regarded as a friendly neutral – was allied with the town. His wife was a handsome woman, whose relations with the enemy were far closer than her husband ever suspected. As for the traitors – Joe, Maire, Brenda, and Peter, the baby – they had voices like trumpets from shouting one another down, and exceedingly dirty tongues to use when the vocal cords gave out.

Joe was the eldest. He was a lad with a great head for whiskey and an even better one for books, if only he had taken them seriously, but it was a convention of the Daly family not to take anything seriously but money and advancement. Like other conventions this was not always observed in practice, but in theory it was always accepted, except by Peter, who later became a Jesuit, and Peter was no advertisement for unconventionality, having something in common with a submarine. He was a handsome lad with an enormous brow and bright blue eyes, and when he was submerged had a tendency to cut you dead in the street. For weeks he sat in his room, reading with ferocity, and then suddenly decided to come up for air and a little light conversation, and argued like a mad dog with you until two in the morning. At the time I speak of he happened to be a roaring atheist, as a result of an overdose of St Thomas Aquinas, and described me to Joe as 'just another belly-thumping image-worshipper'. That, the Dalys said flatly, was what reading did for you.

Yet it was a wonderful house on a Sunday evening when the children and their friends were in, and old Daly concluded an armistice with them for the evening. There was always lashings of stuff, because the Dalys, for all their worldly wisdom, could do nothing in a small and niggardly way. If you asked one of them for a cigarette, you were quite liable to be given a box of a hundred, and attempting to repay it might well be regarded as a deadly insult. Brenda, the younger girl, slouched round with sandwiches and gibes; Joe sang 'Even Bravest Heart May Swell' with an adoring leer at Maire, who played his accompaniment, when he came to 'Loving smile of sister kind', and Maire said furiously: 'Of all the bloody nonsense! A puck in the gob was all we ever got.'

'Really, they are an extraordinary family,' Winifred said with a sigh as I saw her home one night.

I didn't take it as criticism. Having been brought up in a fairly quiet home myself, I sometimes felt the same bewilderment.

'Isn't that what you like about them?' I asked.

'Is it, do you think?' she asked in surprise. 'I dare say you're right. I only wish Daddy thought the same.'

'What does he object to?' I asked.

'Oh, nothing in particular,' she replied with a shrug. '"Just the wrong persuasion, dear." Haven't I nice girls of my own sort to mix with? Don't I realize that everything said in that house is reported in confession? . . . By the way, Dan, is it?'

'Not everything.'

'I hardly thought so,' she said drily. 'Anyhow, they can confess anything I say to them.'

'You're not afraid of being converted?' I asked.

'Oh, anybody is welcome to try,' she said indifferently. 'Really, people are absurd about religion.'

I didn't say that some such ambition wasn't very far from Mrs Daly's mind. I had seen for myself that she liked Winifred and thought her good company for Maire, who was a bit on the wild side, and it was only natural that a woman so big-hearted should feel it a pity that a nice girl like Winifred dug with the wrong foot. It probably wasn't necessary to tell Winifred. There was little about the Dalys that she wasn't shrewd enough to observe for herself. That was part of *their* charm.

But, all the same, her parents had good ground for worry. What began as a friendship between herself and Maire continued as a love affair between herself and Joe. It came to a head during the summer holidays when the Dalys took a house in Crosshaven, and Winifred stayed with them. I went down for occasional weekends, and found it just like Cork, only worse. By some mysterious mental process, Mr Daly had worked out that, as part of a general conspiracy, the property-owners in Crosshaven charged outrageous rents and then encouraged you to dissipate the benefits of your holiday by keeping you up all night, so he insisted on everyone's being in bed by eleven. With the connivance of the neutral power we all slipped out again when he was asleep for a dance in some neighbour's house, a moonlight swim or row, or walk along the cliffs. I was surprised at the change in Winifred. When I had first known her she was prim and demure, and when she was ragged about it, inclined to be truculent and awkward, but now she had grown to accept the ragging that was part of the Dalys' life and evolved a droll and impudent defence which gave the people the impression that it was she who was making fun of them. Irish Catholics don't like to be made fun of, so naturally this line was far more effective.

'She's coming on,' I said to Maire one evening when we were lying on the cliffs.

'She's getting more natural,' Maire admitted. 'At first she'd disgrace you. It wasn't bad enough wanting to pay for her own tea, but when she gave me the penny for the bus I thought I'd die of shame. I was so damn flabbergasted I took it from her.'

The picture of Maire taking a penny made me laugh outright, because she, too, had all the Daly lavishness, and there was nothing flashy or common about it. It was just that the story of their lives was written like that, in large capital letters.

'It's all damn well for you,' said Maire, who had no notion what I was laughing at. 'That damn family of hers must be as mean as hell.'

'Not mean,' I said. 'Just prudent.'

'Prudent!'

'Where is she now?'

'Being imprudent, I hope. Joe and herself are doing a terrible line. She'd be grand for him. She'd keep him in his place.'

'Why? Does he need to be kept in his place?' I asked.

'Joe? That fellow is as big a bully as Father,' said Maire, busy tickling my nose with a blade of grass she had been chewing. 'God, the way Mother ruins that fellow! She'd order you out of the lavatory the way he wouldn't have to wait. Nobody is going to walk on Winifred. Aren't Protestants great, Dan?'

'We'll see when her family hears about herself and Joe,' I said.

'Oh, they're kicking up bloody murder about that already,' Maire said, throwing away one blade of grass and picking another to chew – a most restless woman! 'They think the Pope sicked him on to her.'

'And didn't he?'

'Is it Mother?' said Maire with a laugh. 'Would you blame her? Two birds with one stone – a wife for Joe and a soul for God! The poor woman would die happy.'

After that I watched Winifred's romance with real sympathy, perhaps with a reminiscence of *Romeo and Juliet* in my mind, perhaps already with a feeling of revolt against the cliques and factions of a provincial town. For a time it almost meant more to me than my own affair with Maire.

It didn't last though. One autumn evening when I was coming home from the office I saw Winifred emerge from a house on Summerhill. She saw me too and waved, and then came charging after me with her long legs flying. She always remained leggy and bird-like even in middle age; a tall, thin girl with a long, eager face, blue eyes and fair hair that wouldn't stay fixed. When she caught up on me she took my arm. That was the sort of thing I liked about her: the way she ran, the way she grabbed your arm, the way she burst into spontaneous intimacy with no calculation behind it.

'How's Joe?' I asked. 'I haven't seen him this past week.'

'No more have I, Dan,' she said lightly enough.

'How's that?' I asked gravely. 'I thought you'd be giving us a night by this time.'

'Ah, I don't think it'll ever come to that, Dan,' she replied in the same light-hearted tone, without any regret that I could detect.

'You're not going to disappoint us?' I asked, and I fancy there must have been more feeling in my voice than in hers.

'Well, we've discussed it, of course,' she said in a business like tone. 'But he can't marry me unless I become a Catholic.'

'Can't he?' I asked.

'Well, I suppose he couldn't be stopped if he took it into his head, but can you imagine Joe doing a daft thing like that? You know how it would affect his business.'

'I dare say it would,' I said, and mind you, it was the first time the idea of a thing like that had crossed my mind – I must have been more sentimental than I know, even now. 'But you could get a dispensation.'

'*If* I agreed to have the children brought up as Catholics.'

'Och, to hell with the children!' I said. 'They're all in the future. Why wouldn't you agree?'

'Really, Dan, how could I?' she asked wearily, giving my arm a tug. 'It's all that the parents threatened me with from the beginning. Oh dear! I suppose it was wrong of me to start anything at all with Joe, but no matter how fond of him I am, I can't walk out on them now.'

'It's your life, not theirs,' I said.

'Even so, Dan, I have to consider their feelings as Joe has to consider his parents' feelings. His mother wouldn't like to see her grandchildren brought up as Protestants, and my parents feel just the same. You may think they're wrong, but it would hurt them just as much as if they were right.'

'I think the sooner people with opinions like that get hurt, the better,' I said with a dull feeling of disappointment.

'Oh, I know!' she retorted, dropping my arm and flaring up at me like a real litle termagant. 'I'm a Protestant, so I'm a freak, and it's up to me to make all the sacrifices.'

We were passing St Luke's Cross at the time, and I stopped dead and looked at her. Up to this I thought I'd never felt so intensely about anything. It didn't even occur to me that we were standing outside the church she worshipped in.

'If that's the sort you think I am, you're very much mistaken,' I said. 'If you were my girl I wouldn't let God, man or devil come between us.'

Her face suddenly cleared and she grasped my arm.

'You know, Dan, I almost wish I was,' she said in a curious ringing tone.

Anyone who didn't know her would have taken that for an invitation, but even then, emotional as I was, I knew it was nothing of the sort. I think if I'd tried to slink inside Joe at that moment she'd have hated me for the rest of my life. Whatever it was she had to give was already given to Joe.

The following evening I went for a walk with Joe up the Western Road and we had it out. It was a queer conversation. I was at my worst, and Joe was at his best, and I remember his sensitiveness and my own awkwardness as if it was only yesterday.

'I had a talk with Winifred last night,' I said. 'I hope you won't think me interfering if I mention it to you.'

'I know anything you said would be kindly meant, Dan,' he said gently.

This was one of the many nice things about Joe. However much of a bully he might be, you did not have to skirmish for position with him. It had something to do with the capital letters that the Dalys used as if by nature.

'I think she's very fond of you, Joe,' I said.

'I think the same, Dan,' he agreed warmly. 'And 'tisn't all on one side. I needn't tell you that.'

'You couldn't come to some agreement with her about the religious business?' I asked.

'I'd like to know what agreement we could come to,' he said gravely. 'I can talk to you about it because you know what it means. You know what would happen to the business if I defied everybody and married Winifred in a register office.'

'But you want her to do it instead, Joe,' I said.

''Tisn't alike, Dan,' he said in his monumental way. 'And you know 'tisn't alike. It might have been different a hundred years ago – even fifty years ago. But this is a Catholic country now. Her people haven't the power they had, and they're not going to risk their own position bringing business to a lapsed Catholic. It might mean ruin to me, but it would mean nothing to Winifred.'

'That only makes it worse,' I said. 'You want her to give up a religion that she believes in for one that means nothing to you, only the harm it could do your business.'

'I never said it meant nothing to me,' he said with a smile. 'It means a lot, as a matter of fact. But you've shifted your ground, Dan. That's a different proposition entirely. We were talking about my responsibility to provide for a family.'

'Very well, then,' I said, thinking I saw a way out. 'Tell her that! Tell her what you've told me; that you'll marry her your way and take the responsibility, or marry her her way and let her take it.'

'Aren't you forgetting that a man can't shift the responsibility for a family, Dan?' he asked, laying a friendly hand on my shoulder.

'She can see that as well as I can, and she won't take the responsibility,' I said.

'Ah, well, Dan, she mightn't be as intelligent as you about it, and then I'd have to face the consequences just the same.'

'You won't have any consequences to face, Joe,' I said. 'She's not that sort of a girl at all.'

'Dan, I'm beginning to think you're the one who should marry her,' he said jokingly.

'I'm beginning to think the same,' I said, getting into a huff.

We dropped the subject, and we never discussed it again, but I'd still take my dying oath that if he'd done what I suggested she'd have pitched her family to blazes and married him. All a girl like that wanted was proof that he cared enough about her to take a risk, and after it she'd spend her life seeing that he didn't pay for it. Capital letters are not enough where love is concerned. You want something more. Nowadays I don't blame him, but at that age when you feel a friend must be everything from Solomon to Julius Caesar I felt hurt and disillusioned.

Winifred wasted no tears over him, and in a few months was walking out in a practical way with a schoolteacher of her own persuasion – whoever persuaded them. She still called at the Dalys', but things were not the same. Mrs Daly was disappointed in her. It struck her as strange that an intelligent girl like Winifred could not see the errors of Protestantism for herself, and, from the moment she knew that there was to be no spectacular public conversion, gave her up as a bad job. She told me that she had never approved of mixed marriages, and for once she got me really angry.

'All marriages are mixed marriages, Mrs Daly,' I said stiffly. 'They're all right when the mixture is all right.'

It was about that time that I began to notice that the mixture of Maire and myself wasn't all right. It was partly the feeling that the house was not the same without Winifred there. She hadn't been there when I knew the Dalys first, but that made no difference. These things happen to people and places: some light goes out in them, and afterwards they are never the same again. Maire said the change was in me, and that I was becoming conceited and irritable. Maybe she was right.

But for months I was sore about it. It wasn't Maire I missed so much as the family. My own home life had been too quiet, and I had loved the capital letters, the gaiety and the tantrums. I had now drifted into another spell of loneliness, but loneliness with a new and disturbing feeling of alienation; and Cork is a bad place for a man who feels like that. It was as if I couldn't communicate with anybody. On Sundays, instead of going to Mass, I walked down the quays and along the river. It was pleasant there, and I sat on a bench under the trees and watched the reflection of the big painted houses and the cliffs behind them in the water, or read some book. A long, leisurely book – it looked as though I should have a lifetime to read it in.

I had been doing it for months when, one day, I noticed a man who turned up each Sunday about the same time. I knew him; he was a teacher from the South Side. We chatted, and the following Sunday when we met again he said quizzically:

'You seem to be very fond of ships.'

'Mr Reilly,' I said, 'those that go down to the sea in ships are to me the greatest wonder of the Lord.'

'Oh, is that so?' he said without surprise. 'I just wondered when I saw you here so much.'

That morning I was feeling depressed and resentful, and I didn't care much whom I told about it.

'It happens to be the most convenient quiet spot to the church where my family think I am at the moment,' I said.

'I fancied that from the book you have under your arm,' he said with amusement. 'I wouldn't let too many people see that book if I was you. They might misunderstand you.' Then, noticing a third man we had both seen before, he added: 'I wonder would he by any chance be doing the same thing.'

As a matter of fact he was. It was remarkable, after we got to know one another, the number of educated men who found their way to the Marina Walk on Sunday mornings. Reilly called us 'The Atheists' Club', but that was only swank because we had only one atheist. Reilly and myself were mild agnostics, and the rest were anti-clericals or young fellows with doubts. All this revealed itself very gradually in our Sunday morning talks. It was also revealed to me that I wasn't the only young man in town who was lonely and dissatisfied.

After Winifred got married I visited her a couple of times, and her husband and I got on well together. He was a plump, jolly, good-natured man, fond of his game of golf and his glass of whiskey, and I had the impression that Winifred and himself hit it off excellently. They had two sons. Joe never gave her any great cause to regret him because, though his business prospered, he proved a handful for the girl who got him. Drink was his trouble, and he bore it with great dignity. At one time half the police in Cork seemed to be exclusively engaged in getting him home to prevent his being charged with drunkenness and disorderly conduct by the other half, and except for one small fine for being on unlicensed premises after hours – a young policeman was responsible for that and he was transferred immediately – he never was charged.

But, of course, we all drifted apart. Ten years later, when I read that Winifred's husband was dead, I went to the funeral for the sake of old times, saw nobody I knew there and slipped away again before it reached the cemetery.

A couple of months later, I strolled back from the Atheists' Club one Sunday morning as Mass was ending to pick up two orthodox acquaintances who I knew would be at it. It was a sunny day: the church, as usual, was crammed, and I stood on the pavement, watching the crowds pour down the steps and thinking how much out of it all I was. Suddenly I caught a glimpse of Winifred passing under the portico at right angles in the direction of the back gate. She had the two children with her, and it was only the sight of these that convinced me I wasn't imagining it. I dashed through the crowd to reach her, and the moment she saw me her face lit up. She caught my hands – it was one of those instinctive gestures that at once brought back old times to me.

'Dan!' she cried in astonishment. 'What on earth brings you here?'

'Young lady,' I said, 'I am *not* here, and anyway I'm the one that should ask that question.'

'Oh, it's a long story,' she said with a laugh. 'If you're coming back my way I might tell you, and I'm sure there's a bottle of stout at home . . . Run along, Willie!' she sang out to the elder boy, and he and his brother went ahead of us up the steps.

'I wouldn't have believed it of you,' I said.

'Ah, what is there to keep me back now?' she said with a shrug. 'Daddy and Mummy are dead, and you know how much Ernest cares what I do.'

'Well, you still seem quite cheerful,' I said. 'Almost as cheerful as a roaring agnostic like myself.'

'Ah, but look at you, Dan!' she said mockingly, taking my hand again without the least trace of self-consciousness. 'A bachelor, with nothing in the world to worry about! Why on earth wouldn't you be cheerful?'

I nearly told her why but thought better of it. It was too like her own story, but her way out could never be mine. Besides, if I decided now to try to get on the same terms with her as I had once almost done from blind rage, the position would be reversed. It was I and not she who would have to sign on the dotted line. But for the first time I understood how her life had gone awry. A woman always tries to give the children she loves whatever it is she feels she has missed in life. Often you don't even know what it was till you see what it is she is trying to give them. Perhaps she doesn't know herself. With some it's money, with others it's education; with others still, it is just love. And the kids never value it, of course. How could they when they've never known the lack of it?

And there, as we sat over our drinks in the front room of her little house, two old cronies, I thought how strange it was that the same thing had sent us in opposite directions. A man and a woman in search of something are always driven apart, but it is the same thing that drives them.

Travellers' Samples (1951)

This Mortal Coil

Every Sunday morning, at a time when the rest of the city was at church, a few of us met on the river bank. We were the people who didn't believe in church, and we ranged from a seminarist with scruples to a roaring atheist. It was curious, the discussions and confessions you heard there. I often thought it must have been like that in the early days of Christianity. Youth, of course, will turn anything into a religion – even having no religion at all.

Curious friendships sprang up as well, like the one between me and Dan Turner. Dan was our atheist, and the one I liked best. He was a well-built, fresh-coloured man who looked like a sailor or a farmer, but he was really a County Council clerk. Part of my sympathy for him was because of the way he was penalized for his opinions. Long before, at the age of eighteen, he had had to give evidence in a taxation case and insisted on making a declaration instead of taking the oath. That finished him. Though he was easily the cleverest man in the Courthouse, he would never be secretary or anything approaching it. And knowing this, and knowing all the intrigues that went on against him, only made him more positive and truculent.

Not that he thought of himself as either; in his own opinion he was a perfect example of the English genius for compromise, but the nearest he ever got to ignoring some remark he disagreed with was to raise his eyebrows into his hair, turn his blue eyes the other way, and whistle. A man who might be inclined to overlook a spot of atheism would not overlook a whistle.

'Och, Dan, you take things to the fair,' I said to him once.

'All I ask is that bloody idiots will keep their opinions to themselves and not be airing them on me,' he said in the tone of a reasonable man who was only asking that people shouldn't spit on the dining-room carpet.

'If you want people to behave like that, you should go somewhere you won't be a target for them,' I said.

'And if we all did that, this country would never be anything only a home for idiots,' he said saucily.

'Oh, if you only want to make a martyr of yourself in the interests of the country, that's different,' I said. 'But it seems to me very queer conduct for a man who calls himself a rationalist. I call that sentimentality.'

He nearly struck me for calling it sentimentality, but of course, that's what it was, really. If you ask me, that's what atheism is – sentimental agnosticism. And, for all Dan's brains, he was as emotional as a child. He was cut to the heart by the intrigues against him. He lived in an old house on the quays with a pious old maid sister called Madge who adored him, cluck-clucked and tut-tutted his most extravagant statements and went to Mass every morning to pray for his conversion. He didn't like it, but he knew that she would never marry and that he would have to support her till the day she died, and he was too big a man to emphasize her dependence on him. It was only when she really drove him insane telling him about miraculous apparitions in Donegal that he blew up on her.

'That's not religion at all, woman,' he would shout, slapping the arm of his chair in vexation. 'That's only barbarous superstition.' But Madge only pitied and loved him the more for it, and went on in her own way believing in God, ghosts, fairies, and nutmegs for lumbago.

It wasn't until well into his thirties that Dan fell in love, and then he did it in a way that no rationalist could approve of. Tessa Bridie wasn't very young either, but, like many another fine girl in the provinces, she found that the fellows who wanted to marry her were not always those she wanted to marry. Also, like many another fine girl, she was holding on like grim death to a clerk in an insurance office called MacGuinness, with jet-black curly hair, nationalist sentiments and great aspirations after the religious life, which, I suppose, is the only sort of life a clerk in an insurance office can aspire to.

Dan and Tessa made a nice pair. They both had plenty of character and intelligence, and in a town like ours meeting someone you can fall in love with and at the same time talk intelligently to is a thing you dream about. But the damn atheistic nonsense would keep cropping up. Tessa was convinced for a long time that Dan was the answer to her prayers, but Dan in his simple, straightforward way wouldn't let her be. He had to prove to her that he couldn't be the answer to anyone's prayer, because there was nobody to answer prayers, and it was foolishness – foolishness and worse – to imagine that they could be answered.

Now, Tessa wasn't by any means a bigoted girl: she had several brothers, and she knew that in the matter of religion and politics every man without exception had a slate loose somewhere, but Dan was out on his own. She started a novena for enlightenment, hoping to bring in a verdict in his favour, but she was so acutely aware that he thought there was no enlightenment either that the novena came out the wrong way. With his English tendency to compromise, Dan cursed and swore; assured her that he was the most tolerant man in the bloody world, and that she could believe in any damn childish nonsense she liked so long as she married him, but Dan's compromise frightened her more than another man's intransigence and she got engaged to the insurance man. I thought it a pity, because she was a really nice intelligent girl, and I was sure that a couple of kids would lower Dan's voltage quite a bit.

What the other thing would do to him I didn't know but I soon found out. It seemed he had deserted all his old haunts (he no longer came down the river on Sundays), was off eating and talking, and didn't stir out at night until after dark, when he went for long, lonesome walks in the country. People who had met him talked about the way he passed them without recognition or with a curt nod. I knew the symptoms. I knew them only too well, and I felt it was up to me to do something. One fine evening I called. Madge opened the door, and I could see she had been crying.

'I didn't see Dan this long time, Madge,' I said. 'How is he?'

'Come in, Michael John,' she said, taking out her handkerchief. 'He's upstairs. He didn't stir out this past couple of days. Sure, you know the County Council will never stand it.'

I followed her up the stairs. Dan was lying on his bed, dressed except for a collar and tie, his two hands under his head, apparently studying the ceiling and finding it very unsatisfactory. When I came in he raised his brows with his usual look of blank astonishment as much as to say: 'Can't I have even a moment's peace in this house?'

'Would you like a cup of tea, Dan?' Madge asked anxiously.

'If it's for me you needn't mind,' said Dan with a patient long-suffering air that made it plain what he thought of the suggestion that he could be snatched back from the gates of the grave by a cup of tea.

'Wisha, I'm sure Michael John would like one,' Madge said in a wail.

'You're not feeling well, I hear?' I said.

'I don't know how you heard anything of the kind,' said Dan, rolling his blue eyes to the other side of the room. 'I'm sure I didn't complain.'

'Wisha, Michael John,' Madge burst out, 'did you ever in all your life hear of a grown man carrying on like that on account of a woman?'

'Now, I told you before I wasn't going to discuss my business with you,' Dan said, raising the palm of his hand between them like a partition wall.

'Why then, indeed, she discussed it enough with everybody,' Madge said, not realizing how every word hurt. 'There wasn't much about you that she didn't repeat. How well I could hear it all from a woman in the market!'

'Well, go back and discuss it with the woman in the market,' he retorted brutally. She gave me a tearful smile and went downstairs.

'You have a grand view,' I said, looking down on the quays and the three-master below the bridge in the dusk.

'There isn't the traffic there used to be,' he said grudgingly.

'You never wanted to be a sailor?' I asked.

'I was never asked,' he replied, as if this were one grievance he hadn't thought of. 'No one ever consulted me about what I wanted to be.'

I looked again at the shelf of books by the bed; a few popular books on physics and a fine collection of history and historical memoirs. History is a grand source for unbelievers.

'What you need is a holiday,' I said.

'How can I take a holiday?' he asked, turning his blue eyes wonderingly on me as if he had discovered that I was only another of his persecutors.

'If you go on like this you'll take a holiday whether you like it or not,' I said. 'And it won't be by the seaside either. What about Ballybunion for a week?'

The eyebrows went up again.

'Parish priests.'

'All right,' I said. 'We'll go where there are no parish priests.'

'We'll travel a hell of a distance,' he said despondently, but all the same the idea appealed to him. 'I'd like to see London again. 'Tis ten years since I was there last.'

It almost put him into a good humour, and when I was leaving he put on a collar and tie and walked home with me. I could see that Madge was well-pleased, and I wasn't too dissatisfied myself.

But the pleasure didn't last long. Next morning I was at work when she called for me. She could scarcely speak for terror.

'Michael John, something awful is after happening,' she said. ''Tis Dan. I don't know what to do with him. He tried to commit suicide.'

'He what?' I said.

'He did, Michael John. After he came home last night. He turned on the gas tap before he went to bed. I know because I could still smell it this morning. He's in bed now with a roaring headache.' Then she began to cry. 'Sure, anyone could have told him you couldn't commit suicide with the gas we have in our house.'

I told her I'd be down that night and try to get him away by Saturday. It was all I could think of. Suicide was a thing I had no experience of because in our class a man's family and friends would never let him go so far. It was only when a man or woman had nobody that they were found in the river, and then it was always brought in as accidental death not to depress the neighbours.

I didn't know what the best thing was, so I bought a bottle of whiskey and a few gramophone records. Whenever I feel like committing suicide myself I usually go out and buy something extravagant because after such a tribute of respect to myself I feel less like depriving the community of my services.

Dan was sitting in the front room when I went in, still without a collar and tie, and he barely lifted his eyes to salute me. With the dusk coming down on the river outside, he seemed so lonesome, so shut away in his own doubt and gloom, that he almost reduced me to the same state. Believe me, you can be very lonely in a provincial town.

'Well, I got leave from Saturday if you're ready to start,' I said, trying to make my voice sound as much like a hunting horn as possible.

'I don't know that I'll be able,' he replied in a dead voice, as though the words were merely a momentary interruption of a train of thought that was too strong for him.

'You'll have to,' I said. 'You can't go on like this much longer.'

'I wasn't thinking of going on much longer,' he said in the same tone.

'Why?' I asked, raising my voice and trying to make a joke of it. 'You weren't thinking of chucking yourself in the river or anything?'

'I suppose a man might as well do that as anything else.'

'Ah, look here, Dan,' I said, opening the bottle of whiskey, 'we all think like that at times, and it's only a mug's game. In a week's time you'll be laughing at it.'

'Of course, if you're not there in a week's time, you won't have an opportunity of laughing at it.'

'That's why it's a mug's game,' I said, filling him out a stiff drink. 'Doing something permanent about something temporary is always a mug's game.'

'Life itself is a pretty temporary affair, I always understood,' he said.

'It goes on quite a while, just the same,' said I. 'How old are you? Thirty-five?'

'Thirty-eight,' he said in the tone of an old paralytic telling you he's eighty-three and will be glad when the Lord takes him. 'And what has a man of thirty-eight to look forward to in this country?'

'Being thirty-nine,' said I.

'It's hardly likely to be much pleasanter than being thirty-eight,' he said. 'And that, let me tell you, is no great shakes.'

I sat opposite him with my whiskey, while he continued to look at me moodily, a big, powerful, red-faced man, his hands over the arms of his chair, his head lowered, his eyebrows raised, the blue smouldering eyes in ambush beneath them.

'The trouble with you, Dan, is that you're under two illusions,' I said. 'One is that everyone except yourself is having a lovely time; the other is that when you're dead, your troubles are over.'

That roused him all right.

'That's not an illusion,' he said, raising his voice. 'That's a scientific fact.'

'Fact, my nanny!' I said. 'How do you know?'

''Tis a fact that anyone can see with his own two eyes,' he said, getting angrier and more positive.

'Well, I can't see it for one,' I said.

'You can see it, but you don't want to see it,' he said, tossing his big head as though he was going to gore me. 'It doesn't suit you to see it. You're like all the other optimistic gentlemen who pretend they can't see it. My God!' he said, beginning to splutter with rage. 'The vanity and conceit of people imagining that their own miserable little existence is too valuable to be wiped out!'

Then I began to get angry too. Forgetting he was a sick man, I wanted to take it out on him for his unmannerly arrogance and complacency.

'And who the hell are you?' I asked. 'Who told you you were alive in the first place?'

'Who told me?' he repeated, a bit shaken. 'No one told me. I am alive. If I didn't know that I wouldn't know anything.'

'And what *do* you know?' I shouted. 'As long as you can't tell me who you really are, or what you're doing in this room at this moment, you have no right to tell me in that impudent tone that you know what's going to happen to you when you die.'

He considered that for a moment. I fancy it had never occurred to him in his life before that a man of his strong character mightn't be as real as he thought himself and that he didn't quite know how to answer me.

'I admit there are things you can't explain yet,' he said grudgingly.

'Nor ever will be able to explain,' I said.

'Everything can be explained,' he said, getting mad again.

'Not things that are deliberately intended not to be explained,' said I.

'Oh, so you think it's all deliberate?' he said mocking me.

'If you think at all, you have to think that,' said I. 'You can no more live without doubt than you can live without air – doubt about what's going to happen tomorrow, doubt about what's going to happen next year, doubt about a future life.'

'Plenty of people think they know all about the future life.'

'They have faith,' I said. 'But you can't have faith unless you have doubt.'

'They have more than faith, Mr O'D,' he said saucily. 'According to themselves they have actual knowledge.'

271

'More than faith is no faith at all,' said I. 'They're just like you, pretending to know. Damn it, doubt is the first principle of existence, and ye go round trying to destroy it in other people. If you knew what you let on to know, you wouldn't be planning to go to England on Saturday.'

'I'm not so sure that I'm going to England on Saturday,' he said, getting despondent again.

But the argument did him good; it gave him something to think about. The only mistake I made was in thinking that a man as headstrong as that could ever be impressed for long by an argument. We went on to some music; Madge came into the room to listen, and it was quite like old times. He saw me off at the door. It was a lovely starlit night, and he leaned against the door jamb, talking and cocking his head at the voices of girls and sailors from way down the river.

Next morning, I was barely into work before a couple of the men came up to tell me about the fellow who had been fished out of the river that morning. My heart sank. I didn't need anyone to tell me who it was.

I left word that I probably wouldn't be back and set off down the quays. They were very quiet, and the church and the trees were reflected in the water, almost without a ripple. I was blaming myself terribly for the whole business, though I still didn't see what I could have done. There were a couple of women standing outside the house, gossiping, and there was a trail of water from the quayside to the hall door.

Madge opened the door and put her finger hastily to her lips. I couldn't understand it. She didn't look in the least concerned. She beckoned me up the stairs, and pointed to the wet trail on the carpet. There was a shocking smell of gas. She opened the door of Dan's room, and when we went in, closed it behind us. The window was wide open; the bed had not been slept in, and there was a tea-chest in the middle of the floor.

'What did they do with him, Madge?' I whispered.

'Dan?' she said in surprise. 'Oh, he's downstairs, at his breakfast, I only wanted you to see for yourself. Otherwise you mightn't believe it.'

'You mean they got him out all right?' I asked.

'It was the mercy of God the sailor saw him,' she said with shining eyes. 'He couldn't swim with his boots on.'

'But how the hell did he do it?' I asked.

'Don't you see?' she said, pointing to the tea-chest. 'He had a length of tubing running into this, with a tap on it.'

She raised the tea-chest so that I could see the hole drilled in the side. Beneath it was a pillow and a rug.

'But what's it for?' I asked.

'He bought the tubing and the tap so that he could turn on the gas when he was inside the tea-chest,' said Madge with a smile. 'The notion of him being kept down by a tea-chest, that two men couldn't control when he had the pneumonia! He must have been lifting it off him the whole time. You can see where he got sick through the window.'

'And after going through that jigmareel, he went and threw himself in the river!' I said, marvelling at the stubbornness of the man.

'Ah, that was this morning, Michael John,' said Madge ingenuously. 'Before that, he saw a great light.'

'A great what?' I asked.

'A great light,' said Madge. 'He saw that life was good after all.'

'He saw a hell of a lot,' I said sourly.

'He said suddenly the whole thing became plain to him,' said Madge. 'So to put temptation away from him, he took the tube and the tap to throw them in the river. It was while he was doing that he tripped over the rope.'

'I see,' I said nastily. 'He saw the light, but he didn't see the rope.'

Her eyes filled with tears.

'Don't be hard on him, Michael John,' she said, shaking her head. 'He got a terrible fright, the poor creature. When they brought him in he was sobbing and shaking like a little child. "I thought 'twas goodbye, Madge," he said. Whatever you do, don't upset him again on me. He's the best brother in the world only for the misfortunate books he reads. 'Tis them I'd like to throw in the river.'

She gave a heart-scalded look at the shelf of books by Dan's bed.

I went downstairs in a sort of stupor, not knowing what I was to think or say. Naturally, I didn't believe in the accident. I was only wondering what plan Dan would try next and how I'd stop him.

He was sitting in the kitchen in his best suit, finishing his breakfast and reading the morning paper – a nice domestic spectacle after a performance like that.

'Oughtn't you to be damn well ashamed of yourself?' I said, losing all control at the sight of him.

'Ashamed of myself?' he asked sarcastically, raising his big brows in the old supercilious way. 'I don't see any particular reason for being ashamed of myself. I suppose an accident can happen to anyone?'

'Accident!' I said. 'And wasn't I sitting in this house with you last night, trying to keep you from any more accidents? What sort of way is this to treat your unfortunate sister?'

Suddenly a strange look came over his face. He bowed his head and nodded.

'I admit that,' he said meekly. 'I admit I was headstrong.'

'Headstrong, and inconsiderate, and conceited, and imagining you were the only one in the world who knew anything.'

'I know, I know,' he said. 'I was a terrible egotist. There's a lot of things I have to change in my character.'

At that I didn't know what to say. Dan Turner admitting that there were things in his character he had to change! It was an accident all right.

Of course, Madge wouldn't admit that. She was convinced it was a miracle. It made a different man of Dan, and the funny thing is nowadays he'd squeeze through a keyhole to get away from me. He says I'm a dangerous influence; a man of no conviction. Because now he knows precisely what's waiting for him when he dies, only that it happens to be quite different from what he knew was waiting for him before.

And, of course, I just go on doubting.

The Sentry

Father MacEnerney was finding it hard to keep Sister Margaret from exploding. The woman was lonesome, but he was lonesome himself. He liked his little parish outside the big military camp near Salisbury; he liked the country and the people, and he liked his little garden, even if it was raided twice a week by the soldiers. But he did suffer from lack of friends. Apart from his housekeeper and a couple of private soldiers in the camp, the only Irish people he could talk to were the three Irish nuns in the convent, and that was why he went there so often for his supper and to say his office in the convent garden.

Even here his peace was now being threatened by Sister Margaret's obstreperousness. Of course, the trouble was that before the war fathers, mothers, sisters and brothers as well as odd aunts and cousins had looked into the convent or spent a few days at the inn; and every week, long, juicy letters had arrived from home, telling the nuns by what political intrigue Paddy Dunphy had had himself appointed warble-fly inspector for the Benlicky area; but now it was years since anyone from Ireland had called, and the letters from home were censored at both sides of the channel by inquisitive girls with a taste for scandal till a sort of creeping paralysis seized up every form of intimacy. Sister Margaret was the worst hit, because a girl from her own town was in the Dublin censorship, and, according to Sister Margaret, she was a scandalmonger of the most objectionable kind. Naturally, she took it out on the English nuns.

'Oh, Father Michael,' she sighed one evening when they were walking round the garden, 'I'm afraid I made a great mistake. A terrible mistake! I don't know how it is, but the English seem to me to have no nature.'

'Ah, I wouldn't say that,' protested Father MacEnerney in his deep, sombre voice. 'They have their little ways, and we have ours, and if we both knew more about one another we'd get on better.'

To illustrate what he meant, he told her about old Father Dan Murphy, a Tipperary priest who had spent his life on the Mission, and the English Bishop. The Bishop was a decent, honourable little man, but quite unable to understand the feelings of his Irish priests. One evening Father Dan had called on Father MacEnerney. He was in a terrible state. He had received a terrible letter from the Bishop. It was so terrible he couldn't even show it. He would just have to go home. No, it wasn't so much anything the Bishop had said as the way he had said it. Finally, when Father MacEnerney had pressed him hard enough, he broke down and whispered that the Bishop had begun his letter with 'Dear Murphy'. 'As if he was writing to a farmhand, father.'

Father MacEnerney laughed, but it was no laughing matter to Sister Margaret. She clapped her hand to her mouth and stood looking at him.

'He didn't, Father Michael?' she said in an outraged tone.

So, seeing she didn't understand any better than Father Dan had, Father MacEnerney explained again that this was only how an Englishman would address anyone except a particular friend. A convention, nothing more.

'Ah, you're too simple, Father Michael,' Sister Margaret said indignantly. 'Convention, how are you? "Dear Murphy"? I'm surprised at you! What way is that to write to a priest? And how can they expect their own people to have any respect for religion when they have no respect for it themselves? Oh, that's the English all out! They try to domineer and bully you. Don't I have it every day of my life from them? "Dear Murphy"! I don't know how anybody can stand them.'

Sister Margaret was his best friend in the community: he knew that the other nuns relied on him to handle her for them, and it was a genuine worry to him to see her getting into this morbid state.

'Oh, come, come!' he said reproachfully. 'How well Sister Teresa and Sister Bonaventura can get on with them.'

'I suppose I shouldn't say it,' she said in a low, brooding voice. 'God forgive me, I can't help it. I'm afraid Sister Teresa and Sister Bonaventura are not *genuine*.'

'Now, you're not being fair,' he said gravely.

'And why should I be fair?' she cried. 'They're not genuine, and you know yourself they're not genuine. They're lickspittles, father, lickspittles! They suck up to the English nuns the whole time. They take every sort of gibe and impertinence from them. They simply have no independence. You wouldn't believe it.'

'We all have to accept a lot for the sake of charity,' he said.

'I don't call that charity at all, father,' she replied, obstinately, and her big Kerry jaw stuck out. 'I call that moral cowardice. Why should the English have it all their own way? Even in religion they go on as if they owned the earth. They tell me I'm disloyal and a pro-German, and I ask them: "What did you ever do to make me anything else?" And then, they pretend that we were savages, and they came over and civilized us! Did you ever in all your life hear such impudence? People that were painting themselves all over when we were the Island of Saints and Scholars!'

'Well, of course that's all true enough but we must remember what they're going through,' he said.

'And what did we have to go through?' she asked shortly. 'Oh, now, father, it's all very well to be talking, but I don't see why we should have to make all the sacrifices. Why don't they think of all the terrible things they did to us? And all because we were true to our religion when they weren't! I'm after sending home for an Irish history, father, and mark my words, the next time one of them begins picking on me, I'll give her the answer. The impudence!'

Suddenly Father MacEnerney stopped and frowned.

'What is it, father?' she asked anxiously.

'Just a queer feeling I got,' he muttered. 'I was wondering was there someone at my onions.'

The sudden sensation was quite genuine, though it might have happened in a perfectly normal way, for his onions were the great anxiety of Father MacEnerney's life. He could grow them when the convent gardener couldn't, but, unlike the convent gardener, he had no way of guarding them. His housekeeper was elderly and frightened and pretended not to see what went on for fear the soldiers would take a fancy to her as well.

'They only wait till they get me out of their sight,' he said, and then got down and laid his ear to the earth. As a country boy he knew that the earth is a great conductor of sound.

'I was right,' he shouted triumphantly as he sprang to his feet and rushed for his bicycle. 'If I catch them at it they'll leave me alone for the future. I'll ring you up, Sister.'

A moment later, doubled over the handlebars, he was pedalling down the hill towards his house. As he passed the camp gate he noticed that there was no sentry on duty and knew he had one of the thieves at last. With a whoop of rage he threw his bicycle down by the gate and rushed across the garden. The sentry, a small man with fair hair, blue eyes and a worried expression, dropped the handful of onions he was holding. His rifle was standing by the wall.

'Aha, so I caught you at it!' shouted Father MacEnerney. He grabbed the sentry by the arm and twisted it viciously behind his back. 'So you're the fellow that was at my onions! Now you can come up to the camp with me and explain yourself.'

'I'm going, I'm going,' the sentry said in alarm, trying to wrench himself free.

'Oh, you're going all right,' the priest said, urging him forward with his knee. 'And I'm going with you.'

'Here, you let go of me!' the sentry cried. 'I haven't done anything, have I?'

'You haven't done anything!' the priest repeated bitterly. 'You weren't stealing my onions!'

'Don't you twist my wrist!' screamed the sentry, swinging round on him. 'Try to behave like a civilized human being. I didn't take your onions. I don't even know what you're talking about.'

'You dirty little English liar!' shouted Father MacEnerney, beside himself with rage at the impudence of the man. He dropped the sentry's wrist and pointed at the onions. 'Hadn't you them there in your hand, when I caught you? Didn't I see them with you, God blast you!'

'Oh, those things?' the sentry exclaimed as though he had suddenly seen a great light. 'Some kids dropped them and I picked them up.'

'You picked them up!' repeated Father MacEnerney sarcastically, drawing back his fist and making the sentry duck. 'You didn't even know they were onions, I suppose?'

'I didn't have much time to look, did I?' the sentry asked hysterically. 'I seen some kids in your garden, pulling the bleeding things. I told them get out and they only laughed at me. Then I chased them and they dropped these. What do you mean, twisting my wrist like that? I was only trying to do you a good turn. I've a good mind to give you in charge.'

278

The impudence was too much for the priest, who could not have thought up a yarn like that inside an hour. He never had liked liars anyway.

'You what?' he shouted, tearing off his coat. 'You'd give me in charge? I'd take ten little brats like you and break you across my knee. You bloody little English thief, take off your tunic!'

'I can't,' the sentry said in panic.

'Why can't you?'

'Because I'm on duty. You know that.'

'On duty! You're afraid.'

'I'm not afraid. I'll meet you anywhere you like, any time you like, and put your buck teeth through your fat head.'

'Then take off your tunic now and fight like a man.' He gave the sentry a punch that sent him staggering against the wall. 'Now will you fight, you dirty little English coward?'

'You know I can't fight,' panted the sentry, putting his arms up to protect himself. 'If I wasn't on duty I'd soon show you whether I'm a coward or not. You're the coward, not me, you dirty Irish bully! You know I'm on duty. You know I'm not in a position to protect myself. You're mighty cocky, just because you're in a privileged position, you mean, bullying bastard!'

Something in the sentry's tone halted the priest. He was almost hysterical. Father MacEnerney could not hit him while he was in that state.

'Get out of this so, God blast you!' he said furiously.

The sentry gave him a murderous look, then took up his rifle and walked back up the road to the camp gate. Father MacEnerney stared after him. He was furious. He wanted a fight, and if only the sentry had hit back would certainly have smashed him up. All the MacEnerneys were like that. His father was the quietest man in County Clare, but if you gave him occasion he would fight in a bag, tied up.

The priest went in to his own front room but found himself too upset to settle down. He sat in his big leather chair, trembling all over with suppressed violence. 'I'm too soft,' he thought despairingly. 'Too soft. It was my one opportunity and I didn't take advantage of it. Now they'll all know they can do what they like with me. I might as well give up trying to keep a garden. I might as well go back to Ireland. This is no country for anyone.' At last he went to the telephone and rang up Sister

Margaret. Her voice, when she answered, was trembling with eagerness.

'Oh, father, did you catch them?' she cried.

'Yes,' he replied in an expressionless voice. 'I caught one of them anyway. A sentry.'

'And what did you do?'

'Gave him a clout,' he replied in the same tone.

'Oh, if 'twas me I'd have killed him,' she cried piteously.

'I'd have done that too, only he wouldn't fight,' Father MacEnerney said gloomily. 'If I'm shot from behind a hedge one of these days you'll know who did it.'

'Oh, isn't that the English all out?' she said with hysterical disgust. 'They have so much old talk about their bravery, and when anyone stands up to them, they won't fight.'

'That's right,' he said, meaning it was wrong, and rang off. He realized that for once he and Sister Margaret were thinking alike, and that Sister Margaret was not right in the head. Suddenly his conduct appeared to him in its true light. He had behaved abominably. After all his talk of charity, he had insulted another man about his nationality, had hit him when he couldn't hit back, and only for that might have done him some serious injury – and all for a handful of onions worth sixpence! There was nice behaviour for a priest! There was good example for non-Catholics! He wondered what the Bishop would say if he heard that.

He sat back again in his chair, humped in dejection. His atrocious temper had betrayed him again. One of these days he knew it would land him in really serious trouble. And there were no amends he could make. He couldn't even go into the camp and apologize to the man without getting him into fresh trouble. He faithfully promised himself to apologize if he met him again.

This eased his conscience a little, and after saying Mass next morning he didn't feel quite so bad. The run across the downs in the early morning always gave him pleasure, and the view of the red-brick village with the white spire in a stagnant pool of dark trees below him. The barrows of old Celts showed on the polished surface of the chalk-green hills. They, poor devils, had had trouble with the English too, and got the worst of it.

He was nearly in good humour again when Elsie, the house-keeper, told him that there was an officer from the camp to see him. His guilty conscience started up again like an aching tooth. What the hell was it now?

The officer was a tall, good-looking young man with an obstinate jaw that stuck out like an advertisement for a shaving soap. He had a pleasant, jerky, friendly manner.

'Good morning, padre,' he said in a harsh voice. 'My name is Howe. I called about your garden. I believe our chaps have been giving you trouble.'

By this time Father MacEnerney would cheerfully have made him a present of the garden, onions and all.

'Ah, wasn't it my own fault for putting temptation in their way?' he asked with a sunny smile.

'Well, it's very nice of you to take it like that,' said the officer in a tone of mild surprise. 'The CO is rather indignant about it. He suggested barbed wire.'

'Electrified?' Father MacEnerney asked ironically.

'No, ordinary barbed wire,' Howe said, missing the joke completely. 'Pretty effective, you know.'

'Useless,' Father MacEnerney said promptly. 'Don't worry your head about it. You'll have a drop of Irish? And ice in it. Ah, go on, you will!'

'A bit early for me, I'm afraid,' Howe said with a glance at his watch.

'Coffee, so,' Father MacEnerney said authoritatively. 'No one leaves this house without some nourishment.'

He shouted to Elsie for more coffee and handed Howe a cigarette. Howe knocked it briskly on the chair and lit it.

'Now, this chap you caught last night – how much damage had he actually done?' he asked in a businesslike tone.

The question put Father MacEnerney more than ever on his guard. He wondered how the officer knew about it all.

'Which chap was this?' he asked, fighting a delaying action.

'The chap you beat up.'

'That I beat up,' echoed Father MacEnerney, aghast. 'Who said I beat him up?'

'He did. He expected you to report him, so he decided to give himself up. You seem to have scared him pretty badly.'

However Father MacEnerney might have scared the sentry, the sentry had now scared him worse. It seemed the thing was anything but over; if he wasn't careful, he might find himself

involved as a witness against the sentry, and then the whole
sordid story of his behaviour would emerge. It was just like
the English to expect people to report them. They took every
damn thing literally, from a joke about electrified barbed wire to
a fit of bad temper.

'But why would he expect me to report him?' he asked in
confusion. 'When do you say this happened? Last night?'

'So I'm told,' Howe said shortly. He waited for Father Mac-
Enerney to speak, and when he didn't, raised his voice as though
he thought the priest might be deaf, or stupid, or both. 'I mean
Collins, the man you caught stealing onions last evening.'

'Oh, was that his name?' the priest asked vaguely. 'Of course, I
couldn't be sure he stole them. There were onions stolen all right,
but that's a different thing.'

'But I understand you caught him in the act,' Howe said with a
frown.

'Oh, no,' Father MacEnerney replied gravely. 'That's an
exaggeration. I didn't actually catch him doing anything. I
admit I charged him with it, but he denied it at once. At once!'
he repeated earnestly, as though this might be an important
point in the sentry's favour. 'It seemed, according to what
he told me, that he saw some children in my garden and
chased them away, and as they were running they dropped
the onions I found. Those could be kids from the village, of
course.'

'First I've heard of anybody from the village,' Howe said in
surprise. 'Did you see any kids around, padre?'

'No,' Father MacEnerney admitted hesitatingly. 'I didn't see
them, but that wouldn't mean they weren't there. They're always
snooping around the camp. You know that.'

'I'll have to ask him about that,' said Howe. 'It is a point in his
favour. I'm afraid it won't make much difference though. What
really concerns us is that he deserted his post. He could be shot
for that, of course.'

'Deserted his post?' Father MacEnerney repeated in consternation. This was worse than anything he had ever imagined. This
was terrible! The wretched man might lose his life and for no
reason except that a priest couldn't control his wicked temper.
He felt he was being well punished for it. 'But how did he desert
his post?'

'Well, you caught him in your garden,' Howe replied brusquely. 'In that time the whole camp could have been surprised and taken.'

In his distress the priest almost asked him not to talk nonsense. As if a military camp in the middle of England was going to be surprised and taken while the sentry nipped into a nearby garden for a handful of onions! But that was the English all out! They had to reduce everything to the most literal terms.

'Oh, hold on now!' he said, raising a commanding hand. 'I think there must be a mistake. I never said I caught him in the garden.'

'No, he said that,' Howe replied irritably. 'Didn't you?'

'Oh, no,' Father MacEnerney said emphatically, feeling that casuistry was no longer any use. 'I certainly didn't. Are you quite sure that man is right in his head?'

Fortunately for him, at this moment Elsie appeared with the coffee and Father MacEnerney was able to watch her and the coffee-pot instead of Howe, who, he knew, was watching him closely enough. He only hoped he didn't look the way he felt – like a particularly stupid criminal.

'Thanks,' Howe said, sitting back with his coffee-cup in his hand. Then he went on remorselessly. 'Am I to understand that you beat this fellow up across the garden wall?'

'Listen, my friend,' Father MacEnerney said desperately. 'I tell you that man is never right in his head. He must be a hopeless neurotic. They get like that, you know. Persecution mania, they call it. He'd never talk that way if he had any experience of being beaten up. I give you my word of honour that it's the wildest exaggeration. I don't often raise my fist to a man, but when I do, I leave evidence.'

'I can believe that,' Howe said with a cheeky grin.

'Now, I admit I did threaten to knock this fellow's head off,' continued the priest, 'but that was when I thought he'd taken my onions.' In his excitement he drew closer to Howe till he was standing over him, a big bulky figure of a man, and suddenly, to his astonishment, he felt the tears in his eyes. 'Between ourselves, I behaved badly,' he said emotionally. 'I don't mind admitting it to you, but I wouldn't like it to get round. I have a terrible temper. An uncontrollable temper. He threatened to give me in charge.'

'The little bastard!' Howe said with a surprise that contained a slight element of pleasure.

'And he'd have been perfectly justified,' the priest said earnestly. 'I had no right whatever to accuse him without a scrap of evidence. If I'd been in his shoes, I'd have taken the man who did it up to the guard room and made him repeat it. I behaved shockingly.'

'I shouldn't let it worry me too much,' Howe said cheerfully.

'I can't help it,' said the priest. 'I'm sorry to say the language I used was disgraceful. As a matter of fact, I had made up my mind to apologize next time I met him.'

He returned to his chair, almost weeping.

'This is one of the strangest cases I've ever dealt with,' Howe said. 'You don't think we're talking at cross purposes, do you? The chap you mean was tall and dark with a small moustache, isn't that right?'

For a moment Father MacEnerney felt a rush of relief at the thought that, after all, it was merely a case of mistaken identity. To mix it up a bit more was his immediate reaction. He did not see the trap until it was too late.

'That's right,' he said, and knew at once that it wasn't. Howe smiled and took his time. Then his long jaw shot up like a rat-trap.

'Why are you telling me all these lies, padre?' he asked quietly.

'Lies?' shouted Father MacEnerney, flushing.

'Lies, of course,' said Howe without pity or rancour. 'Damn lies! Transparent lies! You've been trying to fool me for the last ten minutes, and you very nearly succeeded. You're a very plausible liar, padre, but you can't take me in.'

'Ah, how can I remember?' Father MacEnerney said miserably. 'I don't know why you think I should attach so much importance to a handful of onions.'

'At present, I'm more interested in finding out what importance you attach to the rigmarole you've just told me,' said Howe. 'I presume you're trying to shield Collins. I'm blessed if I know why. I thought him a pretty nasty specimen, myself.'

Father MacEnerney did not reply. If Howe had been Irish, he would not have asked such a silly question, and, as he was not Irish, he wouldn't understand the answer. The MacEnerneys had all been like that. Father MacEnerney's father, the most truthful,

God-fearing man he had known, had been threatened with a prosecution for perjury committed in the interest of a neighbour.

'Anyhow,' Howe went on sarcastically, 'what really happened was that you came home, found your garden had been robbed, said "Goodnight" to the sentry, and asked him who did it. He said it was some kids from the village, and then you probably had a long talk about the beautiful, beautiful moonlight. All very interesting. Now, what about coming up to the mess one night for dinner?'

'I'd love it,' the priest said boyishly. It was a great relief to know that Howe didn't really hold it against him. 'To tell you the God's truth, I'm destroyed here for someone to talk to.'

'Come on Thursday,' said Howe. 'And don't expect too much of the grub. It's a psychological conditioning for the horrors of modern war. But we'll give you lots of onions. I hope you don't recognize them.'

Then he went off, laughing. Father MacEnerney laughed too, but he didn't laugh long. It struck him that the English had a very peculiar sense of humour. To him, that interview had been anything but a joke. Here he was, a man who had always hated liars, and he had lied his own head off until even Howe despised him. That was queer conduct in a priest! He rang up the convent and asked for Sister Margaret. She was his principal confidante.

'Remember the sentry last night?' he asked in his gloomy, expressionless voice.

'Yes, father,' she said nervously. 'What about him?'

'He's after being arrested,' he said darkly.

'Oh,' she said. After a long pause she added: 'For what, father?'

'Stealing onions and being absent from duty. I had an officer here, making inquiries. It seems he could be shot.'

'Oh, father, isn't that awful?' she gasped.

''Tis bad,' he agreed.

'Oh, isn't that the English all out?' she cried. 'The rich can do what they like, and a poor man can be shot for stealing a few onions! I suppose it never crossed their minds that he might be hungry? Those poor fellows that never get a proper meal! What did you say?'

'Nothing.'

'You did right,' she said stormily. 'I'd have told them a pack of lies.'

'I did that too,' said Father MacEnerney.

'Oh, I don't believe for an instant that 'tis a sin, father,' she said hysterically. 'I don't care what anybody says about it. I'd say it in front of the Pope. I'm sure 'tis an act of charity.'

'That's what I thought too,' he said. 'It didn't go down too well though. But I liked the officer. I'll be seeing him again, and I think I might be able to get round him. The English are very good like that, when they get to know you.'

'I'll start a novena for the poor man at once,' she said firmly.

Travellers' Samples (1951)

Darcy in the
Land of Youth

1

During the War when he was out of a job Mick Darcy went to
England as clerk in a factory. He found the English as he had
always supposed them to be: people with a great welcome for
themselves and very little for anyone else.

Besides, there were the air-raids, which the English pretended
not to notice. In the middle of the night Mick would be wakened
by the wail of a siren and the thump of faraway guns, like all the
windowpanes of heaven rattling. The thud of artillery, growing
louder, accompanied a faint buzz like a cat's purring that seemed
to rise out of a corner of the room and mount the wall to the
ceiling, where it hung, breathing in steady spurts, exactly like
a cat. Pretending not to notice things like that struck Mick as a
bit ostentatious: he would rise and dress himself and sit lonesome
by the gas-fire, wondering what on earth had induced him to leave
home.

The daytime wasn't much better. The works were a couple of
miles outside the town, and he shared an office with a woman
called Penrose and a Jew called Isaacs. Penrose addressed him as
'Mr Darcy' and when he asked her to call him 'Mick', she affected
not to hear. Isaacs was the only one in the works who called him
'Mick', but it soon became plain that he only wanted Mick to join
the Communist Party.

'You don't want to be a fellow traveller,' he said.

'No,' said Mick. 'I don't want to be a traveller at all.'

On his afternoons off, he took long, lonesome country walks,
but there was nothing there you could describe as country either;
only red-brick farms and cottages with crumpled oak frames and
high, red-tiled roofs, big, sickly-looking fields divided by low neat
hedges that made them look as though they all called one another
by their surnames, and handsome-looking pubs named like the
Star and Garter or the Shoulder of Mutton that were never open

when you wanted them. No wonder he pined for Cork, his girl, Ina, and his great friend, Chris.

But it is amazing the effect even one girl can have on a feeling of home-sickness. Janet Fuller in Personnel was a tall, thin, fair-haired girl with a quick-witted laughing air. When Mick talked to her she listened with her head forward and her eyebrows raised expectantly. There was nothing in the least alarming about Janet, and she didn't seem to want to convert him to anything, so he asked her to have a drink with him. She even called him 'Mick' without being asked.

It was a great comfort. Now he had someone to talk to in his spare time, and he no longer felt scared of the country or the people. Besides, he began to master his job, and this always gave him a feeling of self-confidence. He even began to surprise the others at the factory. One day a group of them, including Janet, had broken off work for a chat when they heard the boss and scattered – even Janet said 'Goodbye' hastily. But Mick just gazed out of the window, his hands still in his trousers pockets, and when the boss came in, he saluted him over his shoulder. 'Settling in, Darcy?' the boss said in a friendly tone. 'Just getting the hang of things,' Mick replied modestly. Next day the boss sent for him, but it was only to ask his advice about something, and Mick gave it in his forthright way. If Mick had a weakness, it was that he liked to hear himself talk.

But he still continued to get shocks. One evening he had supper in the flat that Janet shared with a girl called Fanny, who was an analyst in one of the factories. Fanny was a good-looking dark-haired girl with a tendency to moodiness. She asked how Mick was getting on with Mrs Penrose.

'Oh,' said Mick, 'she still calls me "Mr Darcy".'

'I suppose that's only because she expects to be calling you something else before long,' said Fanny gloomily.

'Oh, no, Fanny,' said Janet. 'You wouldn't know Penrose now. She's a changed woman. With her husband in Egypt, Peter posted to Yorkshire, and no one to play with but George, she's begun to talk about the simple pleasures of life. Penrose and primroses, you know.'

'Penrose?' Mick exclaimed incredulously. 'I never thought she was that sort. Are you sure, Janet? I'd have thought she was an iceberg.'

'An iceberg!' Janet said gleefully, rubbing her hands. 'Oh, boy! A blooming fireship!'

Going home that night through the pitch-dark streets, Mick really felt at home for the first time. He had made friends with two of the nicest girls you could wish for – fine, broad-minded girls you could speak to as you'd speak to a man. He had to step into the roadway to make room for two other girls, flicking their torches on and off before them – schoolgirls, to judge by their voices. 'Of course, he's married,' one of them said as they passed, and then went off into a rippling scale of laughter that sounded almost unearthly in the silence and darkness.

A bit too broad-minded at times, perhaps, thought Mick, coming to himself. For a while he did not feel quite so much at home.

2

In the spring evenings Janet and himself cycled off into the nearby villages and towns for their drinks. Janet wanted him to see the country. Sometimes Fanny came too, but she did not seem so keen on it. It was as though she felt herself in the way, yet when she did refuse to accompany them, she looked after them with such a reproachful air that it seemed to make Janet feel guilty.

One Sunday evening they went to church together. It seemed to surprise Janet that Mick went to Mass every Sunday. She went with him once and clearly it did not impress her. Her own religion seemed a bit mixed. Her father had been a Baptist lay preacher and her mother a Methodist, but Janet herself had fallen in love with a parson at the age of eleven and remained Church till she joined the Socialist Party at the age of eighteen. Most of the time she did not seem to Mick to have any religion at all. She said that you just died and rotted, and that was all anyone knew about it, and this seemed to be the general view. There were any amount of religions, but no beliefs you could put your finger on.

Janet was so eager that he should go to church with her that he agreed, though it was against his principles. It was a little town ten miles from where they lived. Inside the church was a young sailor playing the organ while another turned over for him. The parson rang the bell himself, and only three women turned up. The service itself was an awful sell. The parson turned his back on them and read prayers at the east window; the organist played a hymn, which the three women and Janet joined in, and then the parson read more prayers. However, it seemed to get Janet all worked up.

'Pity about Fanny,' she said when they were drinking beer in the inn yard later. 'We could be very comfortable in the flat only for her. Haven't you a friend who'd take her off our hands?'

'Only in Ireland.'

'Tell him I'll get him a job here. Say you've a nice girl for him as well. She really *is* nice, Mick.'

'Oh, I know,' said Mick. 'But hasn't she a fellow already?'

'Getting a fellow for Fanny is the great problem of my life,' Janet said ruefully.

'I wonder if she'd have him,' said Mick, thinking how nice it would be to have a friend as well as a girl. Janet was as good as gold, but there were times when Mick pined for masculine companionship.

'If he's anything like you, she'd jump at him,' said Janet.

'Oh, there's no resemblance,' said Mick, who had never before been flattered like this and loved it. 'Chris is a holy terror.'

'A holy terror is what Fanny needs,' Janet said grimly.

It was only as time went by that he realized she was not exaggerating. Fanny was jealous; there was no doubt of that. She didn't intend to be rude, but she watched his plate as Janet filled it, and he saw that she grudged him even the food he ate. There wasn't much, God knows, and what there was, Janet gave him the best of, but all the same it was embarrassing. Janet did her best by making her feel welcome to join them, but Fanny only grew moodier.

'Oh, come on, Fanny!' Janet said one evening. 'I only want to show Mick the Plough in Alton.'

'Well, who'd know it better?' Fanny asked darkly, and Janet's temper blazed up.

'There's no need to be difficult,' she said.

'Well, it's not my fault if I'm inhibited, is it?' asked Fanny with a cowed air. Mick saw with surprise that she was terrified of Janet in a tantrum.

'I didn't say you were inhibited,' Janet replied in a stinging voice. 'I said you were difficult.'

'Same thing from your point of view, isn't it?' Fanny asked. 'Oh, I suppose I was born that way. You'd better let me alone.'

All the way out Janet was silent, and Mick saw she was still mad, though he couldn't guess why. He didn't know what Fanny meant when she said she was inhibited, or why she seemed to speak about it as if it were an infectious disease. He only knew that Janet had to be smoothed down.

'We'll have to get Chris for Fanny all right,' he said. 'An exceptional girl like that, you'd think she'd have fellows falling over her.'

'I don't think Fanny will ever get a man,' Janet said in a shrill, scolding voice. 'I've thrown dozens of them at her head, but she won't even make an effort to be polite. I believe she's one of those women who go through life without even knowing what it's about. She's just a raging mass of inhibitions.'

There it was again! Prohibitions, exhibitions, inhibitions! Mick wished to God Janet would use simple words. He knew what exhibitions were from one old man in the factory who had gone to gaol because of them, but if inhibitions meant the opposite, what was there to grouse about?

'Couldn't we do something about them?' he asked helpfully.

'Yes, darling,' she replied mockingly. 'Take her away to hell and give her a good roll in the hay. Then bring her back to me, human.'

Mick was so shocked he did not reply. By this time he was used to English dirty jokes, but he knew this wasn't just one of them. No doubt Janet was joking about the roll in the hay – though he wasn't too sure she was joking about that either – but she wasn't joking about Fanny. She really meant that all that was wrong with Fanny was that she was still a virgin, and that this was a complaint she did not suffer from herself.

The smugness of it horrified him as much as the savagery. Put in a certain way, it might be understandable and even forgivable. Girls of Janet's kind were known at home as 'damaged goods' but Mick had never permitted the expression to pass. He had a strong sense of justice and always took the side of the underdog. Some girls hadn't the same strength of character as others, he supposed; some were subjected to great temptations. He had never met any, to his knowledge, but he was quite sure that if he had he would have risen to the occasion. But a girl of that kind standing up and denouncing another girl's strength as weakness was too much for him altogether. It was like being asked to stand on his head.

Having got rid of her tantrum, Janet cheered up. 'This is wonderful,' she sighed with a tranquil pleasure as they floated downhill to Alton and the Plough – a pleasant little inn, standing by the bridge. Mick didn't feel it was so very wonderful. He had begun to wonder what Fanny had meant by asking who would know it better than Janet, and why Janet had lost her temper so badly. It sounded to him as though there had been some dirty work in connection with it.

While Janet sat in the garden, he went to the bar for beer and stood there for a while unnoticed. There was a little group at the bar: a bald, fat man in an overcoat, smoking a pipe; a good-looking young man with a fancy waistcoat, and a local with a face like a turnip. The landlord, a man of about fifty, had a long, haggard face and wore horn-rimmed glasses; his wife, apparently twenty years younger, was a good-looking woman with bangs and a Lancashire accent. They never noticed Mick while they discussed a death in the village.

'I'm not against religion,' the man with the turnip face spluttered excitedly. 'I'm chapel myself, but I never tried to force my own views on people. All the months poor Harry was paralysed his wife and daughter never so much as wet his lips. That idn't right, is it? That idn't religion.'

'No, Bill,' said the landlord, shaking his head. 'Going too far, I call that.'

'That's fanaticism,' said the man with the pipe.

'Everyone is entitled to his own views, but them weren't old Harry's views, were they?' asked the man with the turnip face.

'No, Bill, they certainly weren't,' the landlord's wife said sadly.

'I'm for freedom, myself,' Bill said, tapping his chest. 'The night before he died, I come in here and got a quart of mild and bitter. Didn't I, Joe?'

'Mild, wadn't it, Bill?' the publican asked anxiously.

'No, Joe, mild and bitter was always Harry's drink.'

'Don't you remember, Joe?' the landlord's wife asked.

'Funny,' her husband replied sadly. 'I could have sworn it was mild.'

'Anyhow, I said to Millie and Sue, "All right," I said. "You run along to chapel, or wherever you want to go. I'll sit up with old Harry." Then I took out the bottle. His poor eyes lit up. Couldn't move, couldn't speak, but I shall never forget how he looked at that bottle. I had to hold his mouth open' – Bill threw back his head and pulled down one side of his mouth with his thumb – 'and let it trickle down. And was I pleased when he died next morning? I said to myself. "That man might have gone into his grave without a drink." No, if that's religion give me beer!'

'Wonder where old Harry is now,' the fat man said, removing his pipe reverently. 'Mystery, Joe, i'nt it?'

'Shocking!' the landlord said, shaking his head.

'We don't know, do we, Charles?' the landlady said sadly.

'Nobody knows,' Bill bawled scornfully as he took up his pint again. 'How could they? Parson pretends to know, but he don't know any more than you and me. Shove you in the ground and let the worms have you – that's all anybody knows.'

Mick was struck by the similarity of Janet's views with those of the people in the pub, and he felt you really couldn't expect much from any of them.

'Isn't it lovely here?' she said when he brought out the drinks.

'Very nice,' Mick said without much enthusiasm. You couldn't feel very enthusiastic about a place while you were wondering who else had been there with your girl.

'We must come and spend a few days here some time,' she said, and it made him more depressed than ever. 'You don't think I'm too bitchy about Fanny, do you, Mick?'

'It's not that,' he said. 'I wasn't thinking about Fanny in particular. Just about the way everybody in the factory seems to behave – fellows and girls going off together, as if they were going to a dance.'

'Having seen the factory, can you wonder?' she asked, and took a long drink of her beer.

'And when they get tired of one another they go off with someone else,' he said drily. 'Or back to the number they started with. Like Hilda in the packing shed. She's tired of knocking round with Dorman, and when her husband comes back she's going to drop him. At least, she says she will.'

'Isn't that how these things usually end?' she asked.

'Oh, come on, Janet!' he said scornfully. 'You're not going to pretend there's nothing else to it.'

'I suppose like everything else, it's just what you choose to make it,' she said with a shrug.

'That isn't making much of it,' he said, beginning to grow heated. 'If it's only a roll in the hay, as you call it, there's nothing in it for anybody.'

'And what do you think it should be?' she asked with a frosty politeness that seemed to be the equivalent of his heat. He realized that he wasn't really keeping to the level of a general discussion. He could distinctly hear how common his accent had become, but excitement and a feeling of injury carried him away. He sat back stubbornly with his hands in his trousers pockets.

'But look here, Janet, learning to live with somebody isn't a thing you can pick up in a weekend. It's not a part-time job. You wouldn't take up a job somewhere in the middle, expecting to like it, and intending to drop it in a few months' time if you didn't.'

'Oh, Mick, don't tell me you have inhibitions too!' she said in mock distress.

'I don't know what they are and I don't care,' retorted Mick, growing commoner as he descended further from the heights of abstract discussion. 'And most of the people who use words like that have no idea of their meaning either.'

'Scruples, shall we say, so?' she asked, yielding the point.

'Well, we can agree on what they are,' he said.

'But after all, Mick, you've had affairs yourself, haven't you?' she added.

Now, this was a question Mick dreaded to answer, because, owing to a lack of suitable opportunities for which he was in no way to blame, he had not. For the matter of that, so far as he knew, none of his friends had either. But coming from a country where men's superiority – affairs or no affairs – was unchallenged, he did not like to admit that, so far as experience went, Fanny and he were in the one boat. He was even beginning to understand why poor Fanny felt such a freak.

'I'm not pretending I haven't,' he said casuistically.

'But then there's no argument, Mick,' she said with all the enthusiasm of a liberal mind discovering common ground with an opponent.

'No argument, maybe, but there are distinctions,' he said knowingly.

'Such as?'

'Oh, between playing the fool and being in love,' he replied as though he could barely bother to explain such matters to one as inexperienced as herself.

'The combination isn't altogether unknown either, is it?'

'The distinction seems to be, quite a bit,' he replied. 'To me, Penrose is one thing and you're another. Maybe I wouldn't mind having an affair with Penrose. God knows it's about all she's good for.'

'But you would with me?' she said, growing red.

'I would,' Mick said, realizing that the cat was out of the bag at last. 'I suppose it's a matter of responsibilities. If I make a friend, I don't begin by thinking what use I can make of him. If I fall in love with a girl I'm not going to begin calculating how cheap I can get her. I don't want anything cheap,' he added earnestly. 'I'm not going to rush into anything till I know the girl well enough to try and make a decent job of it. Is that plain?'

'Remarkably plain,' she said icily. 'You mean you're not that sort of man. Let me buy you a drink.'

'No, thanks.'

'Then I think we'd better be getting back,' she said, rising and looking like the wrath of God.

Mick, crushed and humiliated, followed her at a slouch, his hands still in his pockets. It wasn't good enough. At home a girl would have gone on with an argument like that till one of them fell unconscious, and in an argument Mick had real staying power, so he felt that she was taking an unfair advantage. Of course, he saw that she had some reason. However you looked at it, she had more or less told him she expected him to be her lover, and he had more or less told her that he was not that sort of man, and he had a suspicion that this was an entirely new experience for Janet. She might well feel mortified.

But the worst of it was that thinking it over, he realized that even then, he had not been quite honest. In fact, he had not been honest at all. He had not told her that he already had a girl at home. He believed all he had said, but he didn't believe it quite so strongly as all that – not so as to make exceptions. Given time, he might easily have made an exception of Janet. She was the sort of girl most men made an exception of. It was the shock that had made him express himself so bluntly; the shock of realizing that a girl he cared for had been the mistress of other men. He had reacted that way more in protest against them than against her.

But the real shock had been the discovery that he cared so much what she was.

3

They never resumed the discussion openly, on those terms at least, and it seemed at times as though Janet had forgiven him, but only just. The argument was always there beneath the surface, ready to break out again if either lost his temper. It flared up for a moment whenever she mentioned Fanny – 'I suppose one day she'll meet an Irishman, and they'll spend the rest of their lives discussing their inhibitions.' And when she mentioned other men she had known, like Bill, with whom she had spent a holiday in Dorset, and an American called Tom, with whom she had gone to the Plough in Alton, she seemed to be contrasting a joyous past with a dreary present, and became cold and insolent.

Mick, of course, gave as good as he got. He had a dirty tongue when he chose to use it, and he had considerably more ammunition than she had. The canteen was always full of gossip about who was living with whom, and whose wife (or husband) had returned and found him (or her) in bed with somebody else, and he passed it on with an air of amused contempt. The first time she said 'Good!' in a ringing voice: afterwards, she contented herself with a shrug. Mick suggested helpfully that perhaps it took all those religions to deal with as many scandals, and she retorted that, no doubt, one religion would be more than enough for Ireland.

All the same, he could not help feeling that it wasn't nice. He remembered what Fanny had said about the Plough. Really, really, it wasn't nice! It seemed to show a complete lack of sensibility in Janet to bring him to a place where she had stayed with another man, and it made him suspicious of every other place she brought him.

Still, he could not do without her, nor, apparently, could she do without him. They met every evening after work, went off together on Saturday afternoons, and even went to Mass together on Sunday mornings.

As a result, before he went home on leave, everything seemed to have changed between them. She no longer made snooty remarks about Fanny's virginity and ceased to refer to Bill and Tom altogether. Indeed, from her conversation it would have been hard to detect that she had ever known such men, much less been intimate with them. Mick wondered whether it wasn't possible for a woman to be promiscuous and yet remain innocent, and decided regretfully that it wasn't. But no wife or sweetheart could have shown more devotion in the last week before his holiday, and when they went to the station together and walked arm-in-arm to the end of the long draughty platform, she was stiff with unspoken misery. She seemed to feel it was her duty to show no sign of emotion, either.

'You will come back, Mick, won't you?' she asked.

'Why?' Mick replied banteringly. 'Do you think you can keep off Americans for a fortnight?'

Janet spat out a horrible word that showed only too clearly her familiarity with Americans and others. It startled and shocked Mick. It seemed that the English had strong ideas about when you could joke and when you couldn't, and this was apparently not a time for joking. To his surprise, he found her trembling all over.

At any other time he would have argued with her, but already he was, in spirit at least, halfway home. Beyond the end of the line was Cork, and meat and butter and nights of unbroken sleep. When he leaned out of the window to wave goodbye she was standing like a statue, looking curiously desolate.

He didn't reach home until the following evening. Since he had told no one of his arrival he came in an atmosphere of sensation. He shaved, and, without waiting for more than a cup of tea, set off down the road to Ina's. Ina was the youngest of a large family, and his arrival there created a sensation too. Elsie, the eldest, a fat jolly girl just home from work, shouted with laughter at him.

'He smelt the sausages!' she said.

'You can keep your old sausages,' Mick said scornfully. 'I'm taking Ina out to dinner.'

'You're what?' asked Elsie. 'You have high notions like the goats in Kerry.'

'But I have to make my little brothers' supper, honey,' Ina said laughingly, smoothing his hair. She was a slight, dark, radiant girl with a fund of energy.

'Tell them to make it themselves,' said Mick.

'Tell them, you!' cried Elsie. 'Someone should have told them years ago, the caubogues! They're thirty, and they have no more

297

intention of marrying than of flying. Have you e'er an old job for us over there? I'm damned for want of a man.'

Ina, surprised at Mick's firmness, rushed upstairs to change. Her two brothers came in, expressed astonishment at Mick's arrival, satisfaction at his promotion, incredulity at his opinion that the English were not beaten already, and consternation that their supper was not on the table. They began hammering together with their knives and forks.

'Supper up!' shouted the elder. 'We can't wait all night. Where the hell is Ina?'

'Coming out to dinner with me,' Mick said with a sniff, feeling that for once he was uttering a curtain line.

They called for Chris – an undersized lad with a pale face like a fist and a voice like melted butter. He expressed great pleasure at seeing them, but gave no sign of it, because it was part of Chris's line not to be impressed by anything. He had always regarded Mick as a bit of a softy because of Ina. For himself, he would never keep a girl for more than a month because it gave her ideas.

'Ah, what do you want going to town for supper for?' he drawled incredulously, as if this were only another indication that Mick was not quite right in the head. 'Can't ye have it at home? 'Twon't cost ye anything.'

'You didn't change much anyway,' Mick said drily. 'Hurry up, or we won't get anything at all.'

Next morning, in bed, Mick got a letter from Janet that must have been written while he was still on the train. She said that trying to face things without him was like trying to get used to an amputated limb: she kept on making movements before realizing that it wasn't there. At that point, Mick dropped the letter with a sigh. He wished English people wouldn't write like that. It sounded so unreal.

He wished he could remain at home, but didn't see how he could do it, without a job. Instead, he started to coax Chris into coming back with him. He knew that his position in the factory would guarantee a job for anyone who did. Besides, he had grown tired of Ina's brothers telling him how the Germans would win the war. He had never been very interested in the war or who won it, and was surprised to hear himself replying in Chris's cynical drawl, 'They will, and what else?' Ina's brothers were equally surprised. They had not expected Mick to turn his coat so quickly.

'People here never seem to talk of anything only religion and politics,' he said one night to Chris as they were walking up the Western Road.

'And what better could they talk about?' asked Chris. 'Damn glad you were to get back to them! You can get a night's rest anyway.'

'There's no one to stop you,' Mick said.

Chris stared at him, uncertain whether or not Mick meant what he seemed to mean. Like most other friends, they had developed throughout the years along a pattern of standard reaction in which Mick had played the innocent, Chris the worldly one. Now, Mick seemed to be developing out of his knowledge entirely.

'Go on!' he said with a cautious grin. 'Are they as good-natured as that?'

'I didn't want to say it,' said Mick modestly. 'But I've the very girl for you.'

'You don't say so!' Chris exclaimed, with a smile of a child who has ceased to believe in Santa Claus but likes to hear about it just the same.

'Grand-looking girl with a good job and a flat of her own,' said Mick. 'What more do you want?'

Chris suddenly beamed.

'I wouldn't let Ina hear me talking like that if I was you,' he said. 'Some of them quiet-looking girls are a terrible hand with a hatchet.'

At that moment it struck Mick with cruel force how little Ina or anybody else had to reproach him with. They were passing by the college, and groups of clerks and servant girls were strolling by, whistling and calling. He was sure there wasn't another man in Ireland who would have behaved as stupidly as he had done. He remembered Janet at the railway station with her desolate air, and her letter, which he had not answered, and which, perhaps, she had really meant. A bloody fool!

Suddenly everything seemed to turn upside down on him. He was back in the bar in Alton, listening to the little group discussing the dead customer while he waited to carry the drinks out to Janet on the rustic seat in the garden, feeling that she was unreal and faithless. Now, it wasn't she who seemed unreal, but the Western Road and the clerks and servant girls who just didn't know what they wanted. They were a dream from which he had wakened; a dream from which he had wakened before without even realizing that he was awake.

He was so shaken that he almost told Chris about Janet, but he knew that Chris wouldn't understand him any more than he had understood himself. Chris would talk sagaciously of 'damaged goods', as if there were only one way a woman could be damaged.

'I have to go back to town, Chris,' he said, stopping. 'I just remembered a telephone call I have to make.'

'Fair enough,' Chris said, with an understanding that surprised him. 'I suppose you might as well tell her I'm coming too.'

4

Outside, against the clear summer sky, shadowy figures moved with pools of light at their feet and searchlights flickered like lightning over the battlements of the castle. Chris groaned and Mick gripped his arm confidently.

'This is nothing,' he said. 'Probably only a scouting plane. You get lots of them around here. Wait till they start dropping a few wagons of high explosive!'

It was a real pleasure to Mick to hear himself talk in that way. He seemed to have become forceful and cool all at once. It had something to do with Chris's being there, as though this had given his protective instincts full scope. But there was something else as well; something he could not have believed possible. It was almost as though he were arriving home. Home, he felt, was a funny thing for him to think of at a time like that.

There was no raid, so he brought Chris round to the girls' flat, and Chris groaned again at the channel of star-shaped traffic signals that twinkled between the black cliffs of houses, whose bases opened so mysteriously to reveal pale stencilled signs or caverns of smoky light.

Janet opened the door, gave one hasty, incredulous glance at Chris, and then hurled herself at Mick. Chris opened his eyes with a start – he later admitted to Mick that he had never before seen a doll so quick off the mark – but Mick no longer minded what he saw. While Chris and Fanny were in the throes of starting a conversation, he followed Janet into the kitchen, where she was recklessly tossing a week's rations into the frying pan. She was hot and excited, and she used two dirty words in succession, but they did not disturb him either. He leaned against the kitchen wall with his hands in his trousers pockets and smiled at her.

'Glad to see me?' he said.

'You should try this god-damn grease!' she said, rubbing her hand.

'I'm afraid you'll find I've left my principles behind me this time,' he said.

'Oh, good!' she said, not as enthusiastically as you might expect, but Mick put that down to the burn.

'What do you think of Chris?'

'A bit quiet, isn't he?' she asked doubtfully.

'Scared,' said Mick with a sniff. 'So would you be if your first glimpse of a country was in the middle of an alert. He'll get over that. Should we go off somewhere for the weekend?'

'Next weekend?'

'Or the one after. I don't mind.'

'You are in a hurry, aren't you?'

'So would you be, too, if you'd spent a fortnight in Cork.'

'And Fanny as well?'

'Why not? The more the merrier. Let's go somewhere really good. Take the bikes and make a proper tour of it. I'd like Chris to see a bit of the real country.'

It certainly did make a difference, having someone else there to think for. And a fortnight later, the four of them set off on bicycles out of town. Landscape and houses gradually changed about them, and old brick and flint gave place to houses of small yellow stones, tinted with golden moss. Out of the woven pullovers of wall rose gables with coifs of tile. It all came over Mick in a rush; the company of a friend and of his girl and a country he felt he had mastered. This was what it really meant to feel at home. When the others sat on a bench outside a country public house, Mick brought out the beer and smiled with the pride of ownership.

'Good?' he asked Chris.

'The beer isn't much, if that's what you mean,' said Chris, who still specialized in not being impressed.

In the late evening they reached their destination, and dismounted in the cobbled yard of an inn where, according to Janet, Queen Elizabeth was supposed to have stayed. At either end of the dining room there was an oak dresser full of willow-ware, with silvery sauceboats on the shelves and brass pitchers on top.

'You'd want to mind your head in this hole,' Chris said resentfully.

'But this place is four hundred years old, man,' said Mick.

'You think in that time they'd make enough to rebuild it,' said Chris.

He was still acting in character, but Mick was just a little disappointed in him. Fanny had been thrown into such a panic that she was prepared to hit it off with anybody, but Chris seemed to have lost a lot of his dash. Mick was not quite sure yet that he would not take fright before Fanny, but he would certainly do so if he knew what a blessed innocent she was. Whenever Mick looked at her, her dark sullen face broke into a wistful smile that made him think of a Christian martyr's first glimpse of the lion.

After supper Janet showed them round the town and finally led them to a pub that was on no street at all but was approached by a complicated system of alleyways. The little bar room was full, and Janet and he were crowded into the yard, and sat there on a bench in the starlight. Behind the clutter of old tiled roofs a square battlements tower rose against the sky.

'You're certain Fanny will be all right with Chris?' Janet asked anxiously.

'Oh, certain!' said Mick, wondering if his troops had opened negotiations with the enemy behind his back. 'Why? Did she say anything?'

'No, but she's in a flat spin,' Janet said, clucking with mother solicitude. 'I've told her everything I could think of, but she's still afraid she's got it wrong. If anyone could, that damn girl will. He does understand how innocent she is, doesn't he?'

'Oh, perfectly,' said Mick, feeling that his troops were already sufficiently out of hand. If Janet started giving them orders, they would undoubtedly cut and run.

Back in the bedroom, Chris was so depressed that it came almost as a relief to Mick, because he had no time to worry about himself. Then the handle of the door turned softly, and Janet tiptoed in in her bathing-wrap, her usual, competent, cool self as though arriving in men's bedrooms at that hour of night were second nature to her. 'Ready, Chris?' she whispered. Chris was a lad of great principle and Mick could not help admiring his spirit. With a face like death on him he went out, and Janet cautiously closed the door behind him. Mick listened to make sure he didn't hide in the lavatory. Then Janet switched off the light, drew back the black-out curtain, and shivering slightly, opened the window on the dark inn yard.

5

When Mick woke up and realized where he was he felt an extraordinary peace. It was as though he had laid down some heavy burden he had been carrying all his life. The pleasantest part of it was that the burden was quite unnecessary, and that he had lost nothing by laying it down.

With a clarity that seemed to be another part of his happy state, he realized that all the charm of the old town had only been a put-up job of Janet's. Clearly, she had been here already with another man. He should have known it when she took them to the pub. That, too, was her reason for choosing this pleasant old inn. She had stayed there with someone else. It was probably the American, and it might well be the same bed. Women had no interest in scenery or architecture unless they had been made love to in them, and this showed a certain amount of good sense. They brought one man there because they had been happy with another there. Happiness – that was the secret the English had and the Irish lacked.

He didn't feel quite so sure of this when he realized that what had waked him was Janet's weeping. There she was, crying quietly beside him in the bed. It alarmed him, because he knew that in his innocence he might easily have done something wrong.

'What is it, Jan?' he asked at last.

'Oh, nothing,' she said, dabbing her nose viciously with her handkerchief. 'Go to sleep!'

'But how can I with you like that?' he asked plaintively. 'Was it something I did?'

'No, of course not, Mick. I'm just a fool, that's all.'

The wretchedness in her voice made him forget his doubts of himself and think of her worries. Being a man of the world was all right, but Mick would always be more at home with other people's troubles. He put his arm round her and she sighed and threw a bare leg over him. It embarrassed him, but he reminded himself that he was now a man of the world.

'Tell me,' he said as though he were talking to a child.

'Oh, it's only what you said that night at the Plough,' she sobbed.

'The Plough?'

'The Plough at Alton.'

Mick found it impossible to remember what he had said at the Plough, except that it was probably something silly; but he was used to the way women had of remembering things some man had said and forgotten, and which he would be glad if they had forgotten too.

'Remind me,' he said.

'Oh, when you said that love was a matter of responsibility.'

'Oh, yes, I remember,' he said, but he didn't. What he remembered mostly was that she had more or less told him about the other men and he had been hurt and angry. Now that he was no longer hurt and angry he didn't want to be reminded of what he had said. 'But you shouldn't take it so seriously, Jan.'

'What else could I do but take it seriously?' she asked fiercely. 'Of course I was mad with you for telling me the truth about myself, but I knew you were right. That was the way I'd always felt myself, only I blinded myself, just as you said; taking up love like a casual job I could drop when I pleased. Now I'm well paid for my bloody stupidity.'

She began to sob again, bitterly. Mick felt completely lost. If only the damn situation would stay steady long enough for him to get used to it! He had felt he understood this strange country, and now he realized he hadn't understood it at all. He had accepted all it had to teach him, and now all he got for his pains was to be told that he had been right all the time, and had only made a fool of himself in changing.

'Oh, of course, that's all perfectly true, Janet, but you can take it to the fair,' he said weakly. 'You should see some of the things I've seen at home in the last couple of weeks.' He hadn't really seen anything, and he knew he was making it up, but the warmth of his feelings made it seem as though he had seen nightmares. 'People brought up to look at the physical facts of love as something inhuman and disgusting! If they must believe in some sort of nonsense, it would be better for them to believe in the fairies, as they used to do.'

'Yes, but if I had a daughter, I'd prefer to bring her up like that than in the way I was brought up, Mick. At least, she'd be capable of being serious about something. What can I be serious about? I made fun of Fanny because she didn't sleep round like the rest of us, but if Fanny falls for Chris, the joke will be on me.'

'You don't mean you didn't want to come, all the time?' he asked in consternation.

'It's not that,' she said, beating her forehead with her fist. 'But can't you see that I wanted to prove to myself that I could be a decent girl for you, and that I wasn't one of the factory janes you made fun of? All right. You're not like the others, but how am I to show you? How do you know I won't be back here with another fellow in a couple of weeks' time? I wanted to give you something worth while, and now I have nothing to give you.'

'I wouldn't say that, you know,' Mick said in embarrassment, but he really didn't know what else to say. Clearly this was another of these extraordinary occasions when the aeroplane you had been travelling so comfortably in turned upside down, and you were hanging on to your seat for fear of going through the roof. Here he had been for a glorious hour or so, feeling himself the hell of a fellow, and now he was back where he started, a plain, dull, decent lad again. He did not want to say it, but he knew he was going to say it anyway, and he did.

'We can always get married, you know.'

This threw Janet into something like convulsions, because if she did marry him she would never have the opportunity of showing him what she was really like, and it took him a long time to persuade her that he had never thought of her as anything but a serious-minded girl – most of the time, anyhow. Then she gave a deep sigh and fell asleep in the most awkward manner on his chest. Outside, the dawn was painting the old roofs and walls in the stiff artless colours of a child's paint-box. He felt a little bit lonely, a little bit sorry for himself. He knew that Chris would be furious and with good reason. As a man of the world he was a complete wash-out. He would have liked to remain a man of the world at least for a few months until it came natural to him, and he could scoff at conventions and pretensions from some sort of background of experience.

But it wasn't in his character, and you couldn't escape your character wherever you were or whatever you did. Marriage, it seemed, came more natural to him.

Julian Barnes
Before She Met Me   £3.99

'An intelligent and addictive entertainment . . . Barnes has
succeeded in writing one of those books that keep us up until
2 a.m. reading just one chapter more . . . few will be able to resist
its easy humour and almost insidious readability' NEW YORK
TIMES BOOK REVIEW

'Frighteningly plausible . . . stunningly well done' GUARDIAN

'Graham Hendrick, an historian, has left his disagreeable wife
Barbara for the more agreeable Ann, and is well pleased with
the exchange.He can hardly believe his luck, and spends his time
dwelling on her and listing what she is wearing in a notebook.
This blissful state continues until the day he catches her
committing adultery on celluloid. Ann was, sometime before they
married, a mediocre film actress. Soon he is pouncing on small
clues, examining her books for inscriptions of byegone lovers nd
continually re-seeing the few bad movies she appeared in. It's not
that he blames Ann for having a past before they met, but history
matters to him . . . Funny, sad and faintly ominous . . . making
jealousy tangible and dangerous' HARRIET WAUGH, SPECTATOR

'I find it coming back like a personal memory. Barnes's hilarious
wit is individual, but jealousy (its theme) is unfashionably
universal' PHILIP LARKIN, OBSERVER BOOKS OF THE YEAR

'A remarkably original and subtle novel'
FRANK KERMODE, NEW YORK REVIEW OF BOOKS

'Disciplined and rich. If this were a play there would be a mad
scramble for all the parts'
ADAM MARS-JONES, FINANCIAL TIMES

'It is rare to come across a novel that's so funny and odd, and at
the same time, so resonant and disturbing' NEW YORK TIMES

'There is an irresistible bland of wit and intelligence in his work'
NEW STATESMAN

Graham Swift
Learning to Swim and Other Stories   £3.99

'Swift acquires strength from the interleavings and interweavings of his collection. Almost all the stories are versions of the 'family romance', protective inventions attempting to cope with the tensions and rifts within families, whether children and parents or, by extension, husbands and wives. Children, teenagers, doctors and patients, a refugee Hungarian boy, a Greek restaurant owner – all are clearly yet subtly presented, in their obsessions and deceptions' THE OBSERVER

'An admirable collection. Each story has its subtle nuances of narrative and language which establish a quite distinct character. A most impressive work of fiction' THE TIMES

'. . . among the most promising young writers in Britain . . . Graham Swift should be read by everyone with an interest in the art of the short story' PAUL BAILEY, THE STANDARD

Graham Swift
Waterland   £4.99

'At once a history of England, a Fenland documentary, and a
fictional autobiography . . . a beautiful, serious and intelligent
novel' OBSERVER

'Swift spins a tale of empire-building, land reclamation, brewers
and sluice minders, bewhiskered Victorian patriarchs, insane and
visionary relics . . . a startling cast of characters going about their
business as though it were utterly normal and preparing the way,
down the centuries, for a trio of deaths' BOOKS AND BOOKMEN

'Positively Faulknerian in its concentration of murder, incest, guilt
and insanity' TIME OUT

'One of the most important talents to emerge in English fiction'
GLASGOW HERALD

All Pan books are available at your local bookshop or newsagent, or can be ordered direct from the publisher. Indicate the number of copies required and fill in the form below.

Send to: **CS Department, Pan Books Ltd., P.O. Box 40, Basingstoke, Hants. RG21 2YT.**

or phone: 0256 469551 (Ansaphone), quoting title, author and Credit Card number.

Please enclose a remittance* to the value of the cover price plus: 60p for the first book plus 30p per copy for each additional book ordered to a maximum charge of £2.40 to cover postage and packing.

*Payment may be made in sterling by UK personal cheque, postal order, sterling draft or international money order, made payable to Pan Books Ltd.

Alternatively by Barclaycard/Access:

Card No.

Signature:

Applicable only in the UK and Republic of Ireland.

While every effort is made to keep prices low, it is sometimes necessary to increase prices at short notice. Pan Books reserve the right to show on covers and charge new retail prices which may differ from those advertised in the text or elsewhere.

NAME AND ADDRESS IN BLOCK LETTERS PLEASE:

Name————————————————————————

Address————————————————————————

3/87